# THE RED SYNDROME

# THE RED SYNDROME

a dan gordon
intelligence thriller

HAGGAI
CARMON

Steerforth Press
Hanover, New Hampshire

*In memory of my parents,*
*Ida and Yehiel Carmon,*
*whom I never thanked enough*
*for giving me everything.*

For information about permission to reproduce
selections from this book, write to:
Steerforth Press L.C., 25 Lebanon Street,
Hanover, New Hampshire 03755

Library of Congress Cataloging-in-Publication Data

Carmon, Haggai.
The red syndrome : a Dan Gordon intelligence thriller /
Haggai Carmon. — 1st ed.
    p. cm.
 ISBN-13: 978-1-58642-105-2 (alk. paper)
 ISBN-10: 1-58642-105-0 (alk. paper)
 1. Bioterrorism — Fiction. 2. Food supply — Fiction.
 3. Government investigators — Fiction. I. Title.

PS3603.A7557R43 2006
813'.6—dc22

                            2006009393

Although this book was inspired by the author's work as outside
counsel for the U.S. Department of Justice, it is not an autobiography, but rather a work of fiction. Apart from historical events,
all names, characters, personal history, and events described in this
book have never existed and are purely works of fiction.

**FIRST EDITION**

# FOREWORD

Terrorism has no borders, no authority, no laws, no territory, and no moral considerations. Nothing stands in its perpetrators' ways. Terrorists regard disastrous and devastating consequences as achievements, not failures. They turn their own military weaknesses into strategic might. What good are tanks, missiles, submarines, or nuclear weapons when a determined handful gets access to substances that can kill millions? Many leaders and scientists believe that it is only a matter of time before bioterrorism strikes, causing thousands of casualties.

Bioterrorism uses pathogens, bacterial and viral agents, or biologically derived toxins against people, livestock, or crops. Through the spread of these agents, terrorists seek to inflict massive fatalities. Unlike nuclear weapons, bioterror weapons are relatively easy to make, and unlike chemical weapons, only small amounts of biomaterials are sufficient to wreak havoc.

Is the world ready? I have had the privilege of preparing Israel for the task: As Israel's deputy minister of defense, I took the initiative to make bioterrorism issues a priority in Israel's strategic defense. My communications with other governments led to the realization that many were ill prepared for the prospect of bioterrorism. It is essential for the governments of the free world to develop, test, and implement public policies and operating procedures regarding bioterrorism. The scientific community also needs to be vigilant on this key matter by actively engaging in research to develop countermeasures.

Haggai Carmon has crafted a fictional but all too real tale. It takes place in the clandestine world of bioterrorism, where sinister plots are intertwined with money-laundering schemes. In the book, cooperation between the Mossad and the CIA is all that stands in the way of bioterrorism. By combining keen knowledge of the real-world situation, gained by his personal experience, with a vivid imagination, Haggai Carmon manages to draw the reader's attention to the real risks our modern society faces. This book provides a public service by raising awareness of terror financing and bioterror. What is remarkable is that it does so while telling a damn good story I couldn't stop reading.

— EFRAIM SNEH, M.D.

Dr. Sneh is a member of Knesset, Israel's parliament. During his military service as a medical doctor, he commanded the medical team of Israel's forces that rescued the hostages from their terrorist captors in Entebbe, Uganda. In 1981–82, as brigadier general, he was the commander of the Israeli armed forces in southern Lebanon; in 1985–87 he served as the head of the West Bank's civil administration. Dr. Sneh was elected to the Knesset and served as member of the Knesset's Defense and Foreign Relations Committee, as deputy minister of defense under Yitzhak Rabin, as minister of transportation, and as minister of health. He is currently serving in several Knesset committees, and chairs the subcommittee for Israel's defense strategy.

# ACKNOWLEDGMENTS

The Red Syndrome was written at the urging of people I have never met. Since my first intelligence thriller *Triple Identity* appeared in the United States and Israel, I have been asked repeatedly whether I intended to write a sequel. Though I chose to regard these questions as a compliment, it is also possible that some of my friends wanted to know if they'd have to avoid me and the embarrassing question: "Have you read it yet?" At any rate, I present *The Red Syndrome* in part hoping for a repeat of these encouraging reactions. Readers have also asked since *Triple Identity*'s publication whether the events recounted there really happened. One newspaper reviewer even accused me of writing "too authentic" a novel, while another reviewer praised me for it. How can you argue with them? This book may meet a similar reaction. As to how much of it is "true," I leave it to my readers to decide. I began *Triple Identity* one night in a small hotel in a faraway country, kept awake by jet lag. It turned out not be a fluke; I wrote *The Red Syndrome* because I realized I still had adventures to recount. Like the novel that preceded it, *The Red Syndrome* was inspired by my work for the U.S. government, but is a work of fiction rather than autobiography. During my twenty years as an outside consultant for the U.S Department of Justice and other federal agencies, I have experienced adventure, fear, and most of the time, a great sense of achievement, earning appreciation from my superiors. During those two decades, I was assigned the demanding, sometimes dangerous task of collecting legal intelligence on white-collar criminals who had absconded from the United States. These individuals usually left with the money they stole to another more welcoming jurisdiction, one more accommodating than the United States, which frowns on people who steal millions and launder them. That explains why sometimes, waking up in countless hotels in more than thirty countries, I had trouble remembering where I was. Walking in the long corridors of foreign airports, it was hard to remember whether I was arriving or departing.

Many of my friends read the drafts and made suggestions. My Mossad friend, who must remain anonymous, made helpful comments that once again put me on track. Sarah McKee, former Justice Department general counsel of INTERPOL's U.S. Central Bureau, read the manuscript and helped me avoid pitfalls while describing INTERPOL's work. She also made suggestions based on her distinguished career as a federal prosecutor prior to her top role at INTERPOL. I am grateful for the special efforts she made, and for her unfailing grace and professionalism. My former supervisor and mentor David Epstein retired during the writing of this novel. In eighteen years of guidance he helped achieve that which inspired my novels, and I am grateful to him for that. His successor, Robert Hollis, has smoothly and vigorously assumed the helm without rocking the boat. More on that in the next intelligence thriller. Another friend, a scientist who must remain anonymous, made sure I didn't trip on the medical details. Ariel Blumenthal helped me to get the message straight. My longtime friend Professor Yehuda Shoenfeld was, as usual, supportive and encouraging. My relentless editors, Nicola Smith and Kristin Sperber, Laura Jorstad, and my publisher, Chip Fleischer, knew in a friendly yet professional manner how to move me in the right direction, making it easier for me to delete sections I toiled so hard to write, particularly those that describe events I experienced. But as relentless as I am, a trait inherited also by Dan Gordon, maybe they will surface in my next book, already underway. My thanks to Helga Schmidt and Pia Dewing for their support and to Louise Fili for the unusual book covers. And last but not least, thank you to my wife, sons, and daughters who read the manuscript and made important comments. Most of all, I am grateful for their patience and endurance, because the many hours I have dedicated to writing this book were ones of which they were deprived.

HAGGAI CARMON
New York, 2006

# THE RED
# SYNDROME

# I

## January 2003, Stuttgart, Germany

The prisoner in the red jumpsuit was visibly nervous. He couldn't hide the subtle tremor in his left hand, which gripped a cigarette. He was very thin. Stammheim, the maximum-security prison in Stuttgart, Germany, where Andreas Baader and Ulrike Meinhof had been found dead in their cells in the 1970s, didn't exactly serve gourmet food. Even so, Igor Razov was too thin, as if consumed from the inside. His mustache had nicotine stains, as did his uneven teeth.

"Good morning," I said, entering the visitor's cell and setting down my briefcase, which contained only a yellow pad. The less you carry into the prison, the faster the security check goes. I decided to be as polite as I could, to distinguish myself from this man's interrogators. "I'm Dan Gordon from the U.S. Department of Justice. I'm here with the consent of your lawyer, Dr. Bermann." I looked at his lawyer then at the court-approved interpreter, a heavyset, thirty-something woman who sat quietly in a corner opposite the German prison guard. Dr. Bermann nodded. No wonder he'd approved; I'd paid him five hundred dollars for the honor and promised an additional thousand if his client would give me the information I needed. It was Bermann's only way to get some real money for representing Razov, having helped him avoid extradition from Germany to Belarus, his homeland. There, Razov would have had to face the hangman, following a conviction in absentia for murder. I'd paid, and now the floor was mine.

"I'm sure your lawyer has already told you, but to avoid any misunderstanding I must reiterate that I am not in a position to make any promises concerning your extradition to Belarus or the death penalty you're facing there if you are indeed extradited. The United States is not a party to the legal proceeding against you; your case is entirely in the hands of the German and Belarus courts and governments."

I spoke in English. Bermann had assured me earlier that Igor had learned rudimentary English in Minsk, and had then improved it while living in New York these past few years. Bermann and Igor communicated in English, because Igor didn't speak German and Bermann didn't speak Russian or Belarusian. Bermann had brought in the interpreter, Oksana, as insurance, in case of a failure of communication.

As I spoke, I realized that this statement sounded very formal, full of legal jargon, and was too complex and long. But I had to say it. I had to make sure that both he and — more particularly — his lawyer understood the rules of our meeting. The last thing I needed to hear later was that his lawyer had argued for special consideration because Razov had talked to me. The Belarus government would file a complaint, and I'd find myself having to explain. Again.

"Do you understand that?"

Igor was motionless. He didn't even look at me. I knew he understood by the gaunt, haunted look he cast at the opposite wall. I was betting that his desperate situation would help me crack my case — one of the several international fraud and money-laundering cases I was investigating for the Department of Justice. Igor had to have answers for me because I could no longer ask his two comrades. I'd arrived in Minsk, Igor's hometown in the republic of Belarus, too late to talk to them. They had already been executed. But Igor still had a pulse. At least there was that.

Caveats aside, I had to give Igor a glimmer of hope, something to cling to. Otherwise this interview would be like trying to get a parrot in a pet shop to speak on command. "Helping me would make your life easier, more comfortable," I went on. "It would mean money to buy things at the prison's commissary. I could also ask the warden to let you watch television longer than the other inmates. It could mean a lot of other things that would ease your stay here, but you must help me first."

Igor said nothing. His head stayed down.

The German prison guard shifted in his chair, bored. It crossed my mind that his presence was inhibiting Igor, so I asked him to wait outside. The guard gave me a disapproving look and said, "I'm here to protect you, but I can leave if you want."

"Yes," I said immediately. "Please wait outside, I'll be fine."

Igor, handcuffed and frail, didn't pose much of a threat. I was twice his size, and besides, my favorite class during my training at the Israeli Mossad Academy had been martial arts. Sure, a few decades had passed since then and there hadn't been much use for those particular talents in my current position at the DoJ, but I wasn't too worried.

I asked Igor another question. Still no response.

"Dr. Bermann, would you please come outside with me for a moment?"

We stepped outside the cell, leaving Igor and the interpreter behind.

"I thought you said he spoke English," I said, wondering if my earlier speech had been wasted on Razov.

"He does, he does," Bermann assured me, although I suspected he wasn't that sure.

"Unless he gives me some answers," I said, "our deal is off. I hope you realize that."

"Yes. I don't understand Igor. He promised me he'd cooperate with you. Let's try again."

We went back to the cell, and I continued.

"Are you familiar with Boris Zhukov?

"Have you been working for him?

"You left Minsk and moved to New York in 1994. Why did you return to Minsk? Was it only to whack Petrov, or was it also something to do with Zhukov's money?

"How is Zhukov connected to the wire transfers you were making?"

Not a word.

"We know about your ties to Zhukov, but just knowing him doesn't mean you did anything wrong. I'm not here for your criminal case. I'm interested only in the money side of your relationship with Zhukov. Do you understand that?"

I kept going for another ten minutes. Igor was silent as a grave on a winter's night.

Seeing his thousand dollars slipping away, Dr. Berman made a last effort. "Igor, you promised me you would help Herr Gordon. Nobody is going to find out that you said anything. That's impossible, right?" He turned to me for confirmation.

"Absolutely," I agreed quickly. "I guarantee that everything you say stays in this room. All I need from you is guidance concerning the source of some money transfers that we think are connected to Zhukov."

Igor didn't even look at me. Bermann continued feebly, but to me the effort seemed futile. Bermann inspired no more confidence than a nurse trying to convince a crying boy that the doctor approaching with a syringe big enough to inoculate horses isn't going to hurt him.

I had read Igor's FBI file before coming. I realized that he knew better than to cooperate. He feared his colleagues in the Belarusian mob, on both sides of the ocean, more than anything; certainly more than the wrath of his own lawyer, a pompous scalawag lucky enough to be appointed by the court in this open-and-shut case. What could Bermann do to him if he refused to talk — stop bringing him week-old Russian newspapers? Complain to the prison warden? Write a letter to the editor of the prison's bulletin?

But Misha, Boris, and Yuri — to name just a few of the guys still on the loose — could find a thousand ways to make him wish he'd never been born, to make him pray that his thirty-seven years on this planet would end quickly. He knew that, because he was one of them; he was the one who'd pulled the trigger that led to this mess. Who would have thought that eliminating the president of a trading company in Minsk could cause so much commotion?

This Petrov had refused to pay his dues to Boris Zhukov. So under orders from Zhukov, a thug named Misha had told Igor to go to Stuttgart to await instructions. Misha was a huge person who inspired fear in everyone; his burly resemblance to a raging bear gave his gang the nickname *Mishka*, or "bear" in Russian. The Mishkas were a notorious crime group that had operated in the chaotic streets of Minsk before branching out to New York. Misha took orders from nobody but Zhukov.

Less than a month later, word arrived: Go to Minsk and waste Petrov.

So Igor did. He'd always obeyed orders, first in the Soviet army fighting in the final years of its war in Afghanistan, then as part of the Mishkas. Igor was proud to be considered a member. Indeed, his achievements in Minsk had drawn the attention of Zhukov, who needed more muscle in New York. A quick fictitious marriage to an American woman was arranged; she got a thousand dollars, and Igor got a green card and moved to America. Three years later, Igor had become Zhukov's confidant, and was occasionally sent to foreign countries to carry out "sensitive" jobs. Including this one.

What Igor and friends did not know was that Petrov was married to the daughter of a police chief, who apparently didn't like seeing his daughter widowed. Special orders were immediately sent: Get them! A week later someone ratted to the police that Igor had escaped to Germany. The three other gang members were still at large. An international arrest warrant was issued through INTERPOL. From there it was easy. The German police made inquiries through informers within the local Russian community. Igor was identified and arrested while sitting in a local bar.

As for me, I had traveled from New York in the dead of winter to a German maximum-security prison. I'd had to endure the terrible noise of slammed metal doors and the ominous spectacle of German prison guards clad in long winter coats and leather boots. I'd had to sidestep the vicious-looking German shepherds on short leashes. I'd had to endure sitting in a small room with a guy who reeked of cigarettes — and other odors beyond description. And what did I get in return? Nothing. Igor wouldn't even talk. How inconsiderate could he be?

There wasn't much I could do. Despite all Bermann's pleading, Igor remained silent. He had had his say once, and now it was time to be quiet. Igor wasn't thinking about being reincarnated in this world as a better person. He had far lesser dreams.

When it was clear the situation was hopeless, I left. The security checks exiting the facility were as stringent as those I'd had to clear entering. Given their clientele, and the kind of low lives in their business, the German prison system wasn't taking any chances. They simply wanted to make sure that the Dan Gordon leaving at 11:52 A.M. was the same Dan Gordon who'd entered the prison at 11:04 A.M. — not an inmate assuming my identity to reach the better food, better company, and freedom in the outside world.

Even empty-handed, I was relieved to be out of that place.

It was raining — freezing rain atop the snow already on the ground — and the streets were muddy. Snow might be romantic when you're curled up near a fireplace with a lover, a blanket, or both. Less so when you're in a foreign city with no taxis in sight.

I entered a coffee shop in Aspergerstrasse just outside the prison and ordered hot chocolate. I warmed my hands against the mug. It instantly brought back memories of my childhood in Tel Aviv, when my mother used to make me cocoa in my favorite mug while telling me how she'd escaped the Nazi Holocaust by emigrating from Belarus to Israel seven years before the war broke out. She made it out before every gate was shut to the Jews. My uncles and aunts stayed behind and perished. My uncle Shaya was a student in Stuttgart at the time and thought nothing would happen to him. More than half a century later, I was in the same city where an uncle I had never met was murdered just because he was Jewish.

Snapping out of my reverie, I tried to figure out how to break the news about Igor's silence to my boss, David Stone, the director of the Office of International Asset Recovery and Money Laundering in Washington, DC.

"It's a waste of time trying to make him talk," I'd said to David last week when he'd authorized my trip. "I know these guys. They'd rather die. Any death by execution you'd threaten them with would still be a summer holiday in comparison with the death by slow torture their friends offer."

David had nodded. "Still, we shouldn't let this opportunity slip away."

Igor probably knew that Germany wouldn't extradite him to Belarus until it was sure he wouldn't be executed like his buddies. The extradition treaty between Germany and Belarus provided that anybody extradited to Belarus from Germany must be spared capital punishment because of Germany's opposition to it.

"After Igor is finally extradited to serve a life term in Belarus," David had continued, "he won't even open his mouth to yawn. Our only chance to verify our lead is while he's still in Germany, isolated from fellow gang members and informers. Just the fact that Igor has agreed to meet you could be a good sign — it means he's already taken a huge risk. That might indicate that he'd be willing to take even more chances and give us some info."

"There could be another explanation," I said. "First, I spoke only with his lawyer, Bermann. The smell of money could have clouded his judgment, making him forget to check with Igor; Bermann's consent seemed a little too fast. Second, even if Igor *had* agreed to talk to me, it could still mean that he needed the meeting to signal his friends outside prison that he was sending me back empty-handed. That would serve as proof that he wasn't betraying them."

"I understand," David replied. "Zhukov is in the United States, and unless we have probable cause, we can't arrest him. He will most likely refuse a voluntary interview. He's done that before. But Igor is outside U.S. jurisdiction, so if the German prison authority and his lawyer agree to the interview, what do we have to lose?"

"Okay, you're the boss. You tell me to go, and I will." I could hardly have sounded more reluctant.

"*After* the travel authorizations. You know the rules," added David.

I did. First the Federal Republic of Germany had to authorize my visit; anyone traveling on official U.S. government business must have the prior approval of the host government. Second, under the Federal Chief of Mission Statute, federal employees can operate in a foreign country only with the U.S. ambassador's consent. Although rarely done, the embassy could even assign a representative officer to be present during all of my activities.

As far as I was concerned, all of this was unnecessary red tape. The same music was always being played and replayed: David demanded that I comply with the rules; I tried, but if I couldn't, I left evidence showing I tried. David knew of my tendency to cut corners. He didn't mind pretending that things never happened — as long as I understood that if the shit ever hit the fan I'd be the only one showered. On a good day I might have time to duck.

A few days later the paperwork was complete and I was on my way.

I stirred the hot chocolate, wiping my eyes, which had become teary from the cigarette-smoke-filled café air, and thought that now David would have to concede that I'd been right.

Still, I wasn't the kind of person to rub someone's nose in his mistakes, particularly when that someone was my direct supervisor. Moreover, I knew he'd had a point: Igor Razov could eventually help solve part of my puzzle, even if he was only a pawn. It was just a temporary hurdle; I needed to find a way to jump it.

I ventured back into the relentless rain and returned to my hotel. I changed my business clothes and wrote my report. No accusations, just the tale of a wasted visit to prison. I went outside and called David from a pay phone in a dome that failed to shield me from the wind and rain. When I call people, I observe certain rules, one of which is not to call from my hotel room. It's an old habit left over from my Mossad days: Hotels keep a record of your calls. For the same reason, I rarely use my cell phone when on assignment. I don't think I should be that transparent to foreign governments who think I'm just a tourist.

"Did he talk?" asked David.

"Silent as a husband."

"So the trip was a waste?"

"Well, not yet. While I'm here I want to dig deeper. I have a few ideas, and I'll need INTERPOL assistance."

"What for?"

"I need to see the German arrest file and ask them to issue a search warrant for this guy's local residence. He must have lived somewhere here before his arrest. It might contain some interesting stuff."

David hesitated. Even though I was investigating money laundering, a crime, INTERPOL might not be much help. A U.S. request via INTERPOL could almost certainly get me Razov's German police file. To get it fast, though, I'd have to offer to translate it myself and hope that the Germans would go along. "We might have better luck going through the police attaché at the German embassy in Washington. Still, a search would require a judicial order, so we'll have to send an MLAT request, and that might take more time than we have."

I couldn't help but think about my son, Tom. Before he'd grown to a towering six foot three, sporting a ridiculous goatee and out-of-fashion sideburns, he used to ask me what the meaning of *money laundering* was. He'd grown up hearing the term bandied frequently around the house. "No, it's not a big washing machine that cleans the dirty bills," I used to explain to him. "It's when thieves want to hide their stolen money from the police, so they transfer it from place to place hoping it will become 'clean' in the process and can't be traced back to their criminal activity. Money that criminals made by breaking the law is always dirty, so they want to make it seem like it came from someplace legal."

I told David now, "I think I'll push this forward on my own." Until he decided to request a search pursuant from the Mutual Legal Assistance Treaty in Criminal Matters (MLAT), I could use the time to find out where Razov had lived and with whom he had associated.

"Okay, where can you be reached?" David asked.

"I'm at the Grand Astron Hotel in Stuttgart." I gave him my numbers.

I had little hope that the German police file would contain anything meaningful. After all, Razov wasn't in their prison as a result of a crime he had committed in Germany; they were simply keeping him in escrow until he could be extradited to Belarus. The intelligence on Igor's German activities would be as thin as he was. And of course U.S. investigative agents and police could not conduct criminal investigations outside the United States without the approval of the host country, which is rarely given. But, I reasoned, I was also after the money. That was civil law, not criminal — at least not usually. I only hoped that my so-so legal analysis wouldn't be tested in reality.

At last the rain was letting up. I walked to the nearby city square and asked a local policeman in a black uniform where I could find a café or social club frequented by Russian immigrants.

He gave me an unfriendly look and said, "Try Café Moscow, right off Schlossplatz in downtown Stuttgart."

I finally found a cab, which dropped me off at the café. It was lunchtime. As I entered, heavy cigarette smoke and the smell of vodka assaulted my nose. Posters of old Soviet-era movies adorned the walls, and Russian music was playing.

The café was filled with burly men and a few women with push-up bras and too much makeup. I sat at the bar, squinting through the stinging smoke. I ordered a vodka martini and scrutinized the crowd. Five minutes later I had company. Compared with similar institutions, the response time here was relatively slow.

"How are you, big man?" said a young woman who pulled up a chair to be closer. "American?" She had a pronounced Russian accent.

I nodded. I didn't feel too welcome in Germany as an American. At the time President George W. Bush was trying, without any success, to persuade France and Germany to join the coalition to topple Saddam Hussein. Several street demonstrations against the United States had taken place. In Berlin a remembrance of the World War I antiwar communist leaders Rosa Luxemburg and Karl Liebknecht had turned into a march of ten thousand demonstrators protesting U.S. plans to invade Iraq.

"Buy me a drink?"

Well, despite my nationality, I could apparently still attract the bar broads. I consciously let myself be drawn in. Her agenda might have been the bulge in my pants — my wallet. But I also had an agenda, as she would soon find out.

"What would you like?" I said.

"Buy me champagne?" came the expected response. Next, she'd be served with colored water and I'd be charged for the best French champagne.

"No, dear," I said sternly, "vodka should be just fine." In a softer tone I added, "Isn't it too early for champagne?"

She smiled and asked the bartender for vodka.

I watched him pour from the same bottle he'd used for my drink earlier. As long as I was paying for vodka, let it be that, and not tap water.

"Tourist?" She leaned toward me to give me a better view of her generous breasts. A mixed smell of cheap perfume, bad alcohol, and cigarettes was sufficient deterrent to any thought of taking a two-hour leave from my duty. Two hours? Make that ten minutes.

"Yes, on business just for a few days."

"What kind of business?"

"I'm in microelectronics sales for the computer industry."

"Is business good?" No subtlety there: She was aiming directly at the size of my wallet.

"Business is okay. You sound like you're Russian, am I right?"

She nodded and sipped her drink.

"Do you speak Belarusian? I need somebody who could do some translations for me. Know anyone?"

"I'm from Russia. In Belarus, they speak a different dialect, actually a different language."

"I know, but I was thinking anyone who speaks Ukrainian or Belarusian would have very little trouble understanding the other language. Isn't it the same with Russian?"

She shook her head. "Russian speakers would have difficulty understanding either language. But I could ask here for you."

"Thanks. That would get you another drink from me."

"Nothing else?" There was a tone of seductive disappointment in her voice.

"We'll see about that later," I said, calculatingly ogling her generous cleavage. I hoped I was leading her to expect a financially rewarding transaction, albeit one that had to be postponed. For a millennium, as far as I was concerned.

She got up from the bar stool and walked to a table where four men were playing cards. A minute or two later she returned. "There's a woman in town who came from Minsk, that's in Belarus. I'm sure she could help you."

"Does she speak any English?"

"I don't know."

"What's her name?"

"Oksana Vasilev."

That first name sounded familiar. Could it be the same heavyset woman I had just met in prison? It would be good if I could get her to talk to me.

"And what is yours?"

"Kiska."

I smiled. It meant "pure" in Russian. "Where would I find her?"

"I don't know where she lives, but try the courthouse, across the *platz*. The people here said she was looking for a job as an interpreter and that the court keeps a registry of interpreters. Maybe she's listed."

"Smart girl," I said, and she looked at me to see if there would be any reward other than the drinks.

"I need to go, but I promise I'll be back," I added, slipping a twenty into her cleavage. I never dreamed of coming back for her. My mother's warning rang in my ears: *Don't pick that up, you don't know where it's been!*

I walked to the courthouse a block and a half away and found Oksana's address. Back outside, I hailed a cab and asked the driver to take me on a short tour. Although I didn't think anyone would be interested in what I was doing, old Mossad habits died hard — I needed to be sure.

Stuttgart itself is beautifully located in the Swabian Mountains, at the edge of the Black Forest. Both Porsche and Mercedes have plants there, so the city is home to predominantly working-class neighborhoods.

"Do you want to see the Daimler-Benz Automobile Museum? Perhaps the Mercedes-Benz factory? It is in Sindelfingen, very close to us," asked my cabbie. He was dark with a huge mustache, but his German sounded perfect. A green crescent on the dashboard gave away his country of origin: Turkey.

"No, thanks." I looked at my guidebook. "Why don't you pass through the Black Forest. I'd like to take a short walk."

A few minutes later he drove me to a wide-open picnic area in the forest. It was empty of people. I looked at the sign in German and below it, its English translation, and burst into laughter.

> IT IS STRICTLY FORBIDDEN ON OUR BLACK FOREST CAMPING
> SITE THAT PEOPLE OF DIFFERENT SEX, FOR INSTANCE, MEN
> AND WOMEN, LIVE TOGETHER IN ONE TENT UNLESS THEY
> ARE MARRIED WITH EACH OTHER FOR THIS PURPOSE.

I wished I had a camera. I took a short walk, getting some fresh air — and making sure I had no company.

Next, the cabdriver drove me to the glockenspiel at the Rathaus so I could listen to Swabian music. We continued past the Alte Staatsgalerie, then Killesberg Park, the Schlossgarten, the Ludwigsburg Palace, and the botanical gardens. An hour later, according to what I could make out in the passenger's-side mirror, I was convinced that my paranoia was unfounded.

Finally we arrived at Oksana's address. It was a shabby-looking two-story apartment building in a side street of a working-class neighborhood. Although it was only 4:10 P.M., it was already getting dark; other than passing cars, the street was quiet. It was getting colder and soon snow would cover the broken pavement, giving this place a well-deserved, albeit temporary, face-lift.

There were three mailboxes attached to the wall next to the building's main entrance. Oksana's name was clearly marked on the bottom box. A closer look gave me heart palpitations. Below her name was written IGOR RAZOV, although an effort to scratch it off the nameplate was visible.

So she wasn't just an interpreter. Was she a roommate, a partner, a supervisor, or all these penalties combined? I rang her doorbell and waited a few minutes, but there was no answer. I looked inside the letterbox. Empty. It was time for some action. I went to the back of the house. A small concrete structure housed the garbage cans. I looked around. Nobody was there. It was already pitch dark. Snow started to fall, muffling even the street noises. I opened one trash can, and two cats jumped from the other, petrifying me for five long seconds. I put my right hand deep into the can. I couldn't see much, and the smell wasn't helping. The can contained just two dripping plastic bags with household trash. I dropped them and wiped off my hands with a piece of newspaper. I couldn't tell if they were Oksana's trash bags, but given the freezing temperature and the dripping liquids, the bags had only recently been deposited.

I lifted the lid off the other can. Inside were two plastic trash bags of frozen garbage and one bag of papers for recycling. I untied the latter bag. Russian newspapers were on top. I was getting close, unless there were other Russian speakers in the building. Below these lay a few envelopes, but all with windows — no addressee name. I stuck my hand in again, this time fishing out invoices and handwritten letters in Russian. I emptied the newspapers into the trash can and took the bag with the remaining papers. I hoped that the city of Stuttgart would forgive me for mixing garbage. I hid the trash bag under my coat and hastily walked to the street. I walked up a block, but saw nothing unusual or suspicious. I got on a city bus, getting off a few stops later next to a cab station, where I hailed a cab to my hotel. I must have smelled, because the receptionist gave me a funny look. In my narrow room, I opened the bag and spread its contents on the carpet. I realized I'd hit the jackpot as soon as I started rummaging through.

I meticulously went through every piece of paper, setting aside both empty envelopes without the sender's address and Oksana's utility bills. If I needed proof that I was digging in Oksana's trash and not that of a neighbor, I need go no farther. I dumped the useless junk back into the trash bag — let it rest in peace. Next, I picked up six handwritten letters in Russian script in their original envelopes. They carried a Belarusian stamp and the sender's address. I couldn't tell who the senders were, given my limited knowledge of Cyrillic script, especially handwritten. But the addressee's name appeared Latin letters, probably to help the German letter carrier identify the addressee: Igor Razov.

From my prior Department of Justice cases, I knew that Belarus had a long tradition of using Lacinka, the Belarusian Latin script writing. Until the 1920s Lacinka had been more popular than the Cyrillic alphabet. As the Soviets moved in with their Russification policies, however, Lacinka almost entirely disappeared.

Next were thin, carbon-copy receipts. My heart started racing again. There were banking receipts from Germany, Panama, Venezuela, Saint Kitts and Nevis, and one from a bank in the Seychelles. Most of the papers were second or third carbon copies. Some were slightly torn; others had coffee and other unidentifiable stains. All smelled bad. I opened my room's window. Cool fresh air entered. I breathed in deeply, hoping the smell would go away. Then a sudden wind burst sent the papers on the carpet flying, and I immediately shut the window.

Reviewing these documents had to take precedence over recoiling from the stench. I reorganized the papers and continued.

Next came deposit slips — some of them blank — used-up checkbooks, a three-page handwritten document covered with numbers and Cyrillic script, and two black-and-white family photos. I had no idea whose family.

I sat next to the desk and tried to read the bank receipts. The Justice Department's lab would need to take a better look at them, but from what I could already make out, the numbers were big: At least sixty million dollars was reflected in these documents. On four deposit slips I could clearly identify Igor Razov's name. The other receipts were smudged. My suspicious mind kicked in again. The fact that Razov left behind such compromising evidence looked amateurish. Maybe he'd never thought the German police would arrest him. But once in prison, wouldn't Oksana at least shred the documents? Why did she wait until now to dump these papers? Or maybe Oksana was smarter than that, and was deliberately constructing a false trail for me to follow? I had no answer. Not yet.

I worked for three hours, until my eyes grew sore. I took another look at all the documents I had found, made a list, and put them in a big manila envelope. I returned the trash I had no use for to the original plastic trash bag.

I thought of Alex, my Mossad Academy principal instructor. *We teach you to see in everyday events things that others don't. Underneath anything you hear or see, there are hidden undercurrents. These undercurrents, the minutiae, the details, can direct a careful observer toward evidence or conclusions that the average, unobservant observer would miss. A trail could begin with something mundane and unpleasant. Remember, every finding is only a lead to the next discovery.*

Obviously, today's findings bore out this wisdom.

I leaned back. Was today cleanup day for Oksana? The used envelopes carried postal stamps dated two and three months ago. Of all days, she'd decided to throw out Igor's stuff *today?* Hardly a coincidence. Given the fact that I'd left the prison five or six hours ago, the only possible explanation was that she'd returned to her apartment not long before my arrival and had removed all papers connecting her to Razov. But why? Igor had been in prison for over a month now, and the German police had never bothered to search his home. Had Oksana guessed that my next move would be a request to the German authorities for a warrant to search Igor's apartment? How could she know?

I'd never mentioned getting a search warrant to anyone but David, and that had been from a pay phone in the street. Had it been bugged? Unlikely. I'd chosen it at random. The only remaining conclusion was that *I* was bugged, or that whatever enemies I'd just discovered had planted a mole in David's office.

The latter option was simply not possible. I was up against a criminal organization, not a superpower. The phrase *Never say never* didn't seem relevant here.

I decided to go with the more logical explanation. I turned on the TV and closed the curtains. I completely undressed and went through all my pockets, the jacket lapels, my shirt and tie. Nothing but fabric. I inspected my shoes and socks. Nothing. I sent my fingers through my hair. Just hair and some dandruff.

I unscrewed the telephone handset to see if it had a harmonica bug — those transistorized transmitters that are inserted into the mouthpiece, making it a hot mike. Nothing. I opened my briefcase and emptied its contents on the bed. It all looked benign. I pulled out my radio frequency detector. Today's wireless transmitters are so small that they can be hidden in many common objects, including neckties, eyeglasses, and pens. Thus visual inspection of objects can be insufficient. My detector scanned radio frequency ranges from 30 megahertz to 2.4 gigahertz, which are the ones used by most wireless video and audio devices.

I spread my clothes and shoes on the carpet and scanned them slowly. An amber light on the detector went on, telling me that a device emitting a radio signal was close. I scanned again, but the amber color remained steady. I turned to my briefcase: nothing. So where was it? I threw my coat over the chair and scanned it. The light changed to red. I had a bug in my coat. I kept scanning, carefully — and then I saw it. A pinhead-sized device had been inserted behind the lapel. Oksana had stuck it into my coat when I'd left the prison cell to talk to Dr. Bermann. She'd known who I was and that I was coming to interview Igor.

I washed my hands thoroughly and got dressed. I pulled the tiny transmitter out of my coat and placed it next to the television, blaring at full volume.

*Enjoy the music, comrades,* I thought, and walked out to have dinner. The smell of garbage was still in the air, but the sweet scent of success was already taking over. I took the elevator to the hotel basement and dropped the trash bag into a giant trash receptacle. I went to the reception desk and deposited my newfound treasures in the hotel's safe. The fact that somebody had gone to the trouble of hiding a microphone on my coat lapel indicated I wasn't alone; someone was watching me. As a precaution, I thought about changing my plans to go out and instead have dinner at the hotel restaurant. But then I reconsidered. It was in my nature to be defiant, to ignore doubts, to dispense with routine safety measures. This rebellious streak sometimes got me into trouble but also led me to victories. My ratio of trouble to success wasn't bad.

I walked into the nearly empty snow-covered street, looking for a good German restaurant. As I crossed the road to a corner restaurant, I felt the first blow to my head. Because I'd just turned, the slug lost some impact, although it was still too strong to ignore. I completed the turn and saw two guys built like linebackers, intent on finishing the job. The first guy aimed at my solar plexus. My Mossad martial arts instructor had told us drily: *A blow to the gut could kill. This is one of the best ways to knock out your enemy. And if you doubt me, think of the great magician Harry Houdini. He died from an unexpected blow to his gut.* I instinctively shifted to the side, redirecting the blow to my obliques — the muscles around my ribs. It was painful, but I could tell I'd avoid damage to internal organs. The second guy punched my head directly, hitting my right ear. Against my instincts, but in keeping with my Mossad training, I moved forward. Recoiling backward would actually have resulted in my head taking the punch at full force.

It was time to go on the offensive.

I made a full-body swing and kicked the shorter guy hard in his groin; as he bent forward I kicked him again. My shoe hit his lower abdomen and my knee smashed into his face. That did it. He fell on the sidewalk vomiting. He'd be quiet for a while until his dinner completed its journey onto his clothes and the sidewalk. The other guy shot a quick look at his friend on the ground and realized that fists weren't enough. He pulled out a knife. I had no weapons other than my hands and my experience. Because I was much taller than he, and had longer arms, I jabbed the fingernails of my right hand directly into his eyes; with my left I punched his kidneys so hard I was afraid I'd broken my wrist. He groaned in pain, dropped the knife to the pavement, and tried to push my hand out of his eyes. I let him cover his eyes with his hands as I swiftly picked up the knife and hurried back to my hotel.

The entire episode had taken only a minute or two, and we didn't seem to have attracted any attention. There were no pedestrians around, and the few cars that were passing hadn't bothered to stop. I took inventory: Other than breathing heavily, a ringing in one ear, and my disheveled clothes, there'd been no serious physical consequences. I went up to my room, leaving the front door open so as not to lock myself in with an intruder. When I was certain I had no uninvited company, I bolted the door.

Who were these guys? Was the attack random, a failed robbery of a tourist, or was I the intended target? It had to be the latter. They hadn't tried to rob or kill me; one bullet would have done that. Their purpose had been to intimidate, to send me a message to back off. First the bug in my coat, now the attack. I got the point: Their next move could be less friendly. But I had no intention of taking these hints seriously.

Since I had no further business in Stuttgart, my first instinct was to check out of the hotel and leave Germany. But reason overtook anxiety, and I changed my mind. In any case I would have to find another hotel for the night, or go to the airport immediately. I did not want to meet up again with Igor and Oksana's associates.

I waited in the room until the early morning, then checked out; two porters carried my luggage. I walked between them, making them an improvised protective phalanx, and ignoring their surprised expressions. I took a cab to the Echterdingen airport, checking occasionally to make sure I had no escorts behind my cab. We were alone on the road.

From the airport gate, just before boarding, I called Dr. Bermann. "I'm writing my report and I need your help."

"I am very sorry, Herr Gordon" he said candidly. Well, of course he was; the nincompoop had dragged me all the way to Germany only to realize that his smelly client wouldn't talk. He could have done it over the phone and spared me the trouble.

"I spoke to Igor again. He is not responding to my request to reconsider talking to you. In fact, he won't even discuss it."

"Too bad about that. Anyway, I need to describe our meeting to my boss. Could you please give me the interpreter's full name?"

"It is — " He paused for a minute. " — let me see here . . . *ja*, her name is Oksana Vasilev."

"Got it. And she is an official interpreter?"

"Yes, authorized by the court."

"You were lucky to find a Belarusian interpreter; I don't suppose too many people in Stuttgart speak that language."

"You are correct, Herr Gordon. In fact I think this is her first job. After our first telephone conversation, I asked Igor if he knew of any Belarusian interpreters because we would need one for his court hearing. A few days later, Frau Vasilev called me and said she spoke both German and Belarusian and even some English, so she could be an interpreter in Igor's case. I assumed Igor had sent her. I told her that she had to register with the court first. It took her one week to prepare the application, and now she is an official interpreter with the court. Otherwise she would not have been permitted to enter the prison. If Igor or Oksana were to have any difficulty with English, then I could translate from English to German and Oksana from German to Belarusian."

"Nice of you to think of it, and at the same time to help her," I said, thinking of the chaos a twice-removed translation could cause.

"I think so, too. She told me that she was new in town and needed a job. I paid her fifty dollars just to be in the prison for one hour. I don't think she made that much in Belarus in a month." I could almost see him grinning in self-satisfaction.

I called David from a different airport pay phone; my cell phone could easily have been picked up by a sophisticated listening device. After my encounter with the state-of-the-art bug, I didn't want to take any further chances.

"There have been some positive developments," I said.

"Igor changed his mind?"

"No, something else. I'll send in my report and we can discuss it after you read it. I'm on my way back." I decided not to mention the attack. There were too many people around me waiting to find an available pay phone, or maybe to eavesdrop on me. I couldn't be sure.

Back in my New York office, I forwarded to David in DC my summary of the facts I had gathered from Oksana's trash.

> On December 1, 2002, Igor Razov opened a bank account at the Global Kredit Privatbankiers in Frankfurt am Mein. On the same day, he deposited into that account sixteen cashier's checks totaling approximately $60 million. Four days later, that money was wire-transferred to Barclays Bank in Nevis, the federation of Saint Kitts and Nevis in the Caribbean, into an account owned by Bright Metalwork, Ltd., a Nevis company. A week later, the money continued its route through Panama City to Caracas until it resurfaced as a deposit made by Sling & Dewey Goods and Services, PLC, registered in Australia. Then the money was sent, probably by mail or by courier, to Eagle Bank of New York. Additionally, several checks were drawn on a bank in the Seychelles Islands. The source of the money is still unknown.

I called David two hours later waiting for his litany of praise. Nothing. It had taken a full week of my life to unravel the whirlwind tour of the laundered money around the world. I'd rummaged through garbage, taken a beating, and endured a ringing ear, and this was the thanks I got? Granted, it took me only twenty minutes to actually write my report.

"Good progress," he finally said. "But we need to know why the money traveled as it did. Usually money launderers take one or two interim steps, not five or six. Why so many? And where did Igor get this kind of money, anyway? It's way out of his league."

"No clue. I have no doubt that the money isn't his. Maybe it's Zhukov's."

"We looked into that possibility, too. The whirlwind is also very much unlike Zhukov."

"Maybe this one is different; Zhukov's or not, somebody worked very hard to obscure this money's source. But there could be any number of other possibilities," I said.

"Keep going, then. Sort them out," said David.

## II

I n the beginning it seemed like any other case. A routine audit by FDIC examiners had discovered movements of more than sixty million dollars between the Seychelles Islands and Eagle Bank of New York, all in connection with Sling & Dewey Goods and Services, PLC — private limited company.

But instead of the expected Currency Transaction Reports that the bank should have filed under the Bank Secrecy Act, there were only insignificant reports filed by Eagle Bank regarding smaller amounts and concerning different account holders, not Sling & Dewey. The FDIC report had attracted the attention of a Treasury agent, who had then ordered a report from FinCEN — the Financial Crimes Enforcement Network in Vienna, Virginia, an obscure intelligence agency of the Treasury Department. FinCEN in turn issued Positive Database Extracts, which shed further light on the unusual money transfers and deposits coming into Eagle Bank without any visible, legitimate business purpose. Under normal circumstances, the bank would have had to file a Suspicious Activity Report with its regulatory agency if it suspected it might have been used as a conduit for criminal funds. But no such reports had come in. So the bank itself became the target of an investigation. A phone call by the Treasury agent and a memo to DC had followed. The scope of attention widened.

Now the Department of Justice showed interest. An intelligence report on Eagle Bank of New York was ordered. The report that came back was alarming because it raised suspicion that the massive money deposits were part of illegal activity. The division chief assigned the matter to David Stone.

I reviewed a copy of the case file that David had sent me along with a note: "Dan, take a look. I think you'll be hearing the name of this bank a lot. Call me after your review."

I opened the file. On the top was a FinCEN report, which looked like dozens of others I'd seen.

## FINANCIAL CRIMES ENFORCEMENT NETWORK
### VIENNA VIRGINIA 22182
#### Intelligence Report

Requester: Peter S. Yarmouth; Date of Request: April 21, 2002
Att. Special Agent Ben R. Bailey FinCEN case # 02PPP88660
Requester Case # 02-384
Subject: Eagle Bank of New York, et al.

SYNOPSIS

The Office of Investigative Support searched its financial and commercial databases on Eagle Bank of New York. It is the subject of an investigation resulting from the bank's failure to report suspicious activity to avert further regulatory investigation.

The financial database listed 102 positive Currency Transaction Reports (CTRs) on Eagle Bank of New York totaling $211,011,009 for the month of January 2002 and 33 positive International Transportation of Currency Monetary Instrument Reports (CMIRs) on Eagle Bank of New York for currency arriving at JFK Airport between January and March 2002 totaling $76,556,000. None of these reports concerned Sling & Dewey Goods and Services, PLC. It seems that the bank had failed to report significant suspicious activities concerning money transfers in amounts exceeding $60,000,000. Please see the narrative section of this report and the enclosed database extracts for further details.

Prepared By: G. Walker Bryn
Title: Lead Data Analyst

Reviewed by: Lawrence X. Francis II
Title: Investigative Review Specialist
Telephone: (703) 555-5590
Distribution: DOJ/AR/ML Date: July 28, 2002
Any financial database information contained in this report is
sensitive and is not to be disseminated outside of your organiza-
tion (with the exception of authorized U.S. government attor-
neys who have a legitimate legal interest in such material)
without express approval of the Financial Crimes Enforcement
Network.

## BACKGROUND

Research on the suspects was conducted in databases available to
FinCEN. Below is a description of the databases accessed for
this report on the subjects of your request. Only positive or
inconclusive database results are included in this report. FinCEN
limits its research to only those subjects presented in your
request. Because information may exist on other entities identified pursuant to our research, you are invited to submit another
request on those subjects.

Financial Databases: Bank Secrecy Act information received
from either U.S. Homeland Security or IRS computer centers.

Includes Currency Transaction Reports (CTRs) filed by banks
on transactions of more than $10,000 in cash; reports of
International Transportation of Currency or Monetary
Instruments (CMIRs) — filed by individuals or businesses when
physically transporting or shipping/receiving more than $10,000
in either currency or bearer-negotiable instruments; Currency
Transactions Reports by Casinos (CTR-Cs) — similar to CTRs,
but filed by U.S. persons to report financial interest or signature
authority or other authority over accounts in foreign countries if
the aggregate value is over $10,000 at any time of the year, filed
annually; Suspicious Activity Report (SAR) — reports filed by
banks and other depository institutions under suspicion that one
or more of various financial crimes may have been perpetrated
by, at, or through the financial institution.

Note: One of FinCEN's main objectives is to locate information not normally found or used by law enforcement agents in the field.

NARRATIVE
Attached referral to the U.S. Attorney's Office for the Southern District of New York was made by the regulators once they realized the bank was a huge washing machine for laundered money. FYI.

I took out a yellow legal pad from my drawer, ready to begin planning the investigation, although there wasn't much in the way of hard information. Obviously, my first step should be the perpetrator's last, Eagle Bank of New York. That's where the money had landed. But complicated banking regulations and the need for complete secrecy forced me to reevaluate. I would have to settle for the penultimate step. Sling & Dewey had made huge deposits into Eagle Bank in cash, wire transfers, and checks drawn on a Seychelles bank. *Let's see what I can find out about the depositors*, I said to myself, identifying my first challenge.

I called Jim Lion, a postal inspector assigned to FinCEN in Vienna. Jim and I went back a few years, and he'd always been helpful. I remembered him telling me about his work on a case in the South Pacific, but I couldn't remember if it included Australia.

"Jim, I need some help in Australia. Got any connections?"

"Not personally," he said. "But tell me what you need, maybe I can direct you."

"I need to get info on an Australian company. You know, shareholders, directors, managers, bankers . . . the works."

"Funny you should ask, because FinCEN has recently completed a cooperation project with AUSTRAC. That's Australia's anti-money-laundering regulator and specialist financial intelligence unit."

"Would they help?"

"I think so. Let me check. In the meanwhile, fax me the details you already have about the company."

Fifteen minutes later Jim was back on the line. "The cooperation agreement is between FinCEN and AUSTRAC, so all requests must emanate
from us. I'll place the inquiry once I receive it from you."

I thanked him and went back to the file. Sling & Dewey was the only
solid lead I had so far. Its name had come up in the audit. Just a name,
nothing else. I was hoping that this narrow window of opportunity would
not be shut in the end.

The following day Jim called. "It took AUSTRAC only twelve hours to
come up with a response."

"I'm impressed," I said, thinking how long it would take our own
bureaucracy to react in a similar situation.

"Let me read you what they say . . . 'We attempt to ensure that financial service providers, such as banks, identify their customers to reduce
the occurrence of false name use — '"

"Jim, spare me the niceties," I cut in impatiently. "Do they have anything?"

"Yes, they do," he said coolly, refusing to be pressured. "I'm faxing you
their report."

I walked down the hall to the office fax machine as it started spewing
the report. It was captioned "FTR Information." Below the Australian
agency's emblem it said, "This report is generated in accordance with
Financial Transaction Reports Act 1988 and pursuant to AUSTRAC's
agreement with FinCEN."

I quickly perused the preamble and the caveats and then went straight
to the jugular. Sling & Dewey Goods and Services, PLC, had been incorporated in New South Wales, Australia, on May 12, 2001. The company
listed two shareholders: Advanced Liquids, Ltd., and Regency Portfolio,
Ltd. The company's directors were H. G. Andrews and Sheila McAllister.
Its registered address was Post Office Box 7166, Bondi Junction, New
South Wales. The purpose of the company: international trade. A short
narrative followed.

> Sling & Dewey Goods and Services, PLC, is believed to be a
> shell company. Our enquiry has shown that said postal box has

always been owned by a reputable bookstore which has no connection to any of the listed names. We believe the use of the box was fraudulent. Only Regency Portfolio, Ltd., is registered in Australia. Advanced Liquids, Ltd., is a foreign company registered in the Seychelles. We were unable to find additional local registration in Australia. Regency Portfolio, Ltd., is also a shell company with fake directors. The actual registration of Sling & Dewey Goods and Services, PLC, and Regency Portfolio, Ltd., was made by a service which files, for a fee, the necessary incorporation papers with the local company registrar. Following an enquiry, the service claimed that they were asked over the phone to incorporate the two companies. A messenger brought them the papers ready for filing, with both a money order made out to the company registrar and $750 in cash for their service fee.

That was smart, I thought. Two companies were incorporated in Australia and one in the Seychelles, as an "international company" — one whose shareholders, directors, and beneficiaries were almost impossible to identify.

The Australian service company claimed they had no idea who the clients were. A search in our database of the two names listed as directors of the two Australian companies showed that there are 57 individuals named H. G. Andrews and 23 individuals carrying the name Sheila McAllister. We should interview all these people in the near future.

A waste of time, I muttered to myself. It was all bogus. I'd been there before. These guys knew how to hide their traces. The report concluded by saying that the banking information would follow in a few days. I gave the report to Lan, the office secretary. "File it in the new Eagle Bank file . . . in the cemetery section."

She raised her eyes and smiled. "Dead end?"

I nodded.

Two days later another fax came in from Jim Lion attaching another report from AUSTRAC. On May 13, 2001, two men had come into the First Caledonian Bank of Australia in Sydney to open a commercial account for Sling & Dewey Goods and Services, PLC. The bank's officer handling new accounts demanded picture ID from the two men, which was standard procedure. One man showed him an Australian ID card that, upon later investigation, was determined to be a forgery. The address printed on the card, it turned out, was an empty lot. The second man presented the U.S. passport of one Herbert George Andrews, born in Denver, Colorado, on January 23, 1950. Passport number G967781117. No address was given to the bank.

At last, here was something to work on. I called the Bureau of Consular Affairs at the State Department. Once I'd given them the passport number, I was transferred to Security. Following a quick computer search, a courteous woman told me that the number was a fake. I was about to thank her and hang up when she added, "You may want to check this out with the FBI. I've got a computer message here that all inquiries regarding this passport should be referred to them."

Next, I was on the phone with Donald Romano, FBI special agent. I'd never dealt with him before, and he sounded very reserved.

"Yes, we have a record of this passport as being forged."

"Is there an ongoing investigation?"

"I can't tell you that," he said, cordially but firmly.

"Why?"

"It's classified. Need-to-know basis."

"I need to know. I'm an investigating attorney for the DoJ."

"You still need clearance," he insisted. There was no point in arguing with him. I had been through this bureaucracy before. I called David Stone and asked him to get me a clearance. I told him about the progress I'd made and he said, "I'll get back to you."

Several hours later David called. "You've stepped into a highly sensitive matter," he said in a *telling-you-a-secret* tone. "I had to do à bunch of haggling to get you access. *And* you have to come to Washington to do so, because they refuse to allow the file to be photocopied or removed from the building."

"Okay," I said, wondering why a forged passport was highly classified.

The following morning I went to the J. Edgar Hoover FBI Building. Located on E Street between Ninth and Tenth, it's a huge building occupying an entire city block.

Special Agent Donald Romano met me at the entrance, checked my ID, and walked me through security. He led me to an empty conference room, left me sitting there for a minute, and returned with a government-stock brown file. On its top was a large-font red stamp: TOP SECRET: EYES ONLY. He recorded my name and other details on the inside cover and said, "I hope you understand that you cannot make copies, take notes, or remove anything from this file."

"Sure," I said, with mounting curiosity. I signed a confidentiality statement and was finally handed the file.

A summary of the contents lay on the top. A Cincinnati field office special agent had received a tip from informer GF112-00 that Gregory Lermontov of Evanston, Ohio, was running a home printing facility. A search had turned up eleven blank U.S. passports, fifty-four blank Alien Registration Cards (better known as green cards), and 122 blank social security cards. The FBI forensics lab concluded that the forged passports were almost perfect. Lermontov was arrested and later released on twenty-five thousand dollars' bail.

I went through all the documents, which included several lab reports and affidavits from FBI agents. I paid special attention to a top-secret memo from the assistant special agent in charge in Cincinnati to the assistant director of the FBI. During his interrogation, Lermontov agreed to give up the names of individuals who routinely purchased forged U.S. travel documents from him. In return, he demanded immunity from prosecution and placement in WITSEC, the U.S. Marshals Service's witness protection program. Further investigation by the FBI had unearthed strong ties between Lermontov and Russian mob figures in New York.

In the attached envelope was an FBI internal memo that named Lermontov's main clients: Boris Zhukov and Grisha Grigorev. The same memo went on to note that Lermontov had disclosed the names in an oral interview, but had refused to sign a statement until the immunity agreement was finalized.

The file also described Zhukov's and Grigorev's criminal activity in the United States. It described them as the leaders of two major rival mobs, based in New York, that controlled significant portions of organized crime activity in the Northeast. The report concluded with a recommendation to classify the information because it concerned "two of the most brutal crime gangs in U.S. history."

So that was the basis for the ultrasecrecy: organized crime. The reasons why the mob would need a fresh supply of U.S. passports and other official documents were obvious: smuggling prostitutes, hiding the identity of couriers carrying drugs or cash shipments, and opening anonymous bank accounts, to name just a few opportunities.

Another report tied Zhukov and Grigorev to three additional individuals: Igor Razov, Alexei "Lonya" Timofeev, and Nikita Arkhipov, known members of a Russian gang in New York. The current whereabouts of Timofeev and Arkhipov were unknown; they may have been using forged travel documents. Igor Razov was infamous because of his ruthlessness and his wont for following orders without hesitation. Razov was Zhukov's front man for mob-related financial transactions from which Zhukov wanted to keep a safe distance. He was currently being held in a German maximum-security prison in Stuttgart, awaiting extradition to his native Belarus.

I memorized these names and quickly wrote them down on a small piece of paper as I left the FBI building, heading back into the busy DC streets. The Treasury Department agent's first instinct — supported by David Stone — that this was more than just a violation of banking laws was gaining momentum. I had a hunch it went beyond money laundering. Were the movements of huge amounts of money into and out of Eagle Bank just routine transactions made by a bona fide corporation in the normal course of its business? Were they illegal proceeds of crime deposited in an unsuspecting bank? Or did the Russians have someone inside the bank paving their way — or even the bank itself on their side?

Why? Were they maintaining their huge credit balance for a major crime still on the drawing board?

It had to be a mammoth plan if they intended to spend sixty million on it. The funds were in a checking account, not a savings account, and no securities had been purchased with them. That meant the money had to be available immediately, and for an impending purpose. Clearly these people couldn't have cared less about managing the money, preserving its value and earning interest. This was not how a profit-oriented corporation conducted itself. Further, the bank's conduct raised serious questions; avoiding the reporting was stupid, and banks don't regularly make such foolish mistakes. Something was very wrong. I went directly to David Stone.

David worked in the corner office on the eleventh floor of the Justice Department building. Through his office windows, you could see the red-brick houses of Washington's east side, with high-rises mushrooming through the area.

David took off his glasses and absentmindedly wiped the lenses with his crocheted tie. Although he was nearing his sixtieth birthday, he had almost no gray hair. His calm demeanor masked a bright, quick mind. In his thirty years at DoJ, he had slowly climbed to positions of influence where tenacity and boldness were important assets.

He listened conscientiously to my interim report, scribbling on his pad. He then raised his eyes to mine and grinned. "You thought this case would take you to exotic islands?" he said. "Try Germany. In the dead of winter. In a prison." He couldn't help laughing. "Pack your bags!"

# III

Three days after my return from Germany to the United States, David Stone asked me to go back to Washington to discuss developments on the Eagle Bank case.

"Dan," he said as I entered his office, "I distributed the report you wrote on your Germany visit. Treasury thinks the major money transfers are covering up major criminal activity, and we agree. But we need more evidence."

"Fine," I said. "I'll get right on it."

He shook his head. "The Justice Department has decided to convene a task force. This matter is too big for this office, so other sections of the government are taking over."

I was surprised to hear that. I moved from my chair to the leather sofa at the back, a status symbol in the penny-pinching administration.

"Sixty million is too big? We handle cases of a hundred million!"

"It's not only the money. Look at the individuals involved. This office doesn't fight multinational crime organizations. Our job is to go after their laundered money. The guys upstairs want criminal charges to be filed and these crooks put behind bars."

"I see." I had just started liking this case, and now it seemed to be slipping away.

David read my mind once again. "I'm assigning you to the task force as this office's representative."

"Why a task force? And who's in it?"

"They're hoping to avoid the usual agency turf wars. It'll have the usual members — Homeland Security, the Criminal Investigation Division of the IRS, the FBI, the Postal Inspection Service, Treasury, and Justice. Altogether there will be more than twenty-five active members."

I was pleased I'd be able to participate. Yes, task force assignments usually meant moving to another location, one likely to be less comfortable than my office. Still, I could continue the investigation I'd begun.

But why me? I was pretty well known for my lack of interest in joining a team — any team. Ever since I'd left my three-year service in the Israeli Mossad, graduated from law school in Tel Aviv in the late 1960s, and relocated to the United States in mid-1980s, I'd tried to capitalize on my strengths: I was a lone wolf and I got the best sheep if I hunted alone. My job as a DoJ investigative attorney had been a more or less an ideal fit for me: international legal investigations of complex multimillion-dollar cases that combined my legal and investigative skills and training — and most importantly assured complete independence in my international work. Not to mention a supportive boss.

Now I was being presented with a job that required me to work with others. And even if I were to protest, David wouldn't be responsive.

But why was this matter so complex that it required a task force? I could think of only three reasons, although I was sure there were more. First, the sums involved aroused suspicions of an unusual international spread of criminal activity. Second, the risk to the stability of an American bank was great. Finally — and most strikingly — there was the identity of the front-runner suspect, Boris Zhukov.

The names of Boris, Misha, and Yuri were highlighted on the legal pad resting on my lap while I rode the Amtrak Metroliner back to New York. I knew these guys only too well. We'd never met, at least not yet, but I'd already made close acquaintance with their FBI files. I closed my eyes, shutting myself off from the squeaking of the train on the rails. What I had read about Zhukov's life story began to roll through my mind.

Boris Zhukov felt he'd made it — and with some justification. He'd climbed from a childhood in a penniless family in poverty-stricken Belarus to become a major player in international crime. Belarus, just west of Russia, has always been Russia's poor relative. There Zhukov became a heavyweight. Not in boxing, or maybe that too. Now, resettled in the United States, he was controlling assets exceeding three hundred million dollars. Zhukov didn't like to flash his money, but he still couldn't avoid some of the absolutely necessary trappings: a blond wife flaunting too much gold jewelry, a few diamond necklaces and rings, sables, a black Mercedes S600 with a uniformed chauffer, a penthouse on Central Park West, a 150-foot yacht, a winter retreat in the Florida Keys, and of course a double chin. But Zhukov didn't consider this too lavish. Grisha Grigorev, his former-partner-turned-rival, had a private island in the Caribbean, two mistresses, a triple chin, and an additional thirty pounds of avoirdupois, not counting the gold chain and the diamond ring on his pinkie. Zhukov didn't mind. Ever since he and Grisha had come to terms on how to divide the huge territorial cake they were controlling, things had been calm. Grisha went into prostitution, fuel smuggling, and extortion, while Zhukov liked to be regarded as a banker, money launderer, and facilitator for legitimate American businesses that needed a guided tour into the new world of old Russia. Why worry?

In fact Zhukov had good reason to worry, but he wouldn't realize this until faced with the results of my investigation.

The following morning I went to 26 Federal Plaza in downtown Manhattan, just opposite the federal and New York courts, for my first day on the task force. Some forty people were gathered in a windowless conference room. "All efforts should be made to obtain sufficient evidence to indict Zhukov," said Robert E. Hodson — head of the FBI's New York field office and assistant director in charge — as he addressed the task force members for the first time. Hodson was a tall and heavyset man in his late fifties. He had a full head of white hair, a pinkish face, and an authoritative demeanor. People listened to him.

As I glanced around the room, some of the faces I saw were familiar and some were new. One unfamiliar but intriguing face, as I was later to find out, belonged to Laura Higgins, a green-eyed, red-haired Homeland Security agent who called to mind a jungle feline. There was something tantalizing in the way she walked, the way she moved, even the way she slowly raised her long lashes. *This woman is out hunting*, I thought, but I had no idea what or whom she saw as prey. Bored as usual in the crowded, good-for-nothing meeting, I ogled her as she meticulously wrote down everything that was said. She must be new on the job, new in town, or both.

Bob Hodson raised his voice. "Boris Zhukov dips his hands into anything profitable, legal or not. This is a 'big-business guy.'" He waggled his fingers to illustrate virtual quotation marks.

"Unlike the traditional mobsters on the retail end of crime — prostitution, loan sharking, protection, extortion — Zhukov aims high. His favorite area is international banking, money laundering, and megafraud. Holding himself above common criminals kept him out of the street fights and the city lights and gave him entrée into boardroom struggles. But he doesn't use proxy battles for hostile takeovers; he brings his old comrades from Belarus instead. Of course, their culture of speedy trial is different from ours. Some say it means taking your enemy for a nice long ride, accusing him, trying him, convicting him, and then carrying out justice by dumping him out of your speeding car."

There was a roar of laughter in the crowd. The twenty-five team members and additional fifteen or so support staff looked more like a gung-ho army than a group of legal professionals. All too often guys like Zhukov wriggled out of indictments either by using seasoned lawyers or by taking off. They also took advantage of a public that doesn't perceive white-collar criminals in the same negative light as drug dealers and rapists. That helps when a jury listens to defense teams depicting their clients as honest businessmen who've made a silly mistake or two.

Still, I couldn't help but feeling annoyed at the whole meeting: Instead of cutting to the chase, it was little more than a pep talk. All the pertinent facts had already been included in the encyclopedic EYES ONLY file we'd each received; the FBI had clearly done its homework on these.

Ever since I'd handled genuinely top-secret documents during my Israeli Mossad service, I'd learned to appreciate what was really secret and what was merely an extension of the document author's ego. Zhukov's case was not mislabeled, however; it was truly a confidential matter. A breach of security could risk not only the success of the operation, but also human lives. Although there was no admissible evidence linking them to any violent activity in the United States, Zhukov's gang was known to be ruthless. Their only law was whatever Zhukov decreed. No questions asked. Oh, yes, once there was a guy in Brooklyn who had a question concerning profit sharing . . . may he rest in peace. Meantime, for lack of living witnesses, Zhukov had never been indicted or convicted of any crime in the United States.

Maybe the time had finally come.

"We are dividing the task force into four major teams," rumbled Hodson. "Each team will have an office in this building. On each working day, we'll have a morning briefing session at eight o'clock with one representative of each team attending." Hodson read out the names. I was assigned to the international money-laundering group. With me were Jim Lion, the postal inspector who'd already helped me in tracking down Sling & Dewy; Laura Higgins from Homeland Security; and Peter Vasquez, a clean-shaven IRS agent brought up from Miami.

We walked to our assigned office on the same floor. It was decorated DMV-style with five metal desks, office chairs that had seen better days, and three file cabinets. Still, the view from the window was spectacular; I could see across the East River into Brooklyn. There was no rush for the desks, all standard government stock — that is to say, junk.

I chatted briefly with my team. Laura and Peter reminded me of kids on their first day of summer camp: uncertain and timid, yet rushing to make new friends and claim the top bunk. Before leaving for the day, I put my FBI folder into a desk drawer, but took out the pass provided to allow easy entry into the heavily secured federal building.

I then returned to my midtown Manhattan office to wrap up some other pending cases. None was as urgent as this one. It seemed 26 Federal Plaza would be my headquarters for a few months.

Unlike the shabby government offices so often seen in the movies (good PR for the law enforcement agencies vying for increased budgets), some government offices have, in fact, become quite comfortable of late. Mine was on the twenty-fourth floor of a high-rise with a doorman, fancy elevators, and good-quality carpets, next to a small law firm and an advertising agency.

A sign on my office door read TAT INTERNATIONAL TRADE, INC. I used to joke that the acronym stood for "Thieves and Thugs," but the letters had simply been chosen at random. International trading is a favored front for intelligence and law enforcement agencies when they need to conceal covert activity — even when it takes place in their own country.

Ironically, such covert activity sometimes truly does involve international trading — albeit of information and secrets. My Mossad service, including a lengthy training, had shown me how widespread the trade in information is among governments. Bartering, we used to call it, because no money ever changed hands. Still, it was merchant trading, not the intelligence gathering I'd expected. My Mossad teammate Benny Friedman was particularly good at it. Whenever he thought that a foreign government might be holding information that we needed — clues to the whereabouts of Israeli MIAs, for instance — he made proactive efforts to secure intelligence that he could offer up in trade. The best opportunities had arisen during the Cold War era. The thousands of Jews who'd emigrated from what was then the Soviet Union and Eastern Bloc countries were a fountain flowing with information.

Contrary to popular belief, espionage is not limited to stealing information on an enemy's abilities, capabilities, and intentions. Intelligence means obtaining all sorts of information about a rival: the mood, economy, political undercurrents, and weaknesses of the country and its leaders. If, during the Cold War, the CIA had wanted to know the train schedule between Moscow and Arkhangelsk, an immigrant who'd worked for the train service could provide it without even knowing why.

There were two main sources for information: debriefing U.S. visitors such as asylum seekers, and bartering with foreign intelligence services. The debriefing was always subtle. Rarely was there a direct question that could reveal sensitive planning details. Instead, a query might be posed as a challenge to the person's truthfulness. "I don't believe you ever lived in Arkhangelsk. Prove it. Tell me, for example" — a pause — "what time did the daily train to Moscow pass by?" In fact, Arkhangelsk had been an important Russian seaport — a center for scientific marine research as well as the space-launching site Plesetsk, the nuclear shipyards in

Severodvinsk, and the Russian nuclear polygon on the Novaya Zemlya. Hence, the great interest the West had in this city.

Another immigrant might pass along the name of someone who worked in a restaurant frequented by a particular scientist, perhaps creating an otherwise nonexistent opportunity. If the British MI6 wanted to know the layout of the main spigots in the oil supply from Siberia to the Sea of Japan, someone who'd worked on the pipeline could be helpful. These and other, similar pieces of information might seem completely benign, even insignificant, to a nonprofessional, yet be crucial to analysts trying to fill gaps in the intelligence puzzle.

Such trade in intelligence was only a by-product of the rigorous screening process Israel had adopted when thousands of new immigrants arrived from the Soviet Union in the 1970s — a way to prevent the infiltration of communist agents posing as devout Jews. The process of debriefing the new immigrants was kept top secret; Israel did not want the Soviets halting Jewish immigration, which is what might have happened if they'd found out how much intelligence was being collected as a result.

There are numerous other examples. Following European activity on an unrelated matter, Israeli Mossad operatives were able to inform President Charles de Gaulle about a plot by embittered French army officers in Algeria to assassinate him in the 1960s. De Gaulle was grateful; Israel capitalized on that. Israel also knew where Mehdi Ben Barqa — an exiled, charismatic Moroccan socialist opposition leader — was hiding. French police picked him up in Paris in 1965, and he was never seen again. The Moroccan king was appreciative, and Israel was able to pull more Jews out of Morocco.

From my New York office, of course, we were trading neither information nor anything else. We were simply pursuing absconding bankers who, on their way out, had helped themselves to their institution's FDIC-insured assets, or other major fraudsters and money launderers. Given our abundance of clients — who didn't seek or even want our services — we didn't need publicity. So we kept our identity quiet. This arrangement was just fine with us; it was far more comfortable operating out of a seemingly private office than from a government building. The facade also helped us send and receive mail; our correspondents never knew if we were good guys, bad guys, or somewhere in between. We did, however, limit our activities to locations outside the United States. Local issues were handled by other federal agencies such as the FBI or the Postal Inspection Service.

"You have some messages," Lan, the Vietnam-born office secretary, told me. One of the few good things to come out of the close U.S.–South Vietnam relationship, Lan was loyal, discreet, and, most of all, efficient.

I took the message slips and walked into my office. I sat behind my desk and gazed through the huge glass windows at the motorboats foaming and waving in the waters of the East River. Soon it will be springtime, when nature and people will be emerging from seclusion. But this didn't mean that every rat who'd run away with someone else's money would emerge from hiding. Happily for me, nobody runs away with stolen millions to Albania or Iran. They take their OPM — "other people's money" — to places where the sun shines.

I recorded a new *I'm-out-of-the-office* message for my voice mail, packed a few things from my desk, and returned to Lan's reception area. "I expect to be in the task force office for at least three months," I told her. "But you're not getting rid of me that easily . . . I'll check with you daily for my messages regarding other pending cases. If I'm unavailable, please refer all inquiries to David Stone."

Back at 26 Federal Plaza I took the FBI folder from my drawer and spread out its contents across my wobbly new desk. Some of it was familiar, including the summary I'd prepared myself before the matter had become the focus of such attention. Even in this top-secret folder, the manner in which the intelligence had been gathered was not disclosed. Indeed, intelligence-gathering means are rarely shared, even within an intelligence agency, to limit the possibility of a leak that would compromise the source. Compromise? Nice way of putting it. People get killed.

Of course, nobody knew how I'd collected this intelligence anyway.

When I'd first been assigned to this case, it had seemed a simple attempt by crooks to significantly influence a small New York–based bank by making a huge deposit, thereby rendering the bank more "tolerant" of their wishes, legal or not. But when I'd returned from Germany with the treasure trove from Oksana's trash can, all hell had broken loose, the task force had been convened, and, as I should have known, there was nothing simple about it.

The core document in the folder was an FBI report dated May 23, 2002. The "Background" section told the story of Zhukov and his comrades in mind-boggling detail over four pages. At the top of the report, in bold type, there was the following caveat:

> This background section was translated from Russian. The original Russian document was written by a former gang member as part of his plea agreement. The vital parts have been cross-checked and verified by other sources. However, if you need to rely upon any of the facts given here, it would be advisable to cross-reference with additional sources as well.

I chuckled to myself. This was typical cover-their-asses language. They gave you a story, called the details "facts," and then advised you not to rely on them because they might not actually be so factual.

I read the first page, trying to envisage how the dry words of the FBI report were reflecting reality. It wasn't hard for my creative mind to fill in the gaps.

# IV

oris Zhukov was born in 1945 in Minsk, Belarus. His father, Ivan, was a shop assistant in a shoe factory; his mother, Alla, worked in a local towel factory. Boris was the firstborn. When he was six years old, his sister Ludmilla was born. The family was very proud of a distant relative, Red Army marshal Georgyi Zhukov, conqueror of Berlin in 1945, who later became the defense minister of the Soviet Union. Although there was never any contact between this marshal and Ivan, Boris Zhukov's father, the family still managed to reap some benefits from their famous last name.

Boris grew up in a housing project in the outskirts of Minsk and started his criminal career at the age of fourteen. As the leader of a group of high school dropouts, he extorted money from other children and broke into the cooperative department store to steal cigarettes and vodka. In other words, a capitalist in a communist country. Not an easy status. One day he was caught and brought to trial. In his plea to the juvenile court, Ivan Zhukov asked that his son be spared from prison and that instead, he be sent to boot camp for "re-education" so that he could join the army upon coming of age, and "follow in the heroic steps of Uncle Marshal Zhukov." The judge was duly impressed and sentenced Boris to two years of correction in a youth boot camp.

The boot camp near Lydda in northern Belarus was the ultimate survival school. Boris soon demonstrated his leadership skills when he organized a group of youths, many older than him, to attack their counselor for being too harsh with them. They ambushed the counselor in the wee hours of the night, threw a blanket over his head, and beat him up. The counselor was hospitalized for three weeks and then quickly reassigned to another camp.

Zhukov didn't have much time to celebrate his victory, however. Three of his gang members were also transferred to other camps, and Zhukov himself was put into solitary confinement, or the "Box" as everyone called it. On the outer edge of the camp, a four-foot-square trench was dug in the ground, and covered by a tin sheet with four holes in it for air. The prisoner was then pushed into the trench and the tin cover bolted into the ground with stakes. The prisoner was allowed out once a day for five minutes. The only food and drink was half a loaf of bread and two cups of water thrown daily into the box. One blanket was given to the prisoner for use at night, although temperatures in the spring were only barely above freezing.

Spending a week in the Box was a lesson Boris never forgot. But he also didn't forget Nikita Kerchenko, the superintendent who'd ordered him into the Box. A month later, during a melee in the dining room, Nikita was stabbed to death with a sharpened spoon. No one saw who'd stabbed him, and of course there were no witnesses, although there were more than one hundred "campers" in the dining hall. The investigation led nowhere and the case was closed. But the message was clear: Boris Zhukov was now the uncrowned leader of the camp and all obeyed him, including the instructors. Soon after his discharge from the camp "for good behavior," Boris returned to Minsk. When he'd first left Minsk, Boris was just a troubled youth. When he returned, he had become an angry young man with leadership skills, a criminal propensity, and a ruthless nature.

The underworld of Minsk wasn't exactly waiting for him to take the lead. The city was already ruled by two rival crime groups; there was no room for a third, no matter how angry and competent its leader might be. But Boris wasn't deterred. If he had to fight two rivals at the same time, that was fine with him, even if it meant he couldn't trust anyone. The name of the crime game was smuggling, theft, and extortion.

Boris lured three members from each rival gang and started his own operation. But business was lagging. There's only so much you can rob and extort from a population that barely makes ends meet. Boris's first big opportunity came when American investigators came to Minsk following the Kennedy assassination to make inquiries about Lee Harvey Oswald and Marina Prusakova, his wife, who'd lived in Minsk between 1960 and 1962. Along with the investigators came many others: journalists and intelligence agents from half a dozen countries trying to make sure that JFK's assassination had not been part of a Soviet conspiracy to eliminate the leadership of the free world. Boris, as an up-and-coming local power, was approached by one of these newcomers and was asked if he could get a copy of the KGB report on Oswald and Prusakova. The price tag was very tempting: ten thousand dollars in cash. Boris's father was, at the time, making thirty dollars a month working ten hours a day, six days a week.

Boris was up to the challenge. Within two weeks, he'd handed over a copy of the report that the KGB had prepared after the JFK assassination. This report found its way to the FBI.

Zhukov used the money he earned cleverly. First he paid fifty dollars to the KGB cipher clerk who'd slipped him a copy of the report. That concluded his personal investment in the project, not counting several bottles of local vodka and Boris's reputation for belligerence, which were also part of the effort. Boris then looked for ways to transfer the rest of the money, as well as himself, to the West. This was not a simple task. Foreign-currency smugglers and black-market profiteers were labeled enemies of the Soviet state and were considered lucky to escape a firing squad and to be exiled to Siberia instead. But where there's a will, there's a way. Although Zhukov's position among the crime rings in Minsk was good, he was still just a local power. He needed to go international and the launching pad was in Moscow, five hundred miles away. So Zhukov received a permit from the city commissioner to travel to Moscow. Zhukov never questioned why a Soviet citizen would need permission to travel from one city to the other within his own country; he just accepted it.

Carrying nearly ten thousand dollars in cash was dangerous even for Boris. He wasn't worried about being robbed on the train; he could handle anyone. Rather, Boris was concerned that he would be searched by the police. Carrying such a large amount of hard currency, or *Valuta* as it was called, could send him to Siberia, and Boris had never liked cold weather.

So he left for Moscow, leaving the money stashed in his apartment's *chirdak* — a small storage area built into the hallway ceiling that generally contains the hot-water boiler and can also be used to store small objects.

On a hot July morning, Boris arrived in Moscow for the first time in his life. Although he'd felt like a king in Minsk, where everyone feared him, in Moscow he was the poor relative from the countryside. He was tired after the twelve-hour train ride, but still walked down the wide Moscow boulevards, looked at the old glories of the Soviet capital, and become confirmed in his belief that he was meant to climb higher than Minsk.

Boris went immediately to see Volodia, a freckled red-headed young man he had met at the boot camp. Not having any immediate alternatives, Boris took Volodia up on his invitation to stay with him.

Two cramped days later, which had been spent in the three-room apartment his friend had been sharing with two other families, Boris wanted out. At night Boris succumbed to the shy but persistent looks that Nina Tertsova, Volodia's neighbor, was sending in his direction. So he paid her a personal visit while her husband was toiling on a night shift at the textile factory. But the experience was not too rewarding; Nina was eager, but she lacked the goods and the expertise.

Boris was looking for a local contact in order to get himself and his $9,950 out of the country. But how? You can't just ask someone how you smuggle foreign currency out of the Soviet Union without ending up at the police station or in a mental asylum, or both — without the money.

Boris told Volodia that he wanted to meet people with business connections in the West. The solution came faster than Boris had anticipated. One night Volodia, who spent his days drinking and nights ambushing careless tourists, robbed a friendly drunk. Counting his take, he found $20 in singles, 34 German marks, 123 Swiss francs, and 3,450 rubles. The victim was Russian; of this, Volodia had no doubt. Therefore the only explanation for the amount of foreign currency was the victim's profession. He must be a moneychanger.

"Take me to him," ordered Boris. "I need to talk to him."

"Are you crazy?" asked Volodia while gulping another shot straight from the bottle. "I'm not going to look for him. He'll call the cops."

"Don't worry," said Boris, "he won't turn you in. What is he going to tell the police? That he was carrying foreign currency in Moscow?"

Volodia took Boris to the street corner where he had first seen Vladimir the moneychanger. Boris didn't see him in the street, so he returned the next day and the next; still no Vladimir. Boris was ready to give up when he saw a person fitting Vladimir's description standing on the street corner. He signaled Volodia to beat it.

"Are you Vladimir?" Boris asked as he approached.

The man looked at him full of suspicion. "Who wants to know?"

Boris ignored the question. "I need to buy some *Valuta*," he said abruptly.

"Why do you think I can help you?"

"I know. And that's enough." Boris grabbed him by the throat. "How long would it take to transfer out someone with foreign money to Western Europe?"

"How much?"

"Almost ten thousand dollars."

"Two weeks," gasped Vladimir. He wasn't about to be hit by another stranger, definitely not one twice his size with thrice his temper.

Boris tightened his grip. "Remember me; I'll be back."

Boris got what he wanted. Two weeks later, he met Vladimir at the train station. They sat on a wooden bench in the corner and Vladimir said, "Take this note to Bogdashko Kabanov in East Berlin. He will smuggle you to West Berlin, where you'll get nine thousand in cash. Now give me the money."

Boris looked at him in disbelief. "You mean I'm going to give you almost ten grand in cash in return for a piece of paper hoping that some jerk a thousand miles away will give me money for it? Are you crazy, or do you think I am?"

Vladimir was shaken. "Please don't shout," he said in a low voice, quickly looking around to see if anyone else was listening. "This place is full of informers. Please understand that this is how these money things are done. Read the note."

Boris looked at the handwritten note.

My dear Bogdashko,

I take this opportunity that my childhood friend Boris Zhukov is traveling to Berlin to visit his family to send you this short letter. Everything here is normal, if you can call our mother's bad health as such. The doctor said she needs to take 9,000 mg of vitamin C over a period of one month in small doses. That is a large quantity that we cannot find here. Do you think you can buy the vitamins in Berlin and give them to Boris? He'll bring it over to us when he returns home. Other than that, we all miss you.

Your brother, Vladimir

"What do I do with it?" asked Boris. "And who is Bogdashko Kabanov?"

"Everything will be taken care of," Vladimir reassured him. "Just go to this address in the Nikolai Viertel district of East Berlin. Look for Bogdashko Kabanov and give him this note. He will smuggle you through the Berlin Wall past the East German guards into the American zone of West Berlin. He will give you further instructions as to where to wait in West Berlin for a contact who will give you nine thousand dollars in small bills."

"And the rest?" asked Boris.

"The rest is spent on expenses. You don't expect our comrades in Berlin to work for free, as I do?"

Boris grabbed him by his collar, almost strangling the already trembling Vladimir. "If anything goes wrong, you know what's going to happen to you?"

"Yes," said Vladimir in a choked voice, trying to ease himself from Boris's grip.

"No, you don't," said Boris. "You'll die slowly at my hands. I'll make you suffer until you beg to die. Do you understand that?"

Vladimir managed to nod.

"How do I get to East Berlin?"

"By train, but get your travel permit first. Tell them you're going to visit a sick relative. You must build a credible story, because they might do a check on you."

"I'll give you the money after I receive the travel permit," Boris said as he got up and left Vladimir behind, still slightly panting and grasping for air.

Boris went back to Minsk, received his permit to travel to East Berlin, and within five days was in West Berlin with his money. In Moscow, Vladimir received his share via messenger. The year was 1965.

Coming to the West was easy; reaching the United States was much harder. His visa applications were denied twice, so Boris started planting roots in West Berlin. First he organized a small group of followers, all Russians who offered "protection" to expat Russian shopkeepers and businessmen. Those who refused to participate suffered not-so-mysterious fires in their homes and businesses, not to mention broken teeth and bones. Next, Boris developed a relocation service for people and their money from the communist countries to the West. True, sometimes only the people managed to cross the border and not their money, or at least not the bulk of it. "Lost in transit" was the explanation Boris gave. Another lucrative area was the smuggling of young Russian women to West Berlin for promised jobs as models or nannies. But when they arrived, a completely different career was waiting for them: serving Boris's male clients in his newly opened brothels and nightclubs.

Boris's cash reserve was quickly growing, and he was looking for new investments. Getting into banking was his next move. Of course, his definition of *banking* was different from a civilian's. Sure, he made loans, but the interest rate was just a little higher: 10 percent a month, sometimes more. When the borrower couldn't pay, Boris took his business and, on some occasions, his life. By the early 1990s Boris was very large, both in size and fortune.

In 1991 the Soviet Union collapsed and the United States relaxed its immigration policy regarding Russian immigrants. Boris didn't risk another rejection of his visa application based on his own merits. He married a young woman who had already received a refugee green card, enabling him to become a permanent U.S. resident. Soon they both moved to New York. The rest was history, or it would be soon.

# V

Manhattan, April 2003

My task force team met for the first time the day after Hodson's pep talk. We sat around a rectangular table at a small, windowless office-turned-conference-room. In addition to the table, chairs, and two metal file cabinets, there was a small projector used for visual presentations, and a coffeemaker. We each had a yellow legal pad and sharpened pencils.

"Okay," said the IRS agent. "Let's get to know each other. I'm Peter Vasquez. My area is investigating criminal tax evasion." He was a medium-built Hispanic with thick black hair. He had a wedding band on his finger, and a diver's watch. He struck me as a straightforward guy.

"I'm Dan Gordon, Department of Justice. I'm the international money-laundering guy."

"I'm Special Agent Laura Higgins, of Homeland Security." She paused and added, "I'm new; I volunteered for the task force as my first field assignment. So I guess you'll have to bear with me."

Oh, I could bear with her, I thought. I gave her an appreciative glance; she caught it and lowered her eyes. I was embarrassed.

"Where did you work before coming here?" asked Vasquez.

"U.S. Customs in Brooklyn," she said.

Jim Lion introduced himself, adding, "What do we do next?"

"Let's caucus," said Vasquez. "We have a case of suspected criminal activity involving a small New York bank with money laundered through a maze of six countries. Do we know more?"

"Yes." I said. "Well, not exactly. We have suspicions as to who is behind it."

"Frankly, I'm missing something," said Jim Lion. "Since when does the government convene a task force because of a sixty-million-dollar transfer? Where is the red flag that'd trigger a money-laundering charge?"

"The bank failed to send in some reports?" suggested Vasquez with a straight face, although it was clear he was being sardonic.

"And for that we need forty people?" asked Jim.

"Since I was helping to stir up that commotion," I said, "I must tell you that I support the suspicion that something bigger is going on."

"Like what?" asked Laura and Jim at the same time.

"That's what they expect us to investigate, but this case has several characteristics we usually don't see in simple money-laundering cases. We know that a total of sixty million dollars in several installments went on a whirlwind tour around the world, ending up in Eagle Bank as a deposit purportedly from an Australian company. The bank never reported the transaction as suspicious."

"Was it an oversight or deliberate?" asked Laura.

"I have no idea," I answered. "The regulatory scrutiny of the bank is being done by another team of the task force. Our job is to discover the source of the money, discover whether any U.S. laws were broken, and if so, to identify suspects. The facts we already know indicate that we should investigate outside the United States. That's where it all began. Suspicious activity was the trigger."

"How could a banker know there's something wrong with the client or the transaction? Does the government expect the bank to look into every transaction?" Laura asked again.

"No, of course not," said Vasquez. "But sometimes you'd really need to be blind not to see a problem. In legalese it's called 'willful blindness.'"

"Do we know for a fact that the failure of the bank to file the report was conscious?" asked Jim. "The violation is so outrageous that no sane banker would risk it. There must be some other reason."

"Such as?"

"Such as an internal conflict that stopped the report from being filed, or someone on the inside with a different agenda."

"It's possible," said Vasquez. "But thus far, these are speculations. I'm sure we'll find out more down the road."

"Were the Australian police contacted?" asked Laura.

"Yes," I responded, "thanks to Jim." I indicated him with my hand.

Jim nodded. "I was in touch with the Australian Central Crime Intelligence Bureau in Sydney and with AUSTRAC, their financial intelligence agency. They have recently signed a cooperation agreement with FinCEN and this case was a good opportunity to launch that agreement."

"And?" asked Laura.

"Nothing. Well, almost nothing." I said. "AUSTRAC told us that the shareholders of Sling and Dewey Goods and Services, PLC, used faked names."

At this point I told my team in very general terms about the lead that ultimately sent me to Germany to interview Igor and my subsequent findings; I didn't go into the exact details of how I'd obtained the banking information. My foreign activities are always on a need-to-know basis, and the task force members didn't need to know I was cutting corners.

Laura looked at the list of countries the transferred money had visited. "The Seychelles. What's the story here?"

"Absolutely gorgeous beaches and palm trees and laundered money here and there," joked Lion.

I looked in my notes. "There are six banks there. The Seychelles Savings Bank, Bank of Baroda, Habib Bank, Banque Française, Barclays Bank, and Nouvobanq. I don't remember off the top of my head which bank was used for the money transfer; it's somewhere in the file in my office. What is important for us, though, is why money launderers just loved it during the 1990s. It all started with a decision the Seychelles government made. Their two major sources of income have traditionally been tourism and fishing, but they realized that, given the distance to travel to the Seychelles, American or European tourists could find plenty of similar, closer locations if they wanted a beach and some palm trees. They knew they couldn't run a country's economy on these two income sources alone. They needed additional foreign-currency earnings to meet their increasing import needs. So the government started marketing the Seychelles as an offshore financial center where you could register almost anonymous companies."

Vasquez took some notes on his legal pad. I paused and looked at the other members of the team. They were waiting for me to continue.

"The most glaring attraction of this program is that it permits bearer shares in international business corporations registered in the Seychelles. That obviously facilitates money laundering since it makes it extremely difficult to identify the beneficial owners and directors of these corporations."

"Wait a minute," said Laura. "You mean there's no central registry of shareholders of Seychelles international companies?"

"No," I said. "But the United States doesn't have one, either. The shareholders of private companies are recorded only in the company's books, which are kept by their lawyers."

"So why are you mentioning it?" asked Lion.

"Because here, when criminal activity is suspected, or even during civil litigation over money, you can access the company's records through the discovery process and see who the shareholders are. But with bearer shares, there's no recording of the owners anywhere. Whoever physically holds the majority of shares controls the company. That's the beauty of it if you want real anonymity."

"Is it that simple?" asked Peter.

"No, not at all. Some people have thought that by merely presenting bearer-share certificates in an offshore corporation, they would be automatically recognized as the new owner of that company and all its assets, including its bank accounts. They often had an unpleasant surprise."

"Why?"

"Because there is no vacuum of ownership, meaning that if another person or institution had been controlling the company thus far, and the transfer of shares was not coordinated with them, there could be opposition. Resistance means legal proceedings, meaning open court. And you wind up with what the holder of the bearer shares wanted to avoid in the first place — public attention."

"So the purported benefit of bearer shares is a ploy?" asked Jim.

"No. You simply have to plan ahead."

"Are there any other countries that allow this trick?" asked Laura.

"Off the top of my head I know that Panama, Liechtenstein, and Mauritius allow it, but I'm sure there are many others," I said.

"I need a vacation," said Peter Vasquez, stretching in his chair. "Your talking about these places makes me hungry for sunshine."

I couldn't blame him. The weather outside was bleak. The sky was gray and the temperature in the thirties.

"If we determine the Seychelles are relevant to our case," said Lion in an amused voice, "maybe we could ask to be posted there. With my luck, I always end up in places like Detroit in the winter or Mississippi in the summer. The east coast of Africa doesn't sound so bad."

"It could happen," I said in a tone mixing hope and fact. "Money launderers prefer good weather, and in the Seychelles even the winter is summer."

"How sure are we that the Seychelles was involved?" queried Vasquez.

"We have receipts from a local bank, and AUSTRAC's report that the company that actually made the deposit into Eagle Bank was controlled by two companies, one of them a Seychelles international business corporation. But I don't know if Sling and Dewey simply parked the money in Eagle Bank to launder it or whether there's a stronger connection."

"Wait," said Laura. "How are the Russians you mentioned earlier connected to this?"

"Well, this is precisely why the task force has been convened," I answered. "We must establish the connection to organized crime in New York, if there is one. Without the connection, which until now was just a suspicion, we don't have anything to connect this case to the United States. Cases outside our borders are somebody else's problem, not ours.

"Let's review: We have a Belarusian hit man, Igor Razov, who transferred a substantial amount of money from one suspicious source to the next, all outside the U.S., until it was deposited here. Bad boy, yes, but he's not our boy, because he didn't make the deposits here himself. And at any rate, he's far away and it seems he's going to be a guest of the prison system for the rest of his life, courtesy of the German and Belarusian taxpayers. But if we show that Igor was played by the big guy in New York, then it becomes a U.S. case, because Igor was acting as an agent for Zhukov — who *is* under U.S. jurisdiction."

"It may sound like a stupid question," said Jim, "but why would we care if money was being transferred around? If it's deposited in our banks, the U.S. economy benefits. I chase money launderers because we want to deprive them of the fruits of their crimes. But where's the crime here? No crime, no money laundering."

"Good question," I conceded. "That's what we're supposed to unearth. We have a smoking gun, but no body. If we dig, we may find a body, or we may find nothing at all. But it's our duty to dig. I could offer you a general explanation, but you'll have to bear with me, because I need to get into a global perspective so you can have a broader picture."

"Sure," said Laura, moving in her chair. "Go ahead, I'd like to know."

"Fine," I said. "Because of Russia's economic collapse, everyone is shaking that we'll have a replay of the Cold War. The toppling of financial dominoes from Asia through Russia to Latin America has sent the message that the hands of criminals holding invisible strings could destabilize the world economy. I've been doing this job for more than thirteen years, but recently I've seen a growing number of cases where the crooks take advantage of the weakness of government supervision over a global system that moves vast sums of money electronically, often through poorly regulated offshore banks. We're not talking small potatoes here," I emphasized. "Their money flows hide capital flight that can leave a nation near bankruptcy overnight."

"What are you talking about?" asked Lion. "Did I miss something?"

"What he's saying is that the clandestine money transfers can conceal government corruption and siphon away resources needed for developing economies," said Peter Vasquez.

"Exactly," I said. "We're looking at offshore banks that also serve as shelters for laundering money to finance terror organizations, drug trafficking, and other criminal enterprises. You know, I think the new financial technologies for moving money have in fact dangerously outstripped the abilities of banking regulators to detect fraud, money laundering, and other corruption."

Laura walked to the coffee machine and poured coffee into a Styrofoam cup. I watched her as she moved. She raised her head and saw my gaze.

"Let's descend from world politics," said Lion. "How do we build a case proving that unclean hands tried to use dirty money for some reason yet to be determined?"

"It's not politics," I said. "These events have a major bearing on our case. This could be an isolated incident, but it could also be the first drops of a storm that could flood us. The Russian mafia's intentions have been recognized for years, but have not been handled efficiently. Now things are different, because they're already in our backyard. There's never a power vacuum. When the government is weak, the fringe players are strong, and when they become international some of them come to our shores. When they do, the media calls them mafia, although many are honest businessmen who know how to take advantage of an opportunity."

"The point he's making," said Vasquez, "is that while technology was enabling financial markets to operate beyond national borders, some governments, regulators, and law enforcement agencies were sleeping at home."

"Excuse me, gentlemen," said Laura in a tone I could not pinpoint. "Aren't you going too far in your speculations? This high-level economics talk is very interesting, but aren't we jumping into conclusions without having the benefit of reviewing the facts first?"

"What do you mean?" I asked.

"I mean that we don't know that the Russian mafia made the transfers. And even if they did, we have nothing to tie them to Russia and its failing economy — other than their ethnic background. Besides, we're not some kind of worldwide financial police. We're U.S. law enforcement officers upholding our own laws. Everything else is somebody else's business."

I felt like a schoolboy who'd been reprimanded. We had all gotten carried away and, I had to concede, that was primarily my fault. "You're right," I finally said. "We don't know. In fact, we don't even know if the transfers were made by Zhukov and if they were intended for his own purposes — maybe he was providing a service for a third party. Anything is possible."

Deep inside, I knew that this case was different from the other cases; it had the distinction of being international, suspicious, and ominous. I was the only international animal in our team, and I had to bring some of that experience and those instincts into the conversation, Laura's admonition notwithstanding. But unless my comments were directly connected to our case, anything else I could say about the way the world works could be regarded as condescending, so I kept quiet. For now.

"Let me give you an example to illustrate what the relevance could be," I ventured again. "Before this task force was convened, I traveled on another case to the South Pacific."

I looked at Laura. She looked intrigued. "The money passed through an offshore bank in the Cook Islands. The Cook Islands are beautiful, but they're sparsely populated. So how is it that a population of only eighteen thousand can play host to some three thousand anonymous trusts? They have more trusts than mosquitoes! We suspected that some of these trusts were connected to organized crime and some of the most notorious financial players in the Asia-Pacific region. But I was stonewalled."

"So what did you want the U.S. government to do? Invade? Another Grenada?" asked Laura sarcastically.

"No," suggested Lion. "Simply more international financial safeguards are needed, with punishments for nations that don't meet anti-money-laundering standards."

"Isn't the Financial Action Task Force coordinating these efforts?" said Laura.

"But they're just an intergovernmental policy maker created to assist governments in combating money laundering and allow official travel for 'meetings,'" said Vasquez with a grin. "Seriously, their so-called recommendations have teeth and they can bite any nation that ignores them."

"How?" asked Laura.

"Each country is expected to report compliance with their recommendations," said Jim. "Those member countries that are considered to be lagging behind in their combat against money launderers feel the heat. First, as a kind of hint, the country is asked to deliver a progress report. If that request, along with strongly worded letters from FATF, doesn't help, then FATF sends a mission to the noncomplying member country. If that *still* doesn't do the trick, FATF issues a statement calling on financial institutions to give 'special attention' to business relations and transactions with persons, companies, and financial institutions located in that country. Finally, the FATF membership of that country can be suspended. The country then becomes a financial pariah. Banks and financial institutions stay away. Which could cause a country to collapse."

"How do they define *noncomplying country?*" asked Peter.

"They have a list of requirements," I answered. "Before they take action, they need to determine several things, such as if a country has inadequate regulations and supervision of financial institutions, or maybe excessive secrecy provisions regarding financial institutions."

"So would that attitude work here to make the Seychelles reveal the names of the beneficial owners of the company that indirectly controlled the bank account used to issue checks for sixty million?" asked Laura, looking at me.

"There's nothing we can do," I replied, "officially."

"And unofficially?" She'd read between my lines.

"Well, there are several ways. We need to do more research. Maybe it'll get us to the Seychelles after all."

"I'd like that," said Laura blandly. I was unable to tell from her demeanor whether she'd been picking up on my interest in her, and whether it might be reciprocated.

# VI

It was already dark when I left the building; we'd been holed up in that office all day. I was happy to get some fresh air. A gusty wind was blowing from the East River. Discarded Styrofoam cups and other debris swirled. I walked a few blocks north to my empty but cozy loft in Chelsea. The only living creature waiting for me was Snap. My kids were away in college, and my apartment was just as I had left it that morning. I didn't miss the old days when, upon returning home from work, my wife, now my ex, would be barking at me while my dog was wagging his tail. Now only Snap was waiting, wagging his tail and jumping. I bent down to greet him and he licked my face all over.

A paid dog walker takes Snap out during the day, and I wasn't eager to go back out into the elements for his nighttime walk. I fixed myself a drink and dropped on the couch to read the newspaper, but it quickly became clear that Snap was not going to let me settle into my peaceful evening. Leash in his mouth, his begging eyes bore into mine.

"Okay," I relented, stroking his rich reddish brown coat. "Let's go."

Before stepping from my building, I zipped up my coat and turned up my collar as protection from the wind. But once outside, I realized the wind had already died down. Now it felt delightful by comparison, and my mood lifted as I set out for my ritualistic walk with Snap. It felt good to get the blood flowing after the long day working inside, and the walk was certainly better for me than the drink I'd left behind forming a condensation ring on my end table.

Going up Tenth Avenue, as we approached Chelsea Park my eye was drawn to a MISSING poster affixed to a lamppost. My neighborhood is just north of Ground Zero. Except to retrieve Snap, I was barred from returning to my own apartment for days following the 9/11 attacks. And for many weeks after that, outsiders were kept from entering our neighborhood, lending an eerie ghost-town atmosphere right in the heart of one of the most vibrant metropolises in the history of humankind. Before 9/11, I'd walk past MISSING posters with almost as much indifference as I'd ignore flyers for vitamins, adult education classes, and rock concerts at neighborhood bars. But 9/11 forever changed that. Suddenly the city was plastered with posters that became impromptu, unofficial, and painfully inadequate memorials to the moms and dads, friends and lovers who had gone off to work one Tuesday morning never to be seen again. I started reading every poster I came across, sometimes recognizing the same ones in different corners of the city. People felt so helpless; they couldn't think of anything else to do, because there was nothing more that could be done. Their loved ones were gone, but it had all happened so quickly, unexpectedly, and violently, they couldn't find a way to let go. Not yet. Each eight-and-a-half-by-eleven, computer-generated flyer represented an individual life with children still to be tucked in bed, career goals to be pursued, dreams to be realized, or even dashed, but over the course of a natural lifetime. Typically they featured a photograph of the deceased and a thumbnail sketch of his or her life, loves, and work. Ultimately came the chilling phrase "last seen entering the Twin Towers," followed by the hollow plea that the reader please contact So-and-So with information.

Living so close to the tragedy perhaps made the event even more real for me than for those watching the news from afar, as did my work for the Justice Department. For over a decade my cases had more and more come to involve suspected terrorist activity. Investigations of money trails left by white-collar criminals who had fled the United States with ill-gotten gains, or by narcotics traffickers who were trying to pollute our streets with drugs, were increasingly leading, sometimes quite unexpectedly, to organized terrorism connections. But reading those MISSING posters, more than anything else, transformed the attack for me from a collective massacre to the destruction of individual, beautiful human lives.

My reaction to MISSING posters pre-9/11 had been reasonable enough as a practical matter. Why even look at them? What are the chances that I'd ever see the child on the poster or, if I had, that I'd recognize her? How was I to know whether the missing man hadn't simply abandoned a self-deluding spouse? But 9/11 made me realize that while these weathered pieces of paper might be useless as a law enforcement tool, they can reveal dramatic stories. Someone was deeply emotionally connected to the missing person, and wanted him or her back.

I tugged on Snap's leash and told him to sit, which he dutifully did. This particular poster featured a color photo of a middle-aged man, about my age, in jacket and tie and wearing sensible, office-worker eyeglasses. First impressions are more often right than wrong, and this guy struck me as a paper pusher or bean counter.

MISSING! HAVE YOU SEEN HIM? read the bold type above his image. Underneath were his particulars:

BERNARD LIPINSKY
HEIGHT: 5'6"
HAIR: GRAY, BALDING
WEIGHT: 175 POUNDS
WEARS EYEGLASSES
LAST SEEN LEAVING EAGLE BANK

It took a second for my mind to register what I had just read. Eagle Bank! I had never had any dealings, professional or otherwise, in my entire life with the place before joining the task force, and now here it was cropping up again from an entirely different source. The name *Lipinsky* meant nothing to me, and my brain told me the chances were that the guy was involved in some domestic dispute or misunderstanding, but my gut reminded me that the biggest breaks of my career have tended to come from the most unexpected sources. An investigator would have to be lazy or burned out not to pursue such an unexpected connection. This guy Lipinsky almost certainly had nothing to do with our investigation, but merely taking an active interest in his disappearance would give me a line of inquiry into the world of Eagle Bank that no one else on the task force was pursuing.

I fished a pen from the pocket of my overcoat and was writing down the wife's name and address when I realized I knew the building she lived in. It contained loft apartments not very different from my own, maybe twenty units in all, and was located nearby. I knew the building because my insurance agent Ed Halloran and his wife, Pam, lived there. After my divorce she'd tried to fix me up, inviting me over for dinner a couple of times. The second and last time was with her loudmouthed sister, and the evening went very badly. Several months after Pam had given up on me and my romantic life, Ed died unexpectedly from a heart attack. I couldn't make it to the funeral, I hadn't heard from Pam, and I had no occasion to contact her.

Much to Snap's dismay, I turned around and pulled him along back toward our apartment, all the while thinking about how to approach Pam. I needed to enlist her help with Helen Lipinsky without setting off any alarms, either in Mrs. Lipinsky's vulnerable heart or with my superiors on the task force.

I have to confess, as an investigator I was making cold calculations in my head. I was about to contact Pam for the first time in about a couple of years, and my motivation was that I wanted to use her. If she didn't know Helen Lipinsky and couldn't help me, the fact that I'd missed Ed's funeral and never made a friendly gesture to her after her husband died would rise like an awkward, unpleasant specter between us. But I have thick skin. And if Pam did know the Lipinskys, she'd be so focused on their plight that nothing else would matter.

I dialed Pam's number as soon as I'd taken off my coat and shoes. My drink was still cooler than room temperature, and I took a sip. Pam picked up on the third ring. I got right to the point, telling her that I'd come upon the poster and asking whether she knew Helen Lipinsky or anything about Bernard's disappearance.

Not only did Pam know the woman well, but she'd helped her produce and distribute the posters. "I've been on my own for some time now," she reminded me. "I have time, and so I try to help when I can. Helen was at such a loss. The police told her Bernard's a grown man and he hasn't been missing long enough for them to get involved, unless there's any sign of foul play."

I saw my opening. "I'm on my own, too, you know. I never remarried, I don't have anyone particular in my life now, and the kids are grown. I was walking my dog, the poster caught my eye, and then I recognized the address and thought *What an amazing coincidence! That's Pam's building! Maybe she knows these people!* You were always so nice to me, having me over for dinner, trying to fix me up with the right people . . . You know I always felt bad that I missed Ed's funeral but it couldn't be helped, I was out of the country. So I said to myself, *Dan, this is a sign. Pick up the phone and call Pam. At the very least you can say hello and tell her you were thinking of her and how she was doing.* As for your friend, I'm no cop and I don't know what it is I could do, but I do know law enforcement and bureaucrats and so if you think there's anything I might be able to do to help her, let me know."

"Well I can tell you," Pam said, "it didn't help when the police told her that when a man disappears, he usually doesn't want to be found right away by his wife. Any kind of direction or guidance you could give would be an improvement over that."

"So you don't think this was a domestic dispute or a marriage gone bad?" I had to ask.

"No," she said, then hesitated.

"What?" I asked.

"Her husband seemed troubled during the week before he disappeared."

"Why? How do you know?" I asked.

"She told me that his disappearance could be connected to his work. He was really upset during the past week."

I had to play my hand very carefully. I couldn't let on that the name *Eagle Bank* meant a thing to me. I didn't even mention that I'd seen his place of employment on the flyer. Besides, my experience as an interrogator has taught me that you get your best information when you let the person you're questioning provide it without any prompting.

"Where did he work?" I asked.

. "At Eagle Bank."

"Do you know whether the bank ran an audit to see if he took off with any of their money?"

"I'm not sure if they know he's missing."

My gut told me the chances that Lipinsky was somehow connected to our investigation were getting better and better. "Well, if you think Mrs. Lipinsky would want to talk to me," I volunteered, "I'd be happy to meet with you and her."

"Dan, that's wonderful!" she responded with genuine enthusiasm. "When? I can bring Helen to see you anytime. She's just sitting at home worrying."

"Can you come now?" I suggested. "I have a full day tomorrow at work, but tonight I'm free."

"We'll be right over!"

She sounded a bit overly hopeful, so I reminded her, "Tell Mrs. Lipinsky I don't know what I can do, other than advise her about the next step."

"Understood," said Pam. "That's exactly what she needs. We'll be there in twenty minutes."

About half an hour later, the doorbell rang and Pam walked in with Mrs. Helen Lipinsky, a fifty-something woman with gray hair and sad eyes, now more red than brown. She was holding a wadded handful of tissues.

"Thank you for agreeing to see me with on such short notice," she said apologetically.

"Of course," I said. "Would you like a drink?"

"Just water, please," she said, while Pam added, "Nothing for me, thanks."

I poured Mrs. Lipinsky a glass of water.

"My husband is a good man," she started in. "He would never disappear just like that. He would never change our plans without telling me first; it isn't like him at all. We used to talk several times a day. Two days ago, he vanished. We had tickets for a show and planned to meet for early dinner near the theater." She paused, wiping her eyes.

"And?" I prompted.

"I waited at the restaurant for an hour but he didn't show up. I called his cell phone but got only his voice mail. I called his office and our home, but there was no answer. The bank's switchboard operator told me that there was no one in my husband's office. I was so worried. I had no clue. I went to the theater to see if he'd shown up there with an explanation."

"And he hadn't," I said, trying to make my voice sympathetic.

She shook her head, clasping her hands until her knuckles became white.

"Pam told me earlier that your husband had seemed worried for a few days before he disappeared. Do you know why?"

"He didn't talk much about his work. He was in midlevel management at the bank and handled foreign transactions, something I've always found very boring."

"Why was he distressed?" I wondered if her husband's concerns had anything to do with our investigation. He couldn't have known about it, unless someone had leaked him the information. Still . . . there *could* have been a leak.

"He said something about some strange messages he'd received."

"What about them? Did he tell you their content?"

"There were several of them. Computer messages, all illegible, just a garbled combination of letters that didn't make sense."

"So why was he worried? Sometimes these things happen in wire or computer communications."

"I know. That's what Bernard told me, but what worried him was something else."

I waited, knowing she would go on.

"When he showed the messages to one of his co-workers, he grabbed the messages out of my husband's hands, said they were intended for him, and walked out of his office."

"So what's strange about that, other than the fact that a co-worker was rude?" I asked, keeping my voice bland.

"The co-worker behaved strangely. He wasn't just rude, he was threatening. He told Bernard not to mention the messages to anyone."

"Didn't that immediately telegraph to your husband that something was wrong?"

"It certainly did, but he didn't know what to make of it. He was, after all, just a bookkeeper."

"Did he keep copies?"

"I don't know."

"Did he say anything about why he was concerned? Was it something professional, or personal?"

"He just told me that he was worried about the whole incident. Something just wasn't right. He wasn't used to co-workers being secretive and threatening. He liked his job precisely because it was all about numbers and he didn't have to deal so much with people."

"Do you know if he reported the incident to his superiors?"

"I don't know. He didn't tell me."

"So he felt threatened because of that incident, nothing else? Did he have any reason to feel intimidated other than his co-worker's tone?"

Helen hesitated. "Well, like I said, the man told Bernard not to tell anyone, basically to forget it ever happened."

"Told him or asked him?"

"I think Bernard felt frightened. He said something about the guy's conduct being bad. He didn't threaten him explicitly, but Bernard sensed from his attitude that something shady was going on."

"Do you have the co-worker's name?" I asked, holding my pen.

"Malik Fazal. I think he's from the Middle East."

"The name sounds Afghanistani or Indian."

"Could be," she said. "I saw him once or twice at the bank's New Year's parties and he looked like he could be either of those."

"Have you heard anything since Bernard disappeared? Any phone calls, ransom notes?"

Helen shook her head, blinking back tears. "Nothing."

"Let me have a number where you can be reached. I'll try to interest law enforcement to take this up immediately."

Helen and Pam thanked me and left. I poured myself a new drink, a shot this time. I mulled over the conversation. Was there a connection between our investigation and Bernard Lipinsky's disappearance? Was his disappearance connected to the garbled messages and the incident with the co-worker? Were they all connected?

I called David Stone at home, despite the late hour, and briefed him on the surprising developments.

"What do you want to do?"

"Obviously, I can't call the bank while we're still investigating them. A federal agency's interest in a missing-person case would look unusual and raise questions that could undermine our investigation strategy. I don't think we need outside attention now. I suggest we let the NYPD handle it. But we have to nudge them to take it seriously."

"Did you report this to Hodson?"

"Not yet. I intend to do so tomorrow."

"Dan." There was definite annoyance in his voice. "I don't mind you reporting to me as long as you make sure you also report to Hodson. In task force matters, he's your boss."

"I know," I said gloomily.

"Okay," said David, "I'll make a few calls in the morning. Good night."

The following day, during the morning session of the task force, I reported the contact I'd had the previous evening.

"Do you think there's a connection?" asked Hodson.

"There could be. Everything the wife had to say sounded genuine. I spoke with my director, and he thinks we should let the New York police handle this matter. We didn't think it'd be wise to get the task force or any federal agency involved while we're still in the early stages of our own investigation."

"Keep me posted when you hear from the police," he said.

Hodson turned to his assistant, John Dunn: "John, call the New York State Department of Banking and get anything they have on Bernard Lipinsky and Malik Fazal. Do the same with the FDIC."

I went back to my makeshift task force office, where I found a Post-it note indicating that Helen Lipinsky had called me. I dialed her number. There was no answer. Moments later, David Stone called and informed me that the New York Police Department was already investigating Bernard Lipinsky's disappearance. "They've assigned Detective John Mahoney of the Midtown South Precinct," he said. "You'd better talk to him directly."

I decided to try to get my hands on the garbled messages Lipinsky was holding. They could mean something. Lipinsky's disappearance had given us an unexpected, back-door opportunity to find out whether there was any connection between the two cases without having to approach Malik Fazal prematurely. *Always get intelligence before you move*, said Alex, my former Mossad Academy instructor. *Even when your actual move is to gather intelligence, that by itself should be preceded by intelligence. Get to know your source before any approach.*

I called Mahoney and introduced myself. "I'm calling in regard to Bernard Lipinsky."

"Yes," he said. "We've just gotten the matter. Your name was mentioned as a contact. Is this connected to a federal case?"

"We don't know yet," I said evasively, adding, "but you should know that just before he vanished, Lipinsky had an argument with a co-worker, a person named Malik Fazal. Apparently some garbled messages had come into the bank; Lipinsky stumbled on them, and Fazal snatched them away. There could be something in the messages that points to the origin of their dispute, or maybe even to the subsequent disappearance of Lipinsky. The way it was described to me, something didn't sound right. We'd be most interested in these messages; they could be connected to our case and also to yours."

"So what's the government's role in this?" he asked again.

"All I can say is that Lipinsky could be a material witness in a federal matter. I'm sure you understand there are limits to how much I can discuss. At this point we can't stick our nose into the missing-person case, so I hope you can interview Malik in a benign manner. If you don't mind the suggestion, as part of the routine investigation into Lipinsky's disappearance, you could interview everyone in Malik's department, including him, so that he won't suspect that he is being singled out. I don't want him to take off."

"I hear you," said Mahoney. Any competent detective, of course, could think of this tactic on his own, and wouldn't need me to suggest it. I'd been prepared for him to bristle, but he seemed cool.

"If anything develops," I continued when no objection was heard, "please call me at my temporary office in the FBI in 26 Federal Plaza." I gave him the number.

"All right," he said, and hung up.

# VII

I t was time to call Benny Friedman, my Mossad buddy. He has always been a good sounding board for my ideas. Although many years had passed since we'd trained together at the Mossad Academy, we were still friends, helping each other when we could without compromising our respective allegiances. Benny was one of the few people I've really respected. His shrewd mind, low-key demeanor, and noncondescending attitude made him many friends and only a handful of enemies. His burly appearance didn't reflect the easygoing and no-nonsense top Mossad executive that he was.

I remembered well how Benny and his wife, Batya, gave me moral support and true friendship during my divorce from Dahlia. Although a Mossad career was usually for life, I'd left after only a three-year stint. Things had changed. I'd been burned in an operation in Europe: An Arab informer joining a Libyan diplomat in a rendezvous in Europe turned out to be a former landscaper at my parents' home in Tel Aviv who knew me well. My cover was instantly blown. My future as a Mossad operative was fatally compromised, and the best assignment I could expect after that disaster was a desk job. No thanks. In the dynamic, continually fluctuating profession of intelligence, even if you were sitting pretty, someone would run you over if you didn't keep moving. So I moved. Besides, I needed the change. My divorce, my resolve to turn around my life, all led me to the United States.

But Benny had stayed on and climbed through the ranks. Now he was the head of Tevel, the organization's foreign relations department. Although Israel and the United States exchange intelligence regularly, the direct contact I had with Benny was simple and personal. Each of us knew his own limitations and the other's. I called the Mossad headquarters in Tel Aviv at 10:00 A.M. — 5:00 P.M. in Israel.

"Been awhile, Benny," I said, when I reached him.

"A good friendship never goes stale," he answered. "In fact, I was thinking of coming to the U.S. soon and wanted to call you."

"Something that needs to be done? Or just a decent kosher meal?"

"Both," he said.

"I'm here. When are you coming?"

"Next week. I'll call you a day ahead."

I was glad Benny needed something from me; lately the flow of favors had been unidirectional. I know Benny never kept an accounting, but still.

I then called Helen Lipinsky again at her home.

"Mr. Gordon? Any news?" She sounded worse than she had during our meeting. Her voice broke.

"Not yet. We pushed the New York police to look for your husband. Have they contacted you yet?"

"Yes, that's the reason I called earlier, to thank you. Three detectives came over, interviewed me for two hours, and searched my husband's home office."

"Did you agree to the search?"

"Of course, what do I have to hide?"

"Did they find anything?"

"I don't know. They lifted his fingerprints from his cup, took hair samples from his comb, and a few of his recent photographs from our family album."

"Is that all they took?"

"I think so. Maybe a few more papers from his desk."

"All right. I'll call you if I hear anything, but I suspect you'll be the first to know of any developments in the police investigation."

Fingerprints and hair samples. That sounded like they needed an identification. Had they found a body? I thought of my one meeting with Helen Lipinsky; she had seemed so fragile, and now it sounded as though she would be getting bad news, the worst.

I called Detective Mahoney at the station. "I heard you paid a visit to Helen Lipinsky. Did you find the messages?"

"What messages?"

"I think I mentioned them in our earlier conversation. Lipinsky had gotten some garbled messages and —"

"Right. Let me check, I just walked into my office." He put me on hold.

When he came back on, he sounded somber. "Dan? We have a body and it meets the description of Lipinsky, but the coroner will have to make a final determination."

"Homicide or suicide?"

"You can't commit suicide by putting two bullets to your head and two in your back," Mahoney said drily.

"Where was he found?"

"In a Dumpster in the South Bronx."

"The wife knows?"

"A squad car is on its way to her."

"Any suspects?"

"Still working on it."

"And did you come up with the messages?"

"We took a bunch of papers from Lipinsky's apartment. They could be among them."

"Would you mind if I came over and had a look?"

"Not at all."

Twenty minutes later I was in the Midtown South Precinct at 357 West Thirty-fifth Street. Police cars, including a few unmarked, were parked perpendicularly in front of the building.

Mahoney — a skinny mustached fellow in his early forties — was wearing a blue T-shirt, jeans, and sneakers. His service revolver was tucked in his jeans, and his NYPD badge was hanging from his neck on a thin chain. "These are all the papers we took from the premises." He pushed a thick envelope toward me across his desk.

I opened the envelope and emptied its contents on Mahoney's desk. I sifted through the papers. Each was sealed separately in a plastic bag to prevent contamination of the evidence. I immediately saw what I was looking for: three standard yellow-paper, continuous-form computer printouts with perforated holes at the edges. I pulled the three bagged printouts out from the pile and looked at them through the bag. They were poor-quality carbon copies, probably the bottom ones. The top edge contained the preprinted standard identification details of Eagle Bank of New York with its logo. Below was the date and then forty blocks of letters, each with five letters, without any obvious meaning.

"Can I have copies of these?" I asked Mahoney, as if I didn't know the answer already.

"Sure, but let me do the copying."

I nodded, continuing to rummage through the bagged papers. Nothing else seemed to be connected to the bank, or to have any meaning other than routine. There were personal letters from Lipinsky's sister, a few utility bills, a to-do list with instructions to take the car for inspection, to renew the subscription to a women's magazine, and to buy liquid detergent for the washing machine.

Detective Mahoney returned to his desk and gave me three crisp copies.

I gave him my home phone number. "Please call if any developments occur tonight."

"Like what?"

"Like you find a suspect, or you find that the homicide is definitely connected to his work at the bank."

"Sure."

I hailed a cab and went home. I took off my shoes, uncapped a can of beer, and sank into my couch. I pulled out the printout copies and looked at them. But there was no need for any further scrutiny: The messages weren't garbled, they were simply ciphered. I'd seen hundreds like this during my service in the Israeli armed forces and later at the Mossad. Somebody was sending encrypted messages to the bank; obviously they were out of the ordinary, or at least they'd gotten to the wrong person. Otherwise Lipinsky wouldn't have been so surprised to see them and broken the rules by bringing copies home. Had they brought about his death? Did he see something he shouldn't have? If you send an encrypted message, the recipient must have the key to deciphering the message. Who would that have been? An insider at the bank, or a client? I didn't know. Still, it was a beginning, and I liked the challenge. Even Michelangelo's statue of David started out as a simple block of marble.

My phone rang. "Dan? It's Laura. Is this a good time? I hope I'm not interrupting anything."

"Not at all, not at all," I said, surprised and happy to hear from her. "What's on your mind?"

"Nothing in particular . . ."

I took up the tacit challenge. "Same here, I'm just bored, doing nothing. What about you?"

"I'm going over the notes I took today, getting ready for tomorrow." So she'd received my mental transmissions, and was responding.

"Would you like to do it together, or we could just have a drink, chat or something? I'm having a quiet time at home. Want to join me and Snap?"

"Snap?" she asked.

"My playful retriever."

"Well," she said, slowly, "I don't know if it's appropriate."

"Oh, come on, I promise not to bite, and Snap doesn't, either."

Still she hesitated. "Well, I'm not sure."

"I have good wine and cheese and we could talk about anything. In fact, I was just thinking of you. I had a visitor last night with a troubling story. I have some interesting papers concerning that."

"Anything to do with our case?" she asked.

"Just a suspicion, nothing else. Further investigation is necessary before we know if her story is connected to our case; I'll show you when you come."

An hour later Laura was at my door. Snap was friendly, already wagging his tail. So was I — friendly, I mean. She was dressed in a short tight skirt and a fluffy sweater that did little to hide her attractive body. I got the impression that Laura was very conscious of her appearance and enjoyed the looks it attracted.

She sat on the sofa across from my chair. I poured red wine into her glass, my eyes on her.

She took a sip. "So tell me about your visitor."

I told her about Helen Lipinsky and showed her the copies of the messages I'd received from Mahoney.

"What do you make of it?" she asked, her eyes widening.

"Encryption, plain and simple. Something odd was going on. I have a hunch that there's a connection to our mission, or at least to Lipinsky's disappearance, now homicide —"

"— or to both," she finished. Normally I hate it when people do that, but for Laura it was the first time. "Any idea what these messages might say?"

"No. I'll have to break the code first."

"Why don't you just give the messages to Hodson? He'll know what to do," she suggested.

"Tomorrow morning, but until then, the night is young."

"Can I smoke here?" she suddenly asked, obviously ducking my comment.

"I'm afraid not, if you don't mind."

"Okay, I need to buy cigarettes anyway. I'll go to the corner deli I saw coming here. I'm dying for a cigarette."

Before I could say anything she was gone, leaving behind a trail of her feminine scent. Moments later, I looked out through the window. Laura was standing next to the corner deli talking on her cell phone.

Fifteen minutes later she returned.

"Hi, welcome back, were you able to pick up cigarettes?" I asked.

"Thanks, let's continue," she said, failing to answer my question. She sat next to me on the couch. "Did the NYPD do anything with these messages yet?"

"I have no idea," I said candidly.

"So only NYPD has copies?"

"As far as I know. Why do you ask?"

"Because if NYPD has forwarded copies to other agencies with code-breaking capabilities, we could be wasting our time."

"I agree. Even so, we could still score some points and beat them in the race of breaking the code."

"Do you know anything about encryption?" she asked. Laura knew nothing about my Mossad past, and there was no point in starting to explain now.

"A little. I could try to break the codes, if they're not overly sophisticated."

"Meaning?"

"A cipher is like a locked door between you and the message. To open the door you must have a key."

"I know that much," she said patiently.

"It all depends on the type of key they used," I continued. "If they used a onetime pad, the encryption is unbreakable, unless you get the key first."

"What's a onetime pad?" asked Laura, turning toward me. "Have you ever seen one?"

I nodded. "A onetime pad is a cipher book in which each page contains a unique set of random letters. The sender and receiver have identical pads. Each letter on the pad is used to determine a single letter of the encrypted message. Since the letters on the pad are random, we can't just apply the frequency method by studying the frequency of the letters' appearance."

Laura said nothing, waiting for me to continue.

"The key letters on the pad, and the messages themselves, are typically written in five-letter groups. This helps the communicators to collate and verify the length of the message, and if something was misunderstood, the person at the receiving end could ask for a particular group to be repeated. On each of the onetime pads issued to the user, the key text is printed in different colors: one color for encryption and one for decipher.

"You must link a letter of plain text with the next letter of the key text in the pad to get a letter of encrypted text. There is a three-hundred-year-old system called Vigenère square based on a twenty-six-by-twenty-six table of every single combination of possible monoalphabetical ciphers. It's called a polyalphabetic cipher, because it uses many alphabets. Each alphabet is staggered one letter over from the other, corresponding to a different key letter. So, for example, in the first line, *A* equals *B*, the second line *A* equals *C*, the third line *A* equals *D*, and the rest of the alphabet follows. Thus, success lies in using each alphabet only once for any letter."

"Smart," she said. She seemed to be genuinely interested — in the subject, at least, if not yet in me. I hoped there'd be a smooth transition to that later.

"This is where the onetime pad comes in. It's a guide that tells the recipient which alphabet to use to decrypt a certain letter. So if the first grouping of letters is *BCDEF* — which it would never be, because that's too simple a key — and you were decoding the word *phone*, then for the letter *P* you would encode using the alphabet that starts with a *B*, then for the letter *H* you encode using the alphabet that starts with *C*, and so on, and the word *phone* would become *QJRRZ*. Decryption is extremely complicated and it takes time," I concluded.

I realized as soon as I'd said it that I shouldn't have. From the look on her face, Laura had caught my condescension.

"I'm sorry," I said almost voicelessly, but she heard. "I didn't mean to be such a putz, sometimes when you know something you're impatient with others who don't."

"How do you know these things?"

"I had a prior life," I said. "I'll tell you someday."

That didn't sound good, either. But what the hell, we had a job to do, it was late, and I wasn't in the mood to be politically correct. As if I ever am.

"Please tell me," she asked. She put on a breathy tone: "I promise I won't tell."

I smiled but moved on. "So unless we get our hands on the onetime pad used to encrypt these messages, I'd have more chances of becoming royalty than of breaking it."

"So what's next?" She sounded impatient. "Since we don't have the onetime pads, we can forget about breaking the code?"

"No, because I'm not sure whoever took the trouble to encrypt the messages used onetime pads. Although the method is unbreakable, it has its drawbacks."

"Such as?"

"You need to be a sophisticated user and have some means of communication with the other party. Onetime means onetime, but there should be a way to tell the other side which page you're using. You could include it in the message itself, or pre-agree to select a page according to dates. But, again, that's complicated — which date to choose, particularly when there's a time difference. Was it the date it was written, or the date received?"

"I see," said Laura. "Fine, let's leave it, let the police break it."

I needed no further proof that Laura was a rookie. The police wouldn't have the tools to break ciphers; they would need to outsource it, probably to a federal agency. This time I kept my big mouth shut.

"I don't give up that easily. It could be breakable. I want to give it a try. Wanna help?"

I finally sounded cooperative. That was the right tone to use with Laura. She agreed, but not too enthusiastically. I was somewhat surprised. Was she raising a subtle objection in her behavior so that I'd ask her again?

"So, let's see if these guys are sophisticated enough to have used one-time pads."

"What would they do then?"

"A few options. Let's try the simplest form of encryption. It's called monoalphabetical substitution. There's a single alphabet for the whole document, and each letter is scrambled to be another. The key to breaking this encryption is checking the frequency of the letters, known as frequency analysis. I only hope that the spaces and punctuation haven't been removed, and meaningless spaces haven't been added after every fifth letter, for readability. That could make the text harder to decrypt as we progress."

"I see," she said.

"It's worth a try," I said. "What do we have to lose?"

"Fine."

"Okay, first we need to get some numbers of probabilities."

"This is something I know about," said Laura. "My minor in college was statistics. What do you need to know?"

"The percentage of frequency of each letter of the alphabet in an English text."

"And if the message isn't in English? Then what?"

I had no answer. "Honestly, I didn't think about it. You're right. The encrypted text could be in Portuguese, or Swedish, or *chort znayet*."

"What?"

"Ahh." I smiled. "It means 'only the devil knows' in Russian."

Laura laughed, exposing her perfect teeth. "I thought you were cursing. Do you speak Russian?"

"I picked up a little from a Russian girlfriend I had some years back. But here's what's important now: Every language follows certain linguistic patterns, the most obvious of these being letter frequency. As the length of the text increases, so does the likelihood that it will begin to follow typical patterns. The decoding of the encrypted text is based on comparisons between the frequencies of characters in the encrypted text and frequencies of characters in a plain text."

"Okay, then the statistical tools we should use are summary statistics and sampling. I can't give you numbers off the top of my head. Only linguists could do that."

"Do you know any?"

Laura hesitated. "There's an old professor, Alexander Klebanov. He must have retired by now, but he was always giving us problems that included calculating probabilities of letters in random sentences."

"That's our guy," I said excitedly. "Could you call him?"

"Now?"

"Sure."

She lifted the receiver and dialed the 411 national directory.

Five minutes later Professor Klebanov was on my speakerphone from his Florida home. After the absolutely necessary niceties, including three long minutes of Laura trying to remind the professor who she was, she finally posed the question.

"I need to know in what language you assume the message was written," he answered in a slight accent. "Asking the right question is almost as important as getting the right answers." I imagined him saying that before a class full of college students.

"We don't know, but let's assume it was English."

"Next, I need to know if it was written in American modern English or, say, Shakespearean English."

"Same answer, no idea. If it's English, I'd suspect the language used was modern to be able to include contemporary terms such as *bank* or *currency*," she said.

Obviously, she was right: Shakespeare didn't receive royalties through direct wire transfers into his bank account.

Laura was smart. I liked smart women.

"I think there's simple computer software that analyzes frequency of letters," said Professor Klebanov.

"Does it work in reverse as well?"

"Meaning?"

"Can it decrypt?"

"Maybe," he responded. "But why don't you fax me the document you want to break, and I'll try doing it here. I have always liked these mental games."

"Sure," said Laura.

"Sorry, we can't," I interjected. "Thank you for your kind offer, but this is government material. I hope you understand."

"Of course," said Professor Klebanov. "Well, in that case, I have software in my home computer that does the calculations, so if you give me a random sentence, I could analyze the letters' frequency. That would give you the probabilities you wanted. But to be more accurate I suggest you use the table calculated by Beker and Piper."

"Do you happen to have a copy?"

"I have a book with the table in it. I can fax it to you. I can't tear out the page, so I hope you won't mind me copying it longhand. Do you have a fax machine available?"

"Kind of. I have a fax card in my home computer."

"That'll do it. Give me the number."

I gave it to him.

Laura thanked Professor Klebanov and hung up.

Twenty minutes later a handwritten message came in by fax.

| Letter | % Frequency |
|--------|-------------|
| A | 5.9 |
| B | 1.5 |
| C | 2.8 |
| D | 1.3 |
| E | 3.3 |
| F | 3.2 |

| | |
|---|---|
| G | 2.5 |
| H | 4.1 |
| I | 5.7 |
| J | 0.2 |
| K | 0.8 |
| L | 5.0 |
| M | 4.4 |
| N | 4.7 |
| O | 5.5 |
| P | 1.9 |
| Q | 0.1 |
| R | 5.4 |
| S | 6.9 |
| T | 5.1 |
| U | 2.8 |
| V | 1.0 |
| W | 2.4 |
| X | 0.2 |
| Y | 2.0 |
| Z | 0.1 |

"That's great," I said enthusiastically. "Now let's see if we can get anything out of the text."

Laura was cautious. "Remember that these numbers are based on sample writing. Frequency of certain letters will change from one text to another, but within the margin of error."

I moved to the couch next to Laura, who stretched out her legs, leaving a very narrow space for me, almost touching her body. "I'm comfortable here," she said. "I hope you don't mind."

"Not at all." Her head was close to mine and I could smell her. Although she told me that she'd gone out to smoke a cigarette, there was no tobacco scent; only a gentle perfume.

I took the top message of the three I received from Detective Mahoney, printed another copy of Professor Klebanov's table, and gave it to Laura. I put my copies on the small coffee table next to us.

"It seems that once you break the first ten letters, the rest are like completing sentences in *Wheel of Fortune*," she said.

I felt pressured. I went over the encrypted text, almost praying that the ciphered text was in English and the encryption was not deep. I gulped from my beer and felt the tangy bitterness cool my throat.

"What letter appears in the message most frequently?" she asked.

"Let me count . . . I think the letter *X*," I answered. "So we could assume it was replacing *A*, which according to the table is the most frequently used letter in English." That came as a surprise to me, though. I counted again, "The next most frequent letter in the ciphered text is *Y*."

"It could be *I*." She pointed at the chart, which said *I* is the third most common letter in the English language.

The third most frequent letter was *G*. "According to the chart, I assumed it was an *S*," she said.

I paused. "Something must be wrong," I had to concede. "There is no word in English that starts with the sequence *ais*."

"How about *aisle*?"

"Okay. Any other word?" I asked.

Laura was quick to evaluate the situation. "I don't think so. If it's not *aisle*, then there are at least two explanations. The first is that the ciphered text is in a language other than English."

"And the other?"

"That the text was encrypted in a more sophisticated method than the one we're assuming."

It was possible the work we had already put in was worthless. I took another sip of my beer and started to think about an alternative, more joyful manner to spend the rest of the evening with Laura. I had a sense she thought so, too, hence her apparent unenthusiastic behavior.

Her voice brought me back to the cold reality. "I don't think we have any alternatives at this time."

"So you want to quit?" I asked.

"I think so," she said.

"Well, let's give it a try and continue with the two assumptions, that the text is in English and that the encryption is substituting letters."

"To make things even more complicated," she said with a grin, sensing my frustration, "the chart of frequencies is statistical, and statistics have a margin of error. So although *X, Y*, and *G* are used most frequently, it does not necessarily mean that they were used in that order."

"I know," I confirmed. "We simply can't be certain that *X* equals *A, Y* equals *I*, and *G* equals *S*."

"True," she agreed. "So let's assume for a minute that *X, Y*, and *G* stand for *E, L*, and *R*, because the probabilities are close and the text is relatively short."

I nodded. I saw what she was aiming at and I liked it. I continued her train of thought. "To be more precise, we must look at the letters *next to* the most frequent letters, because grammatical rules limit the probability of a certain letter being next to another. For example, the letter *Q* is almost always followed by *U*, but is never found next to *Z*, unless it's a foreign name."

When Laura just nodded, I added, "And *T* never comes before or after *B, D, G*, and, I think, a few other letters."

"Okay," she said, "I give up, and I'm exhausted. It's too late for me to get a cab to go home. I'm uncomfortable to travel alone that late. Is there a couch I could use?"

"No, I'll use the couch. You take the bedroom."

"Are you sure?"

I wasn't. In fact I hadn't changed my sheets in five days. But what the hell. Let her smell my scent as well. I showed her my bedroom and, for a minute, entertained the idea of suggesting I join her. But she gave me no sign of encouragement, and a rejection at this stage would foul things up. So the complete gentleman, a role I rarely played, I gave her one of my extra-large T-shirts, bid her good night, and fell on the couch in the living room. I closed my eyes and thought of Laura. She was so close, just a few feet away. I tried to think of something less tantalizing. I rolled from side to side but couldn't fall asleep. I got up, turned on my desk lamp, and looked at the encrypted documents. Maybe they had used a onetime pad and I was wasting my time. But what if they hadn't? I decided to give it another try. Maybe Professor Klebanov had erred, or the sampling error had twisted the results.

I decided to calculate the probability of letters that were vowels and consonants. I picked up yesterday's newspaper from the bin, copied twenty sentences, and counted the letters. Half an hour later using my calculator, I had a completely different probability table. Professor Klebanov must have been looking at numbers for a different language.

I looked at the combination *XX*. It appeared twice, but neither *Y* nor *G* appeared doubled anywhere, so that supported the assumption that X was replacing E.

Two hours, half a bottle of wine, and one beer later, I was still struggling. But I'd cracked eleven letters, enough to see that I was on the right path.

I looked at the broken words and thought, *Good! The text was written in English!*

The only conclusion was that the text had been encrypted in monoalphabetical cipher. That was a relief, and a warm sense of achievement came over me.

I put together the letters I'd identified while the still-ciphered letters were substituted with blank spaces. I highlighted the letters I'd identified with a yellow marker.

I read out the text softly, hoping it would make some sense.

*"ma-eth reetr ans-e rs—ni nehun dredt h-usa ndusd —-ar seach t-acc -unth h-tth reeth reeze r—ne at-an -schi —eri nsa-z burgd -n-tn ameap ayeem eeting withc -mrad et-ex chang eison march secon dtran s-ers must- ecomp - eted be-or ethen sa-eh."*

It didn't mean anything, it was crazy. A trace of despair crept over me. And I was tired.

I had a drink of soda and got another idea. Maybe I could break the blocks into normal-sized words of two, three, four, or five letters. Currently the message was broken into five-letter blocks. Nothing is really written like that.

But on a second thought, why two, three, or four letters? There are also English words that have only one letter, *I* or *A*. I continued working on it, trying to keep my eyes open. I was really exhausted. But I wanted to break it more than anything else. Well, almost. Finally, I whispered it aloud:

*"make three transfers of nine hundred thousand usdollars each to account hhkt three three three zero one at bank schiller in salzburg do not name a payee meeting with comrade to exchange is on march second transfers must be completed before that day saleh."*

What the hell? This wasn't plain bankers' talk. What was this bull about a comrade? And the signature, *Saleh*: an Arab or Muslim name? The message reeked to me of conspiracy.

*I should call Hodson*, I thought, but then I looked at my watch: 3:00 A.M. It could wait until morning.

I crawled back to my makeshift bed on the couch. I heard a beep; then another, and another. I couldn't fall asleep with some damn electronic gadget beeping, so I got up and looked around: my cell phone? No. The beep came again. It seemed to come from Laura's purse. It was dark and I didn't want to turn on the light. I put my hand into her purse searching for it, and felt a cold metal. I turned on a desk lamp. It was Laura's service revolver. I emptied her bag and found her phone. As I was about to turn it off, I changed my mind. I pressed the SEND button and wrote down the last number she'd called. Was it just idle curiosity to know whether she had a boyfriend, or was that the persistent suspicious devil in me? I turned off her phone and returned to bed.

Before falling asleep, I thought about Saleh. Who was he? Even more important, who was the guy at the bank who could decipher and follow the instructions? I'd like to talk with him. Then it dawned on me. Very recently I'd read in a magazine that a rare manuscript by Abu Yusuf Yaqub ibn Ishaq al-Kindi had been found in a forgotten archive in Turkey. The story had attracted my attention because the manuscript discussed monoalphabetical encryption. In addition, I knew I'd heard that name before. Mussa, my Mossad Arab customs instructor, came into my mind. With his own unique flourish on combining fables, proverbs, and daily wisdom, he'd told us that the Arabs proudly claim Abu Yusuf Yaqub ibn Ishaq al-Kindi, who lived in Iraq in the ninth century. *The Arabs call him the first Arab philosopher*, he'd said while touching his gray mustache. *All previous known Arab philosophers were not pure Arabs. Al-Kindi was a prolific writer who wrote two hundred forty-one books. Keep their pride in mind, and familiarize yourself with other subjects of Arab pride. Believe me, it will always prove to be an asset when you make a professional contact.* From Mussa we learned that al-Kindi had been a mathematician; now, according to the magazine article, it appeared he had been a clever code breaker as well.

The article described how in the newly discovered manuscript, al-Kindi had outlined exactly the method of breaking an encrypted text in a monoalphabetical cipher. Had the encryption method for the messages sent to the bank been chosen because it was connected to a subject of Arab pride? It would explain why they had chosen such a simple encryption. The connection, if any, was too vague. But still. I combined it with the Arab name mentioned in the decrypted message. *It's a beginning*, I concluded, before falling asleep.

I woke up first with a backache. A garbage truck in the street was making its annoying early-morning noises. I hadn't slept so badly in a long time. I looked in the bathroom mirror: My eyes were red and my cheeks sunken. Not a happy sight to show a woman in whom you're taking a growing interest on your first morning together, albeit after a night spent apart. I was making tea when Laura walked into the living room wearing the T-shirt I had given her. She wasn't wearing a bra. I forced myself to take my eyes off her breasts.

"Do you want tea?"

"Any coffee?"

"Sure. Sleep well?"

"Great," she said while stretching her hands up, lifting the T-shirt above her knees. "Wanna continue breaking the message?" She was energized, while I was still numb. She had slept in a comfortable bed, and I'd been feeling every loose spring on my old sofa.

"We only need to break two. I managed to decipher the first one."

"How did you do that?"

"Professor Klebanov's table was way off the mark. I calculated a new one and the rest was easy."

"Easy?" she repeated.

"Well, not that easy, but I did it in three hours."

We sat at the kitchen table, and while sipping from a thin glass teacup I said, "I'm done."

"These guys aren't that sophisticated," she said.

"I guess not," I answered. "They used the same key again. A big no-no."

"Let me see what the message says," she asked.

I yawned and stretched my arms and hands out. "No, let me read it to you."

WE ARE CONFIRMED THAT THE SCIENTISTS WILL DELIVER THE CARRIERS TO ERADICATE HUNDREDS OF THOUSANDS OF INFIDELS MEETING IN ROME ON FEBRUARY TWENTY AT HOTEL MAJESTIC BE THERE ONE DAY AHEAD OF TIME DO NOT TRAVEL TOGETHER IF THERE IS NO APPEARANCE GO SEVEN DAYS LATER TO PARIS AND WAIT AT HOTEL BRAVADO FOR CONTACT DO NOT ATTEMPT TO CALL US OUR BROTHER IN NEW YORK WILL CHANGE ACCESS CODE TO AUSTRIAN BANK ACCOUNT IF TRANSACTION FAILS SALEH

"That's terror money!" she cried, then grew pale.

"There's no question about it. This is a conspiracy that conducts itself more like an espionage ring than money launderers intent on blackmail," I said, taking new resolve from the facts. "The word *infidels*, the encryption, the secrecy, the alternative meeting places; that's a terror cell buying something lethal, nothing less." Laura was already busy working on the third message with the enthusiasm that she'd lacked last night. But after some time she turned to me again, troubled.

"I can't seem to crack it. They must have used another system of encryption, or applied special cryptography security."

"We should talk to Hodson immediately," I said. This time, it was really urgent. I made the call.

Forty-five minutes later Laura and I were sitting in his office in 26 Federal Plaza.

"What's on your mind?" He sounded almost friendly.

I told him how I'd gotten the ciphered messages, and that we'd been working on them.

"Has it been deciphered by NSA?" Hodson asked. "I didn't see it in today's mail."

"No, it hasn't. We broke it last night."

He gave me a dismissive look, as if to say *Yeah, right.* "And?" he finally said.

"It could be a matter of money laundering as well, but as we see it now, it concerns national security more than anything else."

"What the hell are you saying?"

"I'm saying we're facing terrorists, not run-of-the-mill money launderers."

He sat up in his chair and leaned toward me. "Let me see that!" he ordered.

"The two messages we cracked concerned instructions to someone, telling them to transfer money to a number-coded Austrian bank account to purchase, and I quote, 'the carriers to eradicate hundreds of thousands of infidels.' We haven't been able to break the third one."

"Let me see them," he demanded again.

I gave him the messages, encrypted and deciphered.

"How long have you had these?"

"Since six o'clock last night."

"I didn't see you here last night."

"I made copies of the messages and we worked on it at home after hours."

"Are you nuts?" he yelled at me. "You removed classified information from the office without my permission? What else have you done?" I was reminded of my third-grade teacher, who'd used the same language when she thought I needed to be disciplined. But the mustache made a difference; she had one, Hodson didn't.

Laura was pale and sat there quietly biting her lips.

"Who said it was classified?" I retorted calmly. "The bad guys know what it contains, while we don't . . . I mean, you didn't, until a few minutes ago." I was teasing him; nobody gets to yell at me without a retaliation of some kind, even if he is a top bureaucrat. "So it's the reverse of a leak. The leak's route usually runs from the guys who know to the guys who don't, not the other way around." He couldn't have missed the sarcasm in my voice.

"Now they could know that we know," Hodson pointed out.

"They don't. I kept it for a few hours, worked on it with Laura, and brought it back. Nothing was left behind at my home."

"All right, I'll deal with you later. What's your read on the messages?" he asked Laura.

"As Dan was saying," she said in a subdued voice, "they were coded messages. Not too sophisticated an encryption, I must say, but still it took almost all night to crack them."

"Get to the point," Hodson said impatiently. I was enjoying this cat-and-mouse game, but for a change I was the cat.

"The bottom line," I said, "is that someone in Europe is willing to pay two point seven million dollars for carriers of materials potent enough to kill several hundred thousand people. That person or these people must have had an insider at Eagle Bank who could read these messages; there should also be a source of the money at the bank, a depositor who has sufficient funds available in his account and who can authorize, or authorize someone on his behalf, to withdraw and transfer the money. That doesn't sound like a one-man operation. It reeks of a terrorist network."

"Any more details?" Hodson asked.

"We still need to break the third message. We were unable to," said Laura.

I added, "There could be other messages that didn't pass through Lipinsky; I think we should look for them."

"I'd let the NSA boys do the deciphering job, since it's theirs and not yours," Hodson snapped.

I waited for more berating. I also wondered how NSA's G Group, which is responsible for eavesdropping on all communications emanating from, or being sent to, the United States, had missed these messages.

"Any more bright ideas?" he asked. He was serious, despite the sarcastic tone.

"Yes," I said, "I think we should start working on the bank in Salzburg. It might lead us to the suppliers of the carriers."

"No name of a beneficiary for the money transfer to Austria?"

"No. Just an account number. It could be in the third message, but it seems unlikely."

"Why?"

"Because that's how money launderers work. Why put down the name of a beneficiary when you have a coded account? Maybe Saleh wanted to keep the identity of the ultimate beneficiary secret in case the message was intercepted and deciphered. Simple communication security. There is some talk there about an access code, so we may be talking about two- or three-party transactions, not necessarily your ordinary transfer of funds from one account holder to the other."

"Okay," said Hodson. "I'll talk to the Office of International Affairs at the Criminal Division of the Justice Department to prepare a Mutual Legal Assistance Treaty request to the Austrian Ministry of Justice."

"It might take a long time," I commented.

"I know. We'll let the Austrian desk at State know when the MLAT request goes, and ask it to cable our embassy in Vienna to tell the Austrian Ministry of Foreign Affairs that it's important for the Ministry of Justice to get this executed quickly."

"My experience with the Austrian legal system is that they're extremely bureaucratic. By the time the government is satisfied with the material submitted, which is not guaranteed, they would ask a court in Salzburg to issue a warrant ordering the bank to disclose the account. By that time, I could have circled the globe on foot."

"Dan, you do your job. Investigate. Let the lawyers handle the Austrians."

"Of course," I said. "What I meant is that we have no time. Even if the Austrians surprise us with the speed of their work, it may not be fast enough."

"I hear you. What about the recipient of the messages at Eagle Bank?" Hodson asked. "Anybody we know? The solution could come from that angle."

"Maybe." I reminded him about Fazal, the disappearance of Lipinsky, his death, and the possible connection between the two.

"Detective Mahoney called me this morning about Lipinsky's homicide. Another thing you forgot to report," grunted Hodson. His anger was mounting and his face became red.

"A simple matter of priorities. I was about to tell you, but I thought the alarming nature of the messages should take precedence." There was no apology in my tone.

Hodson didn't comment. But he continued as though nothing had happened. His ability to switch moods from anger to business as usual was remarkable. I should learn how to do that.

"Is it possible that Lipinsky was wasted because he saw the messages? That makes Fazal a prime suspect," I suggested.

"Is anyone sitting on his tail?" Why was Hodson asking me? He should know after his conversation with Mahoney.

I answered anyway. "We're not. NYPD is investigating the missing-person-turned-homicide case, so maybe they're making sure he won't just be in the wind."

"Mahoney told me that you had asked him to question Fazal as a witness, not as a suspect."

"I did. I didn't want to scare him off until we clear the fog. So has Mahoney done that?"

"Apparently."

"Are we doing any independent checks on him?"

Hodson nodded. "We're running a background check. I should have it momentarily."

He pressed his intercom. "Lynn, make sure they include in the Fazal report a search in the Counterterrorism Database, and the CIA's database as well. Also get me FBI's International Terrorism Operations Section; they need to send their representatives here. This matter seems to be going in their direction."

"I hear that there are problems in pooling together the databases," I jumped in, though I knew I was out of line.

Hodson didn't even blink when he snapped, "Dan, I am familiar with our procedures." Reminding him of the rivalry between the agencies, 9/11 notwithstanding, was worse than stepping on his toe.

Hodson pressed the intercom again, "Lynn, get me Detective Mahoney on the phone."

A moment later he continued. "Mahoney? This is FBI Assistant Director in Charge Hodson. I hear you're watching Malik Fazal." Apparently not waiting for an answer, he added, "We're taking over, it's become a federal matter."

Hodson's face color changed all of sudden from red to Irish purple. "What do you mean he disappeared? What kind of police work are you guys doing? When did that happen? Let me talk to your lieutenant. Ask him to call me the minute he walks in." He slammed the phone on its cradle. "The SOB disappeared. Mahoney says Fazal didn't show up to work yesterday morning. They were watching his office, not his home. Budget problems," he muttered in disgust.

"John," said Hodson to his assistant on the intercom, "put out an all-points bulletin on Malik Fazal, and put him also on the lookout list; alert all law enforcement agencies that he's wanted for questioning. Run a computer check on all airlines and passenger ship manifests. But other than that, don't spread the word in the street that we'd like to talk to him. This has to be kept quiet, for now."

Lynn Harris, Hodson's blond all-American assistant, entered the room. "I spoke to the Treasury Department," she said. "According to their records, Malik Fazal was the bank officer who routinely signed the Suspicious Activity Reports for Eagle Bank."

Hodson looked at Laura and me sitting across his desk. "That may explain why there were no reports on these massive transfers. He 'forgot.'"

He pushed a button on his speakerphone. "John, get me Hayes from legal; we need to get search warrants. Then take three messages from Dan Gordon, two of which apparently have been deciphered already. Ask NSA to break the third message and verify the accuracy of the decryption Dan and Laura have already made."

"Right away."

A moment later, another voice came on the speakerphone: "Joe Hayes."

"Joe, I'm sending Laura Higgins to your office. She'll give you all the pertinent details for search warrants we need right away. I want you to complete the paperwork immediately; get it before a federal judge within the hour."

Laura left the room with the messages.

A short time later Joe Hayes, looking barely out of high school, walked into Hodson's office with Laura, carrying a manila folder. Judge McElroy was expected in his chambers in twenty minutes, he told Hodson. If Hodson approved, Hayes would submit to the judge an affidavit, attached to the warrant petition, asking that the entire file be sealed.

"I approve," snapped Hodson.

"The question is whether Judge McElroy will agree to it. He has a reputation for being tough on government search warrants. That could take time," said Hayes.

"Do we have anyone else?" asked Hodson.

"No, he's the duty judge, unless you want to wait."

"No, I don't."

"Then it's Judge McElroy," said Hayes. "Who'll sign the supporting affidavit?"

"I'll sign it," said Hodson. "Make sure the search warrants include wire and computer tapping."

"I already included that," said Hayes. "But from what I've heard so far, we still don't have enough probable cause for an arrest. We need much more, so we may have to do wire and computer tapping first before we force ourselves in."

"No time for that," said Hodson. "Anyway, I hear he's gone already." With that, Hayes handed the documents to Hodson, who gave them a quick look, took out a pen, and signed the affidavit.

Two hours later Joe Hayes he returned to 26 Federal Plaza. "We got it. Old McElroy signed and sealed the warrants."

Hodson nodded, looking relieved, then picked up the receiver and called his assistant. "The Fazal matter: We have warrants. Send three agent squads to his home and two to his office at the bank. Both searches should be done concurrently. Give them an hour to prepare, that's all."

By now I was wide awake, despite my short and uncomfortable night. I felt the same rush of adrenaline that I usually experience during overseas operations. For a change this one was home-based.

"Bob, I want to accompany the search units at Fazal's home," I said, expecting a refusal.

Hodson thought for a minute, then nodded. "Okay, but no independent initiatives. Got it?"

Only two weeks in the task force and he already knew me well. I quickly went downstairs and got in an unmarked FBI car. From the southern tip of Manhattan, we crossed the Brooklyn Bridge and drove to Midwood, Brooklyn, the country's largest residential and commercial Afghanistani neighborhood. Many stores displayed signs offering Afghanistani groceries and delicacies. Others carried signs offering Dari translation services, Afghanistani books, music, and videos.

The streets were crowded with people. It was a late Thursday afternoon. Scores of mothers, many of them *hijab*-clad, were pushing baby strollers with full shopping bags. The neighborhood looked as if it had been imported wholesale from Afghanistan or Pakistan. We passed Makki Masjid, the neighborhood mosque, which stood next to three adjoining brick apartment buildings. As we made a turn into a side street, two other unmarked FBI vans arrived from the other direction.

Sixteen FBI agents jumped out of the vehicles, all wearing blue windbreakers with FBI marked in yellow on the back. The lead agent bounded up a short flight of stairs to one of the redbrick buildings and knocked on the door. Curious passersby and neighbors started gathering to watch.

"Open up. Police," shouted the mustached armed agent as he banged on the door. It was quickly opened by an elderly, Asian-looking woman in a *hijab* and a long, loose-fitting robe who seemed too scared to react. The agent showed her the search warrant and seemed to exchange a few words with her.

"She's Fazal's aunt, it's her home," I heard the agent reporting over the radio.

The woman looked startled and overwhelmed while a female agent silently moved next to her to keep her from compromising evidence.

I got out of the car and went up the few steps to the door, peering into the aunt's face. Why hadn't she asked any questions or protested the search? Was she too stunned and fearful to react, or did she have some inkling of Fazal's activities, in which case her lack of curiosity would be telling? I followed the agents inside. The modest apartment was empty. Fazal was not there. Not a surprise. I was certain he was long gone — "in the wind," as the intelligence community likes to say of a target of surveillance who has vanished.

The small apartment had two bedrooms and one living room joined by a kitchen. The living room was decorated with inexpensive green-upholstered furniture, a small chipped wooden coffee table, and an old TV set. A big photograph of al-Aqsa mosque in Jerusalem was hanging on a wall. The FBI agents went through everything in the apartment, emptying drawers, kitchen cabinets, and bedroom closets. They rolled up the carpets, checking underneath. They inspected the wooden floors to see whether any of the planks had recently been removed. They checked the walls, the ceiling, even the bathroom pipes, using sonic and magnetic sensors to scan for inconsistencies indicating hollow areas that could be used to hide objects. I was impressed with the methodical and efficient manner with which they operated, visibly making efforts not to damage the premises.

During all that time, Fazal's aunt stood silently, her eyes wide open, next to the female agent.

I entered what I assumed was Fazal's bedroom. Two agents were searching the closets. I looked around. There wasn't much to see: a closet, a queen-sized bed with a pinkish marblelike Formica headboard, and two night tables, one on either side. On the left-hand table was a copy of the Koran: The Arabic was printed on the left side, the English translation on the right. A bookmark pointed to the ninth Sura, or chapter. It said:

> Is one who establishes his building on the basis of reverencing Allah and to gain His approval better, or one who establishes his building on the precipice of a crumbling cliff, that falls down with him into the fire of Hell? Allah does not guide the transgressing people.

The agents lifted the mattress from the box spring, but nothing looked suspicious. They checked the seams to see if something had been sewn inside. They passed a metal detector over the bed and the walls, and repeated the process with the sonic sensor. The beeping remained steady.

I was curious about Fazal; I wanted to get into his head. Was he young or old? Was he innocent despite the circumstantial evidence mounting against him? Was he a thread that, if pulled hard enough, would unravel the intricate weaving of a terrorist network?

I went to the front door. The female agent was still standing silently next to the elderly lady.

"I need to ask her a few questions," I said. "Madam, how are you related to Malik Fazal?"

"I'm his aunt," she answered in a strong Afghanistani accent.

"His father's sister?"

"No, my late husband was Malik's mother's brother."

"Does he live here?"

"Yes."

"When is he coming home?" I didn't want to show that we knew he had probably already taken off.

"At about six thirty."

"Did you talk to him today?"

She hesitated, then lowered her eyes. "No, not today."

"Did he sleep here last night?"

"I don't know. I went to sleep early last night. I didn't see him."

"And did you see him this morning?"

"No, he usually leaves early for the morning prayer at the mosque and then goes to work."

"Where is his telephone book?"

"You mean the telephone directory? It's inside, in the kitchen."

"No, I mean the apartment's private telephone book. Where you write up numbers of your friends, your doctors."

"In the kitchen, underneath the telephone directory."

I went inside to the kitchen. It was small and clean. There was no evidence of having been in use that morning. I found the telephone book. Leather-bound, it looked like a prayer book. I flipped through the pages. There were hundreds of numbers and names written in Arabic script.

I returned to the front door, where Fazal's aunt stood quietly. I expected that at some point she'd ask what the hell was going on. *Why are the agents there? What do they want? Am I being accused of something; is Fazal being accused of something?* But she still said nothing. "Where does he keep his passport? Can I see it?"

"I don't know."

"Did he have a U.S. passport?"

"No. He has an Afghanistani passport."

"Any other passports?"

"I don't know."

"I need to see a recent photo of him."

She entered the living room, the female FBI agent following, and took a family album from the coffee table. She pointed to a color photo of Fazal, who looked in the picture as if he were about thirty-five and fairly slight — maybe five foot eight. "That's him."

"How long ago was this taken?"

"I don't know, maybe two or three years ago."

"Does he look the same?"

"No."

"Why?"

"He grew a short beard."

"With a mustache?"

"No."

Back in the living room, I saw two agents pull out of their side pouch two big plastic trash bags, loading them with documents. I handed them the telephone book, the Koran, and the album. His photo would be used in the identikit — a tool used to reconstruct portraits of suspects for whom no current photo is available.

"Please keep the Koran separately," I said. "This is their holy book. Treat it with respect."

The agent put the Koran in a small clear plastic zip-lock bag, and put it in his jacket pocket.

Another agent went to his car and pulled out a folded cardboard box, which he assembled and loaded with files. By now we'd been here two hours, but the agents were still searching the premises. I looked through the window. A crowd had gathered in front of the house, silently watching the agents in action. Four New York police officers stood behind a yellow police line that cordoned off the agents and their cars from the crowd. A resourceful hot dog vendor, sensing the business potential, had moved his cart close by.

The mustached agent once again approached Fazal's aunt, gave her his card, and politely asked her to call him if she wanted to talk to him. "We may have to call you with some more questions. If Fazal returns here or calls, call me. I hope you understand that this is a serious federal matter and anyone who makes any attempt to obstruct justice may find him- or herself in a serious trouble with the law."

She nodded; she understood. The agents loaded four cartons full of documents and three plastic bags into their vans, and we returned to Manhattan.

"When can we see the items you removed from the premises?" I asked the lead agent, sitting in the front seat.

"As soon as we make a complete inventory. I suggest you see Mr. Hodson about arrangements. It's his call."

As I entered the task force office, I saw Laura and Jim Lion in the hallway.

"Any success?" asked Jim.

"The FBI removed about thirty pounds of documents. But I don't know what they include, except for a few items I found. We'll have to wait for Hodson to tell us."

"Anything special?" asked Laura.

"A photo album, a telephone book, and the Koran."

"Why the Koran?" asked Jim.

"There was a particular verse marked. It troubled me."

"Remember what it said?"

"I copied it." I read it to them.

"It sounds like a prophecy," said Jim Lion.

"I hope not," said Laura.

"I hear that the search at the bank turned up empty," said Jim. "Fazal must have cleaned up his office before leaving. He even reformatted the hard disk of his computer to erase all traces of stored data."

"If the formatting has been done recently, we could still retrieve information," I said.

"I know. They brought in the entire computer."

I looked at Laura. She looked lovely, but pale. Either she wasn't wearing makeup or the implications of the case alarmed her.

I entered my office and filled up the time writing long-overdue reports. I glanced at my watch; two more hours had passed, and still no call from Hodson. At five o'clock I went home. Nothing major had been found, I concluded, so I might as well call my children and walk my dog.

# VIII

Next morning, as soon as I entered my office and turned on my monitor, I saw a message from Hodson: There would be an urgent meeting at 9:00 A.M. Attendance was mandatory. As I walked into the conference room, I saw Laura looking at a big board. Twenty other people were already there talking in a low voice. Tension was in the air. The top line written in bold letters read:

MAJOR TERRORIST ATTACKS AGAINST U.S. TARGETS

Below was a list. Some we'd already forgotten:

- September 11, 2001: Four hijacked commercial airlines are slammed into the World Trade Center, the Pentagon, and a field in Pennsylvania, killing 3,020 people, injuring 2,337. Al Qaeda claims responsibility.
- August 7, 1998: Terrorist bombs destroy the U.S. embassies in Nairobi, Kenya, and Dar es Salaam, Tanzania. In Nairobi, 12 Americans and 270 other nationals are killed and more than 5,000 are wounded, including 6 Americans. In Dar es Salaam, 1 U.S. citizen is wounded, 10 people are killed, and 77 are injured.
- June 21, 1998: Rocket-propelled grenades explode near the U.S. embassy in Beirut.
- July 27, 1996: A pipe bomb explodes during the Olympic Games in Atlanta, killing 1 person and wounding 111.
- June 25, 1996: A bomb aboard a fuel truck explodes outside a U.S. Air Force installation in Dhahran, Saudi Arabia. Nineteen U.S. military personnel are killed in the Khubar Towers housing facility, and 515 are wounded, including 240 Americans.

- November 13, 1995: A car bomb in Riyadh, Saudi Arabia, kills 7 people, 5 of them American military and civilian advisers for National Guard training. The Tigers of the Gulf, Islamist Movement for Change, and Fighting Advocates of God claim responsibility.
- February 1993: A bomb in a van explodes in the underground parking garage in New York's World Trade Center, killing 6 people and wounding 1,042.
- December 21, 1988: A bomb destroys Pan Am Flight 103 over Lockerbie, Scotland. All 259 people aboard are killed, including 189 Americans, as well as 11 people on the ground.
- April 1986: An explosion damages a TWA flight before landing in Athens, Greece. Four people are killed.
- April 5, 1986: A bomb explodes in the LaBelle discotheque in West Berlin. One American and 1 German are killed; 150 are wounded, including 44 Americans.
- December 18, 1985: Simultaneous suicide attacks against U.S. and Israeli airline check-in desks at Rome and Vienna international airports. Twenty people are killed.
- November 24, 1985: Hijackers aboard an Egypt Air flight kill 1 American. Egyptian forces later storm the aircraft in Malta. Sixty people are killed.
- October 7, 1985: Palestinian terrorists hijack the cruise liner *Achille Lauro*. Leon Klinghoffer, an elderly, wheelchair-bound American, is murdered and thrown overboard.
- August 8, 1985: A car bomb at a U.S. military base in Frankfurt, Germany, explodes, killing 2 and injuring 20.
- June 19, 1985: In San Salvador, El Salvador, 13 people are killed in a machine-gun attack in an outdoor café, including 4 U.S. Marines and 2 American businessmen.
- April 12, 1985: A bomb explodes in a restaurant near a U.S. air base in Madrid, Spain, killing 18, all Spaniards, and wounding 82, including 15 Americans.
- November 1984: A bomb attack on the U.S. embassy in Bogotá, Colombia, kills a passerby.

- September 20, 1984: A truck bomb explodes outside the U.S. embassy annex in Aukar, northeast of Beirut. The ambassador is injured and 24 people are killed, including two U.S. military personnel.
- March 16, 1984: CIA Beirut station chief William Buckley is kidnapped by militant Islamic extremists in Lebanon. He dies after prolonged torture. His body is found on December 27, 1991, in southern Beirut.
- December 12, 1983: Shiite extremists bomb the French and U.S. embassies in Kuwait, killing 6 and injuring over 80 people. The suspects are members of al-Dawa, a terrorist group supported by Iran.
- October 23, 1983: A suicide car bomb attack against the U.S. Marine barracks in Beirut kills 241 servicemen. A simultaneous attack on a French base kills 58 paratroopers.
- April 18, 1983: A suicide car bombing against the U.S. embassy in Beirut kills 63, including 17 Americans.
- November 4, 1979: Fundamentalist Islamist students take 52 Americans hostage at the U.S. embassy in Tehran, Iran.
- June 14, 2002: Car bomb at U.S. Consulate in Karachi, Pakistan, kills 12.

Laura and the others gazed at the list. She turned to me when she saw me approaching. "What's going on here? Why is that list displayed?" she mumbled in surprise and trepidation as she leaned against the bare wall.

"Beats me," I said, and then it hit me. The documents obtained during the search must have been analyzed. Put together the deciphered messages, the huge money transfers, and Lipinsky's homicide and we apparently had one huge national security crisis on our plate.

Bob Hodson walked into the conference room together with four other men, all in dark blue business suits.

"DC guys," said Laura.

I looked at Hodson's face. I had come to know him a bit during the past few weeks. He looked somber and serious.

"Please be seated," he said. "There has been a major development. As a result of recent combined intelligence and investigation efforts of this task force and several other U.S. federal agencies, the scope of our investigation has been broadened. Although the money-laundering mission of this task force continues to be within our charter, a priority is now given to issues of national security. The FBI director and the secretary of Homeland Security have received the president's instruction to allocate all available means and personnel to crack this impending crisis."

"What is he talking about?" whispered Laura, standing so close to me I could almost hear her accelerated heartbeat.

"I don't know. But those charts are probably connected to what he's about to tell us."

Bob Hodson cleared his throat and continued, "The things I am about to tell you are top secret, I repeat top secret. By that I mean both vertical and lateral confidentiality. All fresh intel you will collect or analyze, you will deny up or down the chain of command, including your peer groups, unless they appear on the disclose list. Reporting will be made only through direct channels to me. Do I make myself clear?" He looked around; a hum of acceptance was sounded.

Hodson continued, "We have credible information that a terrorist organization calling itself the Slaves of Allah is planning to launch a massive attack against the United States. Their first target may be Manhattan. The information we have indicates that they have been using coded messages sent to Eagle Bank of New York to transfer money to an Austrian bank to purchase carriers for materials, which we suspect are biological or chemical, to be used on U.S. soil. Therefore, from now on, the top priority of the Task Force will be to assist the investigation of that threat.

"Investigation outside the country will be carried out by other arms of the U.S. government, such as the Central Intelligence Agency, National Security Agency, and Defense Intelligence Agency. The secretary of Homeland Security and the attorney general have already coordinated with the directors of these agencies, who in turn have sent their representatives to the task force to liaise with us."

The audience was very quiet, looking at Hodson.

"Now, in case you're wondering why this chart is displayed" — he pointed at the wall — "you all know you are here to discuss terrorist activity, but I wanted these events to be displayed as a reminder that we are not dealing with threats. We have enemies that have shown they can cause serious and painful casualties. Let us not give them another opportunity."

At this point, Hodson shifted gears. Without looking at me or Laura, he went on to say that two members of the task force, acting on their own initiative, had cracked two of the ciphered messages sent to Eagle Bank. Normally, of course, he wouldn't approve of such a flagrant breach of the chain of command — particularly since one of the members had actually physically removed the messages from this office — and a conduct review would be forthcoming. This aside, he still wanted to thank Dan Gordon of the Justice Department and Laura Higgins of Homeland Security for their breakthroughs, which now enabled the task force to vigorously confront these dangers.

All eyes were turned to me and Laura. I felt uncomfortable with the attention, but I cherished the moment — well, thirty seconds. Hodson continued, "The task force is therefore being reorganized to face the new challenges. The old teams are disbanded. From now on there will be three working groups. The first group will continue with the original mission of the task force. Look for the source of the money transfers into Eagle Bank; identify any violations of U.S. laws and any suspects. The members of this group are Jim Lion, Laura Higgins, Peter Vasquez, and Dan Gordon. The second group will coordinate intelligence efforts, both receiving and distributing. The third group will oversee international activities, including liaison with foreign intelligence services, and will include representatives from the CIA, the Justice Department, FBI, and NSA. All teams shall report to me only." He listed the new rosters, then continued, "Forget your old allegiances. I will conduct separate daily briefing sessions with each group, starting with Group One at thirteen hundred hours, followed by Group Two at fourteen thirty, and finally Group Three at seventeen hundred. Any questions?"

Jim Lion raised his hand. "Bob, what is the defined role of the task force in its new form?"

"Mainly coordination," stated Hodson. "All U.S. law enforcement, intelligence, and military agencies have been instructed by the president to give top priority to this imminent danger to the United States. The task force will participate in these efforts. Your job is to bring me all the information your particular agency develops and, following my approval, include it in the pool of info we will be collecting here. You will also suggest — I repeat, *suggest* — potential investigative operations with the aim of gathering additional intelligence to protect the United States. If and when approved, specific orders will follow.

"Any more questions?" Hodson was visibly relieved when no one spoke up. "Dismissed."

High politics was not Hodson's forte. Let him chase crooks, drug dealers, or gun smugglers and he beamed; put him on a case where he needed to know what's going on outside the United States and he was lost.

The news was not good — at least for me. How would I endure an assignment that kept me at a standstill while the other guys got all the action?

As I returned to my makeshift office, Lan called from my office in Midtown. "There's a Mr. Ben Friedman on the line; he says that he needs to talk to you urgently."

"Sure, put him through," I said. "Benny, what's up?"

"Dan, I'm in New York. We need to talk. Today if possible."

His tone worried me. What had happened to the lighthearted guy I knew?

"Where are you?" I asked.

"At the Hilton. Fifty-third and Sixth."

"Meet me at the bar. I'll be there in about thirty minutes, depending on traffic, and how crazy my cabdriver is." I hadn't seen Benny for a year. I hoped he hadn't changed, that he was still the easygoing professional with impressive but publicly unknown credentials. In our line of work, very few people know about your capabilities and achievements. Soldiers display decorations on their uniform; what could a spy agency executive like Benny have to show for his pains? Only his failures were reported in the media.

I arrived at the Hilton bar first. A minute later I saw Benny approaching with a gloomy-looking man in his late forties, unfashionably dressed in a tweed jacket and plaid shirt. Benny looked the same as always, tall, heavy, with intelligent brown eyes. Only his mustache had grayed a tad. He was wearing a baseball cap, the custom for observant Jews outside Israel, replacing his knit yarmulke so as not to attract attention — a particularly important objective for Benny.

"This is Gideon, from the Office." Benny introduced the man standing next to him, using the code name for the Mossad. "Let's go up to my room."

Once we got out of the elevator on the twenty-seventh floor, we followed Benny through the long corridor leading to his room. He opened the curtains to a magnificent view of Central Park.

"Dan, we need help," he said.

"Only if it's legal and ethical. If it's fattening, however, I might reconsider."

Benny didn't smile. Bad sign.

"We have two missing operatives in Europe," he said somberly.

"And?"

"We need help finding them."

"Tried to go to my management? Not that I'm ducking the request. But the Mossad has a liaison officer in Washington precisely for matters of cooperation such as this one."

I was a bit surprised that Benny had even asked me for help. This matter was out of my league. I was chasing money launderers, not missing operatives of a foreign intelligence service, even if it was the one I'd served in years ago.

"Of course," said Benny. "We work through channels, and a formal request has already been made. The director of operations — CIA and the deputy director of the FBI have already promised their full support."

"So what could I do that they can't or won't?"

"We don't know why the operatives disappeared, although we assume they were kidnapped. Dead operatives don't talk to their captors, so we estimate that for the time being they are still alive. There could be any number of reasons why we've failed here." He paused, letting me guess. "Nothing, but nothing, is ruled out."

Was Benny implying there was a mole inside the Mossad? I found it hard to believe, given the extremely tight security the organization has always maintained. Something else was on his mind. It was typical of Benny, operating above- and belowboard: filing a formal request and at the same time lobbying his friends. I realized that he hadn't answered my question: *What can I do?* So I took the circular route and asked, "Tell me what happened."

"They were a team of two: Arnon Tal, a Mossad case officer, and Dr. Oded Regev, a biology professor and medical doctor, on loan to us from the Biological Institute, in Nes Ziona."

The Biological Institute is a government-owned facility twenty miles south of Tel Aviv. Citing national security, Israel has for years declined to comment on news reports that the institute has been developing biological and chemical weapons and antidotes — research that dates to the early 1960s, when Egypt used toxic gas during the civil war in Yemen. In the early 1990s the institute, which usually avoids publicity like the plague, gained notoriety when it was revealed that a former deputy director, Marcus Klingberg, had been exposed in 1983 as a Soviet spy and that his trial, conviction, and incarceration had been withheld from the media for more than eight years.

Benny broke my train of thought. "Tal and Regev were going to meet terrorists posing as scientists; the premise behind the meeting was that the two teams of scientists were going to conclude a scientific cooperation agreement. Although all precautions were taken, the operatives vanished in Rome a week ago."

"Before or after the meeting with the terrorists?"

"After. The meeting went well and the parties went their different ways, so our backup team folded and security became more lax. Tal and Regev took a cab back to their hotel, but never arrived."

*Heads will roll*, I thought. Security measures should end only when the operatives are back in their base, not when they leave the battlefield. "What kind of cooperation was discussed in the meeting?"

"Talk to him, Gideon," said Benny as I moved to the sofa.

Gideon was visibly resentful; he didn't like the order or the tone in which Benny had given it. But apparently junior in rank to Benny, he had to comply. It was obvious he didn't like the idea of sharing confidential information with an outsider, even an outsider who used to be an insider.

"Benny, before Gideon says anything further," I said, "you have to tell me if what I'm about to hear is for my ears only or whether I may share it with my superiors. Because if I'm expected to keep the information confidential, it'd seriously limit my ability — which isn't too great to begin with — to help you."

"I know," said Benny. "You may share information with your superiors. But bear in mind that the lives of two of my men are at stake, so act with caution."

"Of course, you know me," I said. I felt the burden of the trust Benny had laid on me.

"Okay," said Gideon. "Are you familiar with hemorrhagic fever?"

That stopped me for a moment. "Well, I know it's one of the most infectious and deadliest diseases known. I've seen terrible footage on TV of people dying quickly and in terrible pain. Wasn't it called Ebola in Congo?"

"Yes, the symptoms are similar, but the causative agents are different. Hemorrhagic fever is considered to be a potentially dangerous biological weapon because it causes serious illness and death."

"So what about it?" I asked, although I suspected the general direction he was taking me in.

"Before there were restrictions, many nations were researching hemorrhagic fever as one of several potential biological weapons. We know that, until the collapse of their empire in 1991, the Soviet Union continued production of strains of hemorrhagic fever that are antibiotic- and vaccine-resistant."

Gideon paused for a moment, as if he was studying my face and attempting to gauge my reaction. But I didn't move a muscle. He continued. "The virus can survive for days and even weeks in decaying animal carcasses. An analysis of dead mice, rats, squirrels, and rabbits can sometimes indicate the existence of the hemorrhagic fever virus."

I was beginning to lose my appetite, which I'd been hoping to satisfy with Benny in a kosher deli nearby after our meeting.

"Any human could contract the disease through bites of infected insects, handling infected animals, drinking contaminated water, or exchanging body fluids with an infected person. Hemorrhagic fever is so contagious that even scientists examining an open culture plate could contract it unless they wear protective gear."

"How do you spread it, making it a bioweapon?" I asked.

"As a weapon, it's not considered particularly effective, because although it's very contagious, contamination is usually made from case to case. One virus carrier infects others. But for bio-weapon purposes, an effective biological agent must be able to kill twenty to forty thousand people in a short period of time. So if hemorrhagic fever is intended for use as a bioweapon, the virus has to be altered to enhance both its ability to spread rapidly and its killing potential — thousands of dead and hundreds of thousands incapacitated. In its current form, the virus cannot do that."

I felt my stomach move, this time not from hunger. "Is death certain?"

He nodded. "It's likely; the survival rates are fairly low. Immediate diagnosis could increase survival chances, but the problem is identifying the syndrome and treating it on time. You could do it with one or two cases, maybe even a hundred, but not with three hundred thousand cases breaking at the same time."

"Syndrome?" I repeated.

"Yes, a group of symptoms that collectively indicate or characterize a disease affecting the body gradually or simultaneously. In this disease, your blood vessels melt. You die of internal hemorrhage."

Benny gave me his characteristic no-nonsense look. "Got the picture?" I nodded.

Gideon must have seen the expression on my face, so he paused for a moment before continuing. "You become sick within three days of exposure to the virus. Once infected, you can pass the infection to others for up to two to three weeks, even if you don't have symptoms."

"Now, if you thought that was bad news," said Benny, "here's the worst part." He nodded at Gideon to continue.

"Although hemorrhagic fever is a killer, it's difficult to use as a bioweapon because under normal circumstances, the virus attacks a few dozen people until medical measures and quarantine put a halt to wide-spread contamination. Also, the virus is aerobic: It needs oxygen to survive, and it's vulnerable to environmental threats such as heat, cold, acids, and the like."

"So what's the bad news?" I wondered.

"If you genetically alter the virus to increase its potency and resistance, thereby amplifying its contagiousness, then you have created a weapon, not just a disease. You can kill thousands in a short period of time."

"Has anyone done that?"

"Theoretically," said Gideon.

"Meaning?"

"If you could successfully match the hemorrhagic fever virus with a pathogen like *E. coli*, then passing the disease on becomes much easier, because *E. coli* thrive in environments that would usually kill the hemorrhagic fever virus."

"Isn't *E. coli* connected to contaminated food?" I asked, thereby exhausting my knowledge in this matter.

Gideon nodded. Here were the basic facts as he outlined them: *E. coli* was a foodborne illness that, in the United States alone, led to nearly seventy-five thousand annual cases of infection and more than sixty deaths. Symptoms included bloody diarrhea. If left untreated, the disease could lead occasionally to kidney failure. Most cases resulted from eating undercooked and contaminated ground beef, but person-to-person contact in families and child care centers could also transmit the infection, as could drinking raw milk or swimming in or drinking sewage-contaminated water.

*E. coli*'s symptoms were quite different from those of hemorrhagic fever; you vomited, had abdominal cramps, and severe bloody diarrhea. Therefore medical treatment usually focused on these symptoms. But if a contaminated person contracted the altered virus of hemorrhagic fever mixed with *E. coli*, the first symptoms would look like *E. coli*, not hemorrhagic fever. That would give the deadly hemorrhagic fever extra time to spread in the body, beyond the point — which was limited to begin with — at which any medical assistance could contain the disease. Death was almost certain, and excruciatingly painful to boot.

"Is there a treatment for *E. coli*?"

Gideon was uncertain, "Well, most patients recover without antibiotics or other specific treatment in five to ten days. But we don't know if the combined hemorrhagic fever and *E. coli* virus will respond to any treatment."

"That's a sinister tool," I agreed. "But how do you spread a genetically engineered virus, making it a bioweapon?"

"By lacing commercially sold food and drink. Since the altered virus can survive in canned food and drink, every can of soda, soup, or tomato sauce would be suspect; every sausage, hot dog, or hamburger could be infected."

"The bastards who kidnapped Regev and Tal need the technology they believed Regev developed to alter the virus. They want to use it to spread death. There could be no other reason for kidnapping him," said Benny, clenching his teeth.

"I'm lost. How, or rather why, did they make contact with Dr. Regev?" I asked.

"Dr. Regev wrote a scientific article about a successful genetic engineering experiment combining the deadly characteristics of hemorrhagic fever with the strong capacity of *E. coli* to withstand the effects of harmful environmental agents," said Benny.

I knew Benny too well. I saw the glitter in his eyes. "Was the scientific research real?" I asked. "Is there really such an engineered virus?"

"No," he said with half a smile. "There *was* research on precisely this topic, and Regev is a legitimate scientist. But the article he wrote — with some changes we suggested — created a misleading picture. And the journal with this article was circulated only to individuals whom we knew that were looking for potential bioweapons as part of their effort to support terrorist organizations."

"You mean you actually enticed them to use bioterrorism?"

"Of course not." Benny was adamant. "We had prior intelligence that they were actively looking for know-how and materials to disseminate bioterror. This edition of the journal was limited. We couldn't risk circulating it to bona fide scientists who might become suspicious. We simply wanted to make the intended recipients use our phony stuff rather than real materials. Their intentions are imminent and real, and the worst thing about it is that we don't know if we've opened a window of opportunity for them" — there came that certain spark in Benny's eyes — "and whether our offer is their only opportunity. Obviously, they could be trying to get it from other sources as well. We knew that we were playing with a wild tiger, but we took measures to contain it, if it got too wild." Knowing Benny, I sensed he had something else hidden up his sleeve.

I could easily think of a situation where other Western foreign intelligence organizations might be using the same stratagem on these terrorists; the bad guys would have a hard time separating the gold from the dross.

I could also understand why the Mossad had hoped to close the deal as quickly as possible: If the terrorists bought into the story, they presumably wouldn't look to other sources — at least until they realized they'd been duped, which, we hoped, would take awhile. I had other questions for Benny, such as what "information" had been included in the article to make it more attractive to the terrorists.

"Easy enough," said Benny. "The article stated that the altered virus could be used as a biological weapon and that it was resistant to known treatment. This, Dr. Regev reassured me, was not true. Yes, the virus carried the disease, but no respectable scientist would alter it so that it could kill millions if it escaped."

"So it's not true?"

"Basically, no. Obviously, the virus carries the disease, but we made sure that nobody in the scientific world could alter a virus that could wipe out a huge chunk of the world's population if it escapes." He saw my puzzled eyes and added, "Don't ask me how."

"Still," I said, sensing there was more to the story, "most scientific journals wouldn't have gone along with Mossad's plan; how did the Office pull it off?"

"True." Benny smiled again. "Most journals wouldn't have gone along with it. Their reputations are critical. But when you're the *publisher* of a journal, you can do what you want." Under Benny's direction, it seemed,

Mossad had started a new scientific journal, filled it with genuine research papers, and then planted the "engineered" article. Circulation was limited; they'd printed only one hundred copies with the phony article. It was a small investment, and a worthwhile one, from their point of view, given the possibility of luring terrorists with the bait.

"And it worked?"

"Yes," Benny replied. A man posing as a biologist working in the United Kingdom approached Regev at a scientific conference in the Netherlands. After a few friendly meetings, the biologist suggested they cooperate on areas of mutual scientific interest. Regev, of course, had been in the loop from day one. He knew that the British biologist had an ulterior motive; Regev had been expecting and hoping for some kind of contact.

"Did the British scientist know Dr. Regev was an Israeli?" I asked.

"No. In the article he used his birth name, István Kovach. He is in his early fifties. He was born in Hungary and migrated to Israel with his parents as a young child. He can speak and write fluently in Hungarian."

"A quick check could have revealed his Israeli background. Maybe he was exposed," I pointed out.

"Maybe. We planted him in Hungary for two years in a university research center. He published scientific articles under his Hungarian name; I don't think anyone in Hungary knew about his additional citizenship."

"What happened next?"

"Regev told the British scientist, who was of course neither British nor a scientist, that he'd be happy to consider a serious offer and asked how he wanted to cooperate. We ran a check on the scientist, who turned out to be a Dr. Abdel Zoheiri, who'd left his rural medical practice in Afghanistan ten years ago to join radical Islamic groups. Zoheiri suggested to Regev that they breed a large amount of engineered virus in a lab and run large-scale tests to enable the development of countermeasure drugs. As incentive, Zoheiri said he was already in contact with a big Asian drug maker willing to invest three to four million dollars in building a fully equipped lab in Italy. He even went as far as suggesting that Dr. Regev become the head researcher.

"Then came the hook: Zoheiri proposed to Regev that they meet in

Rome to negotiate the final details and sign the cooperation agreement together with the sponsoring drug company. In return, Regev was expected to bring a sample of his genetically engineered virus. Once he started breeding it, he'd receive a first payment of nine hundred thousand dollars to purchase a suitable building and the latest equipment. Two additional payments of nine hundred thousand each were promised as the lab was being built. And of course Regev himself will be generously compensated."

"Do you think the drug company was also in the loop?" I asked.

"No," Benny replied. "They'd never heard about their purported intention to invest money; the terrorists brought a person posing as a representative of the company. But the money part was real enough: They gave Dr. Regev the code of a numbered account in an Austrian bank to enable him to withdraw nine hundred thousand dollars once the agreement was signed."

"How do you know? I thought your operatives were kidnapped before they returned to base."

"Dan, we have the entire meeting on video," said Benny.

"So you have the access code," I said.

"Of course."

"Did you withdraw the money?"

"No. Because that would indicate that someone was eavesdropping on the meeting, thereby implicating Dr. Regev and Arnon Tal as more than just two innocent scientists."

It was, I had to admit, a well-thought-out plan. If they could pull it off, the terrorists would kill a number of birds with one stone: They could develop a dangerous biological carrier of a lethal disease, but if the plot happened to be exposed, they could pin the blame on Hungary for allowing its senior scientist to head such a project. And if they knew all along that Dr. Regev was Israeli, they could blame Israel, a much better target from their perspective.

But where did I fit into all this?

"So what do you want me to do?" I asked.

Benny bent over toward me. "We need our men back. Whoever is holding them must not be allowed to uncover their true identity or discover how much Regev actually knows about bioweapons and antidotes. If he talks, since everyone talks in the end, the damage to world security would be significant. We must pull him out together with Tal, who knows so much about the Mossad affairs that I get palpitations thinking what is going to happen when they talk."

"If that was a consideration, and the prospect of these two guys falling into the wrong hands is so dangerous, why you use them in the first place? Did you ask if the risk of them being caught outweighed the benefit of using them?" It was a rhetorical question, of course. There is always an inherent danger to intelligence agents and their country if they are caught. Benny knew it, too, of course. He just gave me that *Oh, come on* look.

I thought Benny was about to conclude that we had to find them now, dead or alive, but he didn't, although I'm sure the thought crossed his mind. Dr. Regev was a scientist, not a combatant trained to sustain investigative pressure if captured. He was likely to talk to his captors in no time. But the distinction between trained professionals and civilians, as far as the ability to resist pressure is concerned, is insignificant: An untrained person would break in a few days; a professional, in a week. The difference is that the professional has been trained to filter the information disclosed, alter important details, and invent legends that his captors are unlikely to discern as false.

"What is Arnon Tal's cover story?"

"Lab assistant to Dr. Regev. He also speaks Hungarian very well. I don't know how long their cover will hold. Although we made arrangements in Hungary to support their cover story, I fear the moment when their captors scratch beneath the surface."

"Had Regev," I asked in disbelief, "actually delivered the engineered virus?"

"Yes and no," Benny answered. "Regev and Tal delivered a virus at the Rome meeting, but not the engineered one; rather, Regev had told Zoheiri that he'd brought unaltered virus samples, in a tightly sealed plastic container with a cement bottom and a wet paper filter, as well as the instructions on how to genetically modify it so that it became a serial killer. It was too dangerous to travel with the altered virus; they would have to wait for the lab to be built first, with all the precautionary measures in place."

"Can the terrorists alter the virus without Dr. Regev's help?"

"Definitely not. He's the one holding the key, and even his knowledge is theoretical. To our knowledge, nobody has done that yet. Our scientists say that even if it were altered, the virus would not have the traits the article purported it would."

"So why the bother? Why did he do the research?"

"To understand the process so that if unscrupulous scientists did do it, new drugs and treatments could be developed ahead of time to effectively contain and limit the damage."

"So the whole story of how the virus can become a guided missile carrying the deadly disease is one big fat lie?"

Benny smiled. "In a way. Obviously, hemorrhagic fever and *E. coli* are dangerous. However, what we gave them was just a sample of the virus, which any lab in the world could get. The idea was to penetrate these terror organizations. The next time they try to obtain bioweapons, they might be more successful; the bioterror might be real, not manufactured. We wanted to begin a dialogue with them, maybe get them to reveal their plans, which would give us the head start we need to try to stall their operation."

"One thing is sure, though," I said. "If Dr. Regev is the only person who could conduct the genetic engineering research, that guarantees his existence for the foreseeable future."

"Only until they realize they've been duped. I wouldn't be surprised if they're testing these viruses right now, even without Regev's help, to see if they can breed the virus without him. And they might be able to do just that, but they definitely can't conduct the genetic engineering to match it with the *E. coli*. What they have now is basically nothing in terms of bioweapons."

"By the way, why the cement bottom of the container? Were the scientists afraid that the viruses might dig a tunnel and escape to freedom?"

Benny gave that half smile again. "No need to worry, for two reasons. First, we buried a surprise inside: a mini transmitter and a direction finder."

"Those things are short-lived without a source of power, and have a short range," I said.

"Dan, it's been awhile since you were exposed to these devices. The miniature transmitter could be picked up by a satellite and the direction finder by a car."

"Have you received any signals?"

"Yes, in Rome, but only for three hours. We lost it due to traffic jams."

"Maybe they discovered the direction finder?"

"Unlikely," said Benny.

"And the satellite signal?"

"Same sad story. The satellite must have a direct, unobstructed view. The virus container could be in the basement of a building with or without Dr. Regev."

"And the second reason?"

"The container was laced with a minute quantity of detergent that will kill the viruses in twenty-four hours."

"What can I do to help?"

"This is an urgent matter," concluded Benny. "We're making our own efforts to find them, but if we wait until our request for assistance from the United States trickles down into the system, it could be too late. I know how big bureaucracy works. Everything takes time, and we don't have much of that. So I thought I'd talk to you also, you know, just in case."

"What can I do?" I repeated. I knew Benny too well. There was something else behind Benny's friendly request.

"Get your task force to listen to vibrations. Following money trails like you do has already proven to be an effective tool in uncovering criminal activity, and terrorists are criminals with a political agenda."

"I usually get the case after the felony is committed, not before it," I said defensively. "To what organization does Dr. Zoheiri belong?"

"The Slaves of Allah, an Iranian-backed terrorist organization that is particularly vile. They want to abolish all symbols of Western civilization, alleging we are transgressors of Allah and deserve to go to hell."

I had frozen in my seat. "The Slaves of Allah?" I repeated.

Benny continued, oblivious to the increase in my blood pressure. "We know that through their terrorist subsidiaries, the Iranians are trying to establish cells for their sponsored terrorist groups in the U.S. They need logistics, money, and means of communication. This isn't easily done in the U.S. without attracting law enforcement attention."

Was Benny just happening to bring up the Slaves of Allah? This was too much of a coincidence.

"What do you mean? What's the connection?" I said, not revealing my suspicion.

"You know that they can't transfer money from Iran to the United States to pay operatives or purchase equipment. Even a transfer of ten thousand gets reported, and carrying cash is risky. They know all that, too. So they 'make arrangements.'"

"Anything you know about?"

Benny didn't respond.

Now I understood. Benny was negotiating a trade-in: information on money transfers made by the Slaves of Allah and Iran — their sponsor — in return for help in finding his missing operatives. Knowing full well that U.S. interests would deem direct involvement in the hunt for the Mossad operatives well beyond the normal quid pro quo of even such a close alliance, Benny had cleverly devised an imaginary or realistic scenario in which the United States did, in fact, have an immediate and pressing interest in assisting Israel with its search for Regev and Tal. Benny had a subterfuge soul, odd as that might sound. He was a highly skilled agent adept at getting what he wanted by making the other guys think they want it, too. He was just plain good at his job. His demeanor misled people into thinking he was soft and yielding. Those who made that mistake paid dearly. In fact, Benny was conniving, tenacious, and results-oriented. Anything alien to his professional goal was tossed aside.

"How do you know about the task force?" I asked. I'd never told Benny about it. Under normal circumstances neither the general public nor other governments would find out the U.S. had convened a task force, even one this large. So how had Benny found out? He wasn't about to tell me. Methods and sources are always out of bounds for anyone outside the inner circle. And I was no longer there.

Benny gave me that maddening smile one more time. "I just know," he said, signaling me to move on.

"I need to talk to my boss and to a few other people," I said.

"Is David Stone still your boss?"

"Yes," I said guessing what Benny would say next.

"Please send him my best regards."

The United States obviously owed Benny big-time for his help years earlier in finding and collecting more than ninety million dollars from an absconding American banker who'd concealed his theft behind a triple identity. On the same case, the Mossad had also benefited from the joint Mossad/CIA break-in into a German bank that yielded substantial sensitive information on Iran's efforts to purchase nuclear material in Europe.

I got the message. Benny had a strong case. "I'll make a few phone calls and get back to you," I said.

"Thanks," he said, escorting me to the door. "Call me when you make progress." He said nothing about having a meal together, as we usually do. I thanked him in my heart for that. I still couldn't think about food. The words *your blood vessels melt* were still ringing in my head.

But the lone wolf in me, very much alive, woke up again. I returned to my task force office and called David Stone in Washington on a secure line.

"David, remember Benny Friedman?"

"Sure. How is he doing?"

"He needs my help urgently."

"Professionally?"

"Yes, it has to do with the task force."

"So why are you asking me?" David sounded slightly annoyed. "You're on assignment with the task force, so ask them."

"I thought I should talk to you before Bob Hodson. He doesn't know what Benny did for us. We need to return a favor, and I think it'd be better if you asked Hodson rather than me. Besides, I suspect there is something in it for us, so it's not just a favor, but more of a trade-off."

"Why can't you speak with Hodson? Are you on a collision course with him?"

"No, but we're not exactly on kissing terms, either. He simply has a different management philosophy than yours."

"What's the hurry?" I had raised David's suspicion level. "Who are you chasing?"

"It seems that U.S. and Israeli interests are going in the same direction again. I have a hot lead on a bioterrorism substance transaction. Now Benny tells me independently that a week ago, two of his operatives — one of them a biologist, the other a Mossad operative — met in Rome with terrorists posing as scientists. The terrorists wanted to lure the Israeli biologist to cooperate with them on research into bioterror. Then the scientist and the Mossad operative disappeared.

"Benny tells me that the terrorist organization that took the Mossad agents is called the Slaves of Allah. That's the same name that appeared in the messages I deciphered, which referred to carriers of materials that could kill hundreds of thousands. I suspect it must be the same organization and the same plan, because the messages alluded to roughly the same amount of money — two point seven million — that Benny talked about. Benny hinted he has intelligence on the terrorists' money movements into the U.S. My read on that is quid pro quo: *Help me find my operatives and I'll give you info on Iranian cells built up in the U.S.* What I think, and frankly I'm not sure that Benny doesn't know it already, is that our case and his are interwoven."

David surprised me with his answer. "Tell that to the FBI. It's their job, not yours."

"I already did. Just before I called you, I spoke with Special FBI Agent Romano. But I don't know what the FBI is doing with it or if they've made the connection. Two weeks with the task force has shown me that by the time a good idea trickles down through all that bureaucracy it — which in our case is just a lead — often fizzles into nothing."

"Not when national security is concerned. I can't let you operate behind Hodson's back. You're stretching my good nature too thin."

"I am not," I protested. "I simply thought we could help Benny out by having you talk to Hodson, and also gain access to information that could help our case."

Although David concluded the conversation with his usual "all right," I didn't know if that meant *Yes, I will,* or *Forget it.*

I went to the file room to catch up on the accumulating intel. Three hours later I returned to my office down the hall.

I thought about the third message. I didn't know if the NSA had already cracked it, so I decided to give it another shot. Laura wasn't in the office; I was on my own. I locked my office door and disconnected my phone. I was glued to my desk for three hours, and when I was done, I copied the message onto a clean sheet of paper. The result was horrific.

THE INFIDELS ARE WATCHING US MAKE SURE YOU IDENTIFY THE SELLERS BEFORE YOU AGREE TO MAKE PAYMENT BY GIVING THEM THE ACCESS CODE TO THE AUSTRIAN BANK ACCOUNT IN CASE OF DOUBT RETURN WITH THE MERCHANDISE TO BASE GOD DOES NOT GUIDE THE TRANSGRESSING PEOPLE SALEH.

I called Hodson and asked to see him immediately. Sensing the urgency in my voice, he agreed. Twenty minutes later I was sitting in Hodson's office, handing him the deciphered message. "I wish I'd broken that earlier," I said.

"We've already read it. NSA deciphered it last night." If Hodson was surprised that I'd broken the code again, it didn't show.

"Oh," I said. "I didn't know. Here is my copy . . . just in case."

Hodson took my note and asked, "How did you do it? Did you do anything different from last night?" He was almost friendly.

"I should have known that they would have tried to confuse anyone trying to break it, something they didn't do in their two other messages."

"So . . . ?"

"One way to make breaking ciphers more difficult is by making the ciphered text more random. I discovered that they'd replaced each space with one of the letters $V, K, Q, J, X,$ or $Z$, chosen at random. These letters are rare in most contexts. They also inserted two random letters before every plain-text letter prior to encryption, making it a nonexisting word. This made no difference to the intended reader but it certainly confused us."

"I see," said Hodson, although his body language showed that he didn't. He was moving in his chair, looking through me impatiently.

"They must have done that because this message was so crucial," I guessed. "Bob, there's something else I think you should know. Mossad played the Slaves of Allah to believe they could supply them with bio-engineered materials."

"An old trick," said Hodson wearily. "We know that. But Mossad's liaison officer tells me that the threat of using bioterror agents against cities is real, obviously not from the stuff they gave them to stall their efforts, but from additional sources that Mossad is still unaware of. And Mossad says their intel shows that the intention and determination of the terrorists is real regardless."

Hodson looked at his papers. "We also received a request from Mossad through our channels to help them find two missing agents. Is that the same case?"

"I think so."

"Okay. Stick around, I need to talk to you soon," he said in a mysterious tone.

I went outside the building to get some fresh air. I stopped next to a hot dog vendor and devoured a wiener with onions and mustard. I completed my meal by gulping down a bottle of overpriced "fresh spring-water," which probably came from some factory tap in the industrial wastes of New Jersey. I took a short walk around the block, but honking Yellow Cabs and jackhammers drilling the asphalt curbed my appetite for more strolling. I looked around at the people, the buildings, and then thought about what they would look like in the aftermath of a bioterror attack. A ghost town, with a cemetery's silence. There will be no people shopping, no kids riding bikes, and plenty of parking.

When I returned to my office, I read the message on my monitor: GO TO INTERROGATION ROOM 7C ON THE FBI FLOORS. I went downstairs and saw Hodson entering the interrogation room — with Benny Friedman. That was a surprise. It seemed Benny had already found his way to management.

Hodson turned to me. "I hear you've already met Benny Friedman."

I nodded.

"We nabbed the bastard," said Hodson. "We found Malik Fazal."

"That's great. Where is he?"

"Right here," said Hodson triumphantly. I followed him inside, into a room with a two-way mirror. I sat next to Benny, Bob Hodson, and two other agents watching Malik Fazal sitting in the interrogation room. Fazal was a slim man in his midthirties, bearded and restless. When we arrived, the FBI interrogator was already in the middle of questioning him. The interrogator was a burly man in his late thirties with a shaved head, dressed in a white T-shirt and cargo pants. To me he looked intimidating. Fazal moved on the chair aimlessly, occasionally biting his fingernails, his black eyes moving swiftly from one side to the other.

The interrogator, sitting across a table, maintained a neutral tone, but Fazal didn't seem too cooperative. In fact, I wondered why he would answer any questions at all. What would his incentive be? But from looking closely at him and the way he was conducting himself, I assumed that he had already been roughed up downstairs. Maybe the FBI put him first in a holding cell with some nuts, telling them Fazal was a child molester or something. Maybe with the fear of returning to the holding cell he was talking. Not much, but still talking.

"When did you first join the Slaves of Allah?"

"In the spring of 2001." His English was good, although heavily accented.

"Was it in the United States?"

"Yes, there were a few of us."

"Who were the other recruits?"

"Some were born in the U.S., others came from North Africa, and also some Afghanistani and Palestinians."

"Who recruited you?"

"A member of my mosque in Brooklyn offered me a trip to Europe to meet other young Muslims."

"Where did you go?"

"To Paris."

"What happened next?"

"We heard lectures about our obligation as Muslims to prepare for jihad, holy war."

"Just lectures, nothing else?"

"Yes."

"How long did you stay in Paris?"

"Two weeks."

"And then? Did you stay in Europe?"

"No. They took us to a military training camp in Yemen."

"Where?"

"Just outside Sana'a."

"How did you get there?"

"We were given airline tickets to fly to Cairo and from there to Sana'a."

"As a group?"

"No. Separately."

"And you thought nothing of it?"

"No, we were told it was all part of being a better Muslim."

"How long was the training in Yemen?"

"Three months."

"Was it all military?"

"No. We studied Arabic and the Holy Koran."

"But was there a military part?"

Fazal hesitated. He looked away from the interrogator and finally said in a faint voice, "Yes, there was also a military part."

"Did they tell you why you needed military training if all they wanted was for you to be a better Muslim?"

"They told us that we must be ready to defend Islam."

"Were you scheduled to return to the U.S.?"

"No. I was willing to stay and fight the infidels and follow the Ayatollah's command."

"So why didn't you stay?"

"Because after the military training was concluded, the instructors started to talk openly of martyrdom."

"What was your reaction to their suicide talk?" asked the interrogator.

"I said that I had no intention of committing suicide. I was willing to fight and even die in battle, but not to walk to my death voluntarily."

"So why didn't you leave?"

"I thought of leaving immediately. But when I asked to leave, I was ushered into a room, where I sat alone on a carpet with the leader of the Slaves of Allah."

"What is his name?"

"I don't know. We addressed him as Ayatollah."

"What was the conversation about?"

"The Ayatollah asked me how my Muslim comrades viewed suicide operations against the West."

"And what was your answer?"

"I answered that we didn't even think about it," he answered tensely. "The Ayatollah said nothing; he only nodded. The meeting ended and I was allowed to return home. After I returned, I used a cover story I was given to explain my absence to my friends and neighbors."

"So why are you now back in their service?"

"The same member of my mosque who initially recruited me knew I was working for a bank and asked if I was willing to help."

"What's his name?"

"I won't tell you," said Fazal decidedly.

The interrogator moved on, preferring not to break the flow. I was sure he'd get back to pressing Malik Fazal for all the missing links later.

Benny looked at Hodson and me and said, "We still haven't figured out the mystery that consumed us throughout the search for Regev and Tal. What, if anything, does the Slaves of Allah have in mind for its foreign recruits like this guy?"

Hodson didn't answer.

The interrogator continued. "Before you went to Yemen, were you willing to fight against the United States?"

"No. We had no plans, no hatred for America," insisted Fazal. "I came here twenty years ago with my family. America has treated me well."

"So why did you go to Yemen?"

"I was curious." Fazal drank some water from a paper cup.

"I'm puzzled," said Benny. "Why do young middle-class Muslims, some of them born in the United States, suddenly leave their homes to spend three months in a terrorist training camp, and then quietly slip back into their previous roles as law-abiding citizens but with a hidden terrorist agenda?"

"Beats me," said Hodson, shaking his head.

"Do you think these terrorist groups are something new?" said Benny. "Think again. These guys are rooted in religious tradition that is centuries old. Their fanatic ideas emerged as a potent political and social factor as early as the 1920s, with the birth of the Muslim Brotherhood in Egypt."

Benny and Hodson looked at the two-way mirror. We could hear the interrogator from the speakers mounted on their desk.

"What were you asked to do at the bank for the Slaves of Allah?" the interrogator was asking.

"I was responsible for receiving donations from Islamic charities in the U.S. and sending the money to my brothers."

"We went through the bank records. There were no deposits to justify the size of the money transfers you were making."

Silence.

"I'm suggesting that you stole the money from the bank to send to your brothers. That's an additional twenty years."

"No." said Fazal quickly. "I didn't steal it. The money is ours."

"So tell me how your bank received it. There is nothing in the records to show small deposits, which are characteristic of charitable contributions. Even if the donations were made to a charity that later deposited the proceeds in the bank, the amounts would still be modest."

"I can't."

"Why? If you're saying that the money was received as donations from Islamic charities, with the aim of sending it to worthy causes outside the U.S., why not just tell me how your bank received the money?" In a reassuring voice he added, "Sending money to worthy causes outside the U.S. is not a crime."

"Because they will kill me."

"Who?"

He didn't answer.

"Your brothers?"

"No. The people who helped us. They told me that they have people inside and if I betray them, I won't be safe anywhere, not even a U.S. prison."

"We know you hired Boris Zhukov to collect the money from the charities and swing it around the world. The money you were sending to your brothers for their reign of terror is the money that Zhukov laundered."

"Did he tell you that?" Fazal asked in panic.

"Maybe. Why are you protecting him?"

Fazal looked startled. It seemed that hearing the name *Zhukov* scared him more than anything else. He was willing to die for his brothers, but facing Zhukov probably meant an even worse ending.

"How did you forward the money?" The interrogator pressed forward, once again trying not to break the rhythm.

Fazal hesitated. "I made wire transfers to locations outside the United States."

"Who gave you the instructions?"

"My brothers."

"How?"

Fazal paused. There was no response.

"We know about the coded messages," said the interrogator. "Is that how you exchanged information?"

I thought that was smart. The interrogator showed he knew about the messages but didn't say whether they'd been broken.

Fazal didn't answer.

"Tell me what's in the messages," repeated the interrogator. Still no reply. Fazal lowered his head.

Wisely, the interrogator moved on. "I thought that the Arabs' struggle was limited to fighting Israelis. Why did you bring your war here?"

Fazal came to life. He raised his head. "You are fools to believe what you hear about the conflicts Muslims are involved in." He was defiant. He probably sensed by now that he was personally doomed, no matter what he said or did, and that realization must have invigorated him.

"Fools?"

"Yes. For example, the Arab–Israeli conflict; it is not the principal cause of our struggle."

"So what *is* the cause, then?"

"Our struggle is against the corrupt values of America. You are all infidels and you try to force your rotten culture on us."

"How were you going to fight it?"

"Can't you see the facts?" Fazal raised his voice. "Our aim, in the simplest terms, is the destruction and expulsion of all Western values and influences — America, Christianity, Judaism, democracy, feminism, capitalism, secular laws, and pluralism — from anywhere they are in contact with Islam."

"What is it about the Western influence that disgusts you and the other members?"

"Your humiliation of Islam after September 11. Your vulgar Western culture, which corrupts our youth. Hollywood, video games, and alcohol is what many of them care about now."

"So the Palestinian struggle is not your cause?"

"Some of it, yes, but only because of our solidarity with other Muslims. So we use some words supporting the Palestinians. But what we really want is all of you converted to Islam or dead."

"To whom do you refer when you say *we?*"

"The Slaves of Allah are at the center of an international network of the Prophet's followers that has plotted and carried out attacks against the West, specifically against the United States. Your end is nearing. Can't you see that? Your civilization is collapsing. You will soon vanish or accept Islam as the only religion."

"So the war against us is a clash of civilizations between the West and Islam? It's us against you?" asked the interrogator. "Our culture against yours?"

"Of course it is. We will win and all infidels will have subordinate status to the followers of Islam, the true faith."

"So how do you explain that several predominantly Muslim nations like Indonesia or Turkey have never participated in or supported terrorism?"

Fazal was not deterred. "Their leaders are agents of the West. Look at the Islamic Republic of Iran. They have always actively supported us. They have shown us the way to ensure Islamic domination."

"What about religious tolerance and human rights?" asked the interrogator.

"We have particular hatred for the American separation of church and state. Why? We live under the mercy of God and his prophet. Your man-made laws, and your equal rights for women and gays disgust us."

"Tell me more. I'm listening," said the interrogator. Fazal was encouraged and played his part in the investigator's old trick, one we had rehearsed at the Mossad Academy: *Let the suspect talk and talk; in the end he'll feel you are his friend, and will dig his own legal grave.*

"Your attempts to promote democratic reforms in the Arab world are an affront to Islam. You are imposing your rotten values on us. This is a new form of colonialism. There are Muslim nations that have allowed your cultural invasion. Their rulers are doomed. You think we are suicidal? Think again. Look at France or Britain."

"Why are they suicidal?"

"Because they in fact allowed us to operate on their territory."

"I thought the French actually cracked down pretty hard on terror cells within their country," said the interrogator drily.

"Nothing like the crackdown of America," said Fazal.

"What was the intended use of the money once transferred?" The interrogator brought the questioning back on course.

No answer.

"Did you kill Bernard Lipinsky?"

No answer.

"Do you know who did?"

No answer.

"I'll have to send you back downstairs," said the interrogator. That definitely sounded like a threat, and it confirmed my earlier assumption.

Fazal looked startled, but kept his silence.

"What is your connection to Boris Zhukov?"

No answer.

"What's the Slaves of Allah's next move?"

"You don't expect me to tell you." Fazal's black eyes glowed in utter contempt. So he wasn't becoming his friend after all.

"Do they plan an attack on the U.S.?"

Fazal looked down.

"Answer me," said the interrogator, raising his voice for the first time. "Don't make me force you."

Fazal raised his head and snapped, "Allah does not guide the transgressing people." He repeated that verse several times like a mantra, closing his eyes.

"Civilians will die? Is that what you're telling me?"

Fazal shrugged.

"Will your conscience be clean when you face your Creator? When you could have prevented the death of innocent people, all killed in the name of zeal? Your zeal?"

"It's not for me to decide," said Fazal quietly. "If Allah doomed them, then who am I to challenge Him?"

"And if you and your family were to be victims of the attack, you would still not prevent it?"

This was a point of no return for Fazal. The interrogator had touched a sore spot. The calm and composed bank employee was transformed into a fiery preacher.

"No! We are Slaves of Allah and you are infidels. You will soon die a painful death. Look at me," he yelled, his eyes ablaze. "You will not be able to do anything! The streets of New York will be empty and desolate and your economy will collapse. That'll be the Slaves of Allah's first blow on your rotten culture and I promise it will not be the last. Remember my words: The Red Syndrome will plague you."

"The Red Syndrome?" asked the interrogator calmly.

"Yes, you'll have red eyes, red skin rash, and then your veins and arteries will explode, you'll vomit blood, and your liver will melt. Red, red, red, all around you, then you will die!" His black eyes rolled in ecstasy; he was no longer present in the room. He had been carried away by ecstatic and passionate hatred that went beyond differences of political opinion. There was no place for misunderstanding. It was black and white, them versus us. Any Christian, Hindu, Buddhist, or Jew, even a Muslim who supported Western civilization was evil, deserving of painful death.

Hodson buzzed the intercom. "Get me the Centers for Disease Control in Atlanta."

Lynn's voice came on the intercom shortly. "Mr. Hodson, I have Dr. Herman Nadler from CDC on line one."

"This is Robert Hodson, FBI assistant director in charge in New York. I need you to identify a syndrome described by a suspect."

Dr. Nadler spoke calmly. "Did he or she identify it by name or symptoms?"

"He called it 'the Red Syndrome' and described exploding arteries and veins, vomiting blood. Is there something in what he said?"

"Well, I don't recognize the term *Red Syndrome*, but the symptoms you're describing sound like hemorrhagic fever. Syndrome is the outbreak of several symptoms together. Hemorrhagic fever is a severe multisystem syndrome caused by a virus. The overall vascular system is damaged; the virus causes the collapse of the blood vessels, resulting in heavy bleeding."

"How is the disease spread?"

"It passes from one infected person or animal to others in close proximity. We don't know of any previous cases of widespread contamination of hemorrhagic fever in North America."

"How contagious is it?"

"Extremely."

"Survival rate?"

"Some people get over it."

"Some?"

"Unfortunately only a few."

"And the rest?"

"Do not."

A chill was slowly making its way down my spine. I looked at Benny. This wasn't news to him; still, I wondered what he felt. He didn't move a muscle.

"I've heard enough," said Hodson. He buzzed the intercom. "Send an immediate alert to the Homeland Security secretary and get me the Federal Emergency Management Agency, the New York governor's office, New York City mayor's office, and the New York National Guard at Stratton Air Guard Base at the Schenectady County airport."

Hodson then called the interrogator's earpiece. "Lean on him, get more details, break a bone or two if necessary. I'll protect your ass."

I looked at Fazal, who was still foaming at the mouth.

Hodson turned to Benny. "I'm going to play hardball with this asshole. The urgency of obtaining information about the potential attacks justifies tightening some bolts here."

Benny and I knew all too well the dilemma posed by a terrorist like Fazal. Fanatics don't listen to reason. In Israel, where the threat of terrorist attack is pervasive, the law has determined that if someone poses an immediate threat — a "ticking bomb" — the security services are allowed to use "measured physical pressure." Torture is generally condemned by law, but in an extreme case, when lives are deemed to be at stake, "special measures" are permitted: sleep deprivation, prolonged shackling — banana-style, with hands and legs tied together behind the back — and the only manner involving actual physical contact: shaking a person repeatedly by holding his shirt.

Hodson muttered, "Using biological agents will likely go unnoticed for days. It's not a lights, bells, and sirens type of incident. We need to move our asses and nail the bastards."

I went out to the hallway with Benny. "Let's get a drink of water," I suggested, meaning, *Let's talk*.

In really tense situations I stay calm. But I must have some mannerism, some habit on which I draw at a time like this to keep me from acting impulsively. And the answer is water. Lots of water. Tension goes high, I gulp a gallon.

"Is the United States ready for a bioterror attack?" asked Benny as we stepped outside.

"Frankly, I don't know," I said. "The sad fact is that civil defenses across the nation are a rudimentary patchwork that could prove inadequate for what might lie ahead, especially lethal germs."

"What about the hospital system? Could it provide help to a large number of people who would need sophisticated medical care?"

"Hell, no."

"Anyway, how would the government even know there *is* a bioattack? Thousands of sick people could indicate widespread disease, but it doesn't necessarily mean it's an attack," Benny pointed out.

"I don't think there are any measures in place," I said. Indeed, the government relies on reports from health care providers that people are seeking medical attention for unusual symptoms. The CDC then issues a national alert calling on public health officials to initiate heightened surveillance for any unusual symptoms or numbers of cases. Still, symptoms of serious illness often appear days and weeks after an infection has begun to spread, when life-saving treatments are no longer effective. "We just heard Hodson talking to them," I added. "He should have done it a lot earlier. The world is simply unprepared to deal with bioterrorism."

"Why does Hodson refuse to link my missing operatives to his investigation?"

"I've only known him for a short time," I said, drinking a whole bottle of water. "But I already know that he follows hard facts, not suspicions. To me and to you, it seems obvious. I don't believe it's just a coincidence that two different Islamic terrorist organizations are planning the same bio-attack on the U.S. I'm convinced it's the same organization that planned the bioterrorism and kidnapped your men. Give Hodson time. The conclusion will ultimately sink in. Anyway, I have to go back to the briefing room. Hodson is about to address the task force. I'll see you later."

"I'll be at my hotel," said Benny and went to the elevator.

When I entered, Hodson gave me an annoyed look for being late. The mood in the room was somber. A major crisis was developing. There was no room for private talk or distraction.

He continued, "Biological weapons, with a few exceptions, are hard to make and use. In 1995 Aum Shinrikyo, a Japanese cult, launched a sarin nerve gas attack in and around Tokyo that was meant to kill millions but in the end killed only twelve and injured thousands. There has always been the fear that some rogue state or terrorist group would successfully deploy germ weapons, as knowledge of how to make deadly weapons spreads, along with the necessary technology.

"I hear from germ-weapons experts that there's a greater risk of dying on the highway than from exposure to anthrax, but terrorists may soon be able to overcome the technical hurdles to mass destruction, especially if aided by rogue states or scientists. A number of terrorist organizations are seeking biological, chemical, radiological, or nuclear agents to attack the West. Bioweapons are cheaper, stealthier, and potentially more devastating than nuclear arms, though hard for terrorists to acquire and use without hurting themselves.

"We have just learned that the imminent threat before us is in the form of a biological agent, probably causing hemorrhagic fever, a virus that kills most people it infects. We've heard it called the Red Syndrome, but the CDC tells us that's likely an ad hoc name for this killer disease. We don't know how they plan to spread it, but we're working on it. The buzzword is *carriers*. We can only guess what this means. It could be contaminated people carrying the disease to our population centers, contaminated organic material, or sick animals. Look for any clues."

I went back to the room overlooking the interrogation cell where the questioning of Malik Fazal continued.

"We don't have much time and neither do you," shouted the interrogator directly in Fazal's ear. "I'm the good guy here. If you don't talk in three minutes, I am going to hand you over to a special interrogation team. They will work you out."

Fazal didn't answer, but he was visibly shaken, looking sideways and moving his hands nervously.

"How do you plan to spread it?"

Not a word. After a few more futile attempts, it was over. "Okay, suit yourself," said the interrogator, and buzzed the intercom. "Take him to Section C."

The door opened and Fazal was roughly removed from his chair. Two refrigerator-sized guards held him by his handcuffs and dragged him along the floor. He was taken to another room down the hall. I returned to the conference room. "That will be a closed session," said Hodson when I asked if I could be present during the aggressive interrogation. "No one is allowed."

Two hours later a different interrogator approached Hodson in the makeshift control room with the two-way mirror. He was a short and stocky fellow in his late twenties — the butcher type.

"He talked."

"What convinced him?"

"You don't want to know. But he told me how they planned to spread the virus."

"How?"

"Contaminate commercially sold food and drink."

"Did he say how they were going to do it?" asked Hodson.

"He refuses to give any details; I suspect he's trying to stall."

"And?"

"Before he lost consciousness he said something about a few of their people working in food-processing facilities."

"Have they already contaminated any food or drink?"

"He didn't say. We'll continue to work on him once he wakes up. As to the money transfer: He conceded being in charge of sending the Suspicious Activity Reports. Apparently he wrote the reports, showed them to Eagle Bank management, but never filed them."

"How long had Fazal been in place at the bank?" asked Hodson.

"Five years," answered the interrogator.

"So when recruited he was already working at the bank?"

"That's what the man said."

"Does Fazal think he was recruited *because* he was working at the bank?"

"I asked him that, but he wouldn't know. He did confirm that it was no hassle to recruit him. He was ready and willing."

"Let a doctor see him," said Hodson.

"Let us finish first. I think we have time constraints here."

"How is he physically taking it?" asked Hodson.

"He had difficulty breathing. Also, his tongue is swollen a bit, and he may need a dentist if he persists in playing games with us," the interrogator concluded with a straight face.

"Okay, but I'll have a doctor ready near the interrogation room. What about Bernard Lipinsky?"

"He denied killing him, but from what we know already there are at least five other members of his cell in the U.S. who could be responsible.

Fazal told me that copies of the messages were given to Lipinsky erroneously. That doomed the man. We have the other members' names, and warrants are being issued as we speak."

"Did you establish any connection to the missing Israeli operatives?"

"Most likely, although we need to clear it up further."

Hodson then called the Centers for Disease Control.

Dr. Herman Nadler said, "It's true. The virus can live in any organic material. When consumed, the virus infects the person immediately."

"Any food and drink?"

"Most foods — if the disease is indeed hemorrhagic fever. Look for scientists who may have genetically engineered the virus, because hemorrhagic fever is unlikely to be used for mass contamination. They may have bred it with another agent that spreads easily."

"Bob," I interjected, "please ask him if it is possible to engineer the virus to mate with an *E. coli* bacteria?"

Hodson posed the question. "It's certainly a possibility," confirmed Nadler.

"If terrorists get a hold of a small strain of the virus, does it have any significance?" Hodson continued.

"You mean if it was genetically altered?

"Yes."

"They'd need to know how to grow it in the lab. With a qualified biologist, you can produce hundreds, then thousands, then millions of deadly strains, and given a combination with *E. coli*, mass contamination becomes a real risk. The viruses work 24/7, and take no sick leave or vacation. They are self-perpetuating time bombs that could go off anytime they meet a human they could infect."

"Is it that easy?" asked Hodson.

"Growing the strains? We need to know first if it was altered."

The interrogator returned to Hodson's office. I couldn't help but notice that his shirt was stained with a few drops of blood. He told Hodson the bastard had talked further. The Slaves of Allah had recruited fourteen men and women working in processing plants throughout the United States. Fazal didn't know specifics, no names or places, just the general plan. The food industry workers would contaminate a foodstuff with small vials of the altered virus just after pasteurization, but before it was actually packaged. Each worker would receive up to twenty vials. Fazal speculated that the workers were pawns of a kind, ignorant of the lethal nature of the virus; they'd been told that lacing the food or drink would result in nothing more serious than a mild outbreak of food poisoning. And if the workers became infected themselves, so much the better; they would be extremely effective carriers because, until they showed symptoms, they'd continue to work in a food-producing environment. Since the virus would spread quickly in organic material, then just one vial in an industrial container could contaminate many thousands of food servings.

Hodson's face turned white. "Squeeze the bastard. Get names and places. I don't care if you make him eligible for disability payments for life — although he won't need it in the place he's going to. Just get me the names!"

Hodson then turned to Lynn, his assistant. "I know the Mossad said that the viruses they gave the terrorists would be dead in twenty-four hours, but we can't take any risks. These bastards may have gotten viruses from other sources. The intention is there." He got up from his chair, left his office, and ran down the hall toward the gathering members of the task force. He stopped, caught his breath, and said, "Prior intelligence has been confirmed. They plan to infect the civilian population by lacing commercially sold food and drink with a deadly virus!"

# IX

returned to my office and saw the message light blinking. The message was from Lynn: "Mr. Hodson wants to see you in his office at three o'clock."

When I walked to Hodson's corner office, I saw two men talking with him. One looked very familiar, but he avoided my eyes. Hodson didn't make any introductions. He went straight to business.

*My firing squad,* I thought. There would be no reward for my breaking the third message, only a reprimand for removing the papers from the office. I was quickly rehearsing my defense.

"Sit down," Hodson said almost politely. His manners were only demonstrated in public, I thought. "Dan, following word I got, I went through your two-oh-one file and CBI and I see you have a history of impersonations." He sounded amused.

Since when had they had a 201 file on me? I'd always thought that CIA 201 files contained personal information only on its staff officers or agents, including any training and operational details, not on people outside the agency. The news surprised me: The CIA must have compiled it even before our previous joint operation to enable them to give me a security clearance. Had the Mossad given them a copy of my personnel file? I found it hard to believe, but still. More surprising was the CBI, a complete background investigation consisting of a local agency check, national agency check, and partial background investigation, all of which were necessary to grant an individual the highest security classification.

"Chasing money launderers needs some innovative and creative thinking," I said.

"I was particularly impressed by what you did in Germany several years ago: using an alias so that you could go one-on-one with a crooked

German banker and also track down ninety million dollars stolen by a man using triple identities."

I thought I'd been called in to be berated and now he was singing my praises?

And who'd told him that? I thought I knew the answer — and he was standing right next to Hodson.

"Could you repeat the show in a new CA?" He used the CIA term for "covert action."

*So far, so good*, I thought. No reprimand. For now. "I'm listening," I said. The tall balding man was still avoiding my gaze. Of course I knew him, and I knew why he was avoiding me.

"David Stone told me about the case. I just spoke with him."

David? I thought he'd been keeping his distance from Hodson. So it wasn't the guy standing next to Hodson who'd talked. "Let me introduce Eric Henderson of the CIA."

"We've already met," I said. It was the same Eric Henderson, CIA chief of station in Munich, who'd given me such heartburn on the triple-identity case. On the other hand, if he'd given me heartburn, I couldn't even begin to think of what I'd given him.

Eric finally raised his eyes to meet mine. "Hi, Dan. How are things?" *That cold-blooded eel has not changed a bit,* I thought. *Life just slips over his skin without leaving a mark. The same tall, receding blond, blue-eyed man who never gets excited.* His tone was as usual — bland.

"Fine, just fine," I said, wondering what Eric's role in this was and whether he was connected to Hodson's earlier conversation with David.

Hodson started, "We need your help in a field assignment. While urgent law enforcement efforts are under way in the United States regarding the bioterror threat, we must continue fighting that war elsewhere as well. Are you ready for some action of the kind you're used to?"

"Go ahead."

"We need to infiltrate, directly or indirectly, into a terrorist group, probably in Europe. Your English, though fluent, has a slight accent, so you could pass for another nationality. One thing is for sure, though: You can't be American or Israeli."

"Does it have anything to do with the deciphered messages?"

"A lot to do with them, and with the outcome of the search warrants at Malik's home and office and his interrogation."

"And Benny's request?" I asked.

Hodson responded, "We spoke with David Stone. We'd like to help Friedman; it's quite possible we're after the same bad guys."

"Only a possibility? I thought you'd established a connection. Do you mean to say that there are two different groups using the same name, *Slaves of Allah*? What, they didn't trademark it?" My sarcasm escaped him; not for the first time, or probably the last.

"No, I mean we don't know for a fact that they're the same group, although it's suggestive. But the disappearance of the Israeli operatives, combined with the potential threat in the deciphered messages and the results of Fazal's interrogation, if corroborated, would imply a joint interest here, and therefore a joint operation against the Slaves of Allah."

"So what do you want me to do?"

"The Department of Justice has agreed to co-opt you to the CIA as an interagency transfer for a specific intelligence assignment."

I nodded.

"A covert action is under way to contact that terrorist group from a completely different angle. You are not involved in that. Independently, we want you to open communication lines with the Slaves of Allah in a very particular manner."

"Such as trying to be recruited? I don't exactly look like a Muslim they would attempt to recruit," I pointed out. "Or maybe you want me to grow a long beard and assume typical Islamic manners. It'll take me a year to adapt. I don't think we have that time. I look too Western."

"No," said Eric. "We have other ideas for getting close to them. If we offered them biomaterials cold turkey, they'd be likely to get suspicious and grab our courier just like they may have snatched the Israeli operatives."

"We don't want that, do we," I said — as if Eric cared what might happen to me if I was the courier.

Eric again ignored my sarcasm. "We want you to gain their confidence as someone who can supply them with other things they might need."

"Like what?"

"Like money. Even terrorists need to eat. They need money to pay their field soldiers and their other staff; they need to rent apartments, rent cars, buy weapons and explosives, transmitters and airline tickets. It all costs money. Big money."

"What about state-sponsored terrorism?" I asked. "Didn't that foot the bill?"

"Sure," said Hodson, "but moving money from point A to point B isn't that simple anymore, particularly when terrorist organizations know governments are tracking the flow around the globe: If you follow the money trail, you get to the bastards; if you stop the money flow, you dry up the terrorists' resources. And if terrorists are preoccupied with getting enough money to eat their next meal, instead of planning how to bomb people, that makes them more vulnerable."

"And vulnerable people make mistakes," I added.

When the International Convention for Suppression of the Financing of Terrorism was adopted by the United Nations, the offenses it cited became extraditable. The convention can help put a lid on both the collection of funds that might be used to commit crime, and the transfer of money to terrorist organizations.

While it's true that terrorists don't care about international conventions, this one did at least set a standard for governments to follow when adjusting their laws to confront new threats. Countries that had been lax before about cracking down on terrorist money sources can't be now.

"The real value in your mission," Hodson said, "if you complete it successfully, would come from your offering to provide the terrorists with new ways of hiding assets and transferring them undetected. That way, we'd have a head start on knowing what their plans are."

"So you want me to pose as a jack-of-all-trades in money movements, hoping the terrorists will take the bait?"

"That's the general idea. We're still working on your legend."

"If you agree, we'd have to send you south of here for one week of briefing and training."

"Do you need my answer now?"

"It'd be helpful. You know the short timetable on this."

"Would I be operating alone?" Somehow I thought that it wasn't such a good idea to be a lone wolf in this adventure: I needed another wolf or, even better, a lamb. On second thought, a feline.

"It all depends on the legend we agree on. Obviously you'll have backup security at all times. We don't want to repeat the Israeli loss of operatives."

"Do you think they're dead?"

"I have no information, but anything is possible in this trade. You know that."

There were other possible complications: If my mission was discovered or even suspected by any members of the cell that Fazal had cracked, it would make things that much more difficult and dangerous. They'd suspect any new contact — even if it came from some purported long-lost relative waving money around. What would happen then? Eric didn't know.

"Fazal isn't in a talking mood now," he said with a straight face, "and we still haven't arrested the other cell members."

I wondered if Fazal still had a workable tongue. Nonetheless, I didn't need to think too long. I have only one life and I prefer it interesting and exciting. The chance to work undercover with Benny and Eric was, as Yogi Berra said, *Déjà vu all over again*.

"Where do I sign?" I asked. "My father taught me that the biggest risk is not taking any." Both Bob and Eric smiled. *A rare occasion*, I thought. *I should have brought my camera.* The third person in the room, still anonymous, smiled as well. I ignored my mother's advice, though: *Don't compromise yourself. You are all you've got.*

"Expect our call later today," Hodson said. "Please do not discuss this conversation with anyone, not even with other members of the task force."

When I left the room, I almost bumped into Laura. "Hi," she said in a certain friendly tone.

"Let's have tea," I said.

"I'd like coffee, if you don't mind," she responded and started walking toward the cafeteria, clearly expecting me to follow. But this time I was not distracted, not even by the way she moved, usually an instant mood changer for me. My mind was already somewhere else.

We sat in the empty office cafeteria. Laura was slowly sipping her coffee. "Why are you so quiet?" she asked. "Did Hodson drop anything on you?"

"Yes, he did," I said.

"And?"

"I don't know what to make of it yet."

"He's giving you trouble because you removed the messages from the office?"

I'd forgotten all about that. "No, it's something else. I can't talk about it right now."

Laura looked at me pointedly, her green eyes narrowed. "Come," she said and grabbed me by my arm. "Let's go."

"Go?" I said. "Where?"

"Let's have an early dinner and maybe a drink later —" She paused midsentence. "You seem like you could use a lift."

Those green eyes and her body language were impossible to ignore. We went outside and headed to a small Italian restaurant in Soho. I was quiet and pensive. Unusual behavior, I had to concede to myself. Laura did the talking. She told me of her childhood in Kansas; about her father, a postal worker, and her mother, a school librarian. Then she wanted to know everything about me, particularly the things I'd done on this case before the task force had convened. But my mind was elsewhere. Laura touched my hand every now and then, as if to attract my attention, but I was still far away. Although the Slaves of Allah were occupying my mind more than the vivacious redhead sitting across from me, I still didn't feel like talking about any of it.

Laura suddenly said, "Come on, let's go."

I didn't ask what was on her mind. I knew. I paid the bill and we walked up Broadway. Soon we were nearing my apartment. "Ask me up for a drink," she said without a question mark at the end.

I opened my apartment door, and before I flicked the light switch on, Laura was in my arms. She kissed me passionately, first on my hungry mouth, then on my neck. I held her tight, and took her jacket off while she was still kissing my neck. I threw my coat to the floor, slipped my hands under her blouse, and undid her bra. I caressed her soft back and moved both arms to cup her breasts. Laura moaned. We were still standing partly in the hallway. "Come," I said. I closed the door behind us and walked her to my messy bedroom. We fell on my bed. Laura rolled me over on my back and sat on my groin. I pulled her down and . . . the damn phone rang.

I thought of ignoring it, but Laura stopped. Reluctantly I picked up the receiver, only to hear Lynn, Hodson's assistant, on the other end of the line, telling me that someone would come by the apartment at ten thirty that night to pick me up. I had to pack a week's worth of clothes, and no one was to know where I was going

"Thanks for giving me such short notice. Besides, I don't know where I'm going, so how could I tell anyone?" I said angrily. I continued as if Lynn was still listening, but she'd already hung up. "And it's just an hour away. I need to find a dog-sitter for a week."

I got up from the bed. "I have to leave," I said. The inconsiderate bastards wouldn't even let me finish.

"Where are you going?" Laura was still on the bed, and sounded as disappointed as I was.

"On assignment, I don't know where. I'll be back soon."

"When?"

"In a week."

"Why can't you tell me where you're going? We work together, remember?"

"You just heard me say on the phone that I don't know. I simply don't." I was annoyed: She was a professional and should know better than to ask me.

"Will you call me?"

"I'll try, but I can't promise."

Laura got up and got dressed. I showed her to the door.

"I'm sorry," I said.

"So am I," Laura smiled. She pecked my lips, we straightened our clothes, and I walked her to the elevator door.

———

A car came for me an hour later, and after a six-hour drive I arrived in the dark of early morning at a military installation. The sign said:

DEPARTMENT OF DEFENSE
ARMED FORCES EXPERIMENTAL TRAINING ACTIVITY

The place looked similar to many other military camps I'd seen, except that here there were very few uniformed soldiers. I realized this must be "The Farm," the ten-thousand-acre site where CIA trainees, also called Career Trainees, took an eighteen-week course in operational intelligence. Those who graduated began working as intelligence and case officers for the CIA's Directorate of Operations.

I was fingerprinted and photographed; I had blood drawn and measurements taken for biometric identification. That done, I was escorted to a different building where I met a man named Joe, if that was indeed his real name; I'd probably never know. He was a well-built man in his forties, with short blond hair, cold gray eyes, and a firm handshake.

"Welcome to Camp Peary," he said with a warmth that contradicted his aloof appearance. "I'll be your instructor for the short period you'll be spending here with us.

"You'll have a weeklong crash course in a few skills. It will not be easy, given the fact that most of our cadets need several weeks for it. For security reasons, you will not be allowed to leave the camp or communicate with the outside world. That means no visitors, no phone calls, no letters, no e-mails."

"I understand," I said. It wasn't the time or place to tell him that some of the skills they were about to train me in I already possessed; I'd been through a similar course during my Mossad training. But times were different then. Among other things, we'd learned Morse code for long-distance communication; today that method was reserved for ham radio fans and visitors to communications museums.

Everything was so organized, I thought. So different from the chaotic and improvisational manner of instruction I had experienced at the

Mossad, typical of the Israeli way of doing things. During the following five days, I was brought up to speed in topics, tools, and tactics I had either already forgotten or didn't even know existed. The use of technology was overwhelming and the lack of budgetary constraints was such a refreshing difference from the frugality drummed into us in Israel. The part that I paid special attention to was communications and emergency procedures. But at night I was alone and lonely. I thought of Laura. On the spur of the moment, I went to the pay phone at the officers' club. I hesitated only for a second. I was certain the phone was constantly monitored by the camp's field security, but, what the hell, I was about to call a co-worker. I wasn't going to tell her where I was or what I was doing. The phone rang but there was no answer. Her answering machine came on, and I left a short message: "Hi, I'm still alive, I'll see you soon." Nobody would reprimand me for such a minimal breach of security.

On the sixth day, when I'd had enough of military food, Joe came to my cabin and suggested we have breakfast outside Camp Peary. After a three-mile drive into the town of Williamsburg, Joe stopped next to a small hotel. I followed him inside. Instead of going into the dining room, as I had expected, he gave me a room key.

"Go to room one forty-one and wait there."

I went through a long hallway to a vacant room on the ground floor. On a small table were a glass jug with orange juice, paper cups, and a basket with thawed mini bagels, the industrial type, a few mini packs of cream cheese, and paper plates. Only the utensils were durable. This was breakfast? Not in my book. There was a knock on the door. A tall darkhaired man in his midthirties walked in. I closed the door.

"Hi," he said shaking my hand. He was dressed like a used-car salesman. "I'm Brian Day. I'll be working and directing you in the operation."

So that was it. For security reasons, the meeting with the handler had been arranged outside Camp Peary. Brian and I couldn't be seen together; it could compromise the operation. And since there are some 256 different terrorist organizations worldwide, depending on what day you're counting, precaution wasn't just a word, it was a way of life. It was apparent that security measures had been heightened since my last contact with the CIA in the early 1990s in Europe, when I'd chased Raymond DeLouise and stumbled onto a plot by Iranian agents to secure nuclear materials. The 9/11 attacks had left their mark everywhere.

Compartmentalizing was a way of life; it insulated people and information. Joe was not allowed to participate in my meeting with Brian Day. Joe had trained me, Brian would handle me. Neither man could meet or be seen with the other.

Brian pulled a big yellow envelope from his briefcase.

"Please make yourself comfortable," he said. "We'll be spending a few hours here."

I sat on the small sofa and Brian sat opposite me on the desk chair.

"The Company has come up with a few ideas as to how to introduce you to the clients without arousing their suspicion. The idea is to form a long-term relationship built on trust and professionalism. We know them as the Slaves of Allah, but you are to refer to them only as 'the clients.'"

"The clients?"

"Yes. The Slaves of Allah, the ultimate client. But forget that name. Use only 'the clients.' Have you heard about them yet?"

"Just recently. I know very little about them. Is it a new organization?"

Brian gave me a quick summary of what was known about them. The Slaves of Allah, backed and sponsored by Iran, had cells in many countries. Iran had state-sponsored terrorism down to a kind of art form: Stay in the dark, use third parties to do the dirty work, deny any connection or knowledge, even offer help and sympathy to the victims, and all the while plan the next attack. The Iranians kept themselves at a considerable distance from organizations like the Slaves of Allah. "Plausible deniability" was scrupulously maintained; if a terror group like the Slaves of Allah was ever exposed, Iran would not only wash its hands of them, but issue harsh condemnations. "Unfortunately," Brian told me, "they will never let go of their zeal. The religious fanatics of Iran continue with their aspiration to defeat the 'Great Satan'" — here he smiled and pointed at himself — "through whatever means available. And their only means are terror."

"Would you ever let them walk with impunity?" I asked. I'd seen that happen before.

"Hell, no. We have proof that the money and the instructions to instigate terror come directly, or rather indirectly, from Tehran. We also know that they maintain a top-secret center in the suburbs of Tehran — Agdassieh Post — for training terrorists in assassination and kidnappings.

"European governments used to claim that they only had evidence of moral support for the terrorists' extremist ideology. They'd turned a blind eye to what Iran was really doing. But that's changed."

"Good morning, Europe," I said mockingly. "Israel has been saying for years that the Iranians are behind the most heinous terrorist organizations, but as long as Europe was spared . . ."

"Right," said Brian. "But a recent report issued by the Germans directly linked Iran to terrorist groups, and pointed a finger at the Iranian embassy in Germany. Maybe it signals a European change of heart."

"So are we targeting the clients or the Iranians, their patrons?" I asked, with mounting interest.

"Both. But first an overview. Specific details are found in the folder I am giving you. Your particular targets are the clients only; the rest is background material."

"Got you," I said cooperatively. He was so different from Eric Henderson, who was zealous in hoarding information, even beyond the necessary shielding of sources and methods.

"Good. There are three branches of the Iranian intelligence establishment: the Ministry of Information, the Qods Force of the Revolutionary Guards, and military intelligence. All three organizations have representatives at the Iranian embassies worldwide. The Iranian Ministry of Information uses the Orwellian name *information* as if they disseminate it. In fact, it's purely an intelligence agency that collects intel and is also used as the clandestine arm of Tehran to do its dirty work. In major countries the embassies might be fronting twenty or more employees from the intelligence services. Apparently when that's not enough, they tap on the other members of the embassy staff for support in their clandestine missions.

"The primary objectives of the three intelligence branches stationed in

145

Europe are to trace and eliminate Iranian opposition leaders exiled there, to purchase technology useful in building weapons of mass destruction, and finally to run Islamic extremist groups in Europe. The two latter activities are directly connected to our case and to your role."

"Have they used any special means to control the rogue Islamic organizations? Usually these people don't take orders from anyone."

"True. But the Iranians are smart. They've steadily infiltrated Islamic educational and cultural institutions, using vast infusions of money to turn them pro-Iranian. Iran couldn't trust the old leadership of these groups to obey Tehran's instructions while maintaining the required strict confidentiality. So they do it cunningly.

"The Iranian intelligence officers use light cover, pretending they're simply arranging cultural activities. Once the officers have a foothold, they can steer the groups in the directions Iran wants."

Brian paused to drink a glass of juice he poured himself from the jug. He seemed very young with his boyish haircut and smooth skin. I wondered why he dressed in such tacky clothes. Could he simply have bad taste, his shrewd mind notwithstanding? At his age, I had served in the Mossad doing similar things. This pattern of recruitment by Iran was similar to the method used to recruit Malik Fazal. That meant that the Iranian recruitment efforts were not limited to Europe; they'd spread to the U.S. as well.

I moved impatiently in my chair.

"You want the bottom line first?" There was no sound of anger or discontent in his voice.

"Yes, if possible."

"Try to think of Iran as a dragon with several heads spitting fire at different times toward different directions. From your perspective, our clients are the Slaves of Allah, not anyone else until we see a definite affiliation. However, we're not letting any of the other organizations off the suspect list, since we still don't know who the Slaves of Allah are. That name surfaced for the first time in the deciphered messages."

"You mean it could be an existing organization simply assuming a new disposable name?"

"That's one possibility."

"And the other?"

"That the captured messages were faked."

"Why?"

"Because breaking the code wasn't that difficult. These guys should never be regarded as stupid or careless."

Although it was an affront to my intellectual ability and the many hours I spent with Laura breaking it while having wine, cheese and erotic thoughts, I had to concede that he had a point. Breaking the code *had* been easy.

"So, let's assume they were faked," I replied. "Then we should ask why and for what purpose. Come to think of it, if they were faked, there is an inherent assumption that the sender knew that the messages would be intercepted and deciphered. That's a higher degree of sophistication. Are you willing to grant it to them?"

"Nothing is conclusive," said Brian patiently. "We simply can't rule anything out. We take the messages at their face value. Treat them as if they are genuine, but continue to suspect they are fake and look for reasons why they bothered, and whether it was a decoy to distract us from the real thing."

"Okay, any other options?" I moved on.

"Yes. It is also possible that they are either a new splinter group that broke off from one of the other organizations, or . . ."

He hesitated, inviting me with his silence to complete his sentence, ". . . or they planned something so horrifying that even they don't want to be identified as the perpetrators." He nodded and I queried, "Terrorists afraid to ruin their monstrous reputation?" My sarcastic remark was left hanging without comment. There was a sudden silence in the room. In our minds, we were digesting what might be at stake. It had the mark of a black operation. A covert operation not attributable to the organization carrying it out. That would be a genuine worst-case scenario in the making.

"I get the picture, I think," I said although I still wasn't sure what my role in this would be. "The deciphered messages were not single-source intelligence, which would make them suspect," I went on. "They were corroborated by Malik Fazal's interrogation. Although even when put together, it doesn't make them anything more than a lead."

Brian nodded. "Fazal's version and the contents of the messages should be regarded as one source. After all, the three messages were in his hands. How do we know that he didn't concoct them as a decoy, while something else, the real thing, is continuing undetected? You probably haven't heard the developments in that matter since you came here, in the week that you've been sequestered."

"It was refreshing to keep away from the noise of phones, faxes, and e-mail for a week," I said, "but I do feel out of the loop."

"The latest is that all agencies involved are confident that the viruses the Slaves of Allah received were too few to cause any immediate large-scale damage; they would need real experts to clone them. The bad news is they can easily recruit any number of biologists who care more about money than any terrorist cause. What these corrupt scientists probably don't realize is that once they've rendered their services, they may become expendable. If they've betrayed once, they might betray again and talk. Terrorists don't like talkative people."

"The Israelis conned the Slaves of Allah into thinking the virus was genetically engineered. Maybe they discovered the hoax?" I suggested

"No. If you think the kidnapping of the Israeli operatives was retaliation for fraud, then look elsewhere for a better reason."

"How do you know that?"

"The task force investigation is not the only source of information for us. In fact, it's a small, albeit important, source," Brian said.

"So has the state of emergency been canceled?"

"Definitely not. The fact that the Slaves of Allah's single operation failed does not mean a failure on their next attempt. We don't even know if there are additional plans that we haven't uncovered yet. We still don't have the other members of their cell in custody."

"It seems there's still a lot of work to do," I agreed.

"Sure. Think of it: We still don't know why Boris Zhukov and his comrades were helping the Slaves of Allah to launder money. Just greed? There could be other reasons, such as strategic alliance. You could be very instrumental in developing that angle."

I nodded, trying to figure out how that could be done, since Zhukov and the Slaves of Allah lived in two different worlds.

"But with things as they are, the interim success is largely thanks to you. I heard that your earlier money-laundering investigation and the subsequent obtaining of the messages made the difference. I heard praise for your work."

"How come I always hear only the complaints?" I was bitching but my heart sang.

"Back to our matter," said Brian, not giving me a chance to relish the moment any longer. "There are a number of plans to combat the Slaves of Allah before more of them reach our shores. But first we need combat-zone intelligence. The part we want you to play concerns your expertise in following the money trail."

"Dry them up?"

"Yes, but that's not enough. We need to track the exact route of the money flow. That would clearly identify who is financing them, thereby facilitating their terror. An open investigation has its advantages. People come and talk to us, supporters are reluctant to be exposed, and potential supporters hesitate more. At the same time we make it difficult to funnel money to fuel their operations. But these are side matters for now. First and foremost, we must identify the operators and their controllers to enable us to facilitate their return to their forefathers in the fastest and most efficient manner." The boyish expression on Brian's face turned iceberg-rigid.

But I smiled. "Now, we'd need plausible deniability for that," I retorted. Brian thawed and smiled, too.

"So, what's my mission?"

"The point is, Iran may be behind the Slaves of Allah. We're sending you as an operative to find out first, if there's an Iranian connection to the plot, and second, why Zhukov is moving money for terrorists."

"And the plan to achieve these goals?" I asked.

"We must take an indirect approach, since organizations of this sort are usually highly suspicious," said Brian. "Frankly, if these guys are like the others in their industry, unless we plan it right, you wouldn't pass their background check and remain alive."

There was tingling in my spine that I couldn't ignore.

"Therefore, infiltration must be indirect."

"Meaning?"

"We will be moving you into a target area while your true affiliation will go undetected. We know and assume two things in that context: We know that a member of a Belarusian group with strong ties to Russian organized crime in New York made huge money transfers, and we suspect that once the money arrived in New York, the clients issued instructions to U.S.- and European-based cells to use the funds for terrorist activities in the U.S."

"You mean the role of Igor and friends in all of this is to act as money launderers for the terrorists?"

Brian nodded. "That's the working assumption at this time. There is no other explanation. In these matters, the intelligence officer doing the tactical planning must always assume the worst-case scenario. Murphy is always right."

The theory coincided with my own early suspicion.

"Do you think Zhukov and his band knew who they were working for, and for what purpose?"

"I don't know. I guess they operated like bankers used to before money-laundering laws were introduced. They asked no questions."

"Is your assumption based on specific info or are you speculating? That the money would be used for attacks on the U.S. presumes the messages were real."

"Maybe, but only as it pertains to their intentions, not their abilities, since we don't know if the method described in the messages was genuine. At a minimum, it could be a ploy to mislead or scare us. Therefore, as I have already said, we work under the assumption of worst-case scenario."

"And Zhukov went along with it?" Somehow it didn't sit well with what I had read about the man in his FBI file, although this was just my gut suspicion.

"As I said," repeated Brian patiently, "he may have been unaware of the true purpose. Even mobsters have some rules, particularly when they live in the area targeted for a major terrorist attack. They could be corrupt and ruthless, but they are not stupid and do not wish to commit suicide. Slow, pleasurable suicide through overeating and drinking is more their style. Zhukov probably planned many more meals, many more bottles of vodka, many more extortions, many more days to count his fortune. No. He was not suicidal, just shortsighted."

"I read his FBI file. You should see his standard of living. He could teach a course on luxury living to any Saudi sheikh who has the cash and is looking to improve his already lofty standards." It was time to cut to the chase. "So what's in the plan?" I asked, sounding too enthusiastic.

He picked up my tone and grinned. "At the end, we want you to provide 'asset-protection services' to Zhukov and his clientele, particularly to the Slaves of Allah."

"Why would they hire me? An unsolicited approach on my behalf would seem highly suspicious."

"You are not supposed to know anything about the extracurricular activities of the Slaves of Allah. You are an expert on money laundering, aren't you?" He didn't wait for an answer. "So be one."

"Sure, discovering and hunting down money launderers, not acting like one."

"Well, do it in reverse. We'd establish you as an expert in asset protection. Trust me, the legend we designed should smooth your entry into Zhukov's money business. Once there, you'll have to find the way, with our remote assistance, to involve yourself in his contacts with the Slaves of Allah."

"And how do you do that?"

"Do what?"

"Build my credentials as an asset protector."

"We install you as a consultant in a Seychelles financial services firm."

"Would they retain me, with no questions asked?"

"Yes, there will be no problem," he said with a smile.

"No problem? What do I say about my qualifications? Service for the U.S. Department of Justice in fighting them? Or you mean I should portray myself as a rogue U.S. agent switching sides?"

He smirked. "We thought of that option, but we can't use it here. We can't allow any connection to the U.S. government. We own the Seychelles firm," said Brian shrewdly. "You have just been hired."

"Ahh," I said, digesting the information. A clever move. Get into the business of money laundering to catch the perpetrators. "Has the business been long established?"

"Long enough. A few years. We are well rooted there. An office, a small staff, a Web site, color brochures. We are legitimate."

"You mean a legitimate business doing illegitimate money laundering?"

"Sort of."

"So every client with dirty money who hires you ends up with his name turned over to his country's police?"

"No, definitely not. That would undermine our own business, which is built on reputation," he said with a straight face, and then smiled. "We keep only the big fish and throw the small ones back into the ocean. We are not interested in sardines. The income tax evaders, the crook bankrupts who stash away money from their creditors, and the husbands with big money contemplating a divorce . . . we keep their information on record; maybe we'll have some use for it in the future. What we're really interested in is the big-time mean guys whose activity could suggest a threat to our national security."

"Okay, so I'm a consultant. I think I could handle that."

"You'll get a few days' worth of instruction from our company's local manager, and then we can place you."

"You haven't answered me: How do I make contact with Zhukov?"

"First, you'll travel to the Seychelles. Get a suntan. Work in the office for a few days. When you feel you're ready, Sunil Bharat, the company's manager, will give you further instructions."

"When do I leave?"

"Tonight. Here are your travel documents." He handed me a folder. "From here to Newark, continuing on another flight to London Heathrow, you'll still be Dan Gordon. In London you'll be met at the gate by Sheila —"

"— who'll recognize me," I finished, forgetting how much I hate it when people do that to me.

"Right. She will escort you through UK immigration, proceeding to collect your luggage. Once past customs and outside the terminal, give Sheila your American passport. She'll give you a new passport and your airline tickets to the Seychelles. She'll also make the final inspection of your luggage. You'll leave Heathrow about three hours later."

"Not that I mind spending time in a tropical paradise, but I need to know if it will be a long stay. I have two children. I can't just vanish."

"Don't worry. They're grown up and used to your long absences."

I had many more questions, but Brian interrupted me. "I need to go now. Here's additional info on the Iranian-sponsored groups. I'll return in about two hours to take it back." He gave me a thick folder; before leaving he added, "Please don't leave this room."

The folder had approximately two hundred pages of text, tables, charts, and photos of leaders of major terrorist organizations. I was so immersed in reading it that only after several knocks on the door did I realize somebody was trying to attract my attention. Brian had returned just as I was done reading.

"Here's your stuff." He put a duffel bag with my clothes on the floor. "Take any notes?" he asked as I handed him back the folder.

"No."

"Good. Please go outside and take a cab to the Newport News airport. The ride will take a few minutes. Your plane leaves in an hour." He offered me a firm handshake. "Good luck. I'll be talking to you sooner than you think. The equipment you'll need will be given to you before you enter your area of operation and actually penetrate Zhukov's organization. We don't want you to travel internationally with these toys. You'll also receive agent authentication stuff — documentation and pocket litter that support and confirm your legend. Good luck."

I opened the door and left. So many things were left open. How would I penetrate the organization? How would I communicate with Brian? I had spent only a week in thorough training and had only received a four-hour overview on Iran's role in promoting terror. I had doubts it was sufficient from an operational point of view. I compared it with my training at the Mossad. Before we left for an overseas rendezvous with potential sources or confronting the opposition, we received far more rigorous and detailed instructions. The CIA couldn't be that shallow, not to say unprofessional, so I hoped the rest and the best was still yet to come. I hoped.

# X

I slept most of the twelve-hour flight from London to the Seychelles and woke up as the cabin crew lifted the window shades . Outside was the approaching hazy view of Victoria. When the doors opened, a blast of hot and humid air swiftly replaced the plane's stale air, with its typical end-of-journey odors of clogged bathrooms and fresh toothpaste. The temperature outside was over ninety degrees. I reset my watch four hours ahead from London time, and walked across the tarmac to the modest terminal.

"Mr. McMillan?" A short dark-faced man in his fifties, sporting a Panama hat and a beige cotton jacket, approached me. It took me a few seconds to realize he was addressing me by my new name, my new identity: Neil McMillan, Canadian businessman specializing in asset-protection services. Divorced; beautiful blond ex-wife, Pat, and two sons: Alec, ten, and Christian, eight (I had the snapshots to prove it); Pat, Alec, and Christian were conveniently out of Canada on a three-month tour of Europe. Just hired by Transcontinental Money Solutions, Limited, of Victoria, Seychelles, to provide financial services to its customers. Ambitious, opportunistic, not above playing fast and loose with the law. A full battery of identification: Ontario-issued driver's license, credit cards, passport, of course. They'd never told me the kind of character McMillan was. Was I expected to be shady? Obviously. But how might McMillan behave differently from me, the fast-moving, unbureaucratic Dan Gordon? Did I have a different persona? Or maybe I was chosen because I fit the character of the imaginative McMillan. I didn't know whether to be offended or flattered.

"Yes, and you are?"

"Sunil Bharat. I'm pleased to meet you," he said with a clear Indian accent. We were outside the terminal and in his car within fifteen minutes. The back of my shirt was already wet. I was not dressed for the equator. Sunil drove on the left side of the winding road through the bustling streets of Victoria. "Let me give you a quick description of this place. The Seychelles are located north of Madagascar and about a thousand miles east of Mombassa, Kenya. There are one hundred fifteen islands in the Republic of Seychelles. This capital city Victoria is on Mahe Island, the biggest, which has a population of about twenty-five thousand. The island is small, only one hundred seventy square miles. The Seychelles were ruled by the French, starting in the mid-1700s. Then forty-some years later the English took over until it became independent in 1977. The population here is a mix of African descendants of slaves and whites of French descent. They are plantation owners and are called 'the big whites.' There are also a few hundred Brits, who are called 'spoiled English' because of their untidy dress." In one minute he had given me the whole history.

"This is Fifth June Avenue," said Sunil as we passed the Victoria bus terminal to commemorate the 1977 revolution. At the Bicentenary Monument roundabout he turned; after a few blocks he stopped next to a red-roofed, two-story white building.

"This is your home. Your apartment is on the second floor. The ground floor is occupied by a family that takes care of the house. They're loyal to us, but obviously don't know who we are or why we are here. So be careful as you would with all strangers."

"Sure," I said; field security was in my genes. I felt the burden of the long day dawning on me.

"I'll pick you up tomorrow at nine thirty. We'll go to the office and get some work done."

I entered the apartment with the key Sunil gave me. It was spacious and nicely decorated. A light breeze came off the ocean as the evening approached. I inhaled it deeply into my lungs as greedily as a heavy smoker lighting a cigarette after many hours of abstaining. With the warm ocean breeze also came a mixed scent of coffee, rum, and flowers. From a distance I could hear rhythmic music and the murmur of the ocean waves. I slipped into the wide, soft bed and was asleep before my head hit the pillow.

A knock on the front door woke me at eight in the morning. I opened the door in my shorts and saw a beautiful young woman. She could not have been more than twenty years old. "Good morning, sir, your breakfast is ready. Would you like to have it on your terrace?"

She didn't wait for my answer, wheeling in a coffee cart with freshly squeezed mango juice, three slices of pineapple, and a bowl of thick yogurt with honey. I ate the meal slowly, looking alternately at the Indian Ocean behind the casuarina trees in bloom, the coconut trees, and the curvaceous young woman who stood silently at the corner of the room.

I had seen casuarinas in Australia, Israel, and now here. I like them: hardy, leafless trees with many toothed sheaths that bear a woody fruit looking much like a nut. Around the base of the tree I could see the fallen nuts and sheaths interconnected by their toothy edges.

"What's your name?"

"Bhamini," she answered shyly.

"Is it Indian?" While driving through the streets on my way from the airport, I could see that many of the island's residents were of Indian descent.

She nodded.

"What does it mean?"

"A beautiful, short-tempered lady," she answered, laughing timidly.

"And —" I paused, searching for the right word. "— are you? Short-tempered? About the beauty I can see for myself."

"That depends," she said with an enigmatic smile.

"How old are you?"

"Twenty-one."

"Went to school here?"

She nodded.

"Will you be serving all my meals?" I didn't know whether the apartment included meal service.

"Yes, if you wish."

"I have to go into town soon, and I don't know today's schedule yet, so I don't know if I'll be back for dinner."

"Mr. Sunil will call me," she said. "He always does."

At that moment there was a knock on the door and Sunil walked in. "I see you have already met my niece."

"Yes," I confirmed. "Bhamini served me a delicious breakfast."

After getting ready, we went to Sunil's car and drove downtown. He parked the car near a four-story building on Revolution Avenue.

"No building can be taller than the coconut trees," said Sunil as we entered the elevator. "It's an old local law." We went directly to the penthouse floor.

The brass plate on the door read TRANSCONTINENTAL MONEY SOLUTIONS, LIMITED. The office suite had six fully furnished offices, but only three employees were present. Sunil led me to a vacant corner office with huge windows overlooking the ocean, and said he would come back after returning a few phone calls.

I sat behind the mahogany desk. Other than the desk, there was only a wall unit with a few books and — much to my surprise — another photo of me and my "adopted" family, Pat, Marc, and Christian. A computer stood on the desk extension. I turned it on and surfed the Internet until Sunil returned.

"I see that you've made yourself comfortable. That's good." He shut the door and sat across the desk. "Don't take any notes. If you don't understand or find it hard to remember, ask me, either now or later. The staff here know nothing about us, other than the fact that we provide financial services to customers from outside the islands. If you can, try to politely avoid all questions concerning your past. Some of the locals can be very nosy."

"Sure. Where do I come in?"

"We establish you as an expert on asset protection with exquisite qualifications, having years of experience in the ins and outs of this business. We have added your name to our Web site as a leading expert on asset protection. We also instructed our asset specialists to mention your name in their communications with third parties."

"Something like 'Our expert Mr. Neil McMillan believes this is the best approach'?"

"Exactly. News of that sort travels fast. You'd be surprised how small this industry is."

"Don't I know it."

As much as I knew about the trade, I still had a lot to learn. My expertise was gained from the hunter's point of view. Now I needed to view it from the deer's perspective. How could he hide from predators and hunters?

Sunil continued. "The legend is that you are a financial consultant who lived on the islands in the distant past and are now returning for a second term of office with a different local company. Your old company went out of business, you moved away, and now you are hired by us."

"What was the name of the now defunct company?"

"World Trusts and Investments Limited. It was managed by an American lawyer who moved here from the British Virgin Islands."

"What was his name?"

"He appeared here as John Walker, but I suspect he adopted that name because he liked the liquor so much. Drinking brought him down, and following a few shady failed deals he just took off. Maybe he found a new location, or maybe his creditors or disgruntled clients finally got him. You were his unsuspecting employee who managed to stay on for only four months before leaving for a better job with a Dutch company in the Netherlands Antilles."

"Okay, I'll need to rehearse my past," I said.

Days went by and the routine repeated itself. I called my children several times through a satellite telephone that showed a U.S. number as the origin of the call. Sunil watched me filling out one-page forms of incorporation, making the clients believe we were working hard. After a week, I'd become used to these lazy days of doing nothing but answering a few phone calls and making myself visible to the bank managers and employees of the Registrar of Companies.

I thought of Laura. I looked at my watch. It was 3:00 P.M. local time, 7:00 A.M. in New York. Time to wake her up. I used the satellite phone to call her home number.

"Hello," came her sleepy voice.

"Laura? It's Dan, did I wake you up?"

"No, I've been up for a while, it's just that I haven't talked to anyone today. How are you?"

"I'm fine, getting some sun for a change."

"Are you still in Virginia?"

"No, actually I'm in the Seychelles."

"The Seychelles? And I thought we'd go there together."

"Maybe one day," I said. "How are things at your end? Still working on the case?"

"Just moving paper from one end of my desk to the other. Since you left, most of the action was moved to other departments. Are you working there on the task force's case?"

"Yes."

"When will you be back?" There was a personal tone to her question.

"I have no idea, but I know I'll go someplace else, probably in Europe, before I return."

"How come you have the fun and I have the paperwork?" she asked with a feigned note of complaint.

"I got lucky, I guess."

"So tell me what you do."

"I can't, not just yet. Maybe when I return."

"I'm curious, give me a hint."

"Remember my presentation and my findings?"

"Sure."

"Then think in that direction."

"Dan you're killing me. Give me more."

"Laura, you know I can't."

"Dan, I need to leave, is there a number where I can call you later on? I need to consult with you on something."

"Personal or business?"

"Personal." She paused. "But it has to do with my work."

"We can't take calls here," I said. "Is it urgent?"

"Kind of."

"I can call you again later at the office."

"No, no," she said abruptly. That answer was firm, and left me wondering why. "Give me your number, I'll call you later."

"I need to go," I said, "talk to you later."

I looked through the window and saw the ocean and coconut trees slowly moving their palm fronds in the wind. The conversation with Laura bothered me: She was withholding something. Of course, I'd refused to tell her what I was doing or to give her my phone number, and I didn't know how she would interpret my conduct. But there was something else.

Sunil came to my office. "Do you feel you are ready yet?"

"I already feel sleazy," I said with a smile. "Does that qualify me?"

"The industry does have a bad reputation," he agreed. "It's full of sleazy people using sleazy methods. But the purpose of 'asset protection' is legitimate: protecting assets against anyone other than their owner."

"The concept may be benign, but most of the people who use it are suspect. That's particularly true with respect to the offshore industry," I said. "I know from more than a decade of chasing these guys."

Sunil chuckled. "I know your reputation."

"Maybe I'll get a different view while assuming, albeit temporarily, my position on the other side of the fence."

"You should familiarize yourself with the terminology used here," Sunil advised.

"I came here to learn," I said in earnest, "and I have gained a lot from working here already. However, there is a question I need to ask you. Do we screen our clients? Or do we provide these services to anyone?" I found it odd that the U.S. government was actually complicit in laundering dirty money.

"Only to a select few," he said with a grin. "Don't forget, we do it as part of law enforcement. A sting, if you will. It is fully authorized by the attorney general."

I smiled in amusement. What a great idea this front company was. Help launderers whitewash their money through us. We get info and control, we discover newly developed tactics and resources, and, best of all, they pay us for the privilege. Brilliant. And just as with a family doctor, the "patients" are financially naked; nothing is withheld.

"I think you're ready to handle the next client who calls in for asset protection," he informed me. He gave me some final technical explanations and instructions then, as if on cue, the receptionist interrupted on the intercom.

"A potential client on line one."

"Take it," said Sunil. "I'll be right here if you need me."

I picked up the phone. "Good afternoon, this is Neil McMillan. How can I help you?"

The voice was of a man perhaps in his sixties, speaking English with a slight German accent. "I need asset-protection information," he said briefly.

"Sure, I'll be happy to help you. May I ask if you need the information for yourself, or maybe you are acting for a third party?"

"For myself, and I need absolute confidentiality."

"You have come to the right place," I said. "Secrecy is our motto. I can guarantee that the information you will provide us shall be treated only by me, and it will be regarded as top secret. We run our operation so as to guarantee that no creditor or government ever penetrates our shields."

"That sounds good," he said.

"Tell me what you want to achieve."

"I have a little argument with the tax authorities of my government, and until I settle it I want to make sure they will not find and seize my assets."

"Fair enough," I said. "Most of our clients need that kind of protection."

"Before we go any farther," said the man, "I need to know the cost of your services."

"We are really very competitive. The fees we charge are more or less the industry standard. This isn't cheap, though. I know some irresponsible companies are offering cheaper services. But we know that people want the best for their money. It must be pampered, and we are the leaders in professional service." I went on to offer a condensed version of the fee schedule Sunil had discussed with me.

The man seemed agreeable. "How do you do it, then?" he asked. "I mean, the actual protection?"

"We help moving the money around until it lands in the legal structure we design — a trust, or an international business company."

"Before calling you, I spoke with a few other competing companies. Is there a compelling reason why should I choose the Seychelles? There are more than thirty similar offshore locations."

"Well, we have similar operations elsewhere. But those who come here do so due to the special benefits the Seychelles government offers. For example, income from international business companies or international trusts is completely exempt from business tax. The Seychelles have a territorial basis for taxation; profits are taxed only if they are derived from a source in the Seychelles. There is no capital gains tax; interest, dividends, and other payments received from abroad are likewise not taxed. Finally, there is no taxation of individual income. Resident, nonresident corporate, and noncorporate businesses are liable to pay business tax only on income derived from the Seychelles. But a company is considered resident only if it is incorporated in the Seychelles, and even then the tax is minimal." I paused and added nonchalantly, "I'm sure most companies avoid even that."

"I see," he said. "Okay, so we start a company or create a trust? Then what? Is the money transferred to the Seychelles?"

"It depends on the level of our involvement. It's your call. Some clients only want incorporation of a Seychelles company, and once incorporated, we never hear from them again."

"Not even for annual reporting?"

"No. Many times the incorporation is made for a onetime transaction, and once completed, the owners abandon the company. We know that because they never answer our letters concerning annual fees. We simply never hear from them again. If you want us to provide you with nominee directors, then we'd continue to be involved. Many clients want to open a bank account locally and ask us to make the arrangements. It's all up to you."

"I need a company as soon as possible."

"We have ready-made shelf corporations. You can have control immediately."

The concept of "shelf" corporations is just another ploy of the sleazy asset protectors that give the industry a bad name. They inform their potential clients that they have a ready-made corporation on the shelf, available for immediate use. What they fail to disclose is that all they have is a computer-generated form, which still needs to be filed with the local Registrar of Companies to make the firm viable.

"Okay, let's move on," said the man, apparently satisfied with my answers. "If I order a shelf company, do you mail out the incorporation papers immediately upon registration?"

"Almost immediately. The shelf company has an open configuration — meaning that it does not yet have any directors appointed and shares allocated. You have to tell us if you'll appoint them or if we should assist you there as well."

"For an additional fee?"

"Yes, but nominal. We charge only one hundred dollars a year for each director." I saw Sunil smiling. Since we handled hundreds of such companies, it was easy to see how we were making money.

"If you would like to open a bank account outside the Seychelles, you'd need the documents to be certified by a notary or legalized by an official stamp, like an official court certification, known as an Apostille."

"What about the directors that you suggested? Who are they?"

"Respectable local individuals that we arrange."

"Are all types of corporations allowed in the Seychelles?"

"No. The business of the company cannot be in banking, insurance, reinsurance, or trust."

"But bearer shares are allowed?"

"Of course."

"Okay," said the man, "let's do it."

I spent the next twenty minutes getting the pertinent details, and the transaction was completed.

"Good job," said Sunil. "Let's go and have dinner. You've certainly earned it."

Another week went by. One late afternoon, after work, I was strolling along Market Street examining the local art displayed on stalls when I suddenly had the feeling I was being watched. The street was bustling with shoppers and tourists. I couldn't see anyone tailing me, but my instinct told me someone was there. The adrenaline surged, and I told myself, *Let's see what he wants.* I continued walking but made a sudden right turn into a side street. While walking, I glanced into a store's window and saw a young man, probably twenty-five, with Indian features, looking in my direction. When I returned to Market Street, he was still behind me by some sixty or seventy feet.

I had to be certain that he was indeed following me for whatever reason. So I applied the first rule of countersurveillance my Mossad instructors had taught me: *Make sure you're being followed and that you're not imagining things, but — just as important — don't tip off the opposition that you've spotted them.* I crossed the street, he crossed the street; I made two left turns, he made two left turns. I crossed the street, he did as well. I turned around and walked back, so did he. It was obvious that he wasn't a pro; I'd spotted him right away. *Okay, my friend,* I said to myself, *let's see how good you really are; so far you're failing.* I pulled from my pocket a bunch of scuba diving brochures I'd collected during my stroll. I surreptitiously tore off one partially printed page, tore off the printed part, and held it on the top of the brochures. I crossed the street again and "accidentally" dropped the torn blank part of the paper in the middle of the road just as I saw a bus coming. The man waited for the bus to pass then bent to pick up the paper off the road. When the bus passed I was out of sight, lost in the crowd, although close enough to see his puzzled look when he realized that he'd lost me. Taking a detour, I entered my apartment building through a side entrance. I couldn't see the young man, or anyone else for that matter. I called Sunil but I got his voice mail. I hung up. However, my .22-caliber pistol was my partner that night.

Sunil called in the morning, and I told him about the previous night's episode. "I don't think I should come to the office," I said. "I don't know when I became a target or if it started only last evening. I shouldn't contaminate the office as well."

Sunil listened attentively and questioned me how I spotted the follower and how I got rid of him. As it happened, he'd been about to tell me that he thought I was ready to move on to the next step: trying to contact Zhukov. This incident only served to speed up the inevitable.

———

That night I was on the plane to Marseilles.

From the airport I took a cab. The weather in Marseilles was calm. The Mediterranean breeze cooled the hot air but also brought high humidity. Flocks of screeching, squawking seagulls were squabbling over scraps thrown overboard by a bearded fisherman gutting fish, while other seamen were unloading crates of colorful, giant shrimp. My cab was maneuvering in the busy avenues where the large population of North Africans was visible. Although physically tired after the long flight, I was mentally alert. I checked into my hotel and, using the approach I'd been told to use, I immediately called Zhukov in New York. It went against all my training to call a target directly from my hotel room, but in this case we wanted Zhukov to be able to trace the call back to me.

"Mr. Zhukov, this is Neil McMillan, I'm calling from France."

"Yes." Although he rumbled just one word, his heavy Russian accent came out strongly.

"I'm a financial consultant, with particular expertise in offshore corporations. I have important information that I need to discuss with you."

"Look," he said, audibly bothered and perhaps a tad cautious, "if you are selling something, talk to my accountant."

This was the make-or-break point: I had to steer him back on course or the conversation would end in ten seconds or less. "Mr. Zhukov, this has nothing to do with selling anything. I'm talking about a security problem. It concerns the Seychelles. I don't think you'd like me to discuss it over the phone."

"Security?"

I'd gotten his interest, but it would keep him interested for only a few more seconds: The spark had to be turned into a blaze. "It concerns certain Australian companies moving money."

Apparently I had, because he immediately responded.

"What do you want?"

"As I said, I'm a financial consultant with an asset-protection operation in the Seychelles, and I recently came across something interesting: a certain activity in a Seychelles bank. I don't think it was meant to be so visible."

"I have no connection to any Australian companies or the Seychelles, so you must have the wrong person. Did my name come up there?"

Bingo. Forget the denial; the latter part of the sentence revealed his concern. He was the right person all right, but obviously he couldn't concede that to a complete stranger.

"I'm sure you'd rather we didn't discuss it now," I repeated for the third time. "It'd be better if we met."

"Let me get back to you. Where can I find you?"

"I'm in Marseilles, France, at the Promenade Hotel." I gave him my numbers.

All of a sudden it felt like my old days with Mossad. Calling sources, pretending to be Joe, waiting in vain for a contact to call, trying to think two steps ahead of your enemy, when sometimes you didn't even know who or where your enemy was.

From a pay phone outside the hotel I called Brian and Eric at the number I'd received and reported that an initial contact had been made. I was told to follow the plan.

Once my business was concluded, I hesitated for only a moment before calling Laura. When it came to Laura, I had to concede that my lust outweighed my logic. I knew I was violating protocol but couldn't help myself. Just a small onetime violation of the rule, I promised myself, the same excuse I use when I devour forbidden food, wiping out weight loss achieved after days of strict dieting.

"Dan, where are you?"

"In Marseilles."

"I hope you mean Marseilles, France, and not Marseilles, Illinois."

"Let me take a look," I said. "Yeah, the steaks here are small, so it must be France."

"Having a good time?"

"Sort of, but it could be better."

"Oh?"

"Feel like a short French Mediterranean vacation?"

She didn't even hesitate. "Sure, you mean now?"

"Why not?"

"On or off duty?"

"Why categorize it? Just come."

"Let me make a few phone calls first. Where are you?"

I gave her my numbers. "I'm registered as Neil McMillan."

I crossed the street back to my hotel and returned to my room. It was getting dark and I started thinking about going out to dinner. But all of a sudden I felt the weight of my weary body. I sprawled out on my bed and fell asleep immediately. French food would have to wait.

The phone rang. I had no idea where I was or why, or what time it was.

"Dan?" came Laura's pleasant voice, "I think I can make it. But it'd have to be private. My visit, I mean. I don't think Hodson would appreciate me joining your assignment without his knowledge. So I simply asked for a few days off."

"As long as you get here quickly. Have a schedule yet?"

"Yes, I'm leaving tonight and expect to arrive at Marseilles tomorrow at noon. I'll take a cab to the hotel."

"Great, see you tomorrow." I put my head on the pillow and fell asleep again in no time.

The piercing ring of the damn telephone woke me up again. Automatically I picked up the bulky white receiver.

"Mr. Neil?" The man spoke with a heavy accent. Russian, probably.

"Yes, this is Neil McMillan. Who are you?"

"Never mind. You called my boss."

"Who's your boss?"

"You know. He told me to arrange a meeting. He will meet you in New York next Monday afternoon."

"I can't. The meeting must be in Marseilles."

"I said my boss wants you here."

"I can't enter the United States. The feds would like to talk to me, but I'd rather talk to you guys."

"You mean they're on to this matter?"

What a language barrier could do. "No. I simply don't want to talk to them; they want me for something else. So I'm staying away from the United States for the time being."

"Are you an American?"

167

"No, Canadian. Could we meet here in two or three days?"

"I have to talk to my boss," he said and hung up.

An hour later he called again. "Okay," he said. "Where do you want to meet?"

"I suggest the Promenade Hotel where I'm staying."

"We'll be there on Thursday, three days from now. If this is some kind of a joke, you should know we have a limited sense of humor."

*And a temper*, I said to myself. "No, it's not a joke. I'm serious, and so is the matter."

It was too easy. Too easy. Although I managed to have it my way, I felt uncomfortable. I wished I could analyze it with David, or Benny. I needed their counsel. Why did Zhukov agree to my dictate? Was the matter I'd brought up so important for him that all of a sudden he'd become a lamb rather than a raging bear? Or maybe the consent to my terms signaled something else I wasn't aware of yet? It bothered me.

I forced myself out of bed and went outside to call Eric and Brian to report, but they weren't available. I left a message.

When I returned to my room, there was a message to call Dr. Jean Pierre Arnaud. *Dr. Arnaud* is the signal that I had been contacted by Eric and/or Brian. I went outside again. Never use a tracks-leaving cell phone in such circumstances.

"Hello, Mr. McMillan," said Eric. I'd expected Brian's friendlier voice.

"Hello, Dr. Arnaud," I said, a bit surprised at the sudden formality; did Eric suspect that someone was listening? "My plans have changed, and I expect to be very busy soon. Could we arrange my appointment immediately?"

"I need to make some arrangements at the clinic. I'll call to tell you when we can schedule an appointment."

I went to the bar to have a drink and within minutes, a hotel employee gave me a note: "Dr. Jean Pierre Arnaud had a cancellation, so he can see you this afternoon at four at his clinic."

The clinic was located in a wide street, but the entrance was inconspicuous. I buzzed the button on the building's main door and the door opened. I took the clunky old elevator to the third floor. The sign on the door read DR. JEAN PIERRE ARNAUD, ONCOLOGIST.

I rang the bell and a nurse opened the door. The place looked like an old-fashioned clinic, with high ceilings and tall windows with wooden shutters painted in white. A strong smell of antiseptics gave the place the final touch. Still, it didn't strike me as a real doctor's office that patients visited. In fact, it was used only as a CIA rendezvous site. There wasn't a receptionist. Other than the nurse, I didn't see anyone.

I followed the nurse to an examination room. There Eric Henderson was standing next to Brian and another person I didn't recognize. Brian just nodded at me, smiling.

"Hello again," Eric said in a bland tone.

"Hi," I said, and thought, *This eel again.*

"This is Martin Levitt, a tech ops officer from OTS, the Office of Technical Service," Brian said; "and you already know Eric."

"Nice to meet you," I said to Martin.

"So," Eric said. "A meeting in three days."

"Yes. They called."

I wondered how he already knew about the meeting. I hadn't told anyone. Zhukov's phone must be tapped.

"Fine," said Eric. "Remember, the purpose of the meeting is to install you as an asset-protection specialist in Zhukov's organization. Nothing else."

I had the feeling that the last two words were meant to deter me from any independent initiatives. I nodded, but mentally I didn't agree: It was my neck and ass on the line, not his. If I needed to go it alone, I would — with or without Eric's blessing. I'd gotten away with it in the past, and other than sending Eric's blood pressure to a new high, there'd been no adverse consequences.

"What I meant to say is that the idea behind the meeting should be cooperation, not confrontation. Remember, the substance of the meeting is a dangle operation. We're enticing Zhukov into thinking you're a bona fide professional. Each of you has an interest in the success of the meeting. But as always, we'll be nearby. We saved your neck once and we'll do it again here, if necessary."

That was Eric's not-so-subtle way of reminding me that during our last joint case, in Germany, they'd sent in the German police at just the right moment — while I was struggling with a colonel from Iranian counter-intelligence.

"The French police may not be as efficient as the Germans," I said. "But at any rate, I think this is a contingency we must prepare for."

"Meaning?" asked Eric.

"If the clients aren't interested in future cooperation, but only in figuring out what I know and how I got it, what then?" I asked.

Brian intervened. "You agree to sell them the information for a hundred thousand dollars. The fee will also include patching the security leak and training their people so that things like that would never happen again."

"They may or may not buy it, but I'm sure they'll be very interested in how I managed to link the money transfers to Zhukov. You and I both know that there was nothing on the money-transfer documents to suggest Zhukov was behind them."

Eric wasn't deterred; as always, he had an answer, satisfactory or not. "That's part of the information you bargain for. Tell them that if you could get it, anyone else who was motivated enough could also obtain it."

"I wouldn't buy that answer, and neither will Zhukov," I said, suspecting that Eric hadn't done his homework before coming here.

The man was exhausting my patience. It was obvious that he was trying to see how far I could go without letting *my* famous temper take over. I didn't give him that pleasure; I kept my big mouth shut.

"Let's see what we have here," Brian stepped in, sensing my mood. "Sling and Dewey, a bogus company, was incorporated in New South Wales, Australia. It had two shareholders: another bogus Australian company and a Seychelles international business company. Sling and Dewey then opened a bank account in the Seychelles, right?"

"Right so far."

"Next, Sling and Dewey asked the Seychelles bank to draw checks made out to Eagle Bank of New York, totaling sixty million."

"Not exactly. Some of the money came as cash. See the FinCEN report."

"Okay, ignore the cash deposits for a moment. But significant amounts were deposited in the New York Eagle Bank through these bank checks."

"Right again."

"Now, do you know who physically went to Eagle Bank to make the check deposits?"

"No."

"Ivan Dimitrov," volunteered Eric.

"Who is he?"

"One of Zhukov's soldiers."

"How do you know that?"

Unexpectedly, Eric was willing to answer a question that revealed a source. "Simple. The teller at Eagle asked Dimitrov to endorse the backs of the checks."

"And he did?" That amazed me.

"Apparently, the teller verified that he was a signatory for the account of Sling and Dewey, and wrote Dimitrov's name and address below his signature on the back of the checks."

"Why? That's not the normal practice."

"In these circumstances it *was* standard procedure, because the checks were drawn on a Seychelles bank and not on an account the Seychelles bank had in a New York bank. Therefore, what Dimitrov did was not 'a deposit' in the true sense of the word but a 'submission for collection.' Eagle Bank simply acted as a collection agent for Sling and Dewey. Only if the funds were indeed cleared would Eagle Bank credit Sling and Dewey's account. To show that the money would be directed to the designated account, there had to be an endorsement of a signatory of the account holder," Eric said.

"I know that much," I retorted. "Eagle Bank couldn't endorse it itself, because under certain circumstances it could be held as a surety, a guarantor for the amount of the check, if it bounced. Eagle Bank would be stupid to do that without knowing whether the check was good."

"Exactly. When Eagle Bank, in the normal course of business sent the checks to the issuing Seychelles bank for collection, it exposed Dimitrov's name and address to the Seychelles bank employees, or anyone else who had access to the banking information — like me. And voilà!" Eric concluded with a rare smile. I'd never seen him so self-satisfied.

"Why did Dimitrov sign?" I asked.

"Apparently he wasn't told about the sensitivity of the deposits. He was told to deposit checks and he did. The teller told him to sign and he did. We checked him out. He's one of Zhukov's chauffeurs."

"So how does it link Zhukov to the account?"

"The address on the back of the check is Zhukov's. It's a single-family town house, and Zhukov is the only tenant."

"Too circumstantial," I said. "I know you're a lawyer, you never let people forget it, but try to think outside the envelope for once; we're not in court."

"Once the checks were sent back to the issuing Seychelles bank with the endorsement, you were able to get the name and address on their back. You quickly discovered through a simple reverse check of the address on Google that Boris Zhukov lives there, and only Boris Zhukov."

"Okay, that's how I explain to Zhukov how I got the info. But how do you know that Dimitrov endorsed the checks?"

"Through a search in the bank," reminded Brian.

"Wouldn't Zhukov suspect that I obtained the information as a result of the search? That would immediately paint me as a federal agent."

"Unlikely. The search was at the bank's archives and was not directed in particular at either Eagle Bank or Zhukov's companies' accounts. I don't know if Zhukov knows about Fazal. It is possible that Zhukov's role ended when the money arrived at Eagle Bank. Furthermore, nobody at the bank knows why the FBI searched their premises. An FBI agent 'accidentally' told them it had to do with telemarketing fraud. The real purpose has been concealed."

"Fine. Now how do I react if they want to see the checks? Suppose they pay, then what?"

"I'm giving you copies of the checks."

"You mean you have them?"

"Yup," said Brian in satisfaction. "Look." He handed me six photocopies. "We made copies from the bank's copy. When a check is sent overseas for collection, the sending bank keeps a photocopy of the check. We got that. But obviously you tell them you got it from a cooperating bank employee in the Seychelles. Once you've shown them the incriminating evidence, I think they'll be committed to retaining your services."

"I'll sound like a sleazeball, like everyone else in the industry," I said.

"That's exactly the impression we want you to give," said Eric. "You can't be a straight arrow. That could make them suspect a sting operation."

"There's another problem," I said. "I was attacked in Stuttgart by two thugs, probably from Zhukov's organization. If Zhukov comes here with any of them, they'll recognize me immediately." I told them about the bug in my coat.

"Nothing to worry about," said Eric. "We know who those guys were: just local hooligans hired to rough you up to frighten you. They're not members of Zhukov's gang. He outsourced the job to locals." He turned to the young man standing next to him. "Martin will give you some toys."

Martin, who'd been quiet all this time, gave me a toolbox-sized carton and meticulously went over its contents with me, giving me step-by-step operating instructions for each gadget.

"You're checking out of your hotel tonight. Do not leave a forwarding address," said Eric.

"I never do. Where am I going?"

"To the Excelsior Hotel."

That piqued my curiosity. "How will they find me? We agreed to meet at the Promenade Hotel, didn't we?"

"You're leaving them a note. You must be out of your hotel immediately, before they're able to arrange a watch on you. Here's the note you're leaving behind." Eric handed me an unsealed envelope with a note written on Promenade's guest stationery: "I moved to the Excelsior Hotel. Please call telephone number 0491 15 41 41. Neil McMillan."

I made a mental note to leave an identical message for Laura. "Is my new room comfortable?" I asked.

"Very, and well equipped. Here is your new room key."

I put the key in my pocket. "You mean equipped electronically?"

"Sure," said Martin. "State of the art, undetectable, and untraceable. Therefore, we want you to suggest holding the meeting in your room. We're positioning eight armed CIA special task agents in two adjoining rooms, four in each. If they determine that you're in danger, they'll intervene."

"And if Zhukov or his men request another location?"

"Stall," said Eric, "and call me again at the same number."

After our meeting I went straight to the reception desk of the Promenade and checked out, leaving my note to Zhukov behind at the desk.

An hour later I returned to the Promenade's lobby, waiting for Laura. The fact that Eric wanted the meeting to take place in my room would complicate things. How would I explain Laura's presence? I'd have to keep her in another room, or a different hotel. This vacation was going to be expensive. But I hadn't yet factored in the benefits in the profit-and-loss column. At noon, she arrived. Red-cheeked, with her red hair curled and waved, and just one carry-on bag, Laura looked stunning in tight jeans and a tee.

She beamed as soon as she saw me, and gave me a peck on the lips. I let out a deep breath. "Welcome to France."

"Shall we go up to the room? I need to freshen up."

"There's been a small glitch. I had to check out and move to another hotel, and there could be a problem if we stay at the same place, so I think you should stay here."

Her face dropped. "You mean not only separate rooms but also separate hotels? You should have told me earlier." There was a distinct tone of disappointment here, with a bit of passive anger.

"I'm disappointed as well, but I have a meeting in my room in a few days. There are a lot of preparations and your presence will be difficult to explain."

"Another girlfriend?" she asked sardonically.

"No. I'm meeting some bad people and you should be kept out of it." I looked at her face. "But," I added, "we have three whole days to have fun together. So it doesn't really matter if we stay in separate hotels."

"I guess I have no other choice." She followed me to the desk, filled in the guest card, and received a key to her room.

"I'll wait here," I said.

Half an hour later Laura returned wearing another tee with white jeans and a baseball cap. "I'm hungry. Let's find a good place to eat."

We took a cab to the old port. We found a small bistro that catered to fishermen. I had always wanted to taste the Marseilles version of bouilla-baisse. Now was my opportunity. "Go ahead," said Laura. "I'll share any-thing you're having."

When the piping-hot bowl was brought to our table, it was worth the wait. It was heaped with jumbo peeled shrimp, plump mussels, sea scal-lops, sea bass fillets, and sliced leeks, white and pale green. I tasted it cau-tiously. The mix of flavors also included dry white wine, saffron, fish fumet, roasted garlic, tomato juice, Pernod liqueur, and a little parsley. Half a loaf of crispy French baguette and a carafe of wine completed the meal perfectly. We didn't talk shop. Whether Laura had finally acquiesced to my gag orders, or maybe had other things on her mind, I didn't know. She told me about her childhood and college, and I listened courteously. One thing that became clear as she told me parts of her personal history was that Laura was a results-oriented person, and a smart woman. A bit inex-perienced, maybe, but clearly driven in life by a one-word agenda: *succeed*.

"So what's the plan?" she asked.

"Take it easy for two or three days," I said, thinking how it would feel to finish the unfinished business I had with her from New York.

She smiled. "I mean business . . . what are you doing here?"

"As I said, I'm meeting a bad character."

"Does it have to do with our case?"

I took a sip of wine. "Yes. Let's forget work for these days, let's just have fun."

"Dan, I'm curious, tell me: Who is he and why are you meeting him?"

"Laura, you're better off not knowing, for your own good."

"Okay, then tell me why you're meeting him. No name, just the reason."

"I want to do business with him."

"What sort of business?"

"Laura!" Her persistence unnerved me.

"Okay, okay, what do you want to do now?"

"Feel like being a tourist? We can go to the Basilique Notre-Dame-de-la-Garde. I read that the views are spectacular from the top — four hun-dred fifty feet up."

Laura's pinched face said *No, thanks.*

"How about the fish market? We can just stroll there, it's very close. We can get fresh sea air, see the yachts and fishing boats. There are some nice sidewalk cafés facing the port. Later, if you change your mind, we could still climb the southern bank to the basilica and get a panoramic view of the city."

"I'd like that," she said. We walked a few blocks, just looking at the stores and the people. The sea breeze was lightly blowing, bringing the familiar scent of seaweed and sea salt. I love that smell. It reminds me of growing up in Israel, near the Mediterranean.

The old port was actually small and looked cramped between the surrounding modern buildings, some of them high-rise. Although the atmosphere should have been a perfect catalyst for creating the right mood between us, it didn't. We walked aimlessly for a while, until Laura said, "I'm tired. I need an espresso."

There was no shortage of restaurants, bars, and nightclubs to choose from. We went into a café that gave us a vantage point to watch the small sailing ships in the harbor, as well as the drunks staggering from the bar next door.

Laura sipped her double espresso while I closed my eyes to smell the sea.

"Dan, did you do anything other than sunbathing in the Seychelles?" came the unexpected question.

I opened my eyes. "Yes, basking in the sun is pretty time consuming." I smiled. "I also talked to people, nothing much. I think management wanted me out of the picture for a while. I don't think they appreciate my unconventional initiatives."

"You mean they exiled you?"

"In a sense. At the beginning I thought I was being asked to do something for the case; you know some of the money moved through the Seychelles. But very quickly, I discovered that the effort to unravel the Seychelles connection was complicated by politics, so it was abandoned."

It was time to stop being so candid with Laura. *Need-to-know basis* means need to know, and she didn't need to know. This was the first time I had bluntly lied to her, my co-worker. But in this case, at last and at least, I was following the rule to withhold information.

She looked at me strangely but said nothing. There was a heavy silence. I had the feeling that she wasn't buying my lie. But as long as she didn't challenge me outright, I was home free.

"I'm tired," she said, "I need to get some sleep." She clearly sounded unhappy with me.

There was no romance in the air, not even lust. The plans I'd made for us seemed irrelevant now. There were no sparks between us, not even a courtship dance. It felt odd.

We took a cab to her hotel. "Good night Dan," she said, "Call me in the morning; maybe we could go to the beach." I should have been disappointed by Laura's coolness toward me, but I wasn't, though it had come as a surprise. I glanced at my watch: 6:30 P.M. I returned to the Excelsior. Personally I didn't care about her attitude, but professionally I was uneasy. Something was happening; I just didn't know what. I decided to sharpen my instincts. They have never failed me before.

I sat at the hotel's bar. My cell phone vibrated. I looked at the display: a local number, 01 49 55 60 00. That was a pay phone's number that signaled me to meet Eric in thirty minutes at a safe apartment in Rue Guibal.

I took a cab to the location. Eric opened the door. I followed him into the sparsely furnished one-bedroom apartment.

"Are you ready?" he asked as we sat down on the only two chairs next to a dining table.

"Yes," I said, realizing I'd made the right decision to put Laura in a different hotel; I was relieved to be free from her company tonight. "Anything new on the Slaves of Allah?"

"Yes, look at this." Eric handed me a manila folder marked TOP SECRET.

I grabbed the envelope and opened it. Scanning the top page quickly, I saw that it was a CIA report on the ongoing investigation into the "Financial Affairs of Imam Abu Ali Hasan" — Fazal's Ayatollah.

The first paragraph caught my attention: "Imam Abu Ali Hasan, a Muslim cleric without a mosque, is soon to be indicted on criminal charges of hiding his ties to terrorist groups in order to obtain U.S. citizenship."

I raised my head in disbelief. "You're holding him on immigration charges?"

Eric smiled wryly. "That's allowed us to conduct a financial investigation into his links to terrorism. We've videotaped his fund-raising activities for the Slaves of Allah. Since last fall, the FBI and the Joint Terrorism Task Force have considered additional potential charges against Abu Ali Hasan, including tax evasion, filing false tax returns, money laundering, mail and wire fraud, and providing material support to designated foreign terrorist organizations as well as other prohibited financial transactions."

"So why file just the immigration charges?"

"Because it's easy to start with, and we need to reveal in court only a very little of the information we've accumulated. No risk of compromising our sources."

I kept reading. When FBI agents arrested the imam at his home in Brooklyn on June 20, 2002, they asked his wife, Fatima, for permission to search the house. Following her consent, FBI agents seized documents, a computer, different computer media such as CDs and disks, passports, and videotapes. The Department of Justice's counterterrorism unit was evaluating the seized documents and computer data as part of their ongoing investigation. The agents also seized political and religious speeches, sermons, and the manifesto of the Slaves of Allah. "This stuff is presumably irrelevant to the immigration fraud case," I said, hating to remind Eric that I was still a lawyer.

"We don't intend to limit the trial to immigration fraud," said Eric, "Now, with what we've seized, we can go after him for the big-ticket items: money laundering and providing support to terrorist organizations. In a trial on those charges, this stuff will be highly relevant."

I could see some serious legal problems in federal court with their approach, but there was no point in arguing with Eric over that. These documents included many speeches, sermons, notes, and articles by Imam Abdul Abu Ali Hasan that were venomously critical of the U.S. government and people. They focused investigators' attention on foreign-language sources that hadn't been previously translated due to lack of funds. One of these, a videotape from early in 1993 that the FBI had seized in another criminal investigation, showed Abdul Abu Ali Hasan soliciting money for the Slaves of Allah from Muslims coming to mosques to pray or attend social events.

I took the videocassette from the envelope. "Let's see it," I said.

Eric inserted the cassette into the VCR in the corner. In a somewhat blurred video, Abdul Abu Ali Hasan was seen urging worshippers to give money to the Slaves of Allah and to murder all infidels, whom he described as the "sons of monkeys and pigs."

"Listen to that," I said. Then, remembering that Eric did not speak Arabic, I explained. "In response to a question from the audience on why the receipts for donations to the Slaves of Allah are from some organization with a different name, Hasan boasted that they are fooling the American infidels by putting the money into a front organization, which will then transfer the money to the Slaves of Allah."

"I know," said Eric. "A translation appears farther on in the report."

Indictments had been filed in March 2003 against a group of people for allegedly supporting the Slaves of Allah operations in the United States. Hasan and others had been charged with racketeering and conspiracy to murder and maim people in the U.S., as well as laundering money and contributing funds to a designated terrorist organization. The imam hadn't been charged with terrorism. The 149-page indictment named him as 'Un-indicted Co-conspirator #1,' and charged him with both planning fund-raising for the Slaves of Allah, and of a fraudulent money-laundering scheme, and with conspiracy to launder money. The report indicated that the wiretaps had been approved by the secret Foreign Intelligence Surveillance Court established under the Foreign Intelligence Surveillance Act of 1978 with legal authority intended for counterintelligence cases. "It looks to me that Hassan's connection to the Slaves of Allah attracted government investigators' attention only after the 9/11 attacks and the passing of the Patriot Act," I said.

"Agencies couldn't share information from different cases before the Patriot Act," Eric said defensively. "I don't think the Patriot Act is perfect, but it's what Congress passed and the president signed, so that's what we use for now, and at least we finally have some tools."

"But the act is written quite cunningly to impede any constitutional

challenge," I countered, playing devil's advocate. "People, supposedly terrorists, are 'disappeared' and held secretly, without being charged with any
crime; they can't reach either the press or, even more importantly, the
courts. The right of habeas corpus is worth zip. We have no idea, none,
how many people have disappeared, and no way of even getting a handle
on the numbers. Furthermore, there's no criterion for who can be labeled
a terrorist and disappeared pursuant to this act. Anyone's fair game."

He wasn't impressed. "European democracies have been employing —
for years now, I might add — the same methods the Patriot Act allows
us now, and nobody calls them undemocratic. To me, it's how you actually apply the law and what the checks and balances are. As long as we
have a free press and an open society, I think American democracy can
survive these restrictions, as long as they are not abused.

"Look at Abu Ali's case," he continued. "If we could've shared the relevant information we already had with the INS, they could have ousted
him ten years ago."

"Monday-morning quarterbacking," I dismissed. "Who knew about
this guy? Should we go into every place of worship and videotape every
sermon of every cleric around the country? It's insane; it can't and
shouldn't be done."

"Listen to me," said Eric. "Abdul Abu Ali Hasan was considered a
moderate. We thought so. But his own flock quietly rebelled against him
because he was too fiery, and wanted him ousted from the mosque."

"So they're the ones who gave you the videotape?" I guessed.

Eric didn't blink. "But there were others who supported him, and he
stayed. This should give you another example of how deeply rooted the
Slaves of Allah are in our country."

He handed me another printed report, a psychological analysis of
Zhukov, which I would read and then destroy after our meeting. We continued going over the various contingencies that could arise during my
meeting with Zhukov. Two hours later we were done. Eric left first. "You
can stay here as long as you wish, but when you're done, burn the report
here." He pointed at the fireplace in the corner.

Since any personal plans for Laura had been scuttled — for now — I opted for the second best option, work. I went through the report Eric gave me. The report's title was "Personality Analysis — Myers-Briggs Types."

The subject's type is: ISTJ; the strength of the qualities are: Introverted: 22%; Sensing 11%; Thinking 67%; Judging 44%.

The subject belongs to a small group of people which logically observes people they meet. People of this type are decisive in the manner in which they conduct themselves. Once they assume responsibility and agree to perform a task, they can be relied upon to complete it. They are very demanding of their subordinates and set high standards for achievement. Their words tend to be simple and down-to-earth, not showy or high-flown. Their home and work are usually clean and neat. Members of this group are thorough and calculated. Usually they honor their word, unless changing circumstances cause them to renege.

I continued reading, but it looked like the psychologist had tried to cover all the bases. There were many *on the one hand*s and *on the other hand*s. Lawyers aren't the only ones who use obscuring double speak.

# XI

Next day the phone rang in the early morning. Half asleep, I picked up the receiver. Why are French telephone receivers so heavy in the morning?

"McMillan?"

There was no mistaking the Russian accent.

"Speaking."

"We are in Marseilles, and received your message about your new hotel."

"Good." I sat up in my bed, trying to focus and collect my thoughts regarding the instructions I'd received from Brian and Eric.

"The boss wants to see you at one o'clock today," the voice said.

Too soon to alert Eric and make the arrangements; I had to stall. "I have another conflicting appointment," I said. "Can we make it later in the afternoon, say four o'clock at my hotel?"

"Wait," he said.

I overhead a muffled conversation. "Okay," came the answer. He hung up.

The man had said *we*, meaning more than one person would be attending. I was surprised that Eric hadn't called me ahead of time, if he indeed had known about the forthcoming call as he'd promised he would. I went outside to another public phone. I called Eric at the clinic, but there was no answer, so I left a detailed message. An hour later I received a short SMS message to my cell phone: "Your message received. We'll be there on time." I heard activity in the adjacent rooms on both sides and presumed Eric's men were making preparations. I didn't attempt to make contact, in case Zhukov's men had put an early watch on my room.

I waited in my room. I thought about Laura. I needed to phone her and make up some excuse why I couldn't see her. I called from my lobby but there was no answer from her room. I left a short message that I'd call later.

At 4:05 P.M. the hotel concierge rang the room: "Monsieur McMillan, there are people here who came to meet you."

"Thanks, I've been expecting them. How many are there?"

"Three."

"Okay, please send them up."

I felt a bit tense. The two minutes were long until I heard a knock, more like a bang, on the door. I opened the door, and three men walked in. I immediately recognized Zhukov from his photos, although he'd gained weight since they'd been taken. But there was no mistaking the man: medium height, almost obese, light receding hair, and clever blue eyes. He was dressed in a gray Hugo Boss suit with a yellow tie, a diamond ring on his pinkie. He didn't carry a briefcase; I found it interesting that he didn't feel the need to carry business accessories. Zhukov nodded, never offered me his hand, entered my room, and sat down on the sofa. He looked around the room, then at me. His thugs checked the doors leading to the other suites where the agents were hiding. I felt my heart race. If they opened either door, the game would be over, and a gunfight could erupt. I looked for the best place to hide if that happened. I had no gun. For Zhukov, I was just an office mouse, a paper pusher holding a pen, not a weapon.

"Who is in the other rooms?" they asked.

"How would I know? I guess other hotel guests."

"Is this room bugged?" asked the other thug.

"Of course not," I said. "Why would I bug you? I'm here to do business, not spy on you."

I glanced at Zhukov. Given the power and money at his disposal, he was in a position to freeze me with his look. But he didn't; instead, he seemed bothered. I could see that his two hulking bodyguards were in awe of him. One gorilla stood next to him while the other guarded the outside door. Even though my room was being heavily monitored, I felt intimidated, which was as they intended. Still, I knew better than to betray any sign of weakness. In a show of self-confidence, I turned my back to them and opened the mini bar. "Would you like a drink?"

"No," he roared. "Cut the bullshit." His accent was an odd mixture of

Russian and Brooklyn. "Tell me how you got the information, or . . ." He nodded in the direction of his two gorilla escorts. So much for the manners typical of top mafia figures — right up to the moment they slit your throat.

I looked him in the eye. "People talk." I repeated my earlier response.

"Who?" he repeated in an ominous tone.

"Who doesn't matter. What you really need to know is how to make sure it doesn't happen again, and I can help you do just that."

"What, whack the guy who spilled?" he said, narrowing his eyes. I was sure he was serious.

"No. I'd make sure none of your foreign business transactions were ever exposed again, whether to complete strangers like me, to the government, or to your competition."

"Start talking, Campbell," Zhukov barked.

"My name is McMillan," I said, keeping my composure.

I remembered a conversation I'd once had with a street vendor of African jewelry in the market of Abidjan, Ivory Coast. I'd wanted to buy a girlfriend an authentic tribal necklace but the price looked excessive. I'd offered him a third of what he had asked. He kept reducing his own offer, but I remained steadfast. He was offended. "Monsieur," he said, "this is an African market, you must negotiate. At the end I'll sell you for a low price but you must negotiate first."

I didn't think Zhukov was in the mood for my stories, so I kept my mouth shut, but I wished he had been. His belligerence was a problem. I knew that I *was* going to relent and show him my cards anyway, but if it came about because of threats, rather than through business negotiation, our relationship would end as soon as he walked out the door. I needed to guarantee a continuation.

"Mr. Zhukov," I said, "I'm a businessman, and I came here to do business. Yelling at me will get you nowhere." I didn't know how many people had ever dared to talk to Zhukov like that and lived to tell. On the other hand, none of them had the advantage of a bugged location or the security of CIA special task agents waiting in adjoining rooms to burst in if things grew hazardous.

My calm demeanor and businesslike attitude must have surprised him. "Show me what you have," he said finally, this time in a slightly less aggressive tone.

*We're getting there*, I thought. But then Zhukov's man, who'd been standing next to him, approached me and lifted me from my chair by holding my shirt collar and neck in a forceful grip. From the corner of my eye I saw the other gorilla just stand there.

"Mr. Zhukov asked you a question, I didn't hear an answer!" he said with a strong Russian accent.

There was no point in resisting. He was about my height and weight, but all muscle, leaving no extra room for brain. "Put me down," I said as calmly as possible under the circumstances; "put me down."

He looked at Zhukov, who nodded. He dropped me back on my chair. "Mr. Zhukov," I said, trying to catch my breath, "I called you hoping to do business. I have something you need, and treating me like that is not helpful."

"I still want to know how you got the information about the Seychelles activity, and how you linked it to me." I'd expected Zhukov to be the kind of man who would litter his speech with obscenities, but he used the manner of a businessman to conceal his thuggery. I knew that his power come from his physical presence, from not saying too much, and from his reputation for ruthlessness. He was on the same level as the other notorious heads of criminal organizations in New York.

I told him about my work in the Seychelles, how I had contacts in the banking industry who showed me the endorsed checks, and how I'd managed through a simple Google search to connect him to the address on the checks. "If I did that, so could anyone else," I said.

"What can you do for me?" he asked. The businessman in him had taken over the hoodlum.

"I want to be your consultant for asset protection; that's what I do for a living. I can bury your money so deep that no one will ever find it; there'll be no paper trail, I can assure you. After many years in the industry, I know all the tricks and the pitfalls."

"How much do you want?"

"One hundred thousand dollars. It's pretty cheap given the millions that can be protected. The hundred thousand will also buy you a few months of continuing assistance from me. If you like my work, then we can discuss a long-term relationship with appropriate compensation."

"And if I don't?"

"Then the information I'm giving you now about my finding, and my added service in the near future, costs you one hundred thousand dollars and we part our ways."

"You've given me nothing, Campbell," said Zhukov.

"McMillan," I corrected calmly, "my name is McMillan. Mr. Zhukov, I've just given you valuable information: Your transactions through the Seychelles are transparent. If you have nothing to hide, then you're right, the information I just gave you is worthless. But if you don't want your business affairs to be so transparent, then you should listen to me."

"Show me documents," he said regaining his aggressive, more thuggish attitude; "what you're telling me could be a fourth-hand recycled rumor, and for that you expect me to pay you a hundred grand? Fucking unbelievable." His face became red. The gorillas moved forward toward me. I kept my composure, but my hands clenched the armrests of my chair.

With an annoyed expression of *Okay, if you must*, I went to the desk drawer and pulled out the check photocopies.

"These are the front and back copies of the deposits Ivan Dimitrov made. The fact that he wrote your address on the back of the checks ties you not only to the deposits, but also to the corporation that wrote this check in the Seychelles, because the address is that of a single-family home, yours."

I looked at his face. Zhukov clearly didn't like what he was seeing. His face was still red. I continued: "If this company is involved in any other illegal activity anywhere on the globe, it will lead to you."

"This is nothing. Bullshit," he groaned, waving the hand holding the photocopies. "Nothing!"

I tried a conciliatory tone. "It might not be enough to indict or convict you, sure, but this is certainly something investigators can start with. If you're comfortable with that, then fine. But if you agree that this information could connect you to anything you don't want to be connected to, then I may be your only way to stem the flood."

Zhukov weighed the information. "And you discovered all that by talking to some bank employees in the Seychelles?" he said in incredulity.

"Sure, it's all there. The deposits lead directly to you. Now, if anyone wants to ask you questions, I think you'd better prepare answers." I went on the offensive.

"What do you mean?" His face was menacing. The gorilla next to him took one step toward me.

"I mean that one day someone from the U.S. government, say the IRS, will knock on your door asking you questions about these transactions; I think you'd better be ready to give them convincing answers. You and I know that the government would love to lock you away and throw the key in the ocean."

The goon standing next to Zhukov moved again in my direction. Zhukov held up his hand.

"Answers?" he asked, focusing on my face. I felt threatened, and I didn't even make an effort to hide it. On the contrary, I even played it up a bit. *I shouldn't be Dan Gordon here. I'm Neil McMillan, a big crook, but with a faint heart.*

"If they link the money to you, then every money-laundering expert in the U.S. government will be all over you. And you know it. I'm sure you know that Al Capone died in prison after being convicted on income tax evasion, not for murder or extortion." I caught a glimmer of satisfaction on Zhukov's face hearing the comparison, quickly replaced by his menacing attitude.

"I think you're a fed," Zhukov shot back. "Only U.S. government agents could have access to Eagle Bank and get copies of the checks."

I let out a nervous laugh. "I don't have anything to do with the U.S. government. It's the other way around. I'm *wanted* by the government, I don't work for them. The checks weren't kept by Eagle Bank; they were sent to the Seychelles for collection. Only the issuing bank receives the checks and returns them to the account owner."

"How do you know that?" he roared.

"Look at the checks. They carry a stamp saying they were sent for collection back to the issuing bank in the Seychelles."

"Maybe you made a deal with the government to bring my head on a platter in return for yours?"

"Look, my record is consistent: I've always helped my clients outsmart the U.S. government; so why would I become a turncoat now? Mr. Zhukov, you read too many detective stories."

The thug next to Zhukov grew restless, but Zhukov halted him.

"And if I catch you being a government agent? Then what?" he said in the amused tone of a card player with a good hand and a big mouth. He was toying with me.

"If I was trying to entrap you," I pointed out, "I didn't have to bring you all the way to France, outside U.S. jurisdiction. I'd keep you in Brooklyn where the FBI could walk in any minute and get you."

I thought I saw some hesitation on his face, and he exchanged looks with his men. That gave me the impression Zhukov was holding something back. But he moved on.

"Okay, let's say I hire you. What do you do next?"

"Well, Mr. Zhukov, I'm embarrassed to say this, but people in my position and prostitutes have something in common: We get paid in advance."

"You'll have your money in a few days; my man will bring it over to your hotel. Now give me these papers." He couldn't have been more aggressive if he had a gun pointed at me.

"I respect your word," I said. I was counting on the agents in the other rooms being ready to burst in with their guns if things got ugly. So I allowed myself a little more chutzpah. "But I'm a businessman, and I cannot give you the documents without the money."

Zhukov's thug came closer to my face, so close I could tell he hadn't brushed his teeth recently. He stepped on my toes and pushed my head with his giant mountain gorilla head, but without the gorilla's grace.

"Give me the documents or I'll tear you to pieces."

"Okay," I mumbled, "get off my feet; I'll give them to you." I handed Zhukov the photocopies. He folded them and put them in his jacket pocket. Since neither Zhukov nor his thugs were carrying briefcases, where else could he put them? It seemed to say something about his character — I wasn't sure what — that he'd treat such valuable evidence that way.

"You'll hear from me soon concerning other business." He left, escorted by his men.

I watched through my fifth-floor window as they entered a limousine and drove away. I stayed in my room in case they'd left behind a scout to spy on me. Ten minutes later the doors of the adjoining suites opened, and Brian and Eric walked in.

"Good," said Eric. "I think he bit."

"Do you think he'll return with the money?" I asked. It felt too simple to me. "Zhukov is a conniving SOB; I find it hard to believe he was maneuvered so cleanly."

"Meaning?" asked Brian. "Sounded to us like you really had to work him, and let him rough you up a bit."

"Brian. These people kill if you cross them. I flashed some attitude knowing I was protected, and even then it was too easy. Zhukov may have something up his sleeve," I said. "There was something in his demeanor that broadcast too much self-assurance for a person who has just been confronted with incriminating evidence."

"Did you read the psychological analysis?" asked Eric. "That's the way Zhukov is."

"I read it. I still hope we're not getting a surprise from his end. I just got a feeling that he was ahead of me."

"You read too many detective stories," said Eric blandly. He'd been paying attention. "Let's wait until tomorrow. We'll see if he comes up with the money and hires you. I need to go out of town with Brian for a few days; you can't call us. But I'll be in touch." I was curious where they were going, and whether it concerned my case. But I didn't ask, knowing I'd get no answer.

"Do you know where he's staying in Marseilles?" I asked.

"Yes, Hotel Du Parc. Why?" Brian asked.

I ducked the question. "Is anyone watching him there?"

"Of course."

"Anything interesting in his room?" I asked with a straight face.

"No. The risk isn't worth the reward, even in a best-case scenario."

"Oh, why is that?"

"Because he came for a few days to hear you out. We don't think he'd be storing anything of interest to us here."

"Okay," I said nonchalantly, but I was already thinking how not to get caught. The stunt I was about to attempt was already a fait accompli in my mind.

After Brian and Eric left, I went to the hotel basement and looked for the laundry room. Amid the steam and the noise of the industrial-sized washers and dryers, I found what I'd been looking for: dry-cleaned doormen's suits with shiny buttons. I picked out a suit approximately my size, and a cap, and wrapped them up with a big bathroom towel to sneak them back to my room. I hid my loot in my closet, put a DO NOT DISTURB sign on my door, went outside to the street, and took a cab to Hotel Du Parc, some seven blocks away. I surveyed the area, the various entrances to the hotel and the best escape route, if needed, then returned to the Excelsior. I carefully removed the hotel's one-letter logo embroidered on the front of the doorman's suit I had borrowed. Donning the suit and the cap, I left the hotel through the service elevator. A cab let me off one block before Hotel du Parc.

I proceeded as if I had a coherent plan. But in fact, I didn't. I felt like a battery-operated toy soldier; neither I nor the soldier had any control over what was going to happen next, but we kept moving anyway. The one thing I did know was that I had to enter Zhukov's room, preferably when it was empty. I had no particular urge to meet his iron-fisted thugs again. But first, I had to know which room he occupied.

I went to the basement to the maintenance manager's office. "Hi, I'm Ivan Krugg. I work for Mr. Zhukov, your hotel guest."

He gave me a bored look. "And?" He cranked his hand in a circle as if trying to make me speak faster. But I intentionally spoke slowly; giving the impression of being a fast thinker is counterproductive in such situations. "Mr. Zhukov does not like the television in his room; he says it doesn't broadcast any Russian stations." I spoke French, and thanked in my heart the French girlfriend I'd once had who insisted I speak my high school French with her. It was rusty by now, but understandable.

He gave me an odd look, as if he couldn't believe I could be so dumb. "Turn the knob on the set. There must be at least two stations in Russian."

"We tried that, but it doesn't work. Mr. Zhukov is very upset," I said, hoping he'd understand my not-so-subtle message: *When Zhukov gets upset, bad things happen.*

"So what do you expect me to do?" He seemed impatient and annoyed.

"Come up to the room and show me what to do. I'm afraid that if Mr. Zhukov returns and doesn't find his favorite Russian station, he will be angry at me." I made a sawing motion across my throat.

"And who are you?" he asked.

"His chauffer," I said.

"*D'accord,*" he relented. "Let's go." He stood and took a toolbox. "What's his room number?"

"Sorry, I don't know. I live in a different hotel. Mr. Zhukov does not believe he should stay at the same hotel as his staff."

"Oh, he's one of those . . ." He gave me the look reserved for a showing of solidarity among members of the working class.

I nodded. "Yes, since he escaped from Russia he hates anything that reminds him of socialism or communism. He believes in separating social classes." I rolled my eyes to show my disdain.

The maintenance manager must have heard enough to sympathize with me, because he muttered something I didn't fully understand, other than the word *merde* repeated three times. He called reception and got Zhukov's room number. I followed him to the service elevator and then to the fourth floor. He knocked on door 411 and, when no response came, opened the door with a master key. The room was in fact a three-room suite with adjoining doors to rooms 412 and 413. There were a few open suitcases, a few packs of American cigarettes, and two half-empty bottles of Stolichnaya vodka. The manager went directly to the television in 413, which was being used as a master bedroom, most likely Zhukov's — I saw his flashy tie on the night table. While he was working I quietly went to the other rooms, calculating how I might return without a personal escort. A minute or two later I returned to the manager's side. "Look," he said, gesturing to the TV. A Russian-language program was on.

"Thanks," I said, "I really appreciate it. Could you tune the other two televisions in the other rooms?"

He didn't answer, but took his toolbox and moved to the next room while I pretended to fine-tune the knobs on the TV in the bedroom. As soon as he entered room 412, I opened two magazines on a coffee table and tore out two subscription postcards. Going to the door, I opened it quietly and inserted a postcard near the latch. I then carefully closed the door and joined the manager in room 412. When he was done there, he moved to room 411 while I returned to the middle room and repeated the process, in case the trick I'd pulled on the bedroom door failed. When I heard the manager close his toolbox, I quickly moved to the window and pretended to look outside. In less than ten minutes we were out of the rooms.

"Thank you so much," I said, slipping him a fifty-euro bill.

He put it in his pocket and said, "Your boss may know how to make money, but he can't turn a TV set knob?"

I smiled. As soon as he'd left me to return to his basement office I headed back to room 413, Zhukov's bedroom. I pushed the door slightly, and it opened. I removed the postcards I'd left in both door latches, then rifled quickly through the four suitcases in the suite. They had a strong odor of expensive cologne. Nothing but clothing. I searched the three rooms, but could find nothing incriminating. Had Zhukov cleaned up his room because he was suspicious? I was disappointed to think that maybe he had nothing to hide. I checked the wastebasket: nothing meaningful there. Then the night table. There was a small writing pad with the hotel's logo on the top. What looked like a telephone number had been scribbled next to some writing in Cyrillic. I tore off the sheet just underneath the written note. I looked at it more closely:. The number and the handwriting were clearly embossed there. It'd do. I carefully put it in my pocket, made sure again that I'd removed the postcards from the latches, and left.

Back on the street, I entered a nearby store and bought a T-shirt and jeans then returned to the dressing room, donned my new clothes, put the uniform in the shopping bag, and dumped the bag in the nearest street Dumpster. I returned to my hotel room and used a pencil to bring out the writing on the note I'd removed. The number was 06 1227 1190, but I couldn't decipher the Cyrillic script next to it. I went out to the street and called Eric. His voice mail came on. "I found something interesting belonging to the fat thug, please follow up on that," I said. "I don't know what your plans are but to minimize contact I'm putting a piece of paper in an envelope, and leaving it at the reception of my hotel, addressed to Dr. Jean Pierre Arnaud."

The following morning I was regretting having asked Laura to join me in France. Her presence was a psychological burden. I called her room again; no response. But then while I was having a late breakfast, she suddenly walked into my hotel's dining room, looking radiant and energetic.

I got up to greet her. "Good morning, Laura, sleep well?"

"Great," she said, "I just feel great." I wondered, *We haven't seen each other for an entire day, and that makes her happy?* I'd been expecting her to be angry at me for not being with her. As I sat down it suddenly hit me: How did she know where I was staying? The day before, when I'd checked out of the Promenade, I hadn't told her that I was moving to the Excelsior.

Laura must have noticed my gloomy expression. "What happened, Dan?"

"Nothing happened," I said, "I'm just so glad to see you." I tried to reflect the appropriate facial expression.

We had a light breakfast, and I quickly read through the *International Herald Tribune*. "It's too cold to go swimming," I said. "The sun is shining, but it says here the water's only sixty-five degrees."

"I know," she said.

"So, what's on your mind?" I asked. I looked at her, but she avoided my eyes. There was something off about her mood, but I couldn't pin it down.

"Nothing, absolutely nothing. Maybe we could rent a car and drive through Provence for a day trip. It's supposed to be pretty country . . . maybe tour a winery."

"Good idea," I said. When we finished our meal, we went to an Avis office and rented a small Peugeot 305. We drove north. The narrow roads were rather empty. Soon the scenery changed from coastal plains to hilly terrain and a winding road.

"Do you have a specific place you want to go?" I asked.

"No, let's go as far north as we can by midday then turn around. I'd like to be back at the hotel tonight."

"Okay. I'll see if we can get as far north as Sisteron."

"Why Sisteron?"

"When I was eighteen, I hitchhiked through Europe with my buddy David. When we couldn't get a ride, we traveled by train. One day we got off the train for the night in Sisteron. In the center of town we found a building with a sign, HOTEL DE VILLE. We went up the stairs, but the place looked more like an office than a hotel. A cleaning lady was sweeping the floor. In a combination of sign language and our limited French, we understood that nobody was there and that we should return in the morning. We found another place, and didn't realize until later what a couple of dumb schmucks we'd been. *Hotel de Ville* of course means 'town hall,' not 'city hotel.' I've never been back and would kind of like to see it again."

Laura just smiled and we drove on in silence. As I drove the narrow road I was thinking how odd the situation was. Here we were alone together for the day. Obviously the emotional connection between us was good. I knew what my motive was. But what was hers?

We did make it to Sisteron, ate lunch, then turned around and cruised back. It was already dark when we returned to Marseilles. Laura asked that I take her straight to her hotel. She didn't even suggest I go up with her, and for that I was thankful. I was thinking of excuses I could make if she had asked me up. My unease with her had only grown during our mostly silent car ride, and if she were to seduce me at this point her motives would be suspect to me at best. I went to do some gift shopping for my children, and then drove to the Excelsior.

When I entered my room, I sensed something was different. The room was made up and clean, but still I had that strange feeling that something was amiss. I opened the wardrobe — my suit was hanging there in peace.

I checked the drawers — my underwear and polo shirts had been slightly disturbed. Hotel chambermaids never open guests' drawers, but this one had been opened. There was nothing to incriminate me, nothing to connect me to the U.S. government or to my assignment. Or was there? The report Eric gave me! I panicked for a moment until I remembered that that I'd burned it in the safe apartment. My passport and my airline tickets were deposited in the hotel's central safe, and besides, there was nothing incriminating there, either. All my documents read *Neil McMillan*.

Was my paranoia getting the better of me? Was the fact that my underwear had been moved an inch sufficient grounds for general alarm? I went to the reception desk.

"I lost my room card key," I said. "Would you please issue me a new one?"

The receptionist quickly prepared another key and handed it to me. "Should I make another key for Mrs. McMillan?"

I was stunned, but only for a second. "Mrs. McMillan?"

She nodded.

"Did my wife have a key as well?" I asked.

The receptionist looked at her computer monitor. "Yes, sir, you called last night to let us know that she was joining you and that we should give her a key. So when she arrived we gave her a key."

"Of course, of course, I forgot all about that. So her key is still good?"

"Yes, the electronic combination hasn't changed."

I walked away and sat on a lobby chair. I had dropped Laura off at the Promenade at 6:30 P.M. She'd gone up to her room, but I didn't get back to the Excelsior until about 9:00 P.M. after my shopping excursion. Had she gone to my hotel and obtained a key to my room? There was no way she could have known I was out on the town unless someone was watching me for her. We'd just spent the whole day together in the car, so unless she had entered my room while I was out shopping . . . She'd also never given me a hint this morning how she knew where I was staying, let alone suggesting she knew I was using a cover name and what it was.

On the other hand — as lawyers like to say — I'd never asked her these questions. The unavoidable conclusion was that, if Laura was connected to the entry to my room, then she might have given the key she obtained to someone else, who'd entered my room while I was traveling with her. That would explain the aimless day trip: to keep me away, and to keep her away from suspicion because she was with me. The receptionist had said *you called*, meaning a man had called the hotel pretending to be me. I felt betrayed and lost. If Laura was indeed the mysterious "Mrs. McMillan," obviously she had an agenda, and most likely an accomplice. But why was she doing this? And for whom?

The thought of double-layer security crossed my mind. Was she a part of a backup team, protecting me and at the same time making sure that I didn't go astray? I remembered Eric's cautioning me not to be independent. I weighed the possibility. It would explain how she'd known where I was staying, and under what name. But I was the one who'd asked Laura to come over to Marseilles. If she were part of a backup team, she'd be here under some pretext.

I composed myself, took a deep breath, and analyzed the sequence of events. It was clear that Laura was up to something. It was conceivable, albeit highly unlikely, that her behavior was personal, motivated by her feelings for me and our relationship. Far more likely, her interests were professional. But was she a friend or foe? There were too many questions.

I thought about the Moscow Rules I had learned about during my Mossad service. During the Cold War, the Soviet Union, and Moscow in particular, was the most dangerous place for a Western spy. Being caught meant, with few exceptions, torture and death. CIA agents going into the Soviet Union were given an informal guide on the "Rules of Engagement," popularly known as the Moscow Rules. There were more than forty but I could remember only a few, all of which I should have followed: *Assume nothing; Never go against your gut; Don't look back; Take it for granted that you are never alone; If it feels wrong, it is wrong, abort any action; Make the opposition think they have the upper hand, but don't harass them; The first time is an accident, the second time is coincidence, but the third time is a hostile action.*

Laura's conduct raised too many red flags to ignore. Even back in the United States, she had tried to dissuade me from continuing working on breaking the code, then told me she was going outside to smoke a cigarette. All I saw was her talking on a cell phone; when she returned she didn't smell of smoke. A quick search I'd made in her purse had shown no sign of cigarettes, matches, or a lighter.

I needed more information before I could confront her. Still, the direction in which this was going seemed ominous. I decided to play her game to see what, if anything, I could get out of her.

I called Eric — aka Dr. Jean Pierre Arnaud — and left a message that I'd had visitors. I went to the hotel's central safe and retrieved the goody box Martin had given me. Back in my room, I took from the box a micro video camera, with the diameter of a dime and the thickness of a silver dollar. I climbed the stylish desk at the far end of the room hoping it wouldn't collapse under me and attached the camera to the smoke detector on the ceiling with the included adhesive tape. It matched perfectly. I hooked a mini signal recorder to the back of the TV. The video camera had motion, sound, and heat detectors: Any change in the room temperature in one spot, any noise, or any movement would start the camera. It also had ultraviolet capacity, enabling it to record in near-complete darkness. The video output would be transmitted to the recorder, which could operate nonstop for thirty-six hours. I went outside to the corridor. When I was sure it was empty, I mounted another micro video camera on the wall-mounted light fixture opposite my door. I then looked around the room to make sure I hadn't left anything behind. I went to the reception desk and rented the room opposite mine.

I left the hotel through the back door, making sure I hadn't gained a tail. After several maneuvers, I was confident I wasn't being followed. I went behind a nearby office building, where I found trash cans full of office debris. I collected a used brown file folder and approximately 150 pages of printed material in French that looked like financial reports and general correspondence, and stuffed them into the folder. I also picked up an empty, used FedEx large envelope that still carried the airbill addressed to

Hector, Nicolas & Freber, Business Consultants, 24B Ave du Prado, 13006 Marseilles, France. I went back to my original hotel room through the main entrance, holding the FedEx envelope in one hand and the file folder in the other. I made a minimal effort to hide the file folder near my bed, but left the FedEx envelope in plain view on the coffee table. But unlike a hunter who stands watch after setting a trap, I promptly went to sleep. The following morning, I went downstairs to a hotel pay phone and called Laura at the Promenade. She answered right away.

"Something's come up," I said apologetically. "I've just received loads of documents concerning my meeting with the bad guys, but in looking through them, I realized that a crucial portion of the file isn't there. So I need to drive to an office in Nice to get the missing documents. I'm afraid our lunch plans will have to be put off. I'm really sorry."

"How could that have happened?" Her tone of voice was a mixture of interest and concern.

"I don't know. Some moron sent one part of the files to an agreed-upon address here in Marseilles as a dead drop, but the rest was sent to Nice. It's a two-hundred-mile drive on narrow roads, but I have to have them."

"Can't someone send it over again?"

"No, it's also a dead drop, I must do it myself. Idiots," I said in contempt.

"Well, shit happens," she said. "I'm disappointed, but I understand. Can I come with you?"

"Sorry, no."

"Then I'll do some sightseeing and wait for you. When are you leaving?"

"Right now, but I'll be back in the evening, and I'll call you. Maybe we could go out to dinner if it's not too late."

"It'd be great if you can make it for dinner," she said.

I noted that although Laura suggested joining me on the day trip, she didn't insist and was complacent upon hearing my refusal. Besides, if she had an accomplice and a key, it didn't matter one way or the other.

I went through the hotel's main entrance to the nearby parking lot and drove the rented car in the direction of the main artery connecting Marseilles and Nice. I made a few sudden turns, including two U-turns, demonstrating the typical behavior of a driver uncertain of the direction he is going, stopping several times to ask for directions — all the while surreptitiously glancing into the rearview mirror to make sure I wasn't being followed. I parked near an office building in the outskirts of Marseilles. I went inside, left through another entrance, and took a taxi back to my hotel, entering through the back. I went to the basement and took the elevator to my floor. I made sure the corridor was empty as I entered my original room. I quickly replayed the video feed, but saw no suspicious activity. I hooked another transmitter to the video reception unit, crossed the hall, and entered my newly rented room. I sat on the couch and turned on my handheld mini video receiver with a color five-by-three-inch monitor. In a moment the monitor's split screen showed me both the hallway leading to my room and the room's interior. I sat patiently. But I wasn't calm. Every now and then my monitor showed people walking through the hallway, all of them either hotel guests entering or exiting their rooms, chambermaids, or maintenance people. No one stopped near my room.

After two hours I was getting bored. Maybe I was overly paranoid. I was also becoming hungry, but I couldn't leave the room or even order room service. So I just sat there. I tried to read a magazine but pushed it aside. I turned on the TV, but after flipping through the channels for five minutes I turned it off. I had to concede that I was nervous. Then I saw her coming. There was no mistake; it was Laura. She walked gingerly down the hallway, looking for a room number. She stopped next to my room and inserted an electronic card key into the slot. The door opened and she entered, looking around to see if anyone was watching her. No one was, of course — except me.

I hoped the way she conducted her search of my room would reveal what kind of animal she was — a pro, or someone who didn't really know what to look for. She looked in drawers and closets. I didn't see her searching for surveillance equipment. After a while she stopped rifling through my clothing and glanced around. She discovered the FedEx envelope near the bed. After examining it, she copied the address on the label. Then she saw the file folder next to it. She picked it up, opened it, and flipped through the papers. After about five or six minutes, she pulled out a few pages, wrote something on a piece of paper, and returned the pages to the folder. She then went through my personal things, making sure she returned everything to its original place, and left. Watching on the monitor, I saw her walk to the elevator.

A minute later I went to the room's window and saw her cross the street and hail a cab. I waited ten more minutes, then took the elevator to the basement and left through the back door. Going in and out of the basement wasn't easy: I had to hide behind ceiling supports three times because security men were patrolling the floor. Out on the street at last, I walked for a few minutes, and after making sure I was alone I took a cab to the spot I'd left the rental car earlier. I called Eric, but there was no answer. So I called Bob Hodson in New York.

"Hi, Dan, what's new?"

"I'm at a pay phone in France, it's not a secure line. But I need to ask you a question that can't wait."

"Go ahead."

"Do you know where Laura Higgins is?"

"Can't stop mixing business and pleasure, Dan?"

"Seriously, Bob. Do you know where she is?"

"She asked for an emergency family leave for a few days. How the heck would I know where she went?"

"So she's not on assignment for you?"

"As I said, she's on a personal leave, but you can also ask Eric; he should be near you."

I returned to my hotel room. I read the newspaper, watched television, and took an hour nap. At 7:00 P.M. I called Laura.

"Hi, I'm back. Are we still on for dinner?"

"Of course. When do you want me ready?"

"I'll pick you up in forty-five minutes." Her voice certainly gave nothing away.

I changed clothes and took a cab to the Promenade. Laura was waiting in the lobby. I looked around to see if she was being monitored from a distance but could see no warning signs.

At the recommendation of the concierge we walked to a nearby French bistro. The food was bland at best, but I wasn't there for the food. I needed to find out what game Laura was playing and why.

"How was your trip?" she asked while leaning back on her chair, and I couldn't help but note her stunning figure in white jeans and a tee. Were her outfit and body language deliberately chosen to distract me? The evening — more accurately, the night — could have played out so nicely if I didn't suspect her. For a moment I even entertained the thought. Why not? Was there a rule against sleeping with a potential subject of an inquiry? Could I label it an *invasive interrogation* and get away with it? But reason mixed with responsibility and — as much as I hated to admit it — work ethics tied my hands. I just couldn't do it.

Apparently Laura had different ideas. Whether conniving or genuine, however, I couldn't say.

"No trip," I answered, "just a long drive behind polluting trucks in heavy traffic. I could never understand why the time of day with the slowest traffic is called rush hour. I found the missing file and drove back. That's all."

"What files are these?"

"Background stuff supporting the material I already have for my meeting."

"About the bad guys you mentioned earlier?"

I nodded.

"What have they done?"

"Laura!"

She smiled, exposing her perfect teeth. "I'm just asking. But seriously, Dan, I'm really frustrated that we can work together, break codes, look for terrorists, and then all of a sudden I'm compartmentalized and shielded from information. It just doesn't make sense. Why can't we pick up from where we left off?"

Did she mean breaking the code or the brief sexual encounter we'd begun before I had to leave?

"I feel the same way, but I can't bend that rule. You saw how Hodson treated me when I dared to remove a coded message from the office. Can you imagine what he'd do if he found out that I'd broken another rule? With you?

"Besides," I went on, "it's quite possible that you or any other member of the task force could get the same assignment I have right now, or something very similar, without knowing about my work."

"Why?" She put her hand on mine.

"To assure independent findings." I pulled my hand to drink the wine. "When we all work on the same team and share information, there's a high likelihood that if the investigation hits a dead end, *everyone* gets stuck. In a team like ours, there are in fact only one or two leaders; the rest just follow and don't engage in independent thinking. That can be bad, particularly bad in a case this serious. I'm sure that upon your return they'll assign you to a task and tell you not to share your methods or tactics with anyone — just report directly to HQ."

Laura nodded lightly. I couldn't tell if she bought my argument. "How long have you been doing this?" She sounded really friendly.

"What?"

"This line of work."

"More years than I care to count. Why do you ask?"

"Because what you say sounds like a conclusion learned from experience, not from the kind of desk training I've been through."

Was she kissing up or leading me on? I couldn't tell. So I decided to change tacks and be the aggressor. "Laura, can I be frank?"

"I wish you would."

"You know I'm attracted to you. I'm going to be very busy tomorrow, so the only time left for us here in France will be tonight and the day after tomorrow, but depending on how tomorrow plays out that may not be an option, either. Let's be together tonight."

"Tonight?" As soon as I'd called her bluff, her tone of voice changed.

"Yes, tonight. Is there a problem?"

She was at loss. I could almost see her thinking. Clearly there was something she had to do tonight, so I pressed my offensive, leaning in at her and taking her hand.

"Dan," she said finally, "I know this is going to sound dumb to you, but my hair, face, and nails look terrible; I was finally able to find a beautician that could do me over. The only time she has available is later tonight. I wasn't planning to be with you after dinner, because I hoped to surprise you tomorrow with a bright fresh look." She got up.

"Where are you going?"

"My appointment is in thirty minutes."

"Come," I said, taking her hand, "I'll take you."

"No need, I'll just take a cab."

"I insist. I want to spend more time with you."

"No, Dan. I mean it. Sometimes a woman needs to be alone. I'm getting beautiful for you."

Her earlier inviting signals had been to lead me on so she could pump for information. But when I leapt at the bait rather than let her coax me to it, she'd gotten flustered — either that or, more likely, realized if she got in any deeper I'd keep her from a prior commitment. I walked with her to the street corner and helped her into a taxi. Our parting was awkward. No kiss; no *see you later*.

As her cab pulled away I approached a motorcyclist parked nearby, a man in his midtwenties. "Want to make a quick hundred euros?" I said in French.

"Doing what?"

"Just follow that cab and take me along."

"You're kidding," he said.

I shook my head. "No, really."

With a funny look, he handed me a helmet. "You must put this on."

"Right, quick," I said, "I can't lose her."

I mounted the backseat and soon we were behind the taxi. "Not too close," I said. "She shouldn't see me."

He said something but I couldn't understand. The combination of the wind, the noisy street traffic, and our helmets made it impossible to communicate from front to back. The taxi passed by the Promenade Hotel, which had a semicircular driveway allowing cars and taxis to stop and then drive off again. But Laura's taxi didn't stop to let her off. Laura looked back through the cab's rear window once or twice, but with the darkness of the night and the helmet on my head, I was sure that even my own mother wouldn't have recognized me.

Finally the cab pulled over next to a hotel building and Laura, looking around, entered the vestibule of its street-level restaurant. I got off and gave my driver a hundred-euro bill; he buzzed away. I waited in the distance behind a parked truck to see what Laura was up to.

A tall blond man approached her from inside the restaurant, and they kissed. Not a friendly peck on the check, either; this was a long, intimate kiss. Was that a pang I felt? I should have been well beyond that by now. I cursed myself for not carrying a camera or any listening device. They went into the restaurant and sat near the window. From a distance I could see that Laura was sipping a drink. Obviously she wouldn't eat two dinners on the same evening. The blond man listened intently while Laura talked. I saw her take and hold his hand. I had to quickly decide what to do next. I needed to speak to Eric, but I had left my cell phone behind and there was no pay phone in sight. I couldn't leave my observation point and risk being detected — or, even worse, lose sight of them. For one thing, I didn't know whether Laura was also being monitored by others who were unknown to me. They could be allies, but just as likely they could belong to the opposition. On second thought I realized I could be facing two different sets of bad guys: Zhukov's gang and the Slaves of Allah. If either saw me observing her, things could get more complicated.

I decided to take a risk. I went to the hotel's main entrance and entered the restaurant through the door connecting it to the hotel. I waited in a dark corner near the side entrance watching Laura and her beau from a distance. Finally, he asked for the bill. I saw him put his credit card on the small plate that came with the bill. That was my opportunity. I approached the hostess with a proposition she could not refuse: a hundred-euro bill in exchange for the chance to copy the name and number on the credit card. "I don't need the card's expiration date or other codes," I said, assuring her I was not an identity thief. "It's a family thing. We want to know who our sister is dating. We've had some bad experiences lately." I put on a sorrowful expression. Now I could not let two people out of my sight; Laura and the hostess. There was not much time, I had to move quickly, and also make sure the waitress wouldn't report me to security. That, and the money, must have persuaded her. In two minutes

I had the name of Laura's friend — Robert Meadway — and his credit card number. As a bonus she also wrote out the name of the card's issuer: Citibank.

Ten minutes later Laura and the man left the restaurant. They hailed a cab, got in. I quickly went out through the same door and stopped another taxi. The ride took ten minutes, and they didn't seem to notice me because their taxi took no evasive maneuvers. Their taxi stopped next to the Promenade Hotel, where Laura got out. "Keep following that cab," I told my driver.

After a few turns into side streets, the other taxi stopped next to Hotel du Parc and Robert Meadway got out. "Wait," I told my cabbie as I handed him the fare. "Please wait for me here. I'll be just a moment." Meadway paid his driver and went inside; I followed. I saw him passing through reception, with the receptionist nodding toward him, and entering the guest elevator.

Obviously I'd followed him as far as I could, so I called Lan in New York from a pay phone. "I need a background on Robert Meadway, male Caucasian, age approximately forty, about six feet tall, medium build. See what you can find."

I went back to my hotel. An hour later my cell phone rang. It was Lan. "I found six men who match the description, but if your estimate of his age is right, really only two."

"Do you have photos?"

"Yes."

"Look for a blond good-looking guy."

"Usually I like them dark," said Lan jokingly, surprising me with an unexpected glimpse into her personal life. All she'd told before was that she'd fled Vietnam and been widowed in the United States. "Three are in their fifties or sixties. Another one is in his early twenties. The two men around forty are both blond and could be described as good looking."

"Okay. Please run a background check on both. I have his Citibank credit card details, if that helps. I need personal history, criminal record, arrest history, names of family members, friends, associates, business affiliations, residence history, you know the drill. Then run a cross-check for both men with the name Laura Higgins, and see what the database brings up. Please transfer the data with the color photos to my care at the Marseilles consulate."

"Why can't you just download it to your computer, once I tell you it's available?"

"The hotel's Internet connection is on dial-up, not broadband — it'll take forever. So for that and other reasons, I'd rather you send it to the consulate."

"Will do," she said.

I woke up the next morning with a headache. Add to my troubles the fact that it was raining — and that I had no idea anymore who Laura was or what she was up to — and I had one pissed-off attitude. Just then a text message came to my cell phone: There was information waiting for me at the consulate. I looked at my watch. It was 9:15 A.M. Lan had been as efficient as always. I went to the consulate and sat there to read the material. I examined the first batch: no resemblance. I gave a glance to the second photo. Shit. Neither man was the guy I'd seen last night with Laura.

I called Eric on his secure line at the clinic. This time he answered after one ring. I intended to give him a report on the developments, but he stopped me. "Dan, I can't talk right now. Just tell me if the hundred thousand dollars was delivered, or if you've heard anything from them. With respect to the rest, I'll talk to you later."

"No," I said. "No contact and no money." He was about to hang up when I stopped him. "I need to ask you. Is this operation double-tiered?"

"Why?" asked Eric.

"I need to know if anyone is watching me on your behalf."

"Dan, forget the conspiracy theories. In this operation what you see is what you get."

"So there's no one else on this here?"

"No. Why do you ask?"

"I just want to make sure first before I jump to conclusions." I still didn't think I should trash Laura with management until I was convinced that what she was doing went beyond bizarre behavior.

I decided it was time to confront Laura; enough with the games and the uncertainty. I reached her in her hotel room: "I just called to see how you were. Are you already as beautiful as ever?"

"Yes, thanks, and much more relaxed, thank you for understanding. How's your day?"

"All went well, and I'm done. Listen, care to have an early drink? I could use a friendly face after today's meetings. I also want to show you something." I tried to sound promising.

She hesitated. "In fact, there's a seat on the flight out tonight and I think I'll take it, so I need time to pack, but I guess I can squeeze in a drink."

"Meet me in my room," I said. I told her the number, not letting on that I knew she already had it. Twenty minutes later there was a knock on the door. Laura entered, dressed in blue jeans and a black tee.

"Thanks for coming," I said, pecked her on her cheek. She sat on a chair, while I sat across from her on the bed. If she'd spent any time with a beautician, I couldn't see a trace of it.

"Laura, I need to ask you a few questions that have been bothering me."

"And what are they?" She was amused and self-confident. She clearly thought that I'd called her to the room to talk about our relationship.

"Have you been snooping on me?" I dropped the bomb when she least expected it.

She seemed to go pale, but I could have been imagining it. "Snoop? You call asking you some questions on our case that you've refused to answer snooping? Dan, really!" Her surprise and protest sounded faked.

"I don't mean only that."

"What else?" Suddenly, there was a hard edge to her voice.

"I mean going through my things?"

"Your things? Now, why would I do that?"

"I don't know. Why don't you tell me?"

"Dan, I didn't come here to be interrogated over some baseless accusations. I'm going to leave now." She got up and walked to the door.

"Laura, I promised to show you something. Here it is."

I pulled out the handheld video monitor and turned it on. "Ever seen yourself on video?" I turned the monitor toward her.

Laura's face completely lost its color when she saw herself entering my room and going through my things. She sat down on her chair again.

"Baseless accusations?"

"Dan, I'm sorry. I shouldn't have done that." I could almost watch the wheels turning as she struggled to come up with a story.

I've seen people try to lie to me many times during my career. I know what people do when they're caught like this and try to wriggle out of it. Almost always, they will lie even more. Breaking down and confessing, especially on the first go-round, happens only in the movies. I wasn't expecting a candid confession here.

"I became suspicious when you avoided me," she finally said. "I came here for you, I fantasized how we'd make love. So I suspected another woman. I'm sorry, but I like you a lot and I was jealous." She came closer to me, threw the monitor on the bed, and touched me slowly. "Can you blame me for that?"

"Laura, please stop that," I said, although I have to admit I was tempted when I smelled her perfume and sensed her body heat. "How did you know what room I've been staying in?"

"I didn't know."

"Laura you took a key to my room from the reception desk and let yourself in!"

"So if you know, why are you asking?" She sounded as if she'd burst in tears. But she didn't.

"I need to know because what you did is serious. I'm not here as a tourist, I'm on U.S. government assignment. So anything out of the ordinary that happens here must be reported. And I can do it with or without your reasonable explanation."

"I've already explained why I did what I did. I can't understand why you're holding against me the fact that I'm attracted to you."

"Laura, cut the bull. Look at the monitor. Were you looking for another woman inside the FedEx envelope, or inside the file folder? Look at yourself going through my personal things; what did you expect to find there?"

She sat on the bed, her eyes tearing. "Dan, please don't report this. I worked so hard to get my job. I'm supporting myself and my ailing mother. I know I made a mistake, but that's only because I wanted you so much."

"Sorry, Laura, it's not enough. Either you tell me the whole story, or I'll report what I know; and the interrogators in the U.S. are a lot tougher than I am."

"Have you discussed this with anyone else?" Although the question was asked in a quiet, almost timid tone, I knew that behind it was a cold calculation.

"Laura, I'm asking the questions here."

She turned around and before I could do or say anything I was looking at the barrel of a .38. I was stunned for a moment. I was prepared for more tears, but not for a gun.

"Dan, don't be stupid, let me have the monitor."

"Sure, take it," I said. I could tell she was surprised by my nonchalance. She turned to the bed to pick up the monitor. The minute her back was turned, I jumped on her and wrestled her to the bed. It was a scenario that I would have welcomed even a few days ago, but not this way, under these circumstances. She fought hard, scratching my face and once kicking my groin. Still, I got the gun from her hand and threw her to the floor. I put the gun under my belt.

"That was a stupid thing to do," I said.

She started crying.

"Tell me the truth: What are you up to and why are you doing it?"

"I told you already," she said, breathing heavily, "I was jealous, and wanted to make sure there was no another woman."

"Laura, for the last time: Who do you work for?"

"No one, I keep telling you. Just the U.S. government."

"Is this a side job you're doing for Eric Henderson or Bob Hodson?" I threw in the bait.

Her eyes lit up. I'd offered her a way out, and she took it. "Yes. I guess there's no point in hiding it any longer. They asked me to snoop on you, but please don't tell them that I revealed that. Please." Even Hollywood would reject such a bad actress, good looks notwithstanding.

"But how is it that they asked you to snoop on me, when I was the one who invited you over? Were you thinking of spying on me long-distance?"

"No. I was about to come anyway, but then you called and made it easy."

This performance was so bad, I almost felt sorry for the woman. Still, I tactically decided to let her know that maybe I could believe her, if she convinced me. "So when were you lying to me? When you told me about being jealous, or now when you told me about Eric and Bob Hodson?"

"Both reasons for coming are true, I swear. Why do you blame me for falling for you?"

"So I'm the only one for you?"

She nodded, wiping her tears.

"Maybe I'm the one who should be jealous now?" I had to put an end to the charade.

She raised her head in surprise. "Why?"

"Because I saw you passionately kissing another man last night. Now, am I still the only one for you?" I asked in contempt.

Laura seemed defeated.

"Either you tell me the truth or my next call is to Hodson. You know what that means?" I didn't wait for an answer. "Most likely indictment for a whole array of felonies and termination of your employment with Homeland Security."

"I can always stay in Europe," she said. The words were defiant, but her tone signaled a possible surrender.

"You'd be extradited to the U.S. in no time. Laura, talk to me before it's too late."

She reflected for a moment. "You'll have to promise to help me out of it," she said. "I've gotten myself into a real mess here."

I backed myself to the television set, moved my hand behind it, and secretly pressed the RECORD button on the transmitter.

"What are you doing?" she asked.

"Unplugging it," I said. "Did you hear it buzzing? It drives me crazy." I showed her the loose cord.

Laura climbed to the bed and leaned her head against the headboard. She was quiet for a moment.

"Tell me about the guy you were kissing last night."

"So you do care about me, you're jealous!" she said, striking a triumphant chord but obviously still grasping at straws. When I didn't react she continued more quietly. "He's a guy I used to date, and now he's trying to reignite our relationship. That's why he came after me to France."

"Who is he?"

"Just a guy."

"How did you meet him?"

"Why is it your business?"

"Everything is my business now. Tell me, what's his name?" I demanded.

"Baird Black. What's so special about him that you're so insistent?

Either Laura was lying or he was using a credit card with a different name. I ducked her question. "Tell me how you met."

"I was investigating a fuel-smuggling case in Brooklyn. He came to my office to tip me off about a web of some Eastern European men who were illegally importing women from Russia to work in brothels. When my boss ordered an investigation, we discovered his information was good. The ring members were arrested and indicted."

"Good for you," I said, "but then what?"

"We started dating."

"Dating?"

"Yes, you know, boy meets girl? I'd come from Kansas to New York. I had no friends or acquaintances, nothing. All I did was work. He was very nice. He complimented me, took me to dinners, sent me flowers, and bought me nice presents. It was a romance."

"Did you fall in love?"

She nodded.

"And?" I was getting impatient when I should have been empathetic.

"I don't know what happened; we sort of grew apart. He was working late most of the time and had less time to see me. We went from meeting four to six nights a week to twice a week, and then barely once a week. Finally I told him it was over. But then he started calling me again, insisting that we were meant to be together."

"How did you end up in the task force?"

"Why?" she asked.

"Because on day one you said you volunteered."

"Yes, that's true. I'd heard of the opportunities in the office. I told Baird about it, and he said that since he was getting into his busy season, he was going to be working late."

"What does he do?"

"He exports flowers. He said I should take the opportunity, rather than wait every evening for him. So I did."

"Was he also in my hotel room?"

"Who?"

"Baird, your friend."

Laura looked startled.

"Answer me!"

She hesitated. "Yes, I asked him to go over your stuff while you and I were traveling to see if there was anything that would reveal what your mission was."

"Why? If you were working for Hodson as you claim, he knows what my mission is."

"Yes, but if I could find out what you were doing by going through your things, that'd mean a breach of security on your part."

Well, all I needed from her here was an explanation I could pretend I believed so that I could move on. This one wasn't plausible even for the feeble-minded.

"He agreed to break into a hotel room just because you asked him?"

"He refused to at the beginning, but I said he'd have to prove that he'd do anything for me. So he searched your room for me, but found nothing."

"How did he enter my room?"

"I asked the receptionist for a key."

"Why would she give a key to a stranger?"

Laura hesitated.

"Let me help you," I said. "Someone authorized the receptionist to give out the key. Who was that?"

"Baird."

"Laura, I'm sorry, but I don't believe you. Our deal is off and now I'm going to call Hodson. Maybe he'll confirm you were working for him."

"Dan, please don't do that. He'll deny it to keep from alienating you about not trusting you. I'm telling you the truth." She paused. "I need to go," she said, getting up from the bed. "My flight leaves in three hours."

I hesitated. I couldn't detain her. Even if Eric was here he'd have no authority to arrest Laura. What could I do? Call the French police? Reveal to them that the U.S. government was engaged in a clandestine operation on their soil, but had forgotten to ask their permission?

"Are you going back home?"

"Yes. Dan, remember your promise to help me."

"What are you going to tell them about my mission here?" I asked.

"Nothing, that I discovered nothing." Finally, one word of truth.

"Wait," I said.

She turned around. "What?"

"Give me back my handheld monitor."

She put her hand into her purse, but instead of my monitor she pulled out a mace canister, spraying my face and yanking her gun from my belt. I rushed to the bathroom and furiously splashed my burning eyes with water, but by the time I came to my senses, she was long gone with my monitor. That bitch had outsmarted me . . . but at least I could still watch the video. I locked the door and checked the device behind the television. It was all there.

An hour later when my vision had improved, I used my laptop to connect to the Internet. I opened a new e-mail account in Yahoo as "John6677878" and sent a plain-language message to Hodson's covert e-mail address: "I believe I have discovered a possible red fur mole. I suggest you run stop-loss efforts immediately. I cannot leave location or speak with you until my assignment is over. Mole said to be returning home tonight, but I cannot verify. She has an accomplice, one Baird Black, aka Robert Meadway, possibly of Brooklyn, New York. Lan has further details about him that I gave her."

I sent the file, purged the temporary Internet file I'd created, and deleted the new e-mail account. I couldn't leave the hotel. I was sure I was under surveillance, and a trip to Eric's clinic or to the consulate to use a secure phone would expose me. I was reluctant to use my cell phone, which was completely unsecured and left a record with the telephone company, and I definitely couldn't use the hotel's phone. I wanted to talk to someone about Laura, but apart from the message I'd sent to Hodson, there was nothing more I could do without jeopardizing my mission. I was also expecting the hundred thousand dollars from Zhukov. In my set of priorities, sticking to my mission was more important than telling on Laura — not to mention confessing my own breach by inviting her to France. That would have to wait until after my next meeting with Zhukov and his men.

Early the following day, the phone in my room rang. Half asleep, I picked up the receiver. A person with a slight French accent said, "This is a message from Mr. Henderson. He asked that you meet him now at Saint-Victor Abbey."

Finally. "Where is that?"

"Take a cab, the driver will know. Once in Saint-Victor Abbey, go inside. Mr. Henderson will be waiting for you." He hung up. The call alleviated my concern over why I hadn't heard from Eric. There was much to discuss now. For the first time I was looking forward to meeting him.

Saint-Victor Abbey was a towering fortress. I entered the huge, cool foyer and looked around, but there was no sign of Eric. Then a woman passed by and discreetly signaled me to follow. She walked quickly down the stairs toward the crypt. I could see a tour guide down there telling a group of Japanese sightseers about the third-century sarcophagus of Saint Maurice. I thought perhaps Eric was shadowing the group, but the tallest person in it was little more than five feet — no match for the six-foot Eric. When I looked back, the woman who'd signaled to me had disappeared. I turned to walk back up the stairs to the main entrance. A big mustached man squeezed past me in the narrow passage, forcing me up against the wall. I was just about to protest when a door in the wall suddenly opened. It was actually a stone door on hinges, leading to another part of the crypt. Two other men pulled me from the inside, pushing and closing the door immediately.

I looked around. Five men were staring at me; two of them were holding my arms and the others were pointing guns at me. I had no escape route. They were guarding both doors of the small hall. There were no windows. I wasn't armed; they were.

"Game is over," said the mustached guy. In fact, everyone in the room had mustaches. They looked Arab. They weren't big men, but there were five of them, and I was by myself. Mustache Guy — as I'd come to think of him — nodded by way of command, and the men holding me frisked me. I had nothing suspicious on me; in fact, everything substantiated my claim that I was Neil McMillan: a wallet, Neil McMillan's Canadian passport, his business cards, a Visa card with his name and my picture, 343 Canadian dollars along with 290 euros, and my hotel card key. A search of my room and my laptop computer would yield nothing — even if they did manage to break my twelve-digit password.

"What game?" I demanded, trying to sound more confident than I felt as the blood left my face on its way to my feet, which by now were cement-heavy.

Nobody responded.

"What's going on? You want my money? You can take it."

I was not dignified with an answer. I knew, of course, that money was not the reason I was here. And they knew I knew it.

Mustache Guy snapped something in an unfamiliar Arabic dialect, quite different from the Palestinian Arabic I understood well. My heart was hammering, my stomach convulsing. I'd been had. I should have been more careful. All the precautionary measures I'd been taught at the Mossad and during my weeklong crash course at The Farm had been in vain . . . and I had no one to blame but myself. I'd violated the Eleventh Commandment of the trade: *Thou shall not get caught.*

I thought about weighing my options, but I didn't have any: My future was in their hands, and it didn't look bright. I heard my captors talking, again in that strange dialect. I could pick up a few words, but not whole sentences. Who were these guys, and what did they want? I refused to admit — even to myself — that I knew exactly why I was in this mess. Nor would I concede the unavoidable truth that someone had outsmarted me. The self-proclaimed invincible American-Israeli attorney and Mossad veteran, with years of investigative experience on behalf of the U.S. Department of Justice, had been brought to his knees by a bunch of . . . well, something lower than lowlifes. I was now lower than them.

I felt a sting in my right arm, and I blacked out.

It was the urge to scratch my face and neck that finally brought me out of unconsciousness. I tried to move my hand, but it didn't go far. I was chained to a bed. *A bed. I'm lying in bed. That means I'm alive.* A positive sign. I couldn't see anything, though. A jute sack over my head blocked my sight and made it difficult to breathe. As I came to, I registered other sensations: the heat of the room, the smell of urine, the itch of the sack against my skin. I moved my legs. They were still in place. Then I felt the headache, a deep-rooted pain in my forehead, just above my eyebrows. I wished I could touch my head to soothe it.

I heard noises and a door opened. A man said in Arabic, "He is awake, take the sack off his head." This time I understood the dialect: It was Palestinian Arabic. Someone approached and aggressively pulled the sack from my head, scratching my ears. Strong daylight flooded my eyes. I instinctively shut them but the world still shone red through the lids.

A man came closer and said in Arabic, "Here is water." Eyes pressed shut, I felt the cup brought to my lips. I drank it slowly. Some of it trickled down my chin.

"*Shukran*, thanks," I said, slowly opening my eyes. I was on a bed in a small room with a high ceiling. The only window had French shutters, and there were no bars on it. Maybe I was still in France.

"Sit up," said a voice on my left. My vision remained blurred, but I could see the speaker. A man in his early thirties, dark-complected, with Arab features. I tried to sit but the chain held me back. Another man unlocked my handcuffs but left my legs chained. I sat up in the bed, feeling dizzy. The room was swinging around me. I closed my eyes as I lay back down.

"Who are you working for?" the voice asked.

"Transcontinental Money Solutions," I answered. My face was immediately thrown to the left from the blow to my right jaw. I felt the taste of my blood dripping from my mouth.

"I ask again, who do you work for?"

"Transcontinental Money Solutions," I repeated, closing my eyes in anticipation of the next blow. It came as expected. Hard and severe. I felt my face swelling. My heart was racing. *Calm down*, I said to myself, *this is still the easy part*. I knew that giving only a three-word answer would suggest that I had had some kind of military or intelligence training, because of both the terseness and the repetition of a single phrase. I could play the role of a kidnapped civilian — asking what my kidnappers wanted, whether they wanted a ransom, then begging them not to hurt or kill me, insisting there had been a terrible mistake, and pleading for release. But I decided to take a different tack. Stoic behavior would not necessarily mean I was a government agent. Perhaps I was a con man who'd been through many police investigations, even served time.

I'd been through a similar experience before. During my Mossad training we'd taken a course on how to survive interrogation by enemy forces. We were told to case a Tel Aviv office building. Our instructors called the police, posing as neighbors complaining that two strangers were scrutinizing the nearby main office of a cash transportation company, taking notes. A squad car arrived, and we were arrested. After about ten minutes of being roughed up, one team member shouted, "Leave me alone, I'm not a robber, I'm from the Mossad, I'm here on assignment." That didn't spare him or me from further abuse. We were brought to the station and released without incident two hours later. Alex, our instructor, admonished the cadet: If he couldn't withstand a rough police investigation, how would he endure an interrogation from a hostile organization? The cadet was ousted from the academy the following day.

"For the last time, who do you work for?"

"Even if you keep hitting me, the answer won't change. I work for Transcontinental Money Solutions; it's a company in the Seychelles. If you're holding me for ransom, I'm sure they'd be willing to pay you, if the demand isn't too high, because we are a small operation."

"Who owns this company?"

"There are two owners, Mr. Sunil Bharat and a group of investors from Russia and Chechnya." I'd quickly decided on that line, hoping to telegraph the idea *people you can't fool around with.*

"Names," he shouted, "I need names."

"My boss is Sunil Bharat; I've never met the other owners. I don't have any other names, I'm just a financial consultant, but I know they have business interests in many parts of the world. You can call Sunil, I'm sure he'd be happy to give you more details."

There was no comment from my interrogator. I asked, "Am I here because I gave you bad advice? Are you one of my clients? If you're unhappy, I'm sure we can work it out."

He ignored this, but his next question told me — as if I'd had any doubts — that the people holding me were the "clients" I'd been seeking.

"How did you find out about the money transfers?"

Now he was talking. Perhaps I could maneuver this one as well. "There was a security breach and I found it. I'm in the business of trying to prevent it from happening again."

This time the blow hit my chest so hard it felt as if all the air had been sucked out of my lungs. I fell on the bed panting, then passed out. A minute later, someone threw water on my face. It was unpleasantly cold, though I was sweating profusely.

"Don't give me smart-ass answers," the man said when I came to. "When I ask a question, you answer it immediately and precisely. Do you understand that?"

Of course I understood. I nodded. The last blow was pulverizing.

"Now answer my question: How did you find out about the transfers?"

"I told you: security breaches. I've lived in the Seychelles long enough to know people in the banking industry and the regulatory agency. For the right price you can find anything you want. I obtain information and contact people, that's all."

He turned from me and cried *"Falaka"* to someone in the room. *Falaka* was the most common corporal punishment in Iran. A man held a bamboo-like wooden stick and whacked my soles while someone else held my feet in place. The pain was so severe that I gasped and dropped my head to my chest. I didn't know how much I could take. But the more a body part suffers torture, the more tolerable it becomes. The seventh and eighth *Falaka* were not as painful as the first and second. Electric shock, our Mossad trainers had warned us, had the opposite effect: Each jolt was more painful than the last.

"I ask again: How did you connect Mr. Zhukov to the transfers?"

Now it was *Mr. Zhukov*. I didn't know what value to assign this information, but for lack of anything else to do, I filed it away.

I repeated the story: the endorsed checks deposited by Dimitrov, and the way in which I'd obtained copies. Apparently he was satisfied with my answer, because no additional beating followed. "Dimitrov endorsed the checks but you called Mr. Zhukov?"

"I called and spoke with Dimitrov first, but as I said, it concerned Sling and Dewey. He said it was Mr. Zhukov's company — so talk to Zhukov."

"You're lying; Mr. Dimitrov isn't listed in the phone book."

"I said I called the telephone number that was connected to the address. Dimitrov answered."

"How were you going to prevent the problem from recurring?"

"I don't know yet. You can't prevent corruption in banking institutions beyond your reach. I suggested they hire me as a financial consultant. I've been in the asset-protection business for several years and I know the industry inside and out. And so far, I've have had no complaints, only compliments."

"Listen to me," he said. He was so close, I could smell the acrid tang of tobacco and sour body odor. "Enough with your bullshit. We know you work for the Americans, and Mr. Henderson is your controller." He was wrong there, but I wasn't about to correct him. My heart rate accelerated and I felt the blood rush from my head. I was dizzy and my vision was blurred. But I did my best to remain calm. I should have expected this. I'd been duped into believing that the man who'd called my room earlier was delivering a message from Eric. So they knew about my connection to Eric. There was no point in denying it.

"Mr. Henderson? Yes, he's a potential client. I think you're right, I think he's American. We agreed to meet in Marseilles; he was highly interested in my services. He said that he's involved in a messy divorce and needs to hide his fortune. He told me that his wife had hired detectives to follow him wherever he went, so he needed to conceal our meetings."

Another *Falaka*; another "Bullshit!"

I held on, after catching my breath. "So was his story a ploy? Does he actually work for you? You didn't have to beat me so hard to acquire my services; an appointment would have done that."

I don't think he liked my answer because the next *Falaka* sent electric vibrations through me. The interrogation continued for several more hours. They asked the same questions again and again, and I gave them the same answers, again and again, and received the same beating, again and again. I wondered how long I could tolerate the torture before it caused permanent health problems.

I tried to disassociate myself from the surroundings. Physically, I couldn't escape, but mentally I was far away. I remembered the mild beatings we'd endured during Mossad training; we'd found them too harsh. The irony didn't escape me now.

*You will be subjected to various degrees of coercive interrogation techniques, most likely coupled with torture*, I remembered Alex saying. *Coercive interrogation aims to reverse the subject's natural resistance. A good interrogator matches the coercive technique to the subject's personality. Individuals react differently. But if you analyze the techniques you'll see that they always include the three important D's: debility, dependency, and dread.*

*The first technique of interrogation would be to ask you straightforward questions. Since any subject's greatest fear is the unknown, they don't have to apply physical force; just the thought of it makes people sing.*

*But once they realize you're a professional, the next technique is applied: playing on your love for your family or even Israel, or your hatred for a rival group. Then they'll try to boost your ego to make you talk. If that doesn't work, they'll insult and degrade you. They'll try to invoke feelings of futility and abandonment — by your friends, family, and country. They'll show you that they already know all the answers to the questions they're asking, and that their only purpose is to catch you lying. They'll fire questions in rapid succession without giving you the opportunity to answer; they'll ask you the same question again and again around the clock while interrogators are constantly being replaced. They'll make you lose track of time. They'll deprive you of sleep; they'll stare at you to frighten you. They'll manipulate your environment, changing the conditions of your detention to make you feel too hot or cold. They'll try to convince you that, in fact, they're not the enemy but allies. They'll isolate you from any human contact or sound. That's the worst torture. Trust me, most people exposed to coercive interrogation will talk, and usually they reveal information that they might not have revealed otherwise.*

My interrogator's voice brought me back. I hoped what I remembered of my Mossad training would serve to steel my nerve, although I knew that nobody can withstand long-term torture — hours, maybe a few days. After that you are becoming a nonperson who'll never fully recover.

"Why did you move out of the Promenade?"

"I wanted to impress Mr. Henderson. Having him meet me in a five-star hotel would show him I was a successful businessman and justify my high fees."

My interrogator moved his head toward me. He reeked. He was intimidating, making Zhukov's gorillas look like puppies — and they at least took showers and used cologne. He had a nasty expression on his face. He was unshaven, not the type you'd be happy to associate yourself with. Mossad training or not, this was the real thing and it looked bad. He said something to the man standing next to him. I felt another needle sting my arm and I blacked out.

When I woke up, I was pitching, then rolling, back and forth, hitting a wall, nearly falling off the edge of the bed I was on. My mouth was dry, my body aching. A piercing headache was tearing apart my forehead from the inside out. My soles burned. I tried to open my eyes but couldn't see anything: that stinking jute sack again! My hands were cuffed. I rolled over; my entire surroundings were moving. I inhaled deeply, but my ribs were so tender and aching that I had to stop breathing halfway through. The room was pitching again. I tried to concentrate, to remember what had happened. I pitched over again and nearly fell off the bed, but the chains restrained me. Was this an earthquake? Then I smelled the familiar distinctive scent of the Mediterranean Sea mixed with the unmistakable scent of heavy-machine oil. I heard an engine's monotonous roaring and clanking. I was on a boat.

My cell was probably belowdeck, because the engine's roar was so close and loud. Other than lie there, there was nothing I could do. I tried to salivate, moisten my parched mouth, but that helped for only a moment. "Hello?" I shouted, "Can anyone hear me? Hello?"

There was no answer. I put my mind into gear, trying to remember what had happened. I resurrected the chain of events that had brought me here: the trap, the abduction, the interrogation. There was no place for self-pity now. I needed to make a plan. The first piece of good news was that I was still alive. Whatever value I had to my captors, it was as a person with a pulse, not as a cadaver. But I wouldn't bet money on it.

I had to quickly create a legend that would be convincing. To do that, I needed to know how much my captors knew and whether there'd been cover erosion. Unless there'd been a security breach within the CIA, the FBI, or the multi-agency task force, there was a possibility, albeit remote, that the first time Zhukov and his comrades heard the name *Neil McMillan* was when I called them five days ago . . . or was it longer than that? I didn't know how long I'd been out of commission. If that was the case, then the only information they could possibly have on me had to have been unearthed only *after* I had called Zhukov.

I hadn't done anything suspicious since then, other than calling the clinic, meeting Eric at the safe apartment, and meeting Zhukov in my room. But the clinic was an unknown: If these people, whoever they were, had prior knowledge that the clinic was just a front, then anyone coming there was exposed and contaminated. The next soft area was the presence of Eric, Brian, and Martin in the clinic and in my hotel. If they were compromised, anyone in contact with them was contaminated and compromised as well. Ditto for the safe apartment. I had no knowledge whether it was Eric's first or tenth visit to the clinic or to the safe apartment. I'd heard that after his service as CIA station chief in Munich he'd been reassigned to another location, but I hadn't known, or cared, what his new position had been, or where. I regretted letting my personal aversion to him impede my professional diligence.

If I knew, for example, that he lived in London and had come to Marseilles only to instruct me, then it would reduce, but not eliminate, the chance that I was involved in whatever other clandestine work Eric was doing. I wondered if they'd captured Eric as well; after all, they'd mentioned his name as my controller. That would have an immediate impact on me and my story, not to mention the devastating consequences if Eric were forced to talk.

This mental exercise was speculative and leading me nowhere, but I had to continue with it. It distracted me from my physical pain, from wondering whether I was going to live or die. My horizon was narrow, particularly with a stinking hood over my head. I had no doubt that my captors were Arabs, although I didn't understand all the dialects. I had no proof, but I guessed that I was in the hands of either the Slaves of Allah or their supporters.

My interrogation had been brutal and unprofessional, with my interrogator substituting sheer force for clever investigatory methods. And he'd made a mistake by revealing that he knew about Zhukov and Dimitrov, thereby placing himself squarely within the framework of my own case. A professional interrogator would never give his subject any information, certainly not before his subject starts talking. Leaving the subject in the dark is the best policy because it undermines his confidence. My interrogator was not clever; maybe he was even stupid. But the reality was, I was the prisoner, and he was the interrogator. Intellectual superiority isn't always helpful when you're chained and your captor holds the key and the whip.

As I continued analyzing, I arrived at the uneasy suspicion that the unprofessional nature of the interrogation had been a sham — that in fact they didn't really need the information at all. I had the sense that they already knew everything they wanted to know and that the sole purpose of the interrogation had been to keep that fact from me, to maintain the charade. But this was conjecture, not fact, so I had to set it aside.

Although I was helpless against brute force, I could still use my intellect to tilt the scales in my favor. My best course was to stick to my story and the explanation for my contact with Eric. I heard metal clicking and a door squeaking open. The jute hood was pulled off my face. I shut my eyes expecting flooding light again, but there was only a single bulb.

"Water, can I have some water?" I said in Arabic in the direction of the sound I heard. The door closed. A minute later it opened again.

"Here," said a young man in Arabic. "Drink this." He handed me water in a cup. When he saw that my hands were cuffed, he brought the cup to my lips. I gulped it down. I looked around. I was locked in a windowless ship's cabin.

"What is your name?"

"Abed," he answered.

"How long have I been here?" I asked.

"No talking," he said in a polite tone that surprised me. He was unshaven, wearing torn jeans and a tee that once upon a time had been white.

"Can I have more water please?" I said, ignoring the no-talking rule. He took the cup and returned with it filled to the brim with water. "I'm hungry," I said. He left the cabin and returned ten minutes later with a bowl of hummus and ful, Egyptian red beans, as well as dry pita bread. He released one hand from the handcuffs, and chained the other to the bed. I devoured the food. Abed collected the bowl and cup and left the cabin, ignoring my requests to leave the water behind. Still, I found comfort in his neglecting to put the stinking jute sack back over my head. I felt hot. There was no fresh air in the cabin.

I tried to figure out where we were going. My best guess was that the boat was midsized, judging from the roar of the single engine and the pitching and rolling. And the distinct smell I remembered so well from my childhood in Israel told me we had to be in the Mediterranean. True, the Atlantic isn't far from Marseilles, either, but the Mediterranean Sea smells different. I'd spent many hours on the beaches of Tel Aviv growing up. If we were crossing the Mediterranean, Morocco, Algeria, and Tunisia were possible destinations, more or less directly across the water from Marseilles. But if we were aiming southeast, we'd end up in Libya or Egypt. There was nothing I could do but wait.

Two more days passed. Other than two meals a day and an occasional visit to the toilet across from my cabin, nothing happened. I didn't see

anyone other than Abed, who brought my meals. On the third day I heard
noises, people shouting, the engine changing gear. We were slowing down,
and then we came to a stop. We had arrived at a port. I heard sounds of
other boats, seabirds perhaps, and now the smell was different, a mixture
of engine oil and diesel fuel. I couldn't even speculate about what port it
might be. The shouting increased in an indistinct vernacular. I was sure it
was Arabic, but again in a dialect I could not make out.

Abed returned to my cell, uncuffed my hand and legs from the bed, and
cuffed my right hand to his wrist while another man entered my cabin.
"We have arrived. You'd better behave yourself or you get this," the
second man said, glaring at me as he displayed a foot-long butcher's
knife. "I'll cut you in half if you try anything." They put the jute sack back
on my head and led me through a corridor, up a flight of stairs where I
banged my head twice, out into abundant fresh air. I was led like a blind
man down a wooden gangway until I felt the ground. I was then helped
into a car that sped away; two men were sitting next to me, one on either
side. They pushed my head down. Soon I heard city noises, motorcycles
passing by, peddlers talking. Cars honked repeatedly, a popular pastime
for Middle Eastern drivers. In the car, I heard the men around me speak
in that same strange Arabic dialect. I could pick up a few words, but I
couldn't understand a full sentence. I did make out one word that sent a
jolt of fear down my spine: *Tripoli*. There are two Arab cities with that
name — one in Lebanon, the other in Libya. I didn't like either option.
Slowly the city noises subsided; I heard nothing but the warm wind
blowing through the open windows and my guards exchanging an occasional word. We seemed to have been driving for hours and hours. The
temperature was high, but the air was dry. The car made a turn to the
right onto a dirt road and filled up with dust. Some time later, we came
to a stop. I was taken out, and the jute sack was removed from my head.
We were in a small village. Around me was nothing but sand dunes and
mud-brick houses. I could see about thirty or forty houses, one dirt road,
and free-roaming white, black, and red chickens busy picking up food off
the ground. Curious barefoot children with big brown eyes wearing dirty
galabiyas ogled me.

Finally someone spoke to me. "McMillan," said an unshaven man standing next to me. I turned to face him. He was short and thin, with a fierce look in his eyes. He was dressed in a long, formerly white galabiya. He had short black hair and chickenpox-scarred face. Judging by the fearful deference the other men showed him, I assumed he was their commander.

"This is a remote village in the desert," the commander said; "there is no point in escaping. If we don't get you, the sun and the heat will. You are six hundred miles from the nearest city. Unless your American president sends a helicopter for you, you will remain here. But then," he added with laughter, "we are beyond the range of your helicopters."

I quickly calculated: The Black Hawk UH-60 has a range of one thousand miles, so for a round trip from a carrier cruising off the coast of Libya, I'd be out of range, provided the commander's information was correct. I was sure he was lying about the distance, though. We'd left a city — probably Tripoli — and driven for about six hours; we couldn't be more than three hundred miles from the harbor. Unless, of course, I'd miscalculated the length of our trip, which was entirely possible. I'd been blindfolded, had no watch, and had lost my sense of time days before.

"If you try anything, my men here have orders to shoot you. Do I make myself clear?"

I nodded. "I'm Canadian, not American. Could you tell me where I am, and why?"

"The Western Desert."

"Where is that?"

"North Africa."

"The Egyptian or the Libyan side of the Western Desert?"

He was visibly surprised at my geographic knowledge. "The Libyan."

"How long will I be here?"

"Until our brothers finish their job in America."

"Who are your brothers?"

I didn't expect an answer, because I knew the answer and feared it, but it still came. "The Slaves of Allah. We will teach all the infidels a lesson they will never forget."

His English was good, although he spoke with a heavy accent. "Where did you learn such good English?" Some flattery wouldn't hurt under the circumstances.

"In America," he answered. He then turned around and was driven away. I just stood there. The sun was setting. The children were still there, looking at me curiously. A middle-aged man, perhaps in his fifties, approached me. *"Ahalan wa'sahalan,"* he said in Arabic, welcome.

*"Shukran,"* I answered. *"Ana Neil, shoo ismak?"* I'm Neil, what is your name?

"My name is Nasser," he said hesitantly in English. "I speak little English I learned many years ago."

"Your English sounds fine to me."

"Thank you. I learned it while working for Standard Oil when they were still here."

"I'm glad to meet you," I said. "What is the name of this village?"

"Bir Tamam."

"Sorry, I've never heard that name before," I said apologetically. "Where is it located?"

"East of Sarir, not far from the Egyptian border."

He saw the expression on my face, although I thought I'd kept it motionless. "We are only two hundred miles from Egypt, but between us there is the Great Sand Sea. The other foreigners here have also asked me the same question. Don't even think about it, nobody can survive the desert."

"Foreigners?"

"Yes, there are two other foreigners here. They were brought here about two or three weeks ago."

"Where are they from?"

He smiled. "We're not supposed to know, but they are from Hungary."

I tried harder to keep my face calm. This time the effort was perhaps more successful because he said nothing. "Who are they?"

"I don't know. The people who brought you also brought them. They told us to keep them in place. And we do. In Libya you don't ask too many questions, and I'm afraid you are doing just that."

I tried to figure out why all of us foreigners would be brought to this

location in particular. Because of its remoteness, I assumed, and its proximity to desert. But what was the Slaves of Allah's connection to this
place? Was it their safe haven? "Thanks for your help," I told him. He
seemed friendly and I did not want to abuse his hospitality. "Who will be
taking care of my needs here? I mean food, water, shelter?"

"I will," he said. "We are poor, but we will share with you what we have.
That hut" — he pointed at the mud-brick hut I'd noted earlier — "is your
home now." I followed him inside. On the floor were a straw rug, a big
bowl of water, and a charred kettle. "We are eating dinner at my home
soon; you are welcome to join us."

"And where is your home?" I asked.

"Over there." He pointed to a mud-brick hut close by.

"I'd be glad to." I was famished.

I followed Nasser into his home. *"Marhaban,"* said Nasser, welcome. It
was spacious and much larger than my hut. His wife, clad in traditional
Arab garb, covered her face as I walked in. Three small children were
standing next to her, peering at me. *"Tfadal,"* please, said Nasser as he sat
down, signaling me to join him. In the middle was a big bowl full of food.
I sat next to him on the rough camel-wool rug. There were no plates or
utensils. All family members waited for Nasser to eat first. He stuck his
hands into the bowl, took a fistful of rice mixed with lamb meat, and ate
it off his hands, telling me, "Please help yourself." I didn't need any further invitation and reached my hands into the common bowl. At the end
of the meal Nasser burped loudly, signaling that he had liked the meal.
His wife then served thick coffee from a small charred bronze finjan, a
Middle Eastern kettle that had been simmering on a small fire in the
corner.

I was tired. Nasser walked with me back to my hut. "Good night," he
said. I thanked him, entered my hut, and fell asleep immediately on the
dirt floor. Sometime in the middle of the night, I was awakened by the
penetrating cold. I'd forgotten how cold the desert could be at night,
winter or summer. I had no blankets or extra clothing to cover myself,
only the lightweight clothes I was wearing when I'd been captured. Now
they were dirty and smelled. An hour later, too cold to stay still, I went

outside. I heard a weapon cock. *"Shoo hada?"* said the man. Who is there? He pointed a gun at me, motioning me to go back inside.

"It's me," I said, "Neil McMillan, I just needed fresh air," and returned to my hut. I sat on the floor, leaning against the hardened mud wall, clenching my teeth, waiting for morning to come. First came the rooster call, then the sound of sheep bells ringing. I opened the door and looked around. The village had awakened. Men in long galabiyas were leaving their huts. Some holding small agricultural tools, some herding a small flock of sheep. I saw four or five women in traditional Arab garb carrying buckets of water. When they saw me they covered their faces with their veils. The men looked at me with curiosity but kept their distance.

I walked to Nasser's hut, my limbs stiff. "Please come in," he said. "Let's have breakfast."

His wife returned to the hut holding a wide tray with flat bread.

*"Gharaiba bil laoz,"* he said, when he saw me looking at the bread. "My wife baked it in the clay oven outside." It was warm and sweet.

Just then two men entered the hut, the other foreigners. I nodded: "Hi," I said in English, "I'm Neil McMillan, from Canada."

The older man, perhaps in his fifties, with a medium build, gray eyes, silver-framed eyeglasses, and an alert, intelligent gaze, answered first. "Hello. I'm Dr. István Kovach, and this is my assistant János Hegedus." He pointed at a man in his midthirties who stood next to him.

"Hungarian?" I asked.

"Yes," they both replied. János Hegedus was athletically built, with brown eyes and short black hair. I shook their hands; one had a soft grip, the other a firm one.

From the moment I'd heard of them, I'd figured that the other foreigners in the village were the two missing Mossad operatives, Benny's guys. Now, seeing them, I was certain. The theory I had suggested to Hodson had turned out to be true. The plan to acquire genetically engineered virus, the kidnapping of Benny's men, the encrypted messages sent to Eagle Bank, the huge money transfers, my own kidnapping, and the threat to hundreds of thousands, maybe millions of New Yorkers and other Americans: The Slaves of Allah *were* behind all of it. There *was* a connection between the Israeli operatives' disappearance and the ciphered messages. The depth of the conspiracy was now revealed to me, though the meaning of it all remained murky. I tried to remain calm but the tension I felt was almost unbearable. We ate our breakfast in silence. While Nasser was listening, there wasn't much to talk about other than the weather. When Nasser finished his meal, he got up and said, "I must attend my herd. I'll see you tonight."

# XII

I went outside. István and János followed. The sun was rising, warming the chilly air. I looked at my wrist, forgetting that my watch had been taken by my captors. From the sun's position I estimated the time to be approximately seven in the morning. We walked silently toward the outskirts of the village until we were a safe distance from the huts. I was about to shock the two Hungarians, and I needed to give them room to react without fear of being overheard.

"In case someone is watching us," I said in English, "please do not over-react to what I'm about to say."

They looked at me in anticipation. I switched to Hebrew: "I'm a friend of Benny's. He asked me to help him find you. Unfortunately, I'm now in the same shit you are."

Dr. Oded Regev — aka István Kovach — opened his mouth to answer, but the younger man, Arnon Tal — aka János Hegedus — stopped him abruptly. "Wait, don't answer. It could be a trap. Who is Benny?" He spoke English.

"I understand your caution," I continued quietly in Hebrew, "but this isn't a ploy; I'm their prisoner as well. You are Arnon Tal from the Office and he is Dr. Oded Regev of the Nes Ziona Biological Institute. You were on an assignment from the Office in Rome." I paused. "Is that enough to satisfy you?" There was no sarcasm in my voice.

"And who are you? You're not from the Office, are you?" The question came in Hebrew, removing any remaining doubt.

"I'm an old friend of Benny's, and I don't work for him. Please don't ask me any more questions about me. You know why." They nodded. They knew that if they were interrogated aggressively, they were likely to reveal what I'd told them, so the less they knew about me, the better. The fact that I spoke Hebrew was incriminating enough.

"The only thing you need to know and all I've told our captors is that I'm a Canadian citizen working as a financial consultant for a Seychelles company. I came to Marseilles to meet a potential client and was kidnapped and brought here."

"Obviously you're Israeli," said Oded. "Your Hebrew is native."

"Please don't ask him anything further," interrupted Arnon.

"I suggest we speak only English among ourselves," I said, "even when we're alone. A slip of the tongue could be dangerous for all of us."

"Sure," agreed Oded.

"Is there a way out of here?" I asked.

"We don't know," said Arnon. "We could be hundreds of miles from civilization. Obviously, that's why they keep us here. Even if we started walking, we wouldn't get far without transportation and supplies. In this desert, nobody could survive without a serious supply of water."

"I keep hearing conflicting numbers on the distance," I said.

"Most of it is disinformation or plain ignorance," said Arnon.

"So why a guard?" I asked.

"Some guard," said Arnon in jeering contempt. "Abdel Rahman is asleep most of the day, or busy chasing off flies and mosquitoes. Once he's convinced you have no escape plans, he won't mind what you're doing. He knows we can't go far."

"But why are they keeping us here?" asked Oded. "Do you have any clue? It seems strange that they'd keep us together."

"Yesterday, the person who brought me here told me I'd be kept here until his brothers taught all the infidels a lesson they would never forget. I think they're a small organization, and perhaps they don't even know we're connected. I think we're simply goods to be traded later for something, and this place is as good as any other to hide us from the world."

"That means that their plan hasn't been averted," said Oded.

"What plan?" I asked.

Oded froze: "You don't know?" I saw suspicion in his eyes.

"Calm down. If you mean spreading hemorrhagic fever, then of course I know. Benny told me."

Oded let out a deep breath. "You frightened me."

"I'm sorry. I said too much. Honestly, from now on all I can tell you are things I heard from my captors, or the little stuff I heard from Benny — and that's only to convince you I'm on your side."

"My read," said Arnon, "is they're going to keep us here until they've carried out their plan."

"And then?" asked Oded in trepidation.

"There could be any number of possibilities, but a trade or killing us are the ones that come to mind."

"No, they won't kill you," I said. "You're worth a lot in the human trade-in business, and you have the scientific know-how they might still need."

"And you?" asked Oded. "How much are you worth?"

"I don't know. I could prove to be a liability rather than an asset, so they might prefer to . . ." I pointed a finger at my right temple.

"Come on," said Oded, "let's get some shade; the sun will come out in full force soon."

"Shade? Here?" I said in disbelief.

Arnon pointed to the east. "Behind this hill there's an oasis with a small pond and palm trees. Why do you think they built this village right in the middle of nowhere? It has water."

We started walking along the sand dune, sometimes knee-deep in sand. When we reached the top of the hill, I saw the oasis, just as Arnon had said. There were approximately twenty palm trees, a few other trees I couldn't identify, and a two-acre pond. Children were playing nearby and two camels were gulping water directly from the pond. "This is their source of life," said Oded. "They use the water for drinking and irrigating their fields; they also water their herds here. They eat the dates of the palm trees, and even burn the dry thin bark that falls off."

"The odor I smelled yesterday from Nasser's fire in his hut didn't come from burning bark. It wasn't pleasant," I said decidedly.

"Oh no," said Oded. "Inside the mud-brick huts they burn dried animal manure."

They saw the expression on my face and burst into hearty laughter simultaneously.

"Let me ask you a question." I looked at Oded hesitantly, not knowing whether he would answer. I knew that his employer, the Nes Ziona laboratory, was considered even more secretive than Dimona, Israel's nuclear research center. Unlikely that he would discuss his work. But I wanted to know things from the terrorists' perspective, and I hoped Oded would answer.

"Why hemorrhagic fever? This disease is so lethal, it could spread and kill their own people. Couldn't they find a more effective virus? Something that would make people want to make love, not war?"

Oded smiled. "Sure. It's no secret many governments are working on the ultimate nonlethal bioweapon; one that would send the enemy to bed, wanting to do nothing but sleep. Something that would take the infected person's energy, cognition, sleep, immune function, and sense of well-being. It's called myalgic encephalomyelitis, or chronic fatigue immune deficiency syndrome, which results from insufficient oxygen availability due to impaired capillary blood flow."

"And what does that all mean in plain language?"

"In healthy people, most red blood cells are smooth-surfaced and concave-shaped, like a bagel. They have the flexibility needed both to move through capillary beds, delivering oxygen, nutrients, and chemical messengers to the body tissues, and to remove metabolic waste, such as carbon dioxide and lactic acid, on the way back. But an abnormal red blood cell lacks the flexibility that allows it to enter tiny capillaries. Scientists believe that, in ME and CFIDS, the mechanism whereby red blood cells are affected by toxic chemicals provides a possible link to environmental illness, and multiple chemical sensitivity. But as I said, everyone is still working on isolating it and a means of dissemination."

"Isn't that what happened to thousands of veterans of the Gulf War?" I asked.

"Maybe," he said. "Gulf War Syndrome symptoms are many: chronic fatigue, severe neurological disorders, muscle and joint pain, shortness of breath, gastrointestinal problems, memory loss, insomnia, rashes, depression, headaches, and other complaints, but what's interesting about it," his tone suddenly became amused "is that Gulf War Syndrome may be a sexually transmitted disease, and is also contagious via the airborne route.

Scientists suspect that soldiers pass the illness on to their wives and family members; there are some indications that their children appear to have an increased incidence of birth defects. So sometimes making love is as dangerous as making war."

"At least it's more pleasurable. But seriously, the question remains, why did they choose hemorrhagic fever and not one of those syndromes that make you tired?"

"I don't know. The Gulf War Syndrome agent hasn't been definitively isolated, so there'd be no way of breeding it in a lab. Hemorrhagic fever in the genetically engineered form they intended to use is reasonably easy to spread and so difficult to prevent or cure."

"On a different note, I tried to understand the dialect they are using, and found it difficult," I said.

"How well do you speak Arabic?" Arnon asked me with interest.

"The Palestinian dialect is no problem, but it gets less certain outside of that."

"They speak Libyan Arabic here, in an Egyptian Bedawi dialect. Only about two percent of the world's Arabic speakers use that dialect."

"That explains why I can't understand it."

We sat under a palm tree, soaking our feet in the water. It felt good. My soles, still injured from the *Falaka* beating, needed soothing. The water was cool, a pleasant surprise. If it weren't for the beatings and the abuse, or the fact that we were prisoners of terrorists, I might have regarded this as an expedition organized by the National Geographic Society.

"I had a short conversation with Nasser," I said, making sure no one else was listening. "Although he didn't say it directly, my hunch is that he's not too happy with Khadafi. I'm not sure why he agreed to keep us here for the Slaves of Allah. Is it for the money? I don't see it in his standard of living."

"He could have other motives," said Oded. "One thing I know, though, is that he's petrified of the Libyan secret police. They make no secret of the pride they take in murdering Libyans at home and abroad who oppose the regime."

"He told you that?" I asked in skepticism. "How could he trust you?"

"He didn't say it directly. Instead, he would say things like 'people say that the secret police are doing such and such,' as if he were quoting others, but then would quickly add, 'but I don't believe it.' I got the impression that the criticism was in fact his. I can understand why. He told me that before the revolution he lived in the city on a nice salary paid by Standard Oil, although he was just a low-level employee. When Khadafi rose to power, kicked out the foreign oil companies, and nationalized their assets, Nasser lost his job. He had to return to his wife's village and live a miserable life, working in the small family field from sunrise to sunset and making zilch. You saw how he lives, so it's little surprise that he's unhappy."

"Perhaps helping the Slaves of Allah is his own expression of his opposition to Khadafi," suggested Oded.

"Could be," said Arnon, "although at the moment they're supported by Khadafi. Maybe they have long-term plans for Libya that Khadafi doesn't realize yet, who knows. Nasser's a brave man: Criticism, even as subtle as his, is like jumping off a skyscraper. They have a law, 'the Protection of the Revolution,' that orders the execution of anyone participating in any expression of opposition against the revolution. All political parties are banned. In 1990 Khadafi passed a law that made any observation or directive by the 'Leader of the Revolution' binding, enforceable, and not subject to review by any authority. Khadafi is above the law, accountable to no one."

"Is that all?" asked Oded. "He didn't pass a law declaring himself God?"

"Have patience," said Arnon, "he's still in power.

"And then," he concluded, "two years ago a new law came about that targets any family, clan, tribe, or community that gives sanctuary to or fails to report any individual opposing Khadafi to the authorities."

"Collective punishment?" I asked.

"It sounds like it," Arnon said. "Communities found guilty would lose services such as water supply, electricity, gas, food, and communication."

"I see," I said. "So if Nasser is found guilty of anything they would disconnect the village's telephone line, broadband Internet connection, and electricity, making their cable TV unusable. I guess they'd have to give the village these services first so that they could disconnect them later."

"Maybe there is an opportunity here," said Oded pensively.

"Did you talk to Nasser about his connection to the Slaves of Allah?" I asked.

"I tried," he responded, "but he refused to say even one word. Apparently he fears them even more than he does Khadafi."

"Or maybe he genuinely supports them," suggested Oded. "I'm puzzled, though, why Khadafi allows these guys to roam free in his country."

"I can only speculate," I said. "I know that Khadafi is perhaps the only dictator who openly and publicly urges his supporters to physically liquidate his political opponents. In doing so, he claims that their death sentences are fated by the will of the people and not his own, since he has no position of authority in the country. His opponents, or 'stray dogs' as he likes to refer to them, have been targeted worldwide. That could explain why he shelters terrorists. They carry out his dirty jobs outside Libya."

A woman came close with a bucket to draw water from the pond. We ceased our conversation and slowly returned to the village. On our way back we saw our guard, the local policeman Abdel Rahman, filling up a small metal container with gasoline from a tanker just outside the village. We exchanged looks. Gasoline.

"Are you thinking what I'm thinking?" I asked Arnon as we walked away.

"The problem of getting out of here is transportation and supplies. If we get his jeep, enough gasoline and water, we could make it to the Egyptian border," answered Arnon.

"And then what? Cross the border?" asked Oded.

"There's only one official border crossing between Egypt and Libya, up north in Sallum, near the Mediterranean Sea," I said, "but we'd have to cross someplace else, because we can't go through the Libyan checkpoint without passports. Since we're hundreds of miles south of the Mediterranean, we should still bear northeast. It's a longer route but it would get us to the northwestern part of Egypt and away from Libyan control. We couldn't just go east. Nasser told me that once a heavily laden camel caravan tried to cross the high undulating dunes of the Great Sand Sea to reach Kufra from the Dakhla Oasis. The conditions were too rigorous and they were forced to turn north and travel in the dune lanes to Siwa in Egypt. We should try the same route," I concluded. "We should also wonder why Nasser would tell me such a thing."

"Indirectly pointing us in the best direction for an escape?" suggested Arnon.

"If that's the case, then we should develop our relationship with Nasser," I said.

"Can we trust him?" asked Oded. "If he turns us in, that could mean our end, or at least put an end to our escape plans. If they didn't kill us, they'd lock us up in some shit hole. We should be very careful. I wouldn't approach him for help at all, unless there's an imminent danger." We all agreed.

Oded continued, "If we succeed getting into Egypt, any problems the Egyptians are liable to give us wouldn't even come close to what we can expect here. The Egyptians hate the Slaves of Allah and all their other satellite fundamentalist organizations. Egypt has diplomatic relations with Israel . . . we'll be much safer in Egypt," he concluded.

"We should take into consideration another danger in the desert," I said. "Land mines."

"Mines?" asked Oded. "Why?"

"The Western Desert of Egypt and its northern part, between El Alamein and the Libyan border, are heavily mined and have been since the fierce fighting in World War II between the British and the Germans."

"How can we avoid mines?" asked Oded.

"Avoid?" I said. "I'd rather find them, preferably before I step on one. Where else can we get explosives?"

From my military training I knew that there are two types of anti-personnel land mines that detonate when someone walks close by. One type is a blast mine, usually laid on or under the ground or scattered from the air. The other is a fragmentation mine activated by a trip wire. Then there is an anti-tank land mine designed to detonate when more than 350 pounds of pressure is applied to it. "You need metal detectors or metal prodders to find them. We don't have any," said Oded.

"We only look for anti-tank mines, not anti-personnel mines. Nothing will happen if a person steps on them," answered Arnon.

"And how do we find them?" asked Oded.

"We'd start looking when we got closer to the border, next to the defense lines that could still be standing sixty years after the war. The wind and weather conditions may have exposed them," I said, "But I'd use extreme caution even getting close to them. Anti-tank mines could be harmless to us, but they could be surrounded by anti-personnel mines to deter guys like us from even approaching."

"We could make some serious bombs if we need to defend ourselves. But let's see if we get that far," said Arnon.

"For now, we need to find and store containers for gasoline and water. The villagers have containers with which they haul water from the pond. We should take a few, fill them up with water and gasoline, and when we're ready steal Abdul Rahman's jeep." I waited for their response.

Oded was the first to react. "We would need to prepare the water and the gasoline very close to the time we plan to leave. These people have so few belongings. If a container went missing, they'd notice it immediately."

He stopped for a moment. "Now let's see, I calculated already that we'd need at least thirty gallons of water, and twenty gallons of gasoline, if the distance is up to two hundred fifty miles."

"That's a lot of containers," said Arnon. "Where in the jeep would we put them?"

"On the backseat and on the roof."

"What would we do about food? We can't save any of it overnight in this heat," Arnon pointed out.

"We could take a chunk of dates off the palm trees; they'll stay edible for a long time, and we should also be able to find additional palms en route. Their sugar content is high; it'll keep us for a few days," I suggested.

"So is this a plan?" asked Oded.

"I think so," answered Arnon.

"When is the next moonless night?" Oded raised his eyes to the clear sky.

I followed his gaze. The moon was visible there during the day as well. "I think the next moonless night will be in three days. That doesn't leave us much time."

The following day we walked through the village and identified the best locations for stealing containers. A one-hour stroll gave us the answer: the local grocery, which was also a makeshift city hall, police station, and barbershop. Behind it was a pile of plastic containers and military surplus five-gallon jerricans.

After a modest dinner, when everyone was asleep — including Abdel Rahman, the snoring police force of one — I quietly left my hut and walked to the outskirts of the village. I chose the hut on the very edge and tried to open the door, but it was stuck. A thin layer of sand had accumulated and blocked the door. I pushed myself in. The one room of the hut had been divided in half; the smaller space must have been used as a kitchen. Just a guess because there were no kitchen implements or cooking utensils to tell me that. The floor was full of debris, remains of human habitation, including two dead birds. Villagers don't leave their land voluntarily. Whoever lived in this hut had died without offspring, or had perhaps been taken away for speaking against the regime. Maybe the owners were the people Nasser told me about. Either way, it was clear that no one had entered this place for some time. I thought it could be suitable for our storage needs. To avoid attention, we'd need to carry one container at a time. I returned to my hut.

On the following three mornings we repeated our routine of carrying containers, one at a time, after receiving the grocer's consent. I guess our explanation — that we needed them to store water to be slowly dripping over the windows to cool off the heat inside — was plausible, because he didn't hesitate for a moment. The containers were mostly used to store sheep's milk and water. We didn't attempt to get the jerricans, which were obviously used for gasoline.

"Tonight," said Oded as we sat with our feet in the pond. "No moon tonight. We'll wait for you before midnight behind the storage hut. Come with the jeep." He handed me his watch. "Use this. I'll use Arnon's."

That evening I sat nervously in my hut weighing all the options, which weren't many; either we would make it or we wouldn't. Time was moving more slowly than usual. I closed my eyes and thought of my children. I ached. Karen was in graduate school, busy with studies and an active social life. With her slim five-foot-eight figure, honey-colored hair, and green eyes, she was truly a beauty. Tom, the younger, heavier built but six inches taller than his sister, was on his college football team. Accustomed to my long absences, they would have had no idea I was in trouble. Whenever I was away, I tried to call at least three times a week. But they knew that if no calls came, it didn't mean I'd forgotten about them, just that I couldn't call.

I thought of my late father, a diffident lawyer during business hours, a researcher of Chinese wisdom in the afternoon, and a loving and caring parent twenty-four hours a day. Twenty years after he'd passed away, I still missed him. He had once entrusted me with a Confucian proverb: "Chi Wen Tzu always thought three times before taking action. Twice would have been quite enough."

At 11:30 P.M. I opened the door of my hut slowly, hoping it wouldn't squeak as it usually did. I looked for Abdel Rahman. He was nowhere to be seen. Probably asleep, as usual. With neither moon nor electricity, the village was completely dark; the twinkling stars were the only source of weak light. Cicadas were buzzing and dogs were barking. The air was warm and dry. I checked the wind direction; it was away from the village. As I came up the hill closer to Abdel Rahman's house, I dropped to the ground and crawled along the dirt road to avoid detection. I was breathing hard and hoped the damn dogs wouldn't direct their barking at me. As it was, luckily, their random barking masked the noise of my approach toward the jeep, which was parked not far from his hut.

I got up off the ground, put my ear to Abdel Rahman's door, and heard what sounded like an espresso machine foaming milk. A machine without electricity? Then I realized it was Abdel Rahman snoring.

I opened the driver's door, which was unlocked. I took a deep breath and slid in. I looked around to make sure all was quiet. No movement was visible. On the backseat were two containers, one with water and the other with gasoline. Rahman was probably preparing for a trip. In my mind, I thanked him for the effort. I released the hand brake and got out; after a light push with my hands the jeep began to slide down the hill, slowly enough that I could jump in again. It stopped about a hundred yards away. I searched for the keys, which weren't in the ignition. I looked on the floor under the mat, on the visor, in the glove compartment. Nothing. That meant I would have to hot-wire it, something I hadn't done since my Mossad training. I quietly opened the hood, holding the jump-start cables that I'd found in the back. Now I had to locate the coil wire in the dark. It knew it should be red, but I couldn't see the colors.

I heard noise — a sound of objects falling to the ground. I ducked under the vehicle and froze, listening for the source. It was coming from the far side of the village, two hundred feet away, to my estimate. I had left the hood open, so if anyone came my way I'd be in serious trouble. I waited two more minutes that felt like eternity. When the noises stopped as suddenly as they had started, I returned to fiddling with the wires. After much effort, I ran a jump-start cable from the positive side of the battery to the positive side of the coil. Now the dash had power. Next, I looked for the starter, following the positive battery cable with my hand. I took the screwdriver that was in the glove compartment and crossed the two wires. The engine started. In the quiet of the desert night, I was sure its noise would wake the dead. Moving quickly now, I closed the hood and ran to the driver's seat. To my horror, the wheel was locked. In desperation, I inserted the screwdriver into the top center of the steering column and started pushing the locking pin away from the wheel. It clicked, and the wheel was free. The temperature outside was getting cooler, but I was sweating, and my heart was racing.

I drove to the dirt road half a mile away without headlights; I veered off the road a few times and was lucky not to get stuck in the dune. As Oded and Arnon heard the jeep approaching, they came from behind the storage hut and waved at me. Once I'd stopped, they quickly and quietly loaded the stored water. It took four long minutes. From there we continued to the tanker, where we filled four jerricans and a few plastic containers with gasoline, which spilled over onto our hands because the tanker's spigot was wider than the mouth of the plastic containers. Again we loaded the containers into the jeep and jumped in. It was cramped, but we weren't going on a joyride.

"Was it difficult?" asked Oded who sat at the back, while Arnon sat in the passenger's seat.

"What, taking Abdel Rahman's jeep or not getting caught?" I asked, feeling much better as we drove away.

"Did anybody notice you?" asked Oded.

"Nobody's chasing us; that's the best sign," I answered. "There was a scary moment when I heard noises like a bunch of things falling while I was wrestling with the Jeep.

"It was us," conceded Oded. "We accidentally dropped a bunch of the jerricans."

"Hell," I said, "I thought we'd be caught red-handed. Thank God these villagers work hard and sleep tight."

I moved the gearshift into first and moved ahead slowly, as if we were tiptoeing away.

"I managed to steal two matchboxes and two shovels from the grocery," said Arnon. "They could come in handy."

"Are you sure we're going in the right direction, heading east?" asked Oded.

"As far as I can remember, we came in from the other way. I was brought from Tripoli, which should be northwest of here. So generally speaking we should be okay."

I kept the engine in low torque until we were no longer within hearing distance of the village, and then accelerated gradually. It was dark, and the road conditions did not allow speeding. I hadn't come this far and survived this much to be killed in a car accident.

The jeep's engine suddenly died. All at once everything went quiet. The jeep rolled for a few more seconds and stopped.

"What happened?" asked Arnon.

"I have no idea," I said. "The engine just died."

I got out and lifted the hood. It was so dark I could barely see the engine. I sent my hand slowly to check the wiring; maybe a connection had worked loose. I couldn't find anything. A warm breeze came, but the silence around us and the black shadows of the nearby hill gave me a chill. We were just a few miles from the village. Unless we got going soon, we could be found easily.

"Do we have gas?" asked Oded.

"When we left, the fuel gauge indicated half full. We couldn't have consumed that much already. But let's check." We unloaded one jerrican and filled up the tank. I hot-wired the engine again and, after a few repeated pumps of the accelerator while we held our breath, the engine roared to life. We jumped in and continued with our journey. "This gauge must be broken," I said. "In fact, it's stuck. It didn't change when we filled up the tank."

"How far do you estimate the Egyptian border is?" asked Oded when he'd calmed down.

Arnon turned his head toward his colleague, who sat cramped on the back bench. "I don't know exactly, but I assume less than two hundred miles," he answered, still sticking to English.

"It's okay, we can speak Hebrew now," I said, and the resulting laughter eased some tension. "Why do you assume that?"

"Because everyone was telling us how far we are from Egypt. I think they were deliberately exaggerating."

"I think Dan is right. The dialect they use here is Egyptian Bedawi, which may indicate we're closer to Egypt than we think."

When we were about ten or fifteen miles from the village, I tried to determine our location. The "main road" was just a plateau, as wide as we could see, though we couldn't see much. To maintain course, I followed the tracks of vehicles that had gone down the road before, hoping they had also aimed northeast. Ten minutes later I turned on the headlights. It was far too dangerous to drive in such complete darkness without lights, maps, or navigational equipment. Driving over a cliff is easy, and then it's too late to go back.

The light made it easier. It calmed us down, although we were still quite tense. It was a strange feeling, driving in such an enormous, empty space, alone in the desert, in complete darkness but for our headlights, with no road nor any sure direction.

"How long do you think we've been gone?" I asked, breaking the silence.

"About an hour," said Arnon. "Since we took the village's only motor vehicle, and without a telephone, it'll be awhile before they can alert the —" He paused. "Who are they in fact going to notify? The Libyan police?

I don't think they even know we're in Libya; the Slaves of Allah? I suspect they don't have a regular post nearby."

"Maybe all they have is some loose contacts in Tripoli. But who knows?" said Oded.

"It's a good question," I said. "Maybe the army, since they control everything here, but I wouldn't write off the Slaves of Allah so fast. I'm sure they're spread all over."

We drove awhile in silence. I was too tense to talk. The horizon was slowly getting brighter behind the hills, and in a few short hours the sun would begin to rise. The dirt road we were taking was more and more difficult to navigate, although we could see better now that we'd become accustomed to the darkness. The terrain was confusing, ranging from sand dunes to salt marsh to gerbel, a highly fragmented rocky terrain. Some areas were flat, while others were undulating plains of gravel or sand. There were several low mountain ranges as well as numerous dry creekbeds that widened out into plains. The air was cool, probably fifty degrees, but I knew it wouldn't last; soon the temperature would climb to ninety or so. Winter in the desert.

"We should stop for the day," I suggested. "It would be faster to travel during the day, but for us it could be too dangerous. We could be spotted."

Neither Oded nor Arnon objected, so I pulled the jeep behind a low hill, in a depression between the dunes next to a bush. I jumped out, stretched my arms, and immediately inhaled a strong smell that reminded me of my childhood days in Tel Aviv: The bush was in fact a mimosa eucalyptus, a tree with yellow flowers, thorny branches, and an intoxicating smell.

"I want to make sure we're heading in the right direction," I said.

"We don't have a map or a compass, and I didn't see any road signs," said Arnon, not hiding his skepticism. "How can you navigate when each hill looks like every other hill?" Apparently desert survival had not been part of Arnon's Mossad training.

It had been part of mine. I looked at the sky; the sun had come out from behind the hills. "I can do without a compass or maps," I said. I took the shovel from the back of the jeep and stuck it vertically in the sand. I marked the top of its shadow with juice squeezed from the mimosa flowers. Approximately fifteen minutes later I placed the shovel's stick in the ground, marking the tip of the new shadow position. I drew in the sand a straight line that joined the two points. "One end is east, and the other west," I solemnly declared. "Anyway we can always tell by looking at the position of the sun."

"So are we going in the right direction?" Oded asked.

"I'm sure we're heading generally toward Egypt," I said. "But whether that's the right direction, I don't know. You saw that the 'main road' we took was in fact ten miles wide."

"It seems a kind of natural passage through the desert rocky hills," said Oded. "But we're nearing the deep desert that divides Libya and Egypt; we might be faced with a mountain of sand. This jeep won't be able to pass over it, and we'd never make it on foot."

"Do you know of anyone who's made it?" asked Arnon. "I'd hate to find out that crossing Antarctica in the winter would have been easier."

"I know of only one successful east–west crossing of the Great Sand Sea. But that was far south of here," said Oded.

"Then what do you suggest?" I asked Oded.

"My guess is that we'll avoid the Great Sand Sea if we aim north," he answered.

"Well," I suggested, "I know U.S. military reconnaissance satellites monitor these areas to track army movements. Libya is a hostile power, Khadafi is unpredictable, and Egypt is a U.S. ally. If we can get there, we could attract their attention somehow."

"We can only hope the U.S. has intelligence showing that we were exiled here; otherwise, we'd probably be regarded by the satellite sensors as nomads on their camels, and ignored."

"Can we try to attract their attention now? Why wait?" asked Arnon.

"Good point. Why wait?" agreed Oded. "We could make some activity and hope."

"I think we should get as close as we can to the Egyptian border first. Anyway, rescue can come only from the Egyptian side."

Oded checked the ground by kicking it with his toes, and picked up some sand in his palm.

"What are you doing?" asked Arnon.

"Looking for the right spot to dig in," I answered for Oded.

Oded nodded. "In the desert, the surface temperature could be almost twenty-five degrees Fahrenheit hotter than the air. We'd better dig in."

I pointed toward a brownish spot. "We should break through the crust here," I suggested. "Once we dig down two feet we get into soft sand, where it could be twenty degrees cooler. Let's build a desert shelter."

I took one shovel and started digging; Arnon took the other and commenced efforts several feet away. Within an hour and a half we had dug a trench two feet deep, seven feet long, and six feet wide. Oded piled the sand we'd dug around three sides of the trench, creating a mound.

"Take your shirts off," I said, while taking off mine. "We need to tie them together to use as cover."

Oded and Arnon crawled in, while I secured the makeshift cover with rocks. I dug in deeper near the end of the trench, which we left without a mound so that we could get in and out more easily. We crawled in. The air was indeed cooler inside.

"I'm dead tired," I told Arnon, who was so close to me I could smell his breath. It smelled of hunger. "You know, the Bedouins say that the desert is like a bad spouse: hot during the day and cold at night."

I looked to my left. Oded was already sound asleep. I closed my eyes.

Oded woke first, Arnon and I soon after. We removed the makeshift cover we'd put over our trench. My muscles were stiff and my bones aching, but we had had a much-needed rest. We each ate ten dates and shared one of the two pita breads we'd hidden in our pockets.

"I'm worried about the safety of the water. We could all get sick, but we must get liquids or we're in real trouble."

We looked at each other, and drank the foul-tasting water out of a container. I didn't know whether the taste was so bad because the container was dirty, the water polluted, or both.

"Where are we?" asked Arnon.

"The odometer isn't working, but I think we drove eighty to ninety miles in about five or six hours. Not bad given the darkness and the conditions of the road," I said.

"Look at that," said Oded calmly, but I sensed a small degree of excitement in his voice. He pointed toward something moving in the sand.

"A snake," I said jumping to my feet. It was approximately two feet long and moved slowly in the sand away from us.

"A sand viper," said Oded. "It usually avoids confrontations and doesn't bite unless it senses danger."

"And when it does?" I asked.

"The venom is hemotoxic; it attacks your blood circulation, destroys blood vessels, and you die from internal bleeding. But if we catch him, he could be a nice meal."

"I'm not that desperate," said Arnon. The wind started blowing stronger, hurling dry bushes into the air. Sand was getting into our eyes.

"A sandstorm is coming," shouted Oded. "Let's get under cover."

The wind became wilder, and the surface of the dunes was awash with billowing sand. The wind sounded like ocean waves breaking on a beach. Arnon ran to our trench.

"No," shouted Oded, "we'll be buried alive, go to the jeep." We jumped inside and closed the canvas door.

"We must cover the hood, or sand will get into the engine and radiator," I said. I ran outside and chased down our shirts, still tied together and barely held down by a rock near our trench. I tied the shirtsleeves over the jeep's radiator. Howling winds whipped up sand, which flew through the cracks in the jeep's fabric top to our faces and hands and got into our eyes, noses, and mouths.

"We must drink," shouted Oded; "these storms suck up any drop of moisture in the air. If you have difficulty breathing, let me know. Most of the time it's caused by a rise in the atmospheric electricity as a result of the sand friction. Don't panic."

Although the jeep's canvas doors were closed, sand and dust still flew in, causing our heads to ache and making us cough. We felt nauseous. We sat in the jeep with our heads down. There was no point in talking because the sound of the storm drowned out everything. One long hour later, the wind subsided.

"Let's go," said Arnon. I looked at the sun; soon it would disappear behind the hills in the west. I shorted the switch by crossing the wires again. The engine cranked twice, and stopped. I tried again while we held our breath. Nothing moved; only the accelerated rhythm of my heart.

I lifted the hood. The coil cable was loose. I fastened it, tried again, and the engine came to life. I shifted into front-wheel drive and we were slowly able to uproot ourselves from the dune, with the double manpower boost of Arnon and Oded pushing.

Although the sandstorm had ended, the air was still full of dust that blanketed our faces, our ears, nostrils, and mouths. Oded looked like he'd fallen into a barrel of flour: His face was almost completely white. "You've aged," I said, smiling.

"You should see yourself," he said, trying to clean his face with his hands. I looked at the side mirror; I was as thoroughly covered with the fine dust as my two partners.

After driving for an hour, just before sundown, I realized we were going nowhere; in fact, I was afraid we were going in circles. Some sights I saw resembled others we had passed earlier — similar hills and desert trees. I stopped the jeep.

"What happened?" they both asked.

"I'm not sure where we're going, and we can't go on like this. We'll use up all of our fuel. We need to be certain where we're going."

# XIII

hear a truck coming," said Arnon. "Let's hope they're friendly." We waved our hands. A flatbed truck slowed down and stopped a short distance away. I realized we'd made a mistake as soon as we saw the two men approaching. One of them held a submachine gun while the other stayed close to the truck, his AK-47 leveled at us.

"Ali," shouted the man who approached with the gun. "These are the Europeans the radio was talking about." That much I understood. "Stay where you are," he ordered, pointing his gun at us. "There's a reward on your heads. You are spies."

"Spies," I said in Arabic, feigning a laugh; "we're agricultural advisers working for the United Nations. We lost our way in the desert."

"I don't believe you," he said. "Show me your hands," he ordered Arnon.

"Look at them," he said, victoriously turning to the man with the AK-47, who started approaching, "these hands have never touched a shovel." I guessed the digging of our refuge didn't count.

"You're right," said Arnon with a candor that frightened me; for a split second I thought he was going to confess. "I've never worked in the field other than while doing my research. But as a scientist I know a lot about agriculture and I teach farmers."

They searched us. We had nothing in our pockets but one dry pita. "Get on my truck," Ali shouted, pointing the gun at us.

I quickly assessed our situation. They were two, we were three. But they had two guns, and we had none. We climbed into the back of the truck. I felt defeated. But only for a moment. I never give up, not here, not ever. Oded and Arnon rode quietly, but I could sense their minds spinning like mine, looking for the next opportunity. Ali's partner — his name was Marwan, we learned — drove while Ali sat next to us with his gun ready.

We were heading back in the direction of the village we'd come from. But then a few minutes later we turned into a small side road, and after about a mile we saw a village with only five or six houses, and a small metal shed that looked out of place among the mud-brick huts.

"Get off," Ali ordered. His face was menacing.

We got off the truck. We needed to move quickly before these guys could make another move. I wasn't concerned about the police. Where would Ali find any? Killing us would be much easier, and the reward from the xenophobic government would be nice.

I'm sure Oded thought so, too, but given the fact that Ali had a gun, he chose the softer approach. "Tell him that I can prove that we're agricultural experts, and that that could be very helpful to him." I translated.

Ali looked at him in suspicion, again raising his gun and pointing it at us.

"*Rooch,*" he said in contempt. "Go." He pushed us into the metal shed and locked the door. The shed, I assumed, was the safest place to lock us up. In these villages, if the huts have doors, they rarely have locks. The shed was dark. It was nighttime, but the heat was sweltering and the stench made it difficult to breathe. Moments later our eyes became used to the dark. Judging by what we could see and smell, the shed was used as storage for agricultural tools and fertilizers.

"We have to get out of here soon," said Arnon. "In a few hours the sun will rise and" — he looked around — "we'll fry."

Oded didn't respond. He was busy rummaging through the fertilizer bags and the containers, releasing additional waves of odor into the air.

"Do you see this fertilizer?" Oded finally said.

"No, but I sure can smell it," I answered. "Let's wait until morning and then maybe then we can get our bearings." We sat in a corner and dozed off.

A few hours later we woke up, tired, thirsty, and hungry. A few beams of sun filtered through small cracks in the roof.

Oded got up and went directly to the other side of the shed. Moments later he returned, wiping his hands on his pants, carrying a small blue plastic container. "This contains acetylene. If we mix it with chlorine, it'll give us great results."

"What are you planning?" asked Arnon.

As always, Oded was calm and patient. "If we mix chlorine with acetylene it will turn into an explosive, acetylene chloride, that could blow up this shed."

"With us inside," I added. "Besides, do they have chlorine stored here?"

"I don't see any; it's too dark."

Arnon went over to Oded, who was sifting through the bags.

"There's something here that says 'NPK five–ten–ten fertilizer,'" said Arnon. "Is that any good?"

"That's a combination of nitrogen, phosphorus, and potassium, a very good start, but for a different solution." I heard the encouragement in Oded's voice. "But for what I have in mind we'd we need an additional compound."

"Come and see for yourself," suggested Arnon. "Some of these bags have no markings at all; maybe you can identify them by their color or smell."

"I need approximately thirty gallons of lime sulfur," said Oded, "a common fertilizer."

Arnon pulled out a green container. "Is this it?"

Oded looked at the label and said, "Yes, great, that's exactly what I need. Now I can prepare a small but unpleasant surprise for Ali and Marwan."

Two or three hours went by. There was no movement outside. We heard only the wind blowing. The heat was unbearable. I started banging on the tin door: "Ali, we need water; we can't breathe here."

There was no response. "I have a better idea than just sitting here," said Arnon. "Let's dig out. We have enough tools here, and this metal shed can't be built deep into the ground. What do we have to lose?"

I couldn't object to that logic. I joined Arnon and we took two shovels from the corner of the shed.

"Here," said Oded, pointing to the ground; "right over here should be a good point to start. It's the back side of the shed, away from the road, and the soil here seems sandy enough." We started digging.

Oded went to the far end of the shed.

"What are you looking for?" I asked while digging.

"A garden hose."

"How can they have hoses here? I bet they have no running water."

"Then I'll think of something else," said Oded cryptically.

An hour later we had a big pile of sand inside the shed, and we'd dug a small passage underneath the side wall that was both wide and deep enough for us to pass through. We didn't have drinking water and the shed was hot as hell. We were dripping with sweat and dying of thirst. I went first, squeezing myself out. It was good to breathe fresh, albeit dusty, air again. I looked around; nothing but desert and barren land. No sign of people. I helped Arnon out.

"Oded," I whispered when we didn't see his head coming out, "come quickly."

"I need to finish this," Oded said from the inside. Two minutes later he pushed out two shovels, and then his head wrapped with his shirt popped out. He crawled out, pressing the shirt tightly over his mouth and nose. He took a shovel and quickly covered up our passage with sand.

"Why bother?" I asked.

"I need to keep the shed as airtight as possible," he said.

I smelled gas.

"Let's move," whispered Oded.

A strong odor of rotten eggs spread in the air.

"Let's get the hell out of here," repeated Oded hurriedly.

We ran past the outskirts of the tiny village in the direction of our jeep. We'd run about half a mile before we stopped to look back. Nothing. No movement. We jumped into our jeep. Apparently our captors hadn't thought to hot-wire it. I got the engine going once again and we sped away in a cloud of dust, though we still didn't know where we were going.

"Tell me what you did," asked Arnon after he'd caught his breath and taken a few swigs from the foul-tasting water container we shared.

Oded smiled. "When you mix lime sulfur with a phosphate-containing fertilizer, you create hydrogen sulfide gas. At very high concentrations, it can kill in only one breath. I filled up the shed with the gas."

"How high was the concentration?" I asked.

"It only takes a level hundred parts per million for hydrogen sulfide to kill. Smaller concentrations cause unconsciousness and respiratory paralysis."

"We didn't need to kill them," I said.

"They won't die," said Oded. "The shed wasn't airtight, and most of the gas will escape by the time they enter. More likely, it'll knock them out for a few hours. By the time they regain consciousness, we'll be far away."

"What would happen if they entered the shed just now?" asked Arnon.

"Respiratory failure," answered Oded drily. "But in another twenty minutes, the gas won't be lethal, given the conditions of the shed, and in three hours, it will have completely evaporated. And we're safe either way."

Arnon gave Oded a confused look.

"If Ali and Marwan enter the shed soon, they'll be unconscious for a few hours, so they won't be able to chase us. And if they don't discover our escape until three hours from now, by which time the gas will have evaporated, we'll have had a head start and be far away," he concluded with a smile. I looked at him in appreciation.

"Remember Arthur Koestler?" I asked.

He looked somewhat baffled, wondering why on earth I'd mention the author given our current circumstances.

"I'm giving you a compliment," I said, seeing his expression. "He said that creativity is a type of learning process in which teacher and student are located within the same person."

We rode for an hour, and when I glanced at the rearview mirror, I sensed trouble. "There's a car speeding behind us, and it doesn't look good."

I accelerated, but the car kept following us, blinking its lights as a signal to stop. I had no intention of doing so. The terrain was solid, with small pebbles that flew back as we spun over them.

The vehicle was gaining on us. I could now make out a white SUV, with a much bigger engine than our jeep. It accelerated and appeared on my left side. "Stop the car," shouted a man from the SUV, in English. "Stop!" I accelerated; we were in open terrain. Both speeding vehicles raised a trail of dust that made it impossible to use the rearview mirror.

The SUV almost passed us, but instead of trying to block us, it slowed until it was near the very rear end, then veered sharply to the right and clipped the jeep's side. We felt the smashing blow, and nearly flipped. Usually the back side of a car is lighter than the front and therefore easier to ram, but our jeep was loaded with water and gasoline, making the back just as heavy. The road, if you could dignify the flat terrain with that name, was very wide. Just as the SUV was about to ram us, I'd anticipated them and moved to the right, softening the blow.

Time to make a move, I said to myself. "Showtime! Hold on to your seats, I'll try to shake them off."

I slowed down. "What are you doing," yelled Arnon, "they'll catch us."

I didn't respond. I stopped the jeep and quickly put the gear in reverse. "Move it," yelled Arnon. "Are you crazy?"

I selected a point ahead of us, a big bush, and began backing up. As the SUV slowed down to see what I was doing, I jammed on the gas pedal, cut the wheel sharply a quarter turn to the left, and immediately put the car into first gear. I stepped on the gas pedal all the way and the jeep leapt forward, passing them. I managed to see their faces in the rearview mirror: three mustached men who looked like soldiers trying to wave away the cloud of dust the jeep had thrown at them.

"You're going back," yelled Arnon.

"I know," I answered coolly. "It's the only way to get rid of them; their car's much faster than ours."

"What now? We can't go back," said Oded with his usual calm, although I was sure he must have been as tense as I was.

"Once we shake them off, we'll bear northeast again."

"I don't think they're going to give up that easily," said Oded.

"We should find a place to hide. I'm sure they're armed," said Arnon.

In confirmation, I heard the first bullet hitting the roof, then a whole barrage that missed us. "If a bullet hits the gasoline containers, we're history," shouted Arnon as the jeep bumped up and down on the dry terrain.

"And if they catch us alive, we won't be any better off; we need to get away," I answered as I tried to maneuver the jeep. They had all the advantages; a faster and bigger vehicle, and guns. We didn't stand a chance. As if to give credence to my thoughts, the next barrage of bullets hit the rear tires, slowing us down immediately until the jeep came to a complete stop. The SUV crossed our path and stopped in front of us. Three men jumped out with Russian Kalashnikov assault rifles.

They pointed their weapons at us and shouted in Arabic *"Ta'al hon!"* Come here!

Overpowered, we left the jeep with our hands raised. They approached and abruptly handcuffed us, not forgetting to hit me and Arnon in our torsos with their rifle butts. They pushed us into the backseat of the SUV and started driving. No words had been exchanged.

"We're in deep shit," whispered Arnon.

The guard sitting next to Arnon hit him in the face with the rifle butt, shouting *"Uskoot!"* Shut up! Blood dripped from Arnon's nose onto his shirt. His jaw was swollen. He wiped away the blood with his hand, leaned his head on the headrest, and closed his eyes.

We drove for more than three hours on the hardened terrain. The air was hot and our lips were dry. No food or water was offered to us. Arnon was moaning in pain. There was nothing I could do for him.

"He needs to see a doctor," I told the guard sitting next to him.

*"Uskoot,"* he shouted again, waving his gun. Oded signaled me to stop; Arnon would be okay.

I looked outside. We joined a paved road. Soon, increased traffic indicated we were entering a populated area. I saw small buildings, mostly commercial. A few people were walking on the side of the road.

A couple of hours later we entered a city. I managed to read a road sign: BENGHAZI. Libya's second largest city, and a major port.

We crossed several railroad tracks without a barrier. Most of the two-story buildings on the main road were shabby. Judging by the hanging laundry, they were residential on the upper floor and commercial on the street level. Many of the stores were selling olives and wool. Live chickens, sheep, and other livestock were displayed in pens out front.

Camels crossed in front of us carrying goods on their backs. The caravan trade entering the city from the interior regions lent an exotic flavor, and snarled traffic. The streets were littered with debris, and only men roamed them. As the sea breeze came through the SUV's open windows, the landscape suddenly changed; wide boulevards stretched in all directions, lined with palm, eucalyptus, and wattle trees in blossom. There were many modern buildings, including what looked like a business center built in the shape of a pyramid. We approached a modern, six-story building separated from the bay by only a narrow coastal road, and surrounded by recently planted palm trees. Our car pulled into the semi-circular driveway and stopped. A uniformed doorman, with an embroidered pocket that read UZO HOTEL, opened the passenger's-side door.

"*Marhaban beekum,*" he said, welcome. Two of our captors got out and said something to the doorman, who shut the car door. They entered the lobby while the two others stayed with us in the SUV. Ten minutes later the men returned with a big envelope, got back into the SUV, and we were off again.

Ten or fifteen minutes later we drove into a side street in an older section of Benghazi, halting in front of a two-story residential house. The driver stepped out of the car and opened the light blue iron gate with a key. We drove into a yard.

A man holding an AK-47 emerged from the house. "Get out," he shouted. We were led into a windowless basement. On the floor were three heavily used and stained mattresses. A guard brought us three plates with sticky, oily rice that was barely edible and cups of water. They'd been expecting us. The door closed behind us and the light went off.

"Are you okay?" Oded asked Arnon at the first opportunity he had to talk without risking a beating.

"Yes, I'm fine. A big headache and a broken tooth, but I'll be all right."

We sat on the mattresses wondering what was coming next. Twice escaped and twice caught; would we have a third opportunity? We fell asleep with the uncertainty of our fate weighing on us.

We awoke when the door opened and the light came on. The same two men from the day before entered, holding their menacing AK-47s.

"Come," said one of them, pointing his gun at us. We climbed out of the basement. We were tired, hungry, and smelly. It was early morning. The SUV was waiting, motor running. Twenty minutes later we arrived at the port. There we boarded a fishing boat: a ninety-foot-long bottom long-liner and set-liner, probably for fishing tuna. We were led into the lower deck. "Stay here and don't move," said our guard. They didn't bother handcuffing us. I guess they presumed we had no place to escape to. Also, bound men attract attention, and maybe they thought they didn't need any. An hour later the boat's engine started and we slowly moved away. Direction unknown.

Two hours later we were allowed to go up to the deck and sit. I counted a crew of seven. The senior-looking man approached us. "I'm Captain Ibrahim. If you make no foolish mistakes, nothing will happen to you." And what would happen to us if we did attempt escape? He must have read my mind because he continued as if in answer, "The sharks would love a free meal."

"Sharks?" I asked, looking at Oded.

"Sure," he said, amused. "Bluntnose sixgill, *Hexanchus griseus.*"

"Very funny," I said. "What is it?"

"A fifteen-foot-long, thousand-pound shark; they're fairly common in this part of the Mediterranean."

We were offered flaked and dried fish and a bottle of water. The journey itself was almost pleasant. The sea was calm, and a light breeze kept us cool in the high temperatures. From the position of the sun I knew where we were going. I couldn't see land, although I figured it couldn't be too far given the seagulls flying above. When evening approached, we were ordered back to the lower deck. A fisherman gave us a loaf of bread, three cucumbers, five olives, and a small bottle of olive oil. "Stay here!" ordered Ibrahim, who'd followed us to our cabin. Compared with our previous diet, this was a gourmet dinner.

After many more hours of uneventful sailing, we slowed down. The engine lowered torque, and the boat rattled until it halted. We heard noises up on deck. A sailor came down the stairs into our cabin, warned us to keep quiet, and locked our door. Two hours later we were sweating profusely in the cramped cabin when the boat started moving slowly again.

"Let me guess," said Arnon. "We've arrived at Port Said, Egypt."

"How can you tell?"

"We were going east. The seagulls indicated we've been near the coast most of the time. A day's sail would get us to Egypt, and Port Said would be a logical place to stop."

"I think you're right," I said. "If we'd been going north, into the sea, we'd have felt it. The waves would have been higher if we'd been out at sea, and we've had a smooth ride. So if we stopped in Port Said and they're now hiding us, we'll probably be crossing the Suez Canal heading south." Port Said is situated a few miles west of the Port Suez bypass approach channel to the Suez Canal.

"Then where are they taking us?" asked Oded.

"Who knows? It could be southern Egypt, Saudi Arabia, Somalia, or Yemen," I said. "And knowingly or unknowingly, any one of these countries could be harboring our terrorists."

We were allowed onto the upper deck after the sun went down, and there was no doubt we were in the Suez Canal. The coastline looked low and flat. We could see Egyptian peasants in the distance. I saw a few fishing boats and for a short minute entertained the thought of jumping overboard and swimming to shore, which looked to be less than two hundred yards away. But the presence of the two gunmen sitting next to me made me change my mind. I had no doubt they would shoot to kill if I tried it — and I still had a life, children, ambition, and unfulfilled plans.

"We'll soon know," I said. "The canal is only a hundred miles long, and at the speed we're going we'll be through in about ten hours."

The fishermen on board fried fish on a small range and gave us fairly large portions to take down to our cabin, where we were ordered to stay. We couldn't talk freely. The boat was too small. But I was sure that Oded and Arnon were doing what I was doing: trying to think of ways to escape. When we talked at all we did so in English, strictly avoiding Hebrew. Far more than the ten hours I'd calculated it would take us to travel the length of the Suez Canal, passing through Lake Manzalah, Lake Timsah, and the Bitter Lakes, had passed, but we still weren't allowed on the upper deck.

"We're going farther south," I said. "Which means that if we passed the lakes and then the city of Suez, we'd be in the Gulf of Suez. Next on our right would be Sudan, Eritrea, and Ethiopia; on our left, Saudi Arabia and Yemen. If we continue south, we'll have to cross the Straits of Djibouti then arrive in Somalia. The boat needs supplies, fuel and water, so we're bound to stop someplace."

The voyage settled into a routine. We were allowed on the upper deck for meals and fresh air several times a day, but were kept down below each time the boat approached other ships or ports, and at night.

On the fifth day, if I hadn't lost count, there was sudden activity on board. We were locked in our cabin. The boat slowed, then stopped. Our cabin door was opened, and we were led to the upper deck. It was late at night. I looked around and could barely make out a dark coastline. A smaller motorboat was approaching us. After an exchange of shouted Arabic, the motorboat stopped next to us and we were told to jump in. Soon we were speeding through the low waves toward the shore. The beach looked rugged and hilly, without any sign of civilization. In addition to the helmsman, there were three gunmen on board. Not a word was exchanged. We entered a small inlet and the engine stopped. The gunmen made us jump into the shallow water with them. After the initial shock, the cool water was quite pleasant. I hadn't had a bath or a shower since dipping into the pond at Bir Tamam's oasis. The water was up to our waists, so I took the opportunity to cleanse myself as much as I could. Arnon and Oded did the same. We walked up the beach, and after climbing a hill saw a flashlight signal.

"Here they are," said one gunman. Not far away I saw a light truck parked on a dirt road. We were told to sit in the back and the truck moved out. After more than a four-hour jarring drive on a rough dirt road, most of it climbing mountains in pitch darkness, we arrived at an inhabited area. It was past midnight. I looked at the few people I could see in the narrow streets, attempting to determine where we were. But customs and dress don't change abruptly just because you cross a political border. We could have been in Eritrea, Ethiopia, Somalia, or any other close location. The truck slowed down; we were nearing a small town. There was a road sign in Arabic. I slowly read it: AL-JUMHURĪYAH AL-YAMANIYAH.

"Guys," I whispered, "we're in Yemen."

"Damn," said Arnon. Yemen was a lawless, remote country, openly cooperating with terrorists of the worst kind and offering them safe haven. Terrorists' strength is in their small number and their lawlessness. They have no sovereign territory, and that makes them hard to trace and difficult to predict. On the other hand, their sparse numbers complicate things when all of a sudden they need to assume duties usually carried out by governments, such as maintaining prisons. I assumed they were moving us around to avoid detection by the outside world.

The truck continued along a winding road, climbing higher and higher. The air became cooler. We passed a few houses built into the hills, and saw very few cars. A few of the homes had electricity, but we were far from what I'd call civilization. We arrived at a three-story building at the top hill of the town and were locked immediately in a room on the ground floor. We got water but no food. The floor was covered by straw. I figured they must have kept sheep there. We made nests of straw to soften the hard ground, and we fell asleep.

Early in the morning we woke up from the cold and the city noises. Muezzins called from the minarets of mosques in all directions, "Hasten to prayer!"

"Where do you think we are?" asked Oded.

"I can only guess," I said. "I would say we are at least five thousand feet high. We must have heard more than ten different muezzins calling, so we must be in a city. If I had to guess, I'd say we're in the capital, Sana'a."

"Why the hell move us here?" asked Oded. The strain was getting to him, his voice tired and weaker.

"They are going to kill us here," he continued, answering his own question in despair.

"I don't think so," I said; "exactly the opposite. They brought us to Yemen to keep us alive. They could have killed us in Libya. I think we're here because nobody knows this country well, not even the locals. You think Libya is primitive? Try Yemen. At least Libya has a government, crazy as it is, that grinds everyone under its boot, even organizations they support. Even as Khadafi's pets, the Slaves of Allah couldn't do anything in Libya without his consent. Since Khadafi is so unpredictable, they couldn't entrust us to him. We're a valuable commodity in the trade-in business."

Although Yemen has a national government, it has no real power. Yemen has been run in the same manner for thousands of years as a loose federation of tribes. Each tribe has a leader with no respect or allegiance to other tribes, and certainly not to central authority. All of this made the country a fine place for the Slaves of Allah to hide their treasures.

"I have no idea which tribe's auspices we're under, but it doesn't matter, because none of them have foreign interests or policies. I wouldn't be surprised if they don't even know or care where Canada or Hungary are," I said.

"So where does that leave us?" asked Oded.

"The Slaves of Allah are smart. They know, given Yemen's lawlessness, that no one will pressure the tribe to release us, since the tribe obeys no one — and as long as the Slaves of Allah pay their price, they will hold us here."

We all knew that Yemeni tribesmen kidnap hundreds of foreigners every year. Their families or employers pay a ransom, and they're released. And if no one pays, *Allah yerahemo*: God will have mercy on them.

An hour later the door opened, and a skinny boy in a long galabiya brought us three bowls of baked beans, three large thin pita breads, and some putrid water. We devoured the food, and had to drink the water for survival. We were then moved to a higher floor, to a room with windows that had bars. Arnon and Oded were made to sit and wait on a wooden bench while I was brought into an adjacent room. A fat man with three small knife scars on his face was behind a desk. I was told to sit on a stool. An armed guard with sunglasses was standing silently in the corner behind me.

"My name is Issam. I hear you made trouble," he said in heavily accented English. "I'll finish you here if you try anything." He looked and sounded capable of being good to his promise.

"Why am I here?" I asked.

"I ask the questions, and you answer," he said, his voice rising. "Understand?"

I nodded and lowered my head.

"Who do you work for?"

"Transcontinental Money Solutions, Limited."

"I've heard that shit before," he said. "I'm going to ask one more time, who do you work for?"

"I already answered you, Transcontinental Money Solutions, Limited, a financial services company in Victoria, Seychelles. I can prove it."

After twenty minutes of unsophisticated interrogation, I could evaluate my interrogator. He was street-smart, but that was it. I crafted my responses accordingly.

"And I say you are a CIA agent working for Mr. Henderson."

"CIA? No way. I'm wanted by the FBI on money-laundering charges. You can easily verify that. In fact, I wouldn't be surprised if my name and photo had been posted on INTERPOL Red Notices as internationally wanted."

Not a bad idea, I thought, as I floated the bold lie. In fact, I wished Eric and Brian had thought of it earlier. Unlike American law, the laws of some countries do allow arrest for international extradition based on a Red Notice. But a Red Notice only says that an INTERPOL member country wants the named fugitive on felony charges; wants help in locating the fugitive; would like any member country finding the fugitive to make an arrest if possible; and will send an extradition request.

Now came the surprise. "I know that," he acknowledged. "We saw your picture posted, but I think it's a ploy." I was encouraged, because his body language indicated that he wasn't entirely convinced it was a ploy. He leaned forward and moved his hands.

So Eric had thought of it after all. My appreciation of him increased slightly.

"Ploy? I wish," I said matter-of-factly. "If I ever set foot in the United States I'll be locked up for twenty years."

"Why?"

"Because I helped too many people avoid U.S. taxes. On two separate occasions indicted individuals made a deal with their prosecutors and fingered me. The U.S. government was more interested in going after the preacher than after his followers. I'm a wanted man."

"Why did you meet Mr. Henderson?"

I still didn't know what this "Mr. Henderson" meant to them. He didn't seem to know Eric's first name. Another promising sign. My previous interrogator hadn't used it, either.

"I met him only once. He wanted to hire my services to hide his assets from his wife. That's what he told me."

"Mr. Henderson is CIA, didn't you know that?"

"Only because my interrogators in France told me. How would I know? A guy calls me on the phone and wants my asset-protection services. I don't ask him for his first name or what he does for a living. Why should I care? If he has enough money to pay me, then I work for him. Plain and simple. For all I care he could be a restaurant chef and I still wouldn't know. I don't even know if his real name is Henderson. Many of my clients assume new names. If he was CIA, do you think he'd tell me?"

My interrogator kept on, and I gave him the same answers. My impression that my captors knew nothing about me other than my initial contact with Eric became stronger. So the legend the CIA had constructed had held water after all. I'd expected violence, but none was forthcoming, or even threatened.

"Tell me about your expertise," he asked again. It had been three hours since the interrogation had started. I was tired and hungry. My interrogator also hadn't had anything to eat or drink, but he'd smoked half a pack of cigarettes and blown the smoke in my face. I had the creeping feeling this was not an ordinary interrogation. They had all the answers; luckily, they asked the wrong questions. I wasn't being forced to divulge tactical or strategic information that might assist them in their causes. It was becoming increasingly clear that they knew very little or nothing at all about me, and that the only reason I'd been kidnapped was because I'd been fingered by Zhukov. But if that were all there was to it, I would have been either killed or dumped. So there had to be another reason why they were holding me and why they showed such interest in my professional skills. Maybe Zhukov had given them only half the story.

So were they trying to recruit me? Not a bad idea. Not at all, not for them, and definitely not for me. I had already demonstrated my corruptibility by directing them to my INTERPOL picture. As far as they were concerned, it would only be a question of time before I offered my services in exchange for my freedom and maybe some cash.

Given that this was probably where they were going, I allowed Issam to put me through my paces, give a show of my expertise. I explained how to establish a trust in Liechtenstein and appoint two local lawyers as your trustees so that they would be bound by attorney–client privilege, in addition to their principality's secrecy laws; how to use a Swiss numbered bank account; how to use nominees in opening bank accounts; and how to use the Internet to make financial transactions anonymously.

Issam was very attentive. Too attentive, I thought. He was taking notes. I wasn't being interrogated, I was being milked. When I sensed where he was headed, I, through the power of suggestion, led him into posing a question. This was a slow and subtle process nurtured by the information I was giving, or hinting at, thereby causing my interrogator to nose around exactly where I wanted him to.

"What's your connection to your two comrades?"

"Connection? Nothing. I just met them in Libya. Never saw them before. They were prisoners like me."

"They are spies," he said in contempt.

"Really? I thought they were Hungarian scientists. We talked a lot about science. The older guy, István, really knows things about biology. I think he is a professor, and the other guy is his assistant. So I'm afraid you could be wrong here as well. Why would the Hungarian government spy on you?"

"Your friends will soon be executed," he said with an evil smile, sending chills down my back. I said nothing. I knew Issam was closely observing my reaction.

"Aren't they worth anything in a trade-off? The Hungarian government will let them die just like that?"

"You could save them, and yourself," said Issam, finally showing his hand.

"How?"

"You mentioned earlier that you could move money through the Internet without being detected. We already know all the tricks. If you're such a big expert, prove it."

"Sure. I could do that. Will you let us go then?"

"No," he said candidly. "But that would delay their execution."

"For how long?"

I was bargaining with Issam. The situation was incredible.

"Until we get a good price for them, or until we just shoot them. It costs us money to keep you here, food and everything."

Was he on such a budget that he couldn't afford to shell out two dollars for our daily meals? This guy was part of a group that had moved sixty million. I knew he was bluffing. From this I learned that he was a poor liar, and that he thought I was stupid. Which usually drives me mad. Here, it served my interests.

"Frankly," I said, "I don't care who you shoot, as long as it's not me. What's in it for me?" I distanced myself from the idea that we were a ring of spies who felt our fates to be tied together.

"Your life," he snapped, apparently surprised I put zero value on Oded and Arnon.

"I'm going to die anyway," I said, bluffing and telling the truth at the same time. "I need more than that. I'm worth more to you alive than dead. There wouldn't be too many bidders for my corpse, except maybe my ex-wife — but since I stopped sending her alimony checks, my corpse isn't worth much."

"If you prove useful, we might consider additional incentives for you. But first you have to convince me that you're as big in your profession as you say you are."

"How? I'm in a cell in what I'm guessing to be Yemen, and the world's financial centers don't exactly have branches here."

"I can give you a computer that would connect you anywhere."

"With a modem?" My interest reached a new high, but my face was bland.

"Yes, a dial-up. If you are lucky you could get connected."

I got up ready to go, but I was sent back to our group cell. Had I been too enthusiastic?

The reception I received from Arnon and Oded was lukewarm. "Were you guys interrogated while I was gone?" I asked them.

They shook their heads. So I had been singled out. Was it a coincidence that they'd chosen me to be the first to be interrogated? How did

Oded and Arnon feel about it? Was their mixed response signaling some-thing? Were they suspicious of me? I was sure they had talked about it. I decided not to raise the issue.

The following morning Issam led me to an office on the second floor. As we passed through the corridor, another door opened and a man exited. I had a glimpse of a room full of weapons and military equipment. When we reached the messy office, an old IBM computer with a mono-chrome monitor was waiting for me.

The piece belonged in a museum, I thought. I turned it on; the Windows 95 operating system came up. I tested the modem and man-aged to connect to the Internet on my third attempt. I turned to Issam. "We're on. What do you want me to do?"

"Show me how to get an anonymous ATM card," he said.

I quickly logged on to a site offering ATM cards that could be used in sixty thousand locations around the world to withdraw cash or make pay-ments in point-of-sale locations.

"Look at that ATM offer," I said; "you could use it in gas stations, department stores, and supermarkets, or even trade securities with it. No ID is required to get the card. You could mail the bank a deposit of five thousand dollars and have the ATM card sent to you anywhere."

"Continue," he ordered.

"The annual fee is two hundred dollars, while the initial setup cost is seven fifty." Clearly someone was capitalizing on people's need for confi-dentiality.

"Fine," he said, writing something in his notebook. "Now show me how to open a numbered Swiss bank account."

I felt that the more and the longer I talked, the better my chances of survival grew. "Most of the civilized world's governments have passed laws against anonymous accounts, where even the banker does not know the account holder's identity. So if a client is willing to identify himself before a bank officer, then most banks, particularly those that offer 'pri-vate banking' or 'wealth management,' don't have a problem calling the account by a different name or just giving it a number. All bank accounts have numbers, so what these institutions simply do is remove the owner's name from open records, such as checkbooks or computer databases available to all bank employees. But when a government agency or a court wants to know who the real owner is, the bank will divulge his or her identity in no time."

"So the trick about a 'numbered account' is just a ruse?"

"Nowadays, pretty much. But —" I paused, building his expectation. "— there are other ways to hide your identity."

"Tell me."

I hesitated. Was I helping a terrorist organization, or simply establishing the authenticity of my legend? I decided to answer. In any case, this information was easily obtained, in how-to books or on the Internet.

"Simple. The bank wants to know you are who you say you are. So give them any identity you can support with documents, such as a passport, or any another government-issued ID. Some small banks would be satisfied with less."

"And how do you do that, other than forgery?"

"Many countries' passports are easily available for a fee or following an investment in their country. Many brokers help you do that. When a foreign government issues you a passport, even if you're not a citizen, give them the alias you've selected. But don't travel with this passport; most countries would require a visa, as well as proof of financial means, such as a pay stub. Use the passport only as identification for opening bank accounts."

"Show me," he said, and pointed at the computer. I logged on to www.passportsforanyone.com; the monitor slowly displayed a list of thirty countries that offered their passports to nonresident aliens. I told him that just because you had a passport from a country didn't give you a right to settle in that country. Countries distinguished between citizens, with their many rights, and passport holders — who simply possessed fancy IDs.

This time Issam seemed to be really satisfied. He smiled in content.

"Okay," he said, "I think we could do business together. Show me how I can get a foreign passport under any name I choose."

I gave him a startled look. "It's not that simple," I finally said.

"But a few minutes ago you told me it was easy." He sounded disappointed and angry. The smile was gone. "Maybe you're not such a big expert after all; maybe the only big thing about you is your ego — and your mouth."

"Okay," I relented, hoping he wouldn't become suspicious that I had given in so easily. "First you start by deciding which country's passport suits your needs best."

"How would I know that? There are thirty countries to choose from."

"You could ask for a brochure from the company that arranges these deals. It would probably include many more details, like requirements and pricing. Once you have more information, you could choose. I can help you with that."

"Fine, ask for a brochure, but don't try anything funny, or you're dead."

"What can I do?" I asked with a shrug, but I knew exactly what I intended to do.

Again I logged on to www.passportsforanyone.com, clicking on CONTACT US.

"Here's the form," I said. "They want to know what the passport's intended use is. What should I write?"

"I want to be able to travel without interruption," said Issam.

I AM AN INTERNATIONAL BUSINESSMAN, I typed looking at Issam for his confirmation, and when he nodded I continued, AND I WANT TO BE ABLE TO TRAVEL UNHINDERED AND WITHOUT INTERRUPTION.

"Where should they send the brochure?"

Issam thought for a moment. "Post Office Box Two-Two-Five, Sana'a, Yemen."

"I suggest you give a name, just any name, or even better the name of a company; it will impress them with your ability to pay their fees."

"Company name?" He scratched his head. "Just make up a company name," he finally said.

"Okay, is 'Snap Dogfood Importers Limited' acceptable?"

"Whatever," he said. I typed it on the form and hit SEND.

"What do you want to see next?" I asked. We were rolling.

"We're done for now. Here is your first reward." I was taken to a different cell and allowed to take a cold-water shower. A barber was brought in to shave my beard and trim my hair. A long white galabiya was given to me. I felt like a bridegroom on his wedding night, although I had a feeling that in the end, I'd be the one to get screwed.

As I returned to our cell, Arnon and Oded looked at me suspiciously. They were dirty and bearded.

"What did you tell them to get so manicured?" asked Oded, with more than a tad of suspicion in his voice.

"They were actually relatively civil to me," I said, adding quietly, "they also threatened to execute you unless I helped them."

"I hope you proved your expertise?" said Arnon, touching his throat.

"Of course. Once it was clear that I was a professional asset protector, they must have realized that I was probably captured by mistake," I said with a wink.

I could see him pick up on my hint.

"I just showed them what I know best: how to shield assets. Maybe they could test your scientific knowledge and see that you are indeed scientists. That wouldn't be difficult, would it?"

"I wish they would," said Oded. Arnon said nothing.

But nothing happened. We had a measly dinner and went to sleep. When I woke up, I saw Oded and Arnon in the corner of the room. Oded was cupping something in his hand.

"What are you doing?" asked Arnon, looking at Oded's hands. "Be careful, those things bite."

Oded looked at him reassuringly. "I know. I've handled hundreds of them before." He brought his hand closer to Arnon. Oded was holding a spider between two twigs. "Isn't she a beauty?"

"That's a far cry from anything I'd call a beautiful . . . and how do you know it's a *she*?" said Arnon, stepping back.

"Years of experience," said Oded. "Let me introduce the black widow."

"The one that eats her male after she has sex with him?"

"That's the one," he answered, holding it with the twigs.

"That's ungrateful. Why is she doing it?"

"Maybe she doesn't want to hear him snoring afterward."

"I didn't know you could find them here. I thought they were only in North and South America."

"Well, there are only two species of black widow that are common in the Middle East, *Latrodectus pallidus*, which occurs from Libya to Azerbaijan, and this one, a *Latrodectus hystrix*, from Aden and Yemen."

"And do they bite like their American cousins?"

"Sure. It's rarely felt, but the area will swell with two visible spots appearing where the fangs have entered the skin."

"So the bite isn't painful?" I asked.

"On the contrary, the bite isn't painful, but the poison is very much so. You can also get a shock, fever, nausea, headache, and elevated blood pressure. You may have difficulty breathing and perspire heavily."

"And then you die?" asked Arnon.

"Not unless you're very young or very old, or already suffer from a heart condition. If left untreated, heart and lung failure could result in death."

"And everybody else?"

"Recovers completely within two days, except for a rare side effect," he said with a grin. "Some men find it difficult to maintain an erection and become impotent for several months."

"Let it go," said Arnon in disgust. "I mean, step on it, I don't feel like being bitten."

"I have other plans for her," said Oded voicelessly, just moving his lips. "The venom of the black widow spider is fifteen times as toxic as the venom of a rattlesnake. All spiders are venomous, but the venoms of most are too weak or minute in quantity to have noticeable effects on humans."

"So what do you have in mind?"

"If we had a cobra, one would be enough. But the next best thing, which happens to be available, is the female black widow. Ten to twenty of these ladies would be enough to take our guards out of commission for hours. I don't think we should sit and wait for our execution; I don't want to be a sacrificial lamb," he whispered.

Silence.

"Okay," I said, keeping my voice low, "so we need female spiders? How the hell can you tell which is which?"

"The female is easy to identify: It has two red spots on the dorsal surface of the abdomen."

"And what do we do with them? Plant them in the guards' clothing hoping they'll bite?"

"No," said Oded, "we can't leave anything to chance. I could extract enough venom from them to cause our guards to run for help, and leave us behind. We could sharpen twigs to toothpick size, dip them in venom, and prick the guards. The venom causes severe pain in the abdomen, to the muscles, and in the soles of the feet. They will also sweat profusely and have swollen eyelids. A spider's venom blocks specific channels in the brain. We'd be the least of their concerns."

"Twigs?" I asked. "Where would we get twigs?"

He pulled out a few long sturdy straws from his pocket. "I picked them up from the room where we slept our first night here."

"We'll be executed if they catch us again, and certainly if we kill our guards," said Arnon, barely moving his lips.

"No, nothing of the sort. It'll be really painful, but they'll live."

"Okay, I'm convinced," I said. "Now go convince the spider to give you its venom without biting you. How do you milk these creatures?"

"In the lab we mist them with carbon dioxide gas to numb them. Then we hold the spider under a microscope, and use electrified tweezers to give it a short electrical jolt. That causes the spider to spew venom from its fangs."

"How much venom do you get out of one black widow?"

"You need six or seven hundred milkings to get one drop," said Oded, "but in the lab we can milk about ninety black widows in an hour. But we don't need production like that. One drop is a lot of poison. All I need are three black widows to neutralize one guard."

"I don't see a microscope or electrical tweezers in our cell," I said. "So how are you going to milk them?"

"We could get the venom either by milking or extracting it from dissected glands. If we don't kill the spider, we need to make it feel danger. When in the threatening stance, tiny droplets of venom can be seen at the tip of each fang. Using suction, a glass pipette connected to a vacuum pump collects the venom droplets at the end of the chelicerae, the first pair of fangs near the mouth that they use for grasping and piercing."

"Oded, we're not in a lab here. Sorry I have to remind you."

"I know. Milked venoms are generally preferred because they do not contain extraneous materials extracted from the glands and tend to be more consistent and easier to work with. However, that is for medical and pharmacological purposes. Here we could use gland extracts because they do not require so much equipment."

"So why the hesitation?" I asked. "Just kill it."

"Not so fast. This one is the first one I caught, so I need to keep it until we have several more, or keep on milking this one."

"So you just smash it?"

"No, look what I'm doing," he said as if I were one of students. "I'm opening the venom apparatus, which includes the fangs and paturons, the basal portions of the upper fangs, the glands, the venom ducts, and the associated muscles." He used a half-inch stone that he chipped from the wall, with a three-inch piece of straw.

"That's too much entomology for me, I give up." I said. "And what do you do for milking equipment?"

"Since I don't have a glass pipette I'm using straw, and we have plenty of that here."

"But how do you pump the venom? You're not going to suck it," asked Arnon.

"No, I saw that Yahye, our guard, uses a dropper for his eyedrops. If you steal it, I'll do the rest."

"We're locked in this crummy cell, and he's behind the door, so how exactly do you propose we steal it?" asked Arnon.

"We could lure him into giving it to us," I ventured. "Does it matter why he's using the eyedrops?"

"He has trachoma," said Oded.

"How can you tell?"

"I'm a doctor," said Oded patiently. "Besides, if you were to look at him, you could also tell. You don't have to be a doctor for that."

"His eyes do look terrible."

"I'm not surprised he has it," Oded said. "The highest incidence of trachoma is in the dry, hot, dusty climatic zones. In some rural villages almost everyone has either active trachoma or scars from an earlier infection."

"What causes it?"

"*Chlamydia trachomatis*. It's a microorganism that spreads through contact with eye discharge from the infected person on towels, handkerchiefs, or fingers, and through transmission by eye-seeking flies. After years of repeated infection, the inside of the eyelid may be scarred so severely that the eyelid turns inward and the lashes rub on the eyeball, scarring the cornea. If untreated, the condition leads to blindness."

"Is there a cure?"

"If used early on in the infection, oral antibiotics can prevent long-term complications. Our guard, had he been treated earlier, could have taken erythromycin or doxycycline and solved the problem. But now it seems that he'd need eyelid surgery for his lid deformities."

"So the eyedrops he uses aren't helping him? Maybe that could be our angle."

"I don't know what he uses. I didn't get a close look at the label. But whatever it is, it can't treat the advanced stage of his disease."

"Good," I said. "Let's try this." I banged on the door.

Yahye opened it. "What do you want?" he responded in a menacing tone. His eyelids looked so awful, I had difficulty keeping my gaze on him.

"Yahye, I don't know if I told you, but this person here" — I pointed at Oded — "is a very famous doctor. He might be able to help you with your eyes."

The expression on Yahye's face changed. "Really?"

"Yes," I said, "he has helped many people."

Gingerly, Yahye entered our cell.

"Why don't you examine him to assure him you are indeed a doctor?" I suggested.

"I can't touch him, I have no gloves, but let's see what we have here," Oded said as I translated. After examining his eyes closely, Oded concluded, "It's chronic trachoma, a bad case, no question about it. Are you taking any medication?"

Yahye nodded.

"Why don't you let the doctor tell you if you are doing the right thing," I suggested.

Yahye left our door open and ran to his desk a few yards away. He returned holding the bottle.

"Let me see that," said Oded, pointing at the small bottle.

Yahye handed him the bottle suspiciously. Oded looked at the label. "That's a steroid," said Oded, shaking his head. "It doesn't help your condition and is likely to cause serious side effects such as glaucoma and cataract." He turned toward Yahye, signaling with his hands, *Don't use it!*

"What's wrong?" I asked, not knowing whether Oded was playing our game of social engineering or adhering to his ethics as a medical doctor.

"Seriously," he said. "He could lose his eyesight. It contains hydrocortisone. That's a steroid that could turn him blind."

I told Yahye what Oded had just said. "He's a doctor. You should listen to him."

Yahye looked confused.

"Ask him who gave him the bottle."

I asked. "He said he saw a foreign tourist using it in the market, and he stole his bag from him."

"That medication was probably prescribed for another condition. See if you could persuade him to leave the bottle in the cell."

"Leave this bottle with the doctor," I said to Yahye, "and the doctor will try to fix something for you."

Yahye hesitated but finally handed me the bottle and hesitantly left our cell.

"First stage successfully accomplished," I declared. "Now what?"

"Now I try to milk this lady," said Oded. "Here, give me that straw."

# XIV

handed him the straw I had picked off the dirty floor. Oded gently milked the spider, restraining it with the two small twigs he kept in his pocket. I stood next to him, amazed.

Suddenly I heard noises and commotion. The roar of a helicopter was too strong to ignore; I climbed up to the window. Three U.S. Navy Seahawk twin-engine helicopters were hovering a short distance from our cell. Approximately twenty soldiers slid down a wire from the helicopter to the roof of the adjacent building. An explosion shook us. The building rattled and filled with smoke. I heard people yelling in Arabic and running through the corridors. I smelled the familiar odor of gunpowder and explosives. Machine-gun shots filled the air. The shouting and yelling became more frantic.

"Help's on the way. This is our chance," I said. "Let's kick this door down."

After the third attempt the wooden door gave way and we spilled into a hallway full of smoke. People were running, waving guns. Nobody paid attention to us. The corridor was empty; Yahye had disappeared.

"Let's run to the roof," said Arnon. "It's only one flight up." On the flat roof, we could hear the beating of helicopter rotors, but the taller building opposite us was blocking our view. The clanking noise of the helicopter's blades grew louder. We looked to the east. "That's where one of them is coming from," yelled Arnon. A moment later a Seahawk was hovering above us. We frantically waved our hands, and Arnon took off his formerly white, now almost black shirt, and signaled *We are here!*

A rescue hoist cable sprang from the Seahawk and two soldiers slid down, automatic rifles tied to their backs. The first soldier, a Delta Force Green Beret, shouted, "Identify yourself!"

"Dr. Oded Regev," yelled Oded.

"Arnon Tal," said Arnon in a hoarse voice.

"Dan Gordon," I said in huge relief.

He asked us to harness ourselves, one at a time, to the end of the cable, while he and the other soldier covered us. Gunfire was all around, and the soldiers returned fire. We flattened ourselves onto the rooftop. The fire stopped. Another hovering helicopter started firing suppression rounds from its machine guns. "Hurry up," the soldiers next to me shouted. Oded went up first, and Arnon followed. Just as it was my turn, we heard more gunfire. I ran to the side wall and sought shelter next to the Green Beret.

"Sir," he shouted, "go to the other side, you'll attract fire aimed at me. I have a gun and flak, and you don't."

"I want to help you," I shouted, "give me your other weapon, you must let me! I see the bastards on the opposite roof. Give me cover and I'll take them out."

"Can't do that!"

"Aren't you here to help us?"

"No. We're here to save your ass. Not to kiss it. Now get to the other side; I'll cover you."

This was no time to argue. I ran to the other side of the roof. The Seahawk slid sideways while Arnon hung on the cable. Oded was already safely inside. Both of the other helicopters were now using their machine guns against attackers on the ground and in the building.

I could easily tell that the fire aimed at us was sporadic and inaccurate. I was not afraid of being hit. In my combat years in the Israeli armed forces, my teammates liked to say that we shouldn't worry, because "every bullet has an address." My response was that I was afraid of the ones that said "to whom it may concern." But here, the bullets all seemed somehow aimless.

The Seahawk overhead spat fire from two 7.62-millimeter machine guns mounted on its windows. The cacophony was music to my ears. I heard another explosion as a Hellfire air-to-ground, laser-guided subsonic missile hit the adjacent building. Smoke and fire erupted as the building collapsed. The gunfire aimed at us ceased again. The cable was lowered and the Green Beret helped me harness myself. Five minutes later we were all aboard. The Seahawk made a complete turn, gained additional altitude, and headed east to the aircraft carrier USS *Constellation* in the open sea, a few miles east of Yemen, with the two other helicopters following.

"Welcome aboard," said the captain as we set foot on the landing deck.

"I'm so glad to be here," I said, "and I speak for the three of us. Thank you very much. I'm glad you came."

"We had just showed up in the neighborhood when your message arrived," he said, smiling. "We'll get you to an airport to return you home. My men here will take care of you," he added as he took in the terrible hygienic condition of Oded and Arnon. He returned to the command deck.

"Message?" asked Arnon. "What message?" We were being led by two sailors through a maze of corridors in the deck below.

"I used a 'hello number,'" I told him, "a procedure where, without identifying myself or my location, I can use a code word to signal an emergency situation to my backup team. While giving Issam a few not-too-secret facts about my trade, I maneuvered him into asking for a brochure from one of those Web sites that lure scumbags like him. Whoever read the message originating in Yemen would also recognize the code word *snap* — the name of my golden retriever. Anything that comes from this part of the world is automatically suspect, and they could see the IP address it was sent from." I thanked in my heart my instructors at The Farm for working with me during the short training I had there on "artifact" communications in distress situations.

After an hour-long shower for us all, haircuts and beard trims for Oded and Arnon, a hearty meal, and a thorough medical checkup by the carrier's doctor, it was time to let go of the tension. I called my children, and, yes, I shed tears. "I'm safe," I managed to say. They cried, too, and I was overcome by emotion. I'd already been through hell in my professional life, but this ordeal had been stronger anything I'd expected. At times I had been sure I'd die, and violently. I'd been trained to confront the possibility of imminent death, or at least I thought I had. Actually staring my mortality in the face turned out to be something I simply didn't know how to deal with. There just aren't words for this experience.

I went out to the deck to calm down and wipe my tears. An hour later, I joined Oded and Arnon, who had also called their families, in the roomy cabin of the carrier, where we embraced our freedom and sipped ice-cold ginger ale. After chatting for a while and exchanging impressions, I remembered something I had never told them.

"Guys," I said, "do you remember the third captured message I told you about?"

"Yes, what about it?" asked Arnon in a disinterested voice.

"I wish I'd broken it earlier," I said. "We could have saved your asses."

That got their attention.

I quoted the message: "'In case of doubt return with the merchandise to base.' Now I know what that merchandise was. It was you!"

Oded raised his head.

"Think about it," I continued. "That message was sent before they met with you to negotiate the 'scientific cooperation'; the message clearly says, if you suspect them, kidnap them and bring them to the base."

"That's Monday-morning quarterbacking," said Arnon. "We didn't know it then. They must have figured out that they were being watched, and we walked into their trap like amateurs."

"If it's any comfort to you, the same thing happened to me. I was careless."

"We weren't careless," said Arnon defensively; "we did everything as planned. But I guess the planning was screwed up."

I had no comment on that. All I knew was what Benny had told me, and that obviously was not the whole picture. Knowing the Mossad, though, I knew there would be an internal investigation, conclusions would be drawn, and at the very least the findings would influence future operations.

After a restful week sailing the Indian Ocean, we arrived in Capetown, South Africa.

"So this is good-bye," I said to Arnon and Oded as we were about to disembark. They were scheduled on an El Al flight to Israel, and my flight was headed to New York.

Oded shook my hand, wanting to say something, but he just hugged me. Arnon came over, gave me his hand, and hesitantly said, "I never asked you who you work for."

"Good," I said conclusively, and he laughed.

As we docked I saw Benny waiting for us on the gangway. "Dan, you lost weight! What, they didn't feed you?"

Since when was Benny a Jewish mother, equating care with feeding? I looked at myself; I must have lost thirty pounds. Nothing a few hearty meals couldn't correct.

He hugged us. "Welcome, and Dan, thanks for helping get my men back."

"It was teamwork," I said. Oded and Arnon walked to the waiting car.

"I'll see you in New York soon," Benny said to me. "I already cleared a debriefing session with Hodson. We must learn from the experience." It didn't sound as if he was admitting that big mistakes had been made, however.

"I have a few unsolved questions I want to ask you."

"Shoot."

"I wonder why you forgot to tell me that the Mossad in fact sent two units to approach the Slaves of Allah: Dr. Oded Regev and Arnon Tal in one, and another three-person team that approached them from a completely different angle."

It had been a long time since I'd seen Benny stunned.

"Who told you that? Even Arnon and Oded didn't know that, for their own protection."

"Remember that worn-out phrase *need-to-know basis*?" I teased him.

"Okay, tell me what you do know and I won't ask how you found out."

"Simple logic. Always look where you are most likely to find the answer."

"And where is that place?"

"The bank account in Eagle Bank. I went over the various deposits and withdrawals and saw one payment of fifteen thousand dollars made to Fabrique National Du Kinshasa Congo, SPLR. The reference on the payment stub was 'raw materials.' I ran a quick search on the firm in Kinshasa's companies registrar and saw that the shareholders were Mr. Ivan Troy of South Africa and G. D. Pierce of Zimbabwe. So I ran a search on these names and discovered an interesting thing. The National Intelligence Agency of South Africa and the Central Intelligence Organisation of Zimbabwe advised us that the passports in question were reported lost or stolen."

Benny smiled.

"Should I tell you where they were lost — in case you don't know? — in Israel. Someone in the Office was careless," I said.

"What's the big deal?" asked Benny. "We had two groups soliciting materials to these bad guys, simply as a precaution in case the negotiations with one team failed."

"But why the fifteen-thousand-dollar payment?"

"Earnest money. We demanded they advance us the money to show their intent to negotiate in good faith . . ." Benny chuckled. "We had expenses, you know, so every dollar helps."

"There must have been a good reason for you to ask for my help. And please spare me the usual explanation of friendship. You were using me as a conduit to offer a trade. We delivered the goods: Your men returned safely."

Benny smiled, paused for a moment, and said, "You mean our meeting at the New York Hilton?"

"Of course."

"I told you we know how the Iranians move money into the U.S."

"I'm listening, go ahead."

"There's a twist to the direction of the flow. In fact, I meant how the Iranians finance their terrorist cells in the U.S."

"I know how — through innocent but-should-have-been-more-suspicious Islamic charities."

"Right. But you asked me why I asked for your help after I had already approached the big guys in Washington, DC."

"I wondered," I conceded.

"We hacked into the computer system of Schiller Bank in Austria and downloaded the details of the numbered account of the Slaves of Allah."

"Leaving no audit trail?"

"Of course," said Benny.

"But you told me that you didn't withdraw the money because you didn't want to expose your men as intelligence operatives."

"True. We hacked into the account just to take a look. We saw how the money was sent from Eagle Bank into the Austrian bank account as well as other deposits and withdrawals. I knew you were a foreign money hunter for the U.S. Department of Justice, so my estimate was that your office, or even you personally, were working on that case."

"Case? How did you know that there was an inquiry into Eagle Bank?" I was really amazed.

"Two things happened. The very extensive flow of money from Eagle Bank to Austria stopped abruptly. We figured there must have been an unusual reason for that."

"There was. Malik Fazal took off. And the second reason?"

"We read newspapers, you know. There was a small item in the New York papers about Bernard Lipinsky, the Eagle Bank employee whose body was found in a Dumpster right after all activity in the bank account seemed to freeze. That was too much coincidence. So my shot in the dark hit the bull's-eye, although it wasn't really that dark and not that much of a shot. So I decided to call you."

"Why not just tell me that at the beginning?"

"Dan, I told you only things you needed to know to help us. That information did not come under that definition."

I knew it was one of the more calculated side effects of intelligence work — keeping allies in the dark when it suits your purpose to do so. I wasn't even angry at Benny for it.

"I think there was another reason," I said.

"What?"

"You withheld that information as future payment to the U.S. government for helping find your men."

"Ah," Benny said. "And if you knew, why the passive anger in your voice?"

"Nothing of the sort. I suspected it from the beginning, and that's how I presented your request to my superiors. A simple trade-in, so now you owe me, for a change."

"No. We're even," he said, opening up his brown leather briefcase and handing me a bulky yellow envelope.

"What's that?" Benny's envelopes always contained pleasant surprises for me: a Jewish version of Santa Claus.

"Open it up," he said. "Payback time."

Inside were numerous documents, mostly in German. "It looks like bank records," I said, after giving them a glance.

He nodded. "These are banking documents reflecting the entire traffic between Schiller Bank and six American banks — including Eagle Bank. These are money changers and financial institutions in the U.S. that have been actively laundering money for the Slaves of Allah for the past year. You have names, addresses, dates, and everything else you'd need to nab and nail the bastards."

"How reliable is the information?"

Benny smiled. "Remember the Mossad's Alphanumeric Source and Information Evaluation System?"

"Sure."

"Then it's B-one."

I remembered Alex, my Mossad instructor, teaching me the system of evaluation of sources and information graded on a descending scale of A through E; *A* means completely reliable, since it is used only for Mossad combatants; *B* means usually reliable; *C* means fairly reliable; *D* means reliability cannot be judged; and *E* means unreliable. The value of information is described on a descending scale of 1 through 3; *1* is eyeball — primary source; *2* is used for information obtained by an agent from a usually reliable informant — that is, secondary source; *3* is rumor-based, or unconfirmed information.

"Why is it only a B?"

"Because the bank may have created false files designated to mislead hackers. Our analysis showed it to be a very remote possibility because we cross-referenced the money movement with other banking institutions that either sent or received the money. It checked. Anyway, give it to your boss. Should I add a card that says 'courtesy of Dan Gordon'?"

"Don't bother. Hodson's not big on niceties."

"Okay, then just give it to him with my thanks for getting my men back. Accounting balance for services rendered: zero."

# XV

New York was both hectic and calm. My children were all over me, and I was hugging them endlessly, while Snap jumped on me with joy, face licking and everything. After three days of debriefing in Langley about my Libyan and Yemenite ordeals, I was called for a meeting at 26 Federal Plaza. Before going to Hodson's office, I went to see my own office at the task force: The space was vacant. I then went to see Hodson.

He was waiting for me with Eric and Brian. To my surprise and delight, David Stone was also present. After exchanging greetings, I asked, "Tell me how it ended." They were seated on chairs in front on Hodson's desk. Frankly, I'd expected a hero's welcome, but when none came, I said to myself, *What the hell, I'm alive and free.*

"Dan, we're trying to tie up some loose ends regarding your capture. Do you know what happened?" Eric was pushy.

"I was tricked into thinking I was meeting you," I said. Didn't he read the first chapter of my Langley briefing?

"Why did they use my name? I know you never said anything to Zhukov about me," asked Eric.

"How do you know?"

"We were listening to your meeting with Zhukov, remember?" answered Eric drily. "Or maybe there was another meeting with Zhukov that we are not aware of?"

It all seemed so long ago. "There was only one meeting with him," I said. "They must have gotten your name elsewhere. I had no idea until I learned during my Langley debriefing that the Slaves of Allah had recruited a sympathizer in my hotel to help them listen to any phone calls to or from my room. They must have heard our short conversation and knew I'd be expecting a call from you. So talking to you exposed me as well."

"They were on your tail well before that," said Brian.

"That's news to me," I said. "When did it start?"

"Remember the Belarusian translator?"

"Sure."

"She was Igor's girlfriend."

"I was the one who discovered that," I reminded him.

"So when Dr. Bermann talked to Igor about your forthcoming visit and asked for his cooperation, Igor agreed. He probably had no intention of talking to you, but wanted to glean from you, through your questioning, what the U.S. government knew or suspected about his services to Zhukov. He wanted to protect Zhukov at any cost, even if it meant spending the rest of his life in prison."

"I can understand that," I said. "Better that than slow torture at the hands of Zhukov's comrades."

"Exactly," said Eric wryly.

"The interpreter used my visit to the prison to plant a transmitter in my coat, probably under Zhukov's direction."

"Right," agreed Brian, "and the attack on you in the street was also his doing. Once you were identified as an investigator looking for evidence on the connection between Zhukov, Igor, and the massive bank deposits, you became a prime target for Zhukov. He could monitor you while you were outside the U.S., but when you returned all his channels of information dried up. He needed inside info." He shot me an accusing look.

I felt as if an ice cube were slowly sliding down my back. What was going on? Did they think I was the insider who'd provided Zhukov with information? Maybe I was imagining things, but Eric and Brian seemed to be coordinated with their subtle accusations and innuendo. It was no coincidence. My stomach moved nervously.

"A garbage run of our files?" I suggested, trying to remember if I'd ever brought home any of the material and then absentmindedly thrown it away. Very unlike me, but shit happens.

"No, the office trash is shredded."

"Wiretapping?" I asked hopefully. I dreaded the moment he'd realize the truth. And I berated myself for having been blind for so long to what Laura was doing, although I'd seen the light and reported her to Hodson. Still, my hands weren't clean. I'd asked Laura to join me in France, which was against the rules, and I'd been slow to correctly label her dubious activities.

"No," said Hodson.

"Dan," Eric said decisively, "we believe there's a mole working for Zhukov."

"You mean, present tense?"

"Yes."

His answer was ominous. They couldn't mean Laura; I'd exposed her. She had to be behind bars. So there had to be another mole. Did they suspect me? As a foreign-born, naturalized citizen of the United States, I could be an easy target of suspicion.

"Laura," I said. "I hope she's under arrest."

"Why Laura?" he asked.

"Bob, I exposed her," I said, "You mean she's not in custody? Didn't you get my e-mail?"

"E-mail, what e-mail? You only called me once to tell me to look for her," said Hodson shortly.

"That's crazy." I raised my voice. "I sent you an e-mail from my hotel room in France telling you that I suspected Laura is a mole, and that she had an accomplice."

"I never got any e-mail from you. Did you copy anyone else?"

"No. It was sent just to you." I told him the address I'd used, and he confirmed that it was correct.

"But I never got any message from you," he continued. "Still, you must have a copy on your laptop . . . Oh, I forgot, you don't have a laptop because it was left behind at the hotel when you were captured." The last sentence dripped with scorn. "Well, I'm sure we can find a copy of your message on your server, that'll be easy enough," he said blandly, looking me in the eye.

"Under instructions I received, I opened a onetime account at Yahoo, and deleted the file after sending you the message, for security reasons. Maybe your spam-blocking software rejected it? Under my instructions, after sending the e-mail I had to delete it and purge the account. If it was rejected by your mailbox I had no way of knowing it." I was becoming increasingly nervous, feeling I was sinking into a black hole.

"So you have no record of ever writing or sending the message?"

"No," I said faintly. For a moment, I was lost for words. "Anyway, I asked you to question Laura; she behaved really strangely." I told them the whole story about Laura, and how I'd exposed her. They listened, but only Brian took notes.

"Laura said the same thing about you," said Eric. I didn't like the tone of his voice. But on the other hand, I'd never liked it.

"What did she say?"

"She said she'd exposed you. She told us that you invited her over, in complete violation of the rules, and when she arrived you tried to talk her into joining forces with you in making a cool million dollars by working for Zhukov."

I couldn't believe my ears. "Is that what she said? That's crazy. I never suggested that, or offered her any such thing. We had a brief relationship while I was still in New York. I was bored in Marseilles, so I invited her over. She wasn't the enemy, I remind you, or at least I didn't think she was when I called her. She worked with me. What's wrong with that? I know I broke a rule, but jumping from that to a conclusion that I betrayed is crazy."

"We don't take these things lightly. What you did was wrong, and you know it," said Bob Hodson in his rumbling voice. "You were engaged in a sensitive operation, and only those actually participating in it were supposed to be in the loop. You breached that and brought an unauthorized person onto the scene. That's outright irresponsible."

"In retrospect, I agree. I was stupid to do it. But that has nothing to do with the false allegation Laura has made. She's covering her tracks. I meant to fully supplement my initial e-mailed report, but then I was kidnapped."

"She's denied any wrongdoing," Eric said. "You had to know that once Laura refused your offer to spy for Zhukov and make a quick million dollars, there'd be an investigation. I suspect that the e-mail you now purport to have sent Bob is actually an alibi you're trying to create after the fact to fend off Laura's accusation." Although Eric's tone was bland, I wouldn't have been surprised if this scene was giving him satisfaction he was working hard not to show.

"This is totally false," I said, feeling I had no air in my lungs. Was it possible I was actually being accused of malfeasance — even a kind of treason? Once again I was faced with a situation I simply didn't know how to deal with. I took a deep breath. I was fighting for my life here. I had to appear confident. "She broke into my hotel room looking for documents. When I confronted her, she concocted a story about being jealous of my relations with other women. When I showed her the video of her searching my room, she said she was working for you and testing whether I was breaching security by leaving behind classified materials in my room. What bullshit."

"Dan," said David in his soft voice, "that attitude is not helpful."

I knew David. He was tacitly telling me that I was digging my grave deeper because of my arrogance. But this was not the time to be Mr. Nice. It was time to get the truth out, no matter what. My defiant and militant nature started kicking in again.

"I presume you don't have the handheld video viewer either," said Eric, in a seemingly serious tone, but the cynicism wasn't far from the surface.

"No. Laura maced me and ran away with the viewer. I know that this story sounds a bit wacko, but that's exactly what happened. Laura had confessed earlier that she'd also sent her boyfriend to search my room. Maybe I also arranged my own kidnapping?" I asked in contempt mixed with rage.

"We're not ruling out anything," said Brian. "Do you have anything to support your story, other than your word?"

"Yes, the message I sent Lan regarding Baird Black, aka Robert Meadway."

"We saw that. We checked the names; neither exist in our database. Maybe you sent the message after Laura refused your offer to work for Zhukov, or maybe you just invented those names."

"It's insane. Why you are you automatically rejecting my evidence? It's like you've already made up your minds that I've betrayed you. Does Laura have anything to support *her* story?" I turned to David. "You know my record. Even when I've taken some tactical shortcuts, I have never taken ethical shortcuts! Can't you judge me by my record of integrity and success?"

"I wish I could," said David. "But from what I hear and see, it doesn't look good."

"Can anyone answer my question? How does Laura support her allegations, other than her word?"

"In fact she does have proof. She gave us papers she found in your room connecting you with a deposit to an account in a French bank. We got assistance from the French police and retrieved copies of the bank statement," said Hodson.

"Laura's framing me, to discredit my testimony against her. Can't you see that?" I almost yelled.

"Frankly, we can't," said Hodson. "The evidence we have shows that you have a one-million-dollar deposit in a bank account in southern France. Do you want to explain that?"

He handed me a two-page document: a bank statement and a signature card with my name on it for an account in Banque Nationale du Provence, in Marseilles.

"See for yourself," he said, "There's only one deposit and no withdrawals. Available balance: one million dollars."

"Inherited money from your grandmother?" asked Eric.

"This isn't my bank account." I said decisively. "I never opened it, and the money in the account isn't mine. Obviously, we're on to something much bigger than Laura. She's in it with someone who put up a million dollars to shut me down and lock me behind bars."

Hodson and David exchanged looks. I heard David say, "Dan, I think you need a lawyer. A real good one."

I felt faint. "A lawyer? Why? I don't need a lawyer, I'm innocent and I can prove it, although I don't have to."

"You're in trouble," said Hodson.

"Am I under arrest?"

"Not yet. Not if you tell us the truth."

"What truth? I've already told you the truth."

"Dan." David was almost apologetic. "I want to believe you. If it were just Laura's statement, it could be explained as her way of settling some score with you. But how do you explain the bank account?"

"Look for someone who wanted me out of commission so badly that he not only arranged for my kidnapping but also framed me."

"Are you willing to confront Laura with your accusations?"

"Willing?" I asked bitterly, "I'm anxious. Where is the bitch?"

"No need to use foul language," remonstrated David. He looked at Hodson again.

Hodson nodded and pressed the intercom. "Send Laura Higgins in."

The door opened and Laura walked in, greeting everyone with a smile but ignoring me. She was dressed in a business suit and looked somber and professional.

"Laura," said Hodson, "Dan denies all your accusations. In fact he is telling us that you are the mole, and that you concocted the story about him to distance yourself from any wrongdoing."

"Of course he said that," she said drily. "What else do you expect him to say to cover his ass?"

"You're lying," I said in contempt.

Laura looked me in the eye. "You called me from France and asked me to join you. Didn't you?"

"Yes, but for fun only."

"Fun? That's a new one. You told me that you had come across alarming information on our case, but that it was so secret that you could not specify over the phone why you needed me."

"That's bull," I said. "Besides, I call and you jump? Wouldn't you have cleared it with Hodson, if such an invitation was connected to our matter?"

"Yes, I must admit that I was surprised you didn't go through channels. When I asked you why, you answered that there were leaks of security in the organization, and until internal security discovered the source, you couldn't share the alarming information with anyone, including Hodson, but you trusted me."

"So you're saying you believed that everyone in this room was a suspect? Is that the level of your trust in your management?" I shot back.

"I didn't know what to think," countered Laura. "The task force assignment was my first. I didn't understand the inner politics, so I came to meet you in France."

"I'm telling you that I asked you to come and have fun with me, or to be more blunt have sex. You on the other hand had another agenda while working for Zhukov and comrades, and maybe even for the Slaves of Allah."

"How dare you!" she shouted. "Sex with you? I wouldn't in a million years." She turned to the men around her. "Ever since I joined the task force Dan has been trying to get into my pants. I rebuffed him. Maybe that's why he's airing these ridiculous accusations about me, hoping to distance himself from his own transgressions."

That was a low blow, an affront to my virility. But now there were more important things on my mind. I confronted Laura with the details of our encounter in my hotel room, the gun, the struggle, the video, and the mace. She vehemently denied everything. "You're imagining things. I guess the period you spent in captivity gave you enough time to concoct these lies about me. It's not going to help you, you're a traitor, and I will testify in court to make sure they lock you up forever."

Woman or no woman, I was so mad I thought of punching her in the face. Hodson sensed what was going to happen and signaled his assistant Lynn, who'd been standing by all this time, to take Laura out.

"Dan, obviously you're upset when confronted with the facts. Can't you confess now, and we'll get it over with? You'll also feel better once you get it off your chest."

"Confess? To what? To being horny? That I admit. Everything else she said was a lie. This woman used and is using her obvious feminine advantages to cloud your judgment. She certainly clouded mine, but not anymore."

"Dan, let's stick to the facts, forget about accusations. Just look at the date of deposit into your bank account," said Hodson. "It was made two days *after* your meeting with Zhukov. Can you explain that?"

"It's a frame. Everything that went on with Zhukov during the meeting was on tape and monitored by Eric from the adjacent room," I pointed out. "How could I have conspired with him?"

"At the end of the meeting Zhukov said his man would come to see you with the money," Eric said blandly.

"Yes, the hundred thousand dollars I was instructed to ask for, as payment for my services."

"Did he ever come up with the money?"

"No. I never met any of them again. I was kidnapped three days later. You know all this."

"Maybe he did return," said Eric. "Maybe he offered you a million dollars to be his mole inside the Justice Department and at the task force. Maybe he told you to plant disinformation that would distance him from charges of abetting terrorism. A million dollars is small change for Zhukov, but not for you. Maybe you agreed, and went with him to the bank to open the account. Maybe you also agreed to be 'kidnapped,' to make it look as if you were above suspicion. And then maybe you returned to the bank during the time you said you were a prisoner, quietly withdrew the money, and worked for Zhukov from the inside?" concluded Eric.

"Dan, if you confess now, maybe I could get you a deal with the U.S. Attorney's office. You'd serve eight to ten years and be a free man soon," said Hodson in a conciliatory voice. "But if you continue to deny it, and you're convicted, it could mean twenty-five to life."

"This is absolutely false. I didn't betray my mission or my country. I was framed, can't you see it? The money is not mine. I never opened that account, I never agreed with Zhukov to be his spy; everything I did was aboveboard. You've accused me falsely. You'd better start thinking of your apology letters when the truth comes out. Are you going to file charges against me?"

"That's a decision for the U.S. Attorney and the grand jury to make," said Hodson. "Get a lawyer."

"Dan, I must ask you not to leave town while the investigation is still ongoing. You are also suspended from your duties at the Justice Department," said Hodson.

"Dan, I'm sorry," said David Stone. "I never believed it would come to this. I must ask you for your Department of Justice ID."

I put my laminated ID card with my picture on Hodson's desk. "This is all wrong," I said in defiance.

I wasn't going to contact a lawyer. I knew I wasn't just in a little trouble here, I was in a lot of trouble. But I would choose the battlefield, and it would not be the courtroom with me as a defendant. Not yet, anyway.

I went home seething. I took Snap for a walk. I needed to clear my head, to do some soul searching and planning. I called no one. I was sure I was under surveillance and my phone was tapped. I knew the old trick: Let the accused walk free when you don't have enough evidence to indict him. Feeling off the hook, the truly guilty guys make the mistakes that bring in the evidence that locks them up. Although I had nothing to hide, I didn't even want to give them the satisfaction that I was seeking outside advice. So I didn't call a lawyer, or even Benny. No one.

I must have walked an hour before I suddenly knew what I had to do. To be stepped on, you have to be on the ground, and I wasn't there yet, though I was close. I knew I was the only person who could prove them wrong. True, as a lawyer I knew they had to prove my guilt beyond a rea-sonable doubt; I didn't have to prove my innocence. Still, the evidence against me so far — although insufficient for conviction — was alarming. Unless I worked fast, more of it would turn up. Whoever had gone to the trouble of investing a million dollars to bring me down wouldn't stop until he'd finished the job; until the stone over my virtual grave was too heavy to lift.

I returned home with Snap. I left him food and water. "Be a good boy," I said as I hugged him. "Help is on the way." I packed a small bag with enough clothes for three nights. I took two passports and five thousand dollars I'd kept for a rainy day. The sun was out, dry and clear, but I felt like I was drowning. Making sure I wasn't followed, I went to Canal

Street and boarded the Chinatown bus to Boston, paying fifteen dollars for the ride.

Once I reached Boston, I used old tactics to make sure I wasn't followed. From there I took a Greyhound bus to Montreal, a ride of about six hours. I alternated between sleeping, being angry, plotting revenge, and calculating how to prove everyone wrong. The seat next to me was empty, so I rode in relative comfort.

When the bus stopped at the Canadian border a Canadian immigration officer came on board, checked the papers of two passengers, and skipped the rest, including me. In Montreal I went directly to the airport and paid in cash for a ticket on an Air France flight to Marseilles, using a genuine U.S. passport the Department of Justice had once arranged for me with the cover name of Peter Wooten. If my movements *were* being monitored, a charge on my credit card for an airline ticket would be flagged immediately. I banked on the assumption that Hodson was unaware of my other passport, and therefore Peter Wooten's name wouldn't show up on the alert list. I called my next-door neighbor, told her I had to leave unexpectedly, and asked that she take care of Snap for a few days. Whenever I could I returned the favor with her cat. She assured me it'd be okay, and that she still had the spare key to my apartment.

I arrived in Marseilles after a sleepless night, but once on the ground there was no time to sleep. I shaved in the men's room at the airport and took a cab to Banque National de Provence.

*"Bonjour,"* said the teller. "How can I help you?" she added in English when I showed her my American passport under my own name.

"I need to withdraw money from my account."

"What's your account number?" she asked.

"I don't remember. But it's under my name."

"Mr. Dan Gordon," she said after clicking on her keyboard; "I'm sorry, your account is closed."

"Closed?" I said in feigned surprise; "I had a million dollars in that account. Where's the money?"

"Let me call the manager." She retreated to a back office. Ten minutes later she returned. "The manager will see you now."

I followed her into the manager's small office. He was a skinny man perhaps in his early sixties with a manicured mustache and kind manners. The nameplate on his desk read JEAN PAUL DASEAU.

"I'm attorney Dan Gordon, and I had a deposit of one million dollars here. Now your teller says the account was closed. Where's the money? I'm a trustee for that money." I showed him my passport.

"Mr. Gordon," the manager said calmly, looking at documents on his desk, "perhaps you don't remember, but you gave a power of attorney to Monsieur Robert Meadway, and under his orders we issued him a cashier's check for one million dollars plus the accrued interest."

"I'm sorry, I must have forgotten it," I said with a show of relief. "May I have for my records a copy of the signature card used to open the account; the power of attorney; Mr. Robert Meadway's written instruction to prepare the cashier's check; and copies of both sides of the check, which I presume was cashed? As a trustee, I must have written records for everything that happens in the account." I paused, "On second thought, will you please put the bank's stamp on the copies to authenticate them? As a trustee, I have to be very careful with other people's money."

The manager nodded toward the teller. "Please make the copies he needs, and stamp them. I'll add my signature to authenticate." Twenty minutes later I was out in the street with the documents. I went to a copy center and made two additional copies. I mailed one set to my home in New York and one set to my sister in Israel, adding a note: "Please keep these for me." I faxed a copy to Robert Hodson in New York with the note "FYI." Nothing else. I faxed another copy to David Stone in Washington. "David, I trust you and I trust you'd know how to examine these documents and reach the correct conclusion. Robert Meadway's name appeared in the info I gave Lan before I was kidnapped. Thanks for helping me out. Dan." I kept the original copies.

My next stop was the Excelsior Hotel, where I went to the reception desk.

"*Bonjour.* I was a guest here a few months ago, and I'm afraid I left the charger for my laptop in the room."

"What room were you in?" asked the pretty receptionist.

"Five eighteen."

"Can I see your passport, please?"

I showed her my Dan Gordon U.S. passport.

She looked at her computer. "I'm sorry, it seems that we never had you as a guest, Mr. Gordon. You must have stayed at another hotel."

I knew I'd stayed there as Neil McMillan. But I had no ID under that name. Those documents were taken by my captors. "Well, I'm certain I was staying here, but come to think of it, my hotel reservation was made by my friend Neil McMillan. Perhaps the record erroneously shows him as a guest? Look, it's only a twenty-dollar charger, but the manufacturer discontinued this model. I have to find it or I can't use my computer."

She relented. "Why don't you talk to housekeeping? Maybe they found it."

"Where are they?"

"On the lower floor," she said and directed me to the stairwell.

There was only one elderly woman in housekeeping. "A few months ago, I stayed in room five eighteen," I said with a smile. "I think I left behind the TV a charger for my laptop computer. Could you please come with me to the room so I can retrieve it?" I slipped a twenty-euro bill into her hand.

"Usually we take all the things guests leave behind to our lost-and-found department," she said.

"I know, but in this case it may be different because I plugged it into the wall behind the TV. That's not a place chambermaids usually look."

She checked the computer. "Okay, that room is vacant. Please follow me."

We took the elevator to the fifth floor. She opened the room with her master key. My heart was pounding. I went straight to the TV and checked behind the set. It was still there: the recorder and my proof. "*Merci,*" I told the housekeeper. "I found it." I wanted to jump up and down for joy, but I kept my cool. I left the hotel and climbed into a cab without even knowing where I was going. I was clasping the recorder as if it were treasure. I needed to make a copy. But where? After consulting a classified directory at a nearby bistro, I had the driver drop me off at a studio that turned out to be a modeling agency. There were ten or twelve skinny teenage girls in the reception area, all either overdressed or under-dressed. I asked the receptionist if I could see the manager, and explained that I wanted to copy a video feed onto a DVD.

"Of course, monsieur, why don't you leave it here and come back tomorrow," the manager said. He was a young medium-built, dark-skinned man, probably North African.

"I can't wait, and I must be present. I'll give you five hundred euros if you do it now."

There was a spark of understanding in his eyes: "A woman is in the video?"

"Yes," I said, truthfully enough. I followed him to a back studio, where he hooked up the recorder to his desktop computer. The video showed my room at the Excelsior, and there was Laura with me in her leading role from *Frame Your Opponent*. It was all there. Even the audio was clear. I had her dead to rights.

"Pretty lady," said the studio manager in appreciation, "but why was she fighting you?"

Apparently he didn't understand English. "Lovers' quarrel," I said.

After a pause in the video, the recording continued briefly, showing me sitting on the bed and talking to the anonymous caller who'd sent me to the Saint-Victor Abbey to meet Henderson. "I think that's it," I said.

"Wait," said the manager. "My computer shows that there is more data on the disk."

Probably just a still video of my room, I thought, but I didn't stop him. My eyes widened when I saw the new video feed: Laura entering my room with Baird Black, aka Robert Meadway.

They were searching the room, opening drawers and closets.

"Nothing here but his luggage," Black/Meadway said.

"It must be here," countered Laura. "He showed me on the handheld monitor the video of me entering his room earlier. So there has to be a camera somewhere sending the feed to the handheld, or it could also be recording independently. I must find it and get rid of it."

She looked up at the ceiling. "There's something on the smoke detector. I think that's it."

Black/Meadway climbed onto the desk and retrieved the camera, holding it near his eye and thereby giving me a close-up of his face. He was good looking, the bastard.

"You can relax," he said; "it's just a camera. It's too small to include any recording device. So since you already have his handheld monitor, you're safe."

He gave the camera to Laura, who put it in her pocket or purse — I couldn't tell, because the monitor at the studio went black. The sound recording continued. "Okay," I heard Laura say; "I'll get rid of it as well. You can tell your friend that we destroyed the evidence."

"Mr. Zhukov was very upset when I told him that you were captured on a video. It took a lot of effort to dissuade him from whacking you."

Laura's voice sounded apologetic. "Baird, I kept my promise to you, didn't I? Now I want you out of my life."

I heard the room door slam and an elevator door open. The recording ended there.

"Are you a detective?" asked the manager. "Is he her lover?"

"Yes, I'm a private detective. Can I please have three copies of this recording on DVDs?"

An hour later, I paid him five hundred euros, took the DVDs, and went to the post office, mailing one copy to David Stone by FedEx and another to my sister in Israel. I took the next flight out to New York.

The following morning I called Hodson. I'd needed a day to cool off and plan ahead.

"Dan, I don't know what to say," he started. Should I let him eat his words, or just get to the point?

"I guess David Stone gave you the DVD," I finally said, matter-of-factly.

"He did, and I also saw the fax you sent with the bank records."

"And?"

"I'm glad you were able to pull this through so fast." He forgot to berate me for leaving town in violation of his instructions.

"I need to see you and Eric," I said.

"He'll be here at three. Is that a good time?"

"Sure."

I called David Stone in DC. "Dan, I never believed them to begin with," he said. Knowing David as well as I did, I knew he was being truthful. I could only guess why he hadn't come to my defense at the meeting.

"I'm meeting Hodson and Eric at three o'clock in New York," I said. "You were present during my crucifixion, so perhaps you'd want to be present during my resurrection."

"I'll be there."

At 3:07 P.M. I walked into Hodson's office. Eric Henderson, David Stone, and Brian Day were also there.

I didn't waste time. "The only thing I can say is that I'm disappointed that you gave even an iota of credibility to Laura's accusations."

"Dan, we were dealing with an accusation supported by what appeared to be credible evidence," said Hodson. "Even you would have to concede that the banking documents appeared genuine."

"Genuine? My foot! Couldn't you see that my signature on the signature card was forged? Didn't you see there was a power of attorney for the account indicating that there was more than one person involved? Did you made *any* effort to investigate that?"

"In fact, we didn't know there was a power of attorney; the French police never sent it to us," said Hodson. "There was only the deposit slip Laura gave us, followed by the bank statement and the signature card that the French police gave us."

"And my forged signature on the deposit slip and the signature card? Even a five-year-old could see it's not mine."

"The forensic lab is backlogged," said Hodson in an apologetic tone. "Anyway, we didn't think the evidence was sufficient to indict or even to arrest you. We did have our doubts."

"Your accusations didn't reflect any doubt," I said bitterly. "Did you make any effort to trace the account where the French bank's check was deposited?"

"Yes, the back of the cashier's check you faxed us shows it was deposited into a Swiss bank account of a Liechtenstein trust. A request is going out to the principality of Liechtenstein and to the Swiss government through INTERPOL."

"It will lead to Zhukov, I can assure you of that," I said, although I had no proof, just a hunch.

"We think so, too, but let's wait for the responses from Liechtenstein and Switzerland."

David handed me back my ID. "Dan, you are hereby reinstated. And for the record, I'm glad it ended the way it did." I decided not to rub it in. David's calm demeanor could restart me as if I were a computer.

"Give me the chain of events before you were kidnapped," David asked.

"I received several phone calls at my hotel. The first was from a guy with a Russian accent telling me that the meeting with Zhukov would be in Marseilles. He telephoned me again once they'd arrived in Marseilles, and a meeting with Zhukov was set. Then there was another call from Eric, as well as a subsequent message from him to come to the clinic. The last call came the next day and purported to be a message from Mr. Henderson. Since that message coincided with my previous agreement with Eric to meet in a neutral location, I had no reason to suspect the caller. When I went to the meeting, I was drugged and kidnapped. And you know the rest."

A thought occurred to me. "What about Laura?"

"She was arrested this morning," said Hodson.

"Is she in the building?"

Hodson and David exchanged a look, and David nodded. "She is being interrogated now."

"I want to see her reaction when confronted with hard evidence."

Hodson hesitated.

"Bob, I think Dan can be useful in the interrogation," said David.

"Okay," relented Hodson. We walked to the room adjoining the interrogation cell and sat behind the double mirror. Laura was sitting next to a metal table, and an African American female agent in her midthirties was interrogating. The room was similar to the one in which Fazal had been interrogated, except for a twenty-seven-inch TV monitor mounted on the wall seven feet above the floor. The screen was turned off.

We heard the agent continue with a line of questioning that must have been going on for some time.

"You claim that you were blackmailed."

"Yes," said Laura.

"What were they trying to get from you?"

"Inside information on the task force."

"And if you refused?"

"They said that my elderly mother would be hurt."

"When did the blackmail start?"

"When I was investigating a fuel-smuggling case in Brooklyn. Baird Black came to my office and tipped me off to a web of ambitious young Eastern Europeans who were smuggling Russian women with forged documents through JFK to work as prostitutes. I told my supervisor, and an investigation commenced. We discovered that the information Baird Black had given me was accurate. The ring members were arrested and indicted."

"And then?" asked the interrogator.

"We started dating."

"Dating?"

"Yes, I came from Kansas to New York and had no friends or acquaintances, nothing. All I did was work. Baird was very nice to me. He complimented me, took me to dinners, sent me flowers, and bought me nice presents."

"So he was buying your cooperation?" asked the interrogator.

"No!" Laura raised her voice. "It was a love affair."

"Tell me about your romance," asked the interrogator gently.

"At the beginning of our relationship, I didn't suspect Baird of anything. But then I was approached by the blackmailers, and as time went by, I started suspecting Baird as being the link to them."

"Why?"

"Because it was his idea that I ask to join the task force."

"How did he know there was a task force?"

"Oh, I told him that. When my department put the word out asking for volunteers, I wondered whether I should. So I asked Baird. He *was* my boyfriend, or so I thought, and the posting made it clear that long, unpredictable hours would be required. Baird encouraged me to apply. He was moving into his busy season in his flower-exporting company and said he'd be busy during the coming months. So I did."

"And then what happened?"

"Soon I started getting phone calls threatening to kill my mother in her nursing home in Kansas unless I became an informer."

"Why didn't you report the threats?

"I was afraid for my mother. She is so frail and vulnerable, I couldn't imagine putting her at risk."

The investigator didn't buy that. "And as a trained federal agent, you just believed the callers and yielded immediately? Besides, your mother could have been given protection."

"I told you I felt I had no choice."

"I see," said the investigator. "Did they tell you exactly what information they wanted?"

"All the details about the investigation Dan Gordon was conducting outside the U.S. They promised me they'd stop contacting me once the task force case was over."

"And you agreed."

"I was torn. I was afraid for my mother's life and also for my own."

"Did you discuss the blackmail with Baird?"

"Yes."

"And what did he say?"

"Obviously he said I should do what the callers asked. I didn't know he was one of them. You must believe me, I was looking for a way out, and in fact I told them very little about Dan's work."

"Little," I snorted. "Kidnapping, torture and imprisonment, barely escaping death: If that's little, I'd hate to see what a lot means to her."

Hodson and David didn't comment, and of course Laura and the inter-rogator couldn't hear me.

Laura said, "I need to go to the bathroom." The interrogator buzzed, and a female agent entered the room and took Laura with her.

"Zhukov killed two birds with one stone," Hodson said. "By using Baird to lure Laura with genuine information about a rival gang, he both eliminated a rival group in Brooklyn and gained surreptitious access to law enforcement. He needed that badly to install an early-warning system in case the task force investigation came close to him."

"I can understand that he used Laura through Baird to eliminate a rival gang, but how could he possibly have known that Laura would be assigned to a task force investigating him?" asked David.

"He didn't," Hodson answered. "He was just looking for Homeland Security info that could help in his business and stifle the competition. But he saw an opportunity when Laura told Baird about the task force."

"It's bullshit," I said. "Unless Zhukov had an independent source, there was no way he could have guessed that he was being targeted. You also assume that Baird Black worked for Zhukov. But that's what Laura says, and she is a proven liar. I think there's more to this matter than we know. Zhukov may have had additional motives."

There was a sudden silence in the room.

I continued. "I'd squeeze Laura and Zhukov on that. Something's missing here. Obviously I don't believe Laura's claim that she gave little information to her blackmailers. I think she's guilty of big-time treason. It wasn't just the information she gave them — she actively obstructed my work."

"Why did you suspect her?" asked Hodson.

"A few things about her made me feel uneasy, but I didn't add them up at first," I said. "I ignored the rule *Trust all men, but cut the cards.* She was a woman and I was interested in her. I admit it. What more can I say? I made a judgment error. I think she's lying now about volunteering for the task force. In my experience, it doesn't usually happen that way, particu-larly given her status as a rookie. You get assigned, and that's it. Typically they send more senior agents, so she must have lobbied hard for the assignment."

"For your information," said Hodson, "there were three other Homeland Security agents in the task force. You're right, though, she made many efforts to be assigned. But back to your suspicions. Please be more specific."

Eric and Brian entered the room apologizing for being late. I acknowledged Brian with a nod but ignored Eric.

I continued, "There was a much bigger concern that came too late for me to do anything about it."

"What do you mean?" asked David.

"I had plenty of time to think and reconstruct the chain of events that brought me down while I was a prisoner. Frankly, I should have listened to my instincts rather than automatically trust a co-worker."

"Or obeying your hormones," said Eric. I gave him a cold look.

I told them about Laura's unsuccessful attempt to get me off track through Professor Klebanov. "He may have been working for the opposition. Come to think of it, he may not even be a genuine professor."

"Of course he was in with her," said Eric. "He was a real professor, but not Laura's. He once worked for Zhukov as a private English tutor, and was hired to get you off track." Eric continued, "When Laura left your apartment telling you she was going out to smoke a cigarette, she called Baird Black and told him about the coded messages you'd obtained. Black called her back ten minutes later and told her to return to your apartment, pretend to cooperate with you in breaking the code, but in fact stall you, and then suggest enlisting Klebanov. In the meanwhile Black called Klebanov and instructed him to pose as Laura's professor."

"I guess Klebanov sang," I said.

Eric smiled. I continued. "I think Laura did it to put me off track and convince me that the encoded messages were garbage and not genuine, so that I wouldn't even bother sending them to NSA, who could break it in microseconds. I didn't rely on Klebanov's tables because they were bad. I cracked the code independently."

"They didn't know you'd be that persistent," Eric responded. "So they failed in their effort to convince you that the messages were garbage, and they went to plan B, which was to stall you long enough to alert the

Slaves of Allah to the impending investigation, give them time to go under or leave the country. That's why Fazal vanished."

I told them about the phone conversations I'd had with Laura. "When I called her from the Seychelles, she asked me if I was still in Virginia. Even at the time that was suspicious."

Eric didn't seem to get it. "What's the significance?"

"I never told her I was going to Virginia."

He weighed the information. "Do you think you were followed there?"

"No. I called her from a pay phone at the club in Camp Peary." I looked at Brian apologetically. "I know you told me not to use the phone, I'm sorry."

He didn't react, but after all, I was the one who'd paid the price for my mistake.

"Did you talk to her from Virginia?"

"No. There was no answer, so I left a short message on her voice mail, just sending my regards; nothing else."

"Her machine couldn't have recorded the calling number and tied you to Virginia," said Eric. "The pay phones in the Company installations have their caller ID blocked. There must have been another way for her to find out where you were calling from."

"How stupid of me," I admitted. "I called her again from the Newport News–Williamsburg airport just before boarding to go to London and Victoria. Again I got her voice mail, so I didn't leave a message. But the caller ID of that pay phone probably wasn't blocked, and her phone captured the number even though I'd hung up. Then while I was in the Seychelles I called her again, using the satellite phone. This time we spoke and I told her I was in the Seychelles. I should have never trusted that bitch with any information," I said bitterly.

I told them how Laura came to meet me in Marseilles and her sudden appearance at the Excelsior while I was having breakfast, although I'd never told her where I was staying; all she knew about my hotel accommodations was my initial stay at the Promenade. I'd planned to leave her a note that I was moving to the Excelsior, but in the end I didn't, instead simply waiting for her at the Promenade. Only Eric, Brian, and Martin of the CIA knew about my new hotel reservations.

Eric didn't move a muscle.

"Did Laura say what she did with the miniature video camera?"

Brian smiled. "She said that she tried to understand how it worked, but couldn't get a signal."

"Of course she couldn't," said Eric. "The signal is civision, an enciphered television signal. Since the broadcast from the camera to the recorder is wireless, all television sets within a perimeter of three hundred feet could show what was going on in your room unless we encrypted the signal. Professional labs have the deciphering software."

"After finding out I was in the Seychelles, did she send Zhukov's thugs there as well?"

"Yes, but they never made it."

"You mean they lost their way, or what?"

"They were arrested at Heathrow after an X-ray machine discovered concealed weapons in their luggage. What worried us was the type of ammunition they were trying to smuggle."

"What was it?" I had a right to know how they were planning to kill me.

"Assassins' bullets with a plastic sabot over them to prevent the marking of the bullet by the pistol barrel, making ballistic identification extremely difficult."

"If they're such professionals, how were they caught?"

"Even professionals make mistakes," he said, giving me a snide look. "They wrapped the weapons in an X-ray-masking container, and as an added precaution had a baggage handler remove their luggage from the conveyor belt that led to the X-ray machine and put it back at the other end of the machine. What they didn't know was that the baggage handler was already under surveillance by the British police in connection with drug smuggling, and he was caught on video removing the baggage from the belt. He was arrested and so were Zhukov's assassins, who were already seated in the plane waiting for takeoff."

"So nobody was after me in the Seychelles?" I asked. Then the shadow I thought I saw was just in my imagination.

"Sort of. When Zhukov heard about the arrest of his men in London, as plan B he called a Seychelles private investigator to trace you and see what you were doing until he could arrange to send over another team."

"A private investigator? I saw some poorly trained man follow me just before I left the Seychelles. But I dry-cleaned him."

Through the double mirror we saw that the agent had returned with Laura, and the interrogation continued.

"You know that Baird was working for Zhukov, and both were helping a terrorist organization. Didn't you have any qualms about helping terrorists plan an attack on the U.S.?"

"I did no such thing," said Laura quickly. "I had a romance with a man, and was blackmailed. At the beginning I didn't know he had any connection to Zhukov. When I was in France, Baird showed up all of a sudden. Only then did I realize that there was a connection."

"How did you learn that?"

"Baird told me he was a member of Zhukov's organization, but claimed his relationship with me was originally unrelated to Zhukov. He said that only after Zhukov discovered Baird was dating me did he tell Baird to use me for information. I agreed with Baird that my cooperation would be limited to Dan Gordon's activities, meaning his efforts to discover the source of the money, while withholding any information on the bio-attack. We never told Zhukov that Dan Gordon and Neil McMillan were the same person. Zhukov met only a McMillan, not a Gordon."

"That's bullshit," I muttered. "Zhukov didn't need that information anyway. In Germany I met Igor as Gordon, the attack on me was as Gordon. Then I appear as McMillan, and Baird must have given him my real name — courtesy of Laura, who knew both names." I wished the interrogator could have heard me. But Hodson made a note of my comment.

"I never met Zhukov," continued Laura. "All my contacts were with Baird. But maybe Zhukov also wanted to distance himself from the Slaves of Allah and save his own skin. So he wanted to know what Dan was doing, what his plans were, what information he was able to gather that could put him at risk, and then . . ." Laura paused.

"Then what?"

"Eliminate Gordon."

"How do you know that?"

"Baird told me."

"When?"

"While we were in France and I told him I wanted out."

Hodson turned to me. "What Laura doesn't know is that Zhukov confessed that when his plan to have his men kill you in the Seychelles was botched, he suspected that he was under surveillance and wanted to distance himself from a direct hit on you. So he outsourced the job of eliminating you to the Slaves of Allah, keeping one huge card up his sleeve.

"He had two good reasons to want you dead. Your testimony as a key witness against him, and your findings in Germany, could send him to a federal prison for many years. But a much better reason from his perspective was his fear of the Slaves of Allah."

"What was the card he withheld from them?"

"The fact that you were Dan Gordon, a U.S. agent. He told them you were Neil McMillan."

"Why?"

"Not to protect you. He was afraid of the consequences. Telling the Slaves of Allah about Neil McMillan, an asset-protection expert who after the fact is suspected as an outside informer of the CIA, is one thing, but let the Slaves of Allah discover that Zhukov knew the truth about your identity early on was negligence of a kind that could have cost him his life."

"Why?" I asked although I knew the answer.

"Because if Neil McMillan — a sleazeball from the Seychelles — betrays Zhukov and then reports to the CIA, it's not necessarily Zhukov's fault, but to fall for a U.S. government sting operation would be just too much for the Slaves of Allah to swallow. Not only because Zhukov was careless in moving their money and in agreeing to meet you, but because he would become a significant security risk for the Slaves of Allah if he were arrested. He might plea-bargain, spill too much information about the Slaves of Allah. So Zhukov just told them half the truth about who you were, hoping it'd be enough for them to take care of Neil McMillan."

"Then why didn't the Slaves of Allah kill me? They had plenty of opportunities while I was their prisoner. Did Zhukov's check bounce?" I asked sardonically.

"No. They didn't take orders from Zhukov. For them he was just a service provider, a subcontractor to launder money. When he told them about your skills, they thought they'd have a better use for you than as a dead body."

"Using me as their asset protector?"

"Exactly. They didn't know your true identity, and Zhukov certainly wasn't going to tell them. Funny enough, we've come full circle. The whole idea was to use Zhukov to infiltrate the Slaves of Allah, and as it turned out they actually wanted you to do the job."

"Cutting out the middleman is a Middle Eastern custom," I said.

"Until your head was on the chopping block, they thought that you could provide them with a much-needed service."

I touched my neck. Then I turned to Laura's interrogation again.

"What's your mother's name?" asked the interrogator.

"Edna Higgins."

"Is that Edna Norma Higgins born in Kansas in 1935 to Emily and Harold Higgins?"

"Yes."

"And you are her only child?"

"Yes."

"And where is your mother now?"

"In a nursing home in Topeka, Kansas. What are all these questions about my mother? Is she okay? Has anything happened to her?" asked Laura in a concerned voice.

"Laura," said the interrogator in a stern voice, "I think it's time for some truth here."

"What do you mean?"

"I'm afraid your mother is dead," said the interrogator, "and she's been dead now for five and a half years. She died of cancer and you arranged for the funeral."

Laura burst into tears. The interrogator didn't seem to be affected. "So the blackmailer couldn't threaten you with killing your mother, because she was already dead."

Laura wiped her tears. "I'm sorry I lied, but I was blackmailed. My own life was threatened. I added my mother to the story when Dan caught me in France and then I just stuck with to make it more believable. I didn't know what he had already told you. I just didn't know what to do."

"Do you have Baird Black's address?"

"Eleven twenty-nine Hillside Avenue, Brooklyn, New York."

"That address is in Queens, not Brooklyn."

"That's the address he gave me. We always met at my place, I never visited his apartment."

"Do you have his phone number?"

The interrogator dialed the number Laura gave her. She gave the receiver to Laura to listen; I guess she'd tried that number earlier. The recording said that the telephone was not in service.

"Well," said Laura, "actually I used to call his cell phone number, but I don't remember it."

I turned to Hodson. "His real name could be Robert Meadway; it's the same name that appears on the power of attorney used at the bank to deposit and withdraw the million dollars as well as on the Citibank credit card I saw in France. That means he has some ID with that name."

"Go on."

"If Laura called him using her mobile phone. I can help you with the number."

I pulled a piece of paper from my pocket. "Write that down. It looks like a New York cell phone number."

"How come you have that?" asked Hodson.

"While we were trying to break the code in my apartment, Laura suddenly went outside, ostensibly to smoke a cigarette. I saw her through my window talking on her cell phone. But when she returned, I didn't smell any tobacco on her, although I'm very sensitive to that odor. That night, she left her purse in the living room. When her phone beeped to indicate the battery was low, on a hunch I pressed the REDIAL button and wrote down the last number she'd called."

"Good thinking," said Brian.

"No, good training," I said. "Didn't you subpoena Laura's phone records?"

"We did, but there's nothing there. Laura told us earlier that the blackmailers gave her a cell phone and ordered her to use it only to call them," said Hodson.

"Where's that phone now?" I asked.

"She said they took it away from her," answered Hodson.

"Did she give you the number?"

"She did, but it led nowhere. The phone they gave Laura was stolen from an old lady who never realized it was stolen and therefore didn't report it until we came to see her. She said there were no charges on her phone bill so she thought it was somewhere around her house."

"Weren't there any calls?"

"There were so few and the charges were so small that the old lady didn't even notice them."

"A dead end," I concluded.

They nodded.

"But if the number I just gave you is indeed Robert Meadway's, he must have called others using his phone. You can get the records."

"Right." Hodson pressed the intercom and asked the person at the other end to run a check on the number I had given him.

Laura, meanwhile, was drinking water from a plastic cup.

"Let me tell you something," said the interrogator. "Your lie about the threats on the life of your now dead mother is minor in comparison with your other lies."

"Where else did I lie?" Laura sounded defiant.

"About your motives and the extent of you involvement in telling your alleged blackmailers about Dan Gordon. You'd better come up with the truth."

"I have no idea what you're talking about," insisted Laura.

"Okay," said the interrogator calmly, "let me play a short recording. You are the major player; costarring is Mr. Zhukov." She pressed a button on the phone and said something we couldn't hear. But soon a recording came on.

A dial tone, then a series of ten beeps.

"Hello?" came a voice in heavily accented English.

"This is me. Is he in?" That was Laura's voice.

"Hold on."

*"Da,"* said a voice.

"Boris?"

"I can't make it tonight. Gordon has asked me to come to his apartment."

"For what?"

"He promised to show me something. It could be connected to Lipinsky. He's been working on it with NYPD."

"Destroy anything he finds on that. If necessary, I'll destroy Gordon also." I could identify the voice as Zhukov's.

"Boris, please let me run things the way I understand is best for your interests. What about your promise?

"What promise?"

"You said you'd transfer me an additional quarter million dollars. Last night I logged on to my bank account in Luxembourg and the money wasn't there."

"It will be, don't worry."

"I'm afraid you'll be the one to worry if the money isn't there by tomorrow. You know I can be bad, and I can be even worse. I can have the book thrown at you. Don't get me started."

"Okay, check your account tonight."

A dial tone.

"I'll be damned," I said. "Not only wasn't Laura blackmailed by Zhukov, she in fact blackmailed him." I thought the situation hilarious, but given the serious faces of the people in the room I kept my mouth shut.

Everyone was stunned but Hodson. "Zhukov was under a federal surveillance for some time," he confided, "but for budgetary reasons we didn't transcribe the recordings until this week. You heard what we found. I understand there are additional recordings."

"What do you say to that?" the interrogator asked Laura.

"I want a lawyer," said Laura.

The interrogation stopped and Laura was taken from the room. We returned to Hodson's office.

"What about Zhukov?" I asked

"Let me call Agent Burton. He'll give you the interesting details," said Hodson, pressing his intercom.

A tall young agent wearing a blue suit and eyeglasses came into Hodson's office.

"So you're Dan Gordon," he said. I couldn't tell whether that was said appreciatively or not.

"Tell him about Zhukov," Hodson urged with a grin.

The agent cleared his throat. "Tim Kelly, an FBI special agent in my team, approached Zhukov's table at a crowded fancy restaurant in Coney Island, Brooklyn. He kept shoveling beef stew into his mouth but was otherwise very gracious. He confirmed his identity to Kelly, with his mouth full, and invited him to sit and have a drink. Kelly had backup with him, of course, and Zhukov ordered more chairs for the table.

"But Kelly told Zhukov that he'd have to come with them. Kelly never introduced himself, but no introduction was necessary. I think Zhukov knew exactly who we were. He'd been through it before many times. But usually it was only a matter of hours before his lawyer got him out. 'Indict him or release him,' Nathan King used to challenge our agents when we would come to pick up Zhukov. Of course, it was always 'release' because the witnesses for 'indict' tended to suffer amnesia where Zhukov was concerned. Better that than an obituary.

"But this time it was different. Five other agents carrying shotguns stood near the club's exits. Tim repeated that Zhukov must come with him, and that there was a warrant for his arrest.

"'Can't I finish my meal?' Zhukov asked.

"Kelly was respectful but unyielding. Reluctantly Zhukov followed him to the car outside with the other agents circling him. When the agents left with Zhukov, two stayed behind to make sure no one left until Zhukov was in the car. But I heard that the diners pretended not to notice what was going on.

"'What's the charge this time?' asked Zhukov mockingly.

"'You're in deep shit,' said Tim Kelly. 'This time, you're not getting off that easy. National security charges aren't something the court takes lightly.'

"'National security?' Zhukov feigned surprise. 'What do I have to do with that?'

"'You'll soon find out,' answered Tim.

"Zhukov was emotionless as they handcuffed him and shoved him into a waiting car. As had happened many times before, Zhukov was taken to the Metropolitan Correctional Facility behind the Federal Court House in downtown Manhattan. Following routine, he was brought to a windowless interrogation room on the second floor. But this time, Zhukov could sense the seriousness of purpose. The detectives had a somber look, and although they were polite, they didn't even try to play the nice guy. There were no jokes. I'm sure he felt the shift," concluded Burton.

"And that was enough for Zhukov to cooperate?" I asked. Odd that Zhukov, the hardened criminal, should have gone soft.

"No, not at all. We let him stew in his own juices, so to speak," said Hodson in self-content.

"Meaning?"

"After telling him what he could expect for aiding and abetting terrorists, he plea-bargained. He was looking at life without the possibility of parole in a federal maximum-security prison, like the one in Marion, Illinois," explained Burton.

"What does he know about Marion?"

"We took him there for a visit. We showed him his future cell, six feet by eight, which is hardly big enough for his potbelly, not to mention his ego. He was told that prisoners like him are kept in solitary confinement for twenty-two to twenty-three hours a day. There are no standard vocational, educational, or recreational activities. Physical contact is prohibited during visits. Phone calls for prisoners generally cannot exceed ten minutes a month. No group dining, exercise, or religious services are permitted. Prisoners are shuffled through remote-controlled electronic doors to their destination, without ever seeing another human being," Burton said.

"I guess he got the message," I said in appreciation.

"Quickly. He asked to sign an agreement immediately, even without his lawyer present. We couldn't allow that, but it was all done in two days. He told us about the transactions with the Slaves of Allah, the money transfers, everything."

"Did he tell you also about my kidnapping and the ordeal in the desert? Or had that slipped his mind?"

"In fact, there were several things he said he didn't know. First, he told us he'd thought that the Slaves of Allah were a political group fighting the French over the French government's refusal to allow Muslims a greater cultural autonomy in southern France," said Hodson.

"And you believed him?" I asked.

"Of course not, but we let him continue with the charade because we wanted him to dig his own grave deeper."

"So what else did he say he didn't know?"

"He claimed he had absolutely no knowledge about the plan to kill hundreds of thousands of people by spreading a deadly virus," said Burton.

"What about me? He must have been the one who gave my name to the Slaves of Allah; I was kidnapped the day after our meeting."

"He confessed to that. He simply wanted to preempt your investigation. He told the Slaves of Allah about you, as Neil McMillan, and said you were a sleazeball from the Seychelles selling information on their financial affairs to the CIA. He hoped the Slaves of Allah would kill you," said Burton. "He didn't tell them he knew you were Dan Gordon."

"Remember the envelope you left for Eric at your hotel's reception?" asked Brian.

"Yes, there was a number, most probably a telephone number, I'd found in Zhukov's room. There was something else on that note written in Russian. Of course I remember," I said.

"It's a cell phone number that the French police seized when they arrested Saed Safe-Eldin, later identified as the ring leader of the Slaves of Allah in southern France. We believe Zhukov called him to take care of you," said Eric.

"So you tied Zhukov to Safe-Eldin?" I asked

"Yes. We showed that scrap of paper with the phone number on it to Zhukov during his interrogation. He then implicated Saed Safe-Eldin. They are now trying to establish his connection to Iran. We have intelligence, but not evidence, that he took his orders from Tehran, but we still need more. However, Zhukov's testimony, together with additional evidence we and the French had, will put Saed Safe-Eldin behind bars for the next millennium."

"I still don't understand: Why didn't they kill me when I was their prisoner?" I asked. "Not that I'm complaining."

"They had bigger plans for you. First, you were going to solve some money-transfer problems, and then they were going to put you up for sale on the trade-in market. We believe that they were waiting for an outcry to erupt when you disappeared, and then ask for a hefty ransom. But when no ransom demand was made, we became concerned about your safety. For national security reasons we could not let the media know you were missing."

"What about my children? Didn't they raise hell when they realized I was missing?"

"They contacted David Stone when they didn't hear from you. David asked them to be patient. A few days later they started pressing, so we brought them here," said Hodson. "I explained to them that for your safety they must keep quiet, and that we were doing everything we could to find you."

"And they agreed?

"Reluctantly, they gave us little more time, but said they'd eventually start a media campaign."

"We met the deadline," Hodson said. "You were rescued one day before it expired. You should be proud of your children, they put up a real fight."

"I am," I said. Tom and Karen had already told me of their efforts; I put more faith in Hodson, since his story was in line with these unimpeachable sources. "What efforts did you make to find me?"

"Too many to detail, and most of them were made by the CIA and NSA using sophisticated intelligence methods. We also decided to get INTERPOL to issue a Red Notice for you, as a person wanted by the police. We hoped that once your captors realized you were a wanted felon, they'd understand that no ransom would be paid for your release."

"That could have convinced them to get rid of me."

"There was some risk," conceded Hodson, "but since we suspected that the motive for your kidnapping wasn't money, then failure to pay ransom wouldn't be a reason to kill you. In fact, we believed that asking INTERPOL for a Red Notice could strongly support your legend."

"Was Zhukov part of it?"

"Zhukov claimed that he didn't know that end of the story, because all he did was finger you," said Hodson. "But when we pressed him, he admitted that he placed a call to these guys in Marseilles immediately after meeting you, telling them you were a money-laundering expert who'd stumbled across a money trail leading to Islamic organizations. He also told them that he'd rebuffed your offer to sell him the information, and that you threatened to go with it to the CIA. In fact, Zhukov claims that he even suspected you were working for the Slaves of Allah."

"Really?" I was amused. "Why?"

"He thought that your contacting him was a test by them to see whether he had betrayed them by failing to report a breach of security. Therefore, Zhukov reported your call immediately," Hodson said. "You called him from Marseilles and Zhukov's contact with the Slaves of Allah was also in Marseilles, so he felt he had to report the conversation without any delay, thinking that the fact that both contacts were in Marseilles was not a coincidence."

"Wasn't he afraid to report my purported discovery of a security breach for which they could hold him responsible?"

"Apparently not. Zhukov's fear of being accused of disloyalty by failing to report your approach exceeded his fear of being accused of negligence. After all, he took reasonable care in protecting the money transfers by whirling them around the globe. Even terrorists understand that there is no such thing as absolute protection, but they do know what intentional betrayal and disloyalty mean."

"So CIA's selection of Marseilles for my meeting was not coincidental?" I asked.

"Definitely not," answered Brian. "We knew about their active cells there, although they were operating under different names."

"So how was my connection to Eric discovered?"

"Following Zhukov's call, they put their local contacts into gear. A sizable percentage of the population in Marseilles is Muslim, and many of them are supporters of the Slaves of Allah. With the help of a supporter who worked in the hotel's switchboard they listened to your phone conversation with Eric from your hotel room and knew you were expecting his next call."

"Did Eric identify himself on the phone as Henderson?" I asked.

"Eric called the hotel and asked to be transferred to your room. When asked for his name, he said 'Henderson.' That was the conversation that was listened to."

I gave Eric the look I usually reserved for noisy children. So he wasn't perfect after all. He didn't seem to care.

"Did they follow me to my meeting with Eric at the clinic? That would have doomed not only Eric, but the rest of the operation as well."

"We don't know for sure, but judging from the result, they probably didn't, or else they lost you en route."

"How did you get to put in the rescue message that led us to you?" Hodson asked.

"I managed," I said. "I played turncoat for two hours, just about enough to whet their appetite and postpone any dire plans they may have had for us."

The intercom buzzed; Lynn had a message for Hodson. "Agent Goldberg needs to have a word with you."

"Send him in," he said. He turned to us. "That's Zhukov's interrogator."

The door opened and a stocky, middle-height, spectacled man walked in. When he saw us, he hesitated.

"Go on," said Hodson, "tell me what you've got."

"We confronted Zhukov with the recording of the phone conversation with Laura and asked for his comment. I have his statement here." He handed a folder to Hodson.

"Give me the bottom line," asked Hodson. "I think these gentlemen would also be interested in hearing it."

"The bottom line is that Zhukov claimed that he was blackmailed by Laura to the tune of two million dollars. She approached him and told him she had incriminating evidence on his illegal activities in fuel smuggling. She wanted money in return for her silence. He paid. He has records showing money transfers he made to her bank account in Luxembourg. But what Laura didn't know was that he sent one of his more handsome men to befriend her and control her moves."

"Do you have his name?"

"Zhukov said he had several names, he suggested we check Baird Black or Robert Meadway," said Agent Goldberg. "He also gave us his address. We picked him up six hours ago."

"Any prior arrests?" asked Hodson.

"Not as far as we know. We're fingerprinting him now. Maybe we'll discover more."

"That's the man," I said. "I got his credit card information in Marseilles, and the name *Robert Meadway* also appears on the power of attorney used to deposit and then withdraw the million dollars you thought was mine.

"Before we leave," I continued, "I need to know whether the Slaves of Allah cell members here in the U.S. have been arrested."

"All but one," answered Hodson. "They were arrested in Florida as they were making plans to flee the country to Cuba by boat. Kind of a reverse immigration trend. We're still looking for one who's missing. Fazal is in federal prison awaiting trial for murder, money laundering, and other counts too numerous to list."

"I'm glad there's a happy ending," I said.

"Not so," said Hodson. "This case demonstrated how vulnerable we are to terrorism."

"What's going to happen to Laura now?" I asked.

"If she were sentenced according to her stupidity, and the gravity of her offenses, then she'd spend a life time behind bars," said Hodson.

"Too bad. I liked her at the beginning," I said.

"She'll pay for her mistakes," Eric said.

"Just be aware that the entire case is still under seal," Hodson cautioned. "The public doesn't know anything. That's one of the reasons we agreed to a plea bargain with Zhukov — to avoid a public trial."

"How much is he in for?" I asked.

"Ten to twenty in a medium-security prison."

"He'll lose weight. Look what he did for my figure." I patted my deflated stomach.

Hodson's phone rang. He listened. "Fight it," he finally said and hung up. "Damn. Major media is asking the federal judge to unseal the gag order. I suspect parts of this case will soon be out. Don't give any interviews without prior DoJ approval. As to your weight," he continued without a pause, "keep it that way."

"We'll see."

As I headed toward the door, I stopped. "Bob, please get that Red Notice canceled! Otherwise I'll have a dickens of a time doing any international travel for years to come."

Hodson smiled. "Don't want to spend time in a Turkish prison?"

"Turkish or any other kind. Plenty of INTERPOL member countries will arrest me with the Red Notice still valid."

"Ah." Hodson leaned back. "I said Turkey, because we had a similar story once. One perfectly innocent Israeli businessman, a dual citizen of the U.S. just like you, unfortunately had the same name and close to the same birthdate as a wanted U.S. fugitive on whom there was an old Red Notice." He chuckled. "The poor guy was arrested in Turkey. He later told INTERPOL that the Turks do not provide food for prisoners, though they'll get takeout for you if you pay for it; water comes only in communal slop buckets; and it took days before the Turks would even contact the U.S. embassy, in violation of the Vienna Consular Convention, to confirm his identity. He figured the Turkish commandant was waiting for a bribe."

"That must have been years ago," I said. "Last time I was in Turkey I was amazed how they'd adapted their procedures to comply with the European Union's standards. Anyway, I need a personal, notarized copy of that cancellation notice to keep with me at all times! I've had enough of cells."

Hodson's phone rang. "Hold on, let me write this down." He scribbled on his pad. "Thanks." He turned back to me. "The number you gave me belongs to a cell phone that was reported lost. It was seized by New York police last week during a drug bust in Brooklyn."

"On whom?"

"On a lowlife named Jerome P. LeBlanc. He has a record as long as they come." Hodson turned to his monitor and clicked a few keys. The photo of Baird Black, aka Robert Meadway, aka Jerome P. LeBlanc appeared.

"That's him," I said. "That's the guy I saw in France."

"Seems like him," said Hodson. "He also looks like the guy on your video."

"So he was the honey they used to trap Laura," I said.

"He was already out on bail when we picked him up again a few hours ago. The file says he's a soldier in Zhukov's gang," said Hodson. "Now he'll be just another nail in Zhukov's legal coffin." He smiled in satisfaction.

"Has he talked?"

"He only said that Zhukov told him to befriend Laura and bilk her. He said Zhukov needed incriminating information on Laura so that he could pressure her to cooperate, if the romance ploy failed."

Hodson stood up, signaling that the meeting was over. "Thank you all," he said shortly.

What a twist, I thought. Truth really was more incredible than fiction. Laura and Zhukov were manipulating each other. Laura was blackmailing him. Zhukov sent her a honey trap to seduce her and get inside information, *and* incriminating evidence about her to countermeasure her blackmail. Zhukov wanted me dead, Laura wanted me imprisoned, and now both were in custody as I walked. I thought of a verse from the seventh Psalm: *He hath digged a pit, and hollowed it, and is fallen into the ditch which he made.*

The next afternoon I walked into my Midtown office and Lan welcomed me. It was business as usual.

"There's a collect call from a Homeland Security agent."

"Who's the agent? Tell him to call again sometime next week."

"This is one Agent Laura Higgins, who says you have unfinished business."

"Agent? She's not an agent anymore, at least not with the U.S. government. Where is she calling from?"

"Metropolitan Correctional Facility in Manhattan," said Lan.

"Put her on."

"Dan?"

"Yes."

"Dan, I'm so sorry, very sorry."

"Really?" I replied with heavy sarcasm.

"Yes, I truly am. Can we talk? I want to explain."

"Sorry, I'm kind of busy."

I hung up. Laura certainly had chutzpah, I had to give her that.

"Oooff, it's hot in here," I said to Lan. She looked outside the window. January in New York, a foot of snow on the ground, but too hot for me inside the building. I shed my jacket, loosened my tie, unbuttoned my collar, and rolled up my sleeves.

I turned on my computer. The first message was from David. "See immediate results. David." To his e-mail was attached a clipping from the *Washington Post*:

> The Office of the U.S. Comptroller of the Currency, a Treasury Department agency, said today that Eagle Bank of New York, a small commercial bank in New York, has inadequate controls against money laundering and has been ordered to stop transferring funds or opening new accounts.
>
> In an unusual move the regulators said the bank cannot continue with its traditional banking activities until remedial steps are taken. The bank also faces several lawsuits in the United States filed by relatives of terrorism victims who allege it has supported terrorist attacks by funneling money to terrorist organizations.
>
> "The inadequacy of the bank's controls over its funds transfer activity is particularly worrisome due to the high-risk nature of many of the transfers," the comptroller's office said in the order. In a statement, John Sheehan, the bank's chief financial officer, said that "the bank has agreed to accept the U.S. regulators' conditions because they are likely to strengthen our internal controls and will give the public confidence in the bank's adherence to banking regulations."

I turned the television to *NBC Nightly News*. After a commercial break, anchor Brian Williams came on.

*"And in other news, Israeli warplanes bombed what an Israeli military spokesman called a Slaves of Allah training base in Yemen on Friday. Slaves of Allah is an Islamic radical group that claimed responsibility for several terrorist attacks on Israeli villages and U.S. interests in Yemen. The Israelis say the operation was a success and that all of their intended targets were destroyed. It was the first Israeli attack deep inside Yemeni territory, a thousand miles from Israel's border. Israel, which accuses Yemen of harboring the Slaves of Allah, said it would strike terrorist bases anywhere in the region.*

*"A statement by the Israeli military also accused Libya of hosting training camps belonging to the Slaves of Allah, adding that Israel 'will act with determination against all who harm its citizens.'"*

I turned off the TV.

Lan came into my office and put a pile of that day's newspapers on my desk. "See what you did," she said in irony.

I took one copy off the top.

### Ten Held in Money Laundering Investigation
### of Eagle Bank of New York

New York, January 16, 2004. As a lateral part of a money laundering investigation of Eagle Bank of New York, FBI agents arrested more than 10 people suspected of involvement in a network which laundered millions of dollars through Caribbean, Australian and South Indian Ocean banks and companies. This was the second wave of arrests following last week's arrest of Boris Zhukov, the ring's suspected kingpin. A federal court in Manhattan ordered a freeze on 96 bank accounts in several New York banks. The arrests followed earlier suspicions that the large-scale laundering of money obtained illegally by ethnically Arab businessmen was being done through seemingly legitimate businesses. A spokesman for the U.S. Department of Justice said tonight that the arrests grew out of an investigation that had begun by looking into Russian organized crime in Manhattan,